THE DIFFERENCE

THE
DIFFERENCE

Suzanne Goodwin

St. Martin's Press
New York

THE DIFFERENCE. Copyright © 1994 by Suzanne Goodwin.
All rights reserved. Printed in the United States of America.
No part of this book may be used or reproduced in any manner
whatsoever without written permission except in the case of
brief quotations embodied in critical articles or reviews.
For information, address St. Martin's Press, 175 Fifth Avenue,
New York, N.Y. 10010.

Library of Congress Cataloging-in-Publication Data

Goodwin, Suzanne.
The difference / Suzanne Goodwin.
p.   cm.
ISBN 0-312-13051-1
I. Title.
PR6057.O585D54   1995
823'.914—dc20   95-14707   CIP

First published in Great Britain by Little, Brown and Company

First U.S. Edition: August 1995
10   9   8   7   6   5   4   3   2   1

PART ONE

1972

Chapter One

Somebody had told her you could wake a person if you stared hard at them. It was worth a go. Leaning forward, elbows on her knees, she looked at him steadily. Come on, Hugo, thought Eleanor as she stared harder. She visualised green rays shooting from her eyes. No luck. He slept on.

Suddenly a thrush flew down from the top of the hedge and alighted at her feet. When she moved it made a loud angry cluck-cluck-cluck. Bird succeeded where girl failed. Hugo opened his eyes.

She couldn't help laughing.

'Why, it's you,' he said, the words slurred with sleep.

'So it is.'

He did seem tired.

'I'm so glad,' said Hugo, finally waking and putting out his hand. She took it – it was cold.

'Your father rang my Dad. When I heard you'd come home I couldn't resist surprising you.'

'I'm so glad,' he said again.

'You're jet-lagged, poor Hugo.'

'Yes, the journey was long. But it's great to see you.'

They made a contrast: the girl with her brilliant face, her vitality, a dress of turquoise and russet, and the white-faced white-clad man.

,She regarded him dispassionately and remarked that he looked pretty awful. 'Perhaps you should be in bed sleeping it off.'

'I prefer the garden. And it's wonderful to see you.'

He meant it, for his waking thoughts were sad.

'I always go green after long flights,' he said, as if apologising. 'The plane was held up for hours at Dallas Fort Worth. Tell me about yourself, Eleanor. It's so long since I saw you.'

Glad to amuse him, she began to chat – about Somerville and the American friend with the room next to hers at college; about the tutors, some eccentric, some disinterested and one plainly mad. Hugo listened, but she had the idea that part of him was not exactly here. She felt disappointed and somewhat guilty.

'I talk too much. I'm wearing you out. I must go.'

She sprang up, radiant with energy and, thought the man, a troubling restlessness.

'Don't go.'

When he stretched out his hand again, Eleanor reacted. She never refused a request for her company, just as she never said no to friends who wanted to borrow money or clothes, books or records. She had a careless profligacy, and a good deal of money.

'Okay. Ten minutes.'

'Not more?'

'No. I shall time it.'

She sat down and began to talk again, interrupting herself with 'six and a half minutes left', or 'down to five now'. He relaxed as he listened to what she called her mini adventure of the previous week.

'Would you believe that I was a prisoner in the Oxford Botanical Gardens?'

'Impossible.'

'Unfortunately not. How was I to guess that they padlock the beastly gates at sunset?'

Discovering this, she had climbed a tree, only to find that there was a twelve foot drop on the other side of the wall down to the pavement.

'It was ages before someone hove into view, I kept thinking "Where *is* everybody?" Then along came this guy. He looked staggered when he saw me on top of the wall.'

'So he hauled you down.'

'Not precisely. He was about 12.'

'A good sturdy 12?'

'No such luck. Small and puny and I had to stand on his shoulders, poor little beast. I nearly squashed him flat.'

There was the sound of an ancient stable clock.

'Five. I must go. And *you* get some rest.'

'Shall I see you tomorrow?'

''Fraid not. Due back at college.'

He stood up, much taller than she was, and looked down at her. She had an olive skin and long remarkable eyes. Her Latin appearance was of the kind that the Irish claim comes from Spanish heroes wrecked on their rocky coasts during the Armada. She could have easily been Italian, Greek, even Cornish.

'But you'll come over to see Agnes when she's back?'

Agnes, his sister, was Eleanor's close friend.

'Oh sure. And so we'll meet then and you can tell me all about Peru.'

She patted his arm and darted away under an arch of yews like a dragonfly.

When Eleanor arrived home she wondered why she had been in such a hurry to leave him. She would be back at

Somerville tomorrow morning, which was a relief – it was lonely here by herself. The house had always been too large for one middle-aged man, his daughter and two self-sufficient Spaniards. Built in the eighteenth century, Ferne Place was meant for gentry with many children and servants and bustle; with entertainments, coaches clattering up the drive, music at night, long elaborate meals. Now it was a grey and ponderous silence.

The house had been Eleanor's home for ten years, but she never spent much time here, she was always packing and unpacking. There had been boarding school and holidays spent with her friend Agnes who lived close by. Now that she was older Eleanor went to parties in London and for weekends to friends in other parts of the country. Last year it had been finishing school in Switzerland, now it was Oxford – more packing.

Eleanor did not dislike the settled pattern of being unsettled. It amused and surprised her to see her friends stay put when off she went again. The only drawback to her varied life was how little she saw her father. 'Of course he can't spend time with me when he's swallowed alive by work,' she said to new friends and to old. Her love and admiration for her father were passionately felt; he was always in her thoughts. When she did see him, and they briefly talked, usually when he was leaving to fly to Washington or New York, she felt the same familiar stab of heartache. She used small traps to make their conversations last – just a little longer. Just after that call from the States, just before he left for London, but he was always in a hurry and always brief.

Walter Nelson had been born in America and had never taken out British citizenship, although he had lived in the UK for forty years. He was the rare man of business who

had travelled to success on a route other than the tradi-
tional one – Walter had taken a ship from New York to
England. He had begun his working life in a Madison
Avenue advertising agency being a messenger – as good a
way as any to learn the trade. The agency believed piously
in educating the junior staff, and there were weekly talks on
Aspects of Advertising. The talks were given after office
hours and many of the younger staff ducked out. But
Walter attended every one. He sat quietly at the back of the
conference room, listening and paying attention. One talk
was by a director who had just returned from London,
England.

'Boy,' said the speaker, 'could we show them a thing or
two!'

Walter went home, looked at his savings and talked to his
parents. Sad and impressed, they lent him the extra money
he needed.

London in the early 1930s was tough, with twenty men
after every job, but Walter had a plus: he was an American.
He had another valuable advantage, not a trace of humour.
What he had, and later brought to every client in jobs
which rose in promotion and pay, was a dedicated seriousness. He was never kidding; he gave his clients the
confidence that their interests, balance sheets and products
were what he cared about. Still relatively young, he decided
to start his own advertising agency, which he named
Nelson's.

It was during his starry ascent to success that Walter
married Sara Freston; the only time in his life when he did
not use his head. He did not behave like Walter Nelson at
all. He married for passion. He was crazy about the young,
beautiful, changeable, empty-headed and spoiled girl. He
did laughable things: ordered a dozen red roses to be

delivered to her home every day, little knowing how she, her family and even the housemaids groaned at their arrival. Buckets and saucepans in the kitchen were always filled with roses. He telephoned Sara twice a day. He wrote her love letters – Walter, who had never written a letter of love in his life. He was at her sexual mercy and Sara, who liked it, kept him out of her bed until the day they married. After that, for a while it was bliss indeed.

It could not last. Sara had been as attracted to Walter, as moved by his adoration and as satisfied with his sex as a woman could be; even his excesses, the roses and later the diamonds, touched as well as pleased her. Absorbed in work as he was, he never forgot to make tribute to the goddess. But his ambition bored her, it became a great granite presence in every room of their flat. She disliked the clients Walter brought home for champagne cocktails, the long dinners at the Dorchester, the politenesses necessary towards men putting business her husband's way. She had never respected advertising and soon did not bother to hide that she thought most of its practitioners were vulgar. She was beautiful, and rich with her husband's money, and she had one or two affairs. In the end, tempted by a man richer than Walter and both idle and glamorous, she left.

Walter never forgave her. He detested her and venomously tried to wipe her from his mind. He was also appalled at being landed with a child he scarcely knew, a responsibility – the baby had been Sara's idea – he had never wanted. Even the sound of his daughter laughing or shouting in the corridor got on his nerves.

His answer to the problem was money. If anything went wrong – if the child caught chicken-pox, if she was at a loose end, hung round him too much, he paid somebody to cope. Poverty-stricken as a boy, he knew the uses of hard cash.

At the time Sara left him, the agency which he had founded was doing very well indeed. Nelson's advertising was tough and stylish, clever and deceptively matter-of-fact. The biggest clients began to swim into Walter's nets like great lustrous fish. By the time the 1960s came, the men heading huge companies – already multi-national – saw Walter as one of themselves. But advertising no longer satisfied Walter. His eyes turned to a world of real power – politics. He was drawn to its complexities, its dubious morality and its challenge. He wanted to be part of all that and – still the same Walter who had come to London as a young man – he was not kidding.

Changing gear was not as difficult as it might have seemed. His partner Giles Burnett was a Truman to his Roosevelt, a money man with an unexpected imagination. Walter was soon flying to Washington, and knee-deep in Senators.

Eleanor had never been close to her mother when they had lived as a family in the enormous dark flat in Sloane Street. Sara was usually out, or on her way out. Eleanor would hear her mother laughing with whoever had come to collect her; primped up by the nanny, the child would be pushed into the drawing room to be kissed by Sara and greeted with a certain irony by one man or another. They all seemed handsome and usually had black hair.

As soon as she was old enough, Eleanor was sent to an expensive day school; the nanny stayed on to take her there and collect her and iron Eleanor's wardrobe of party dresses. In the evenings they shared the silliest TV programmes.

Suddenly everything changed. The nanny left for another job; the dark flat changed into Ferne Place, with grounds which needed two gardeners – a change indeed.

Before they left London, Eleanor had found her father alone in the drawing room amid signs of departure; Persian mats rolled up and tied with string.

'Dad. Where has Mum *gone*?'

'To South America. She is going to live there.'

Eleanor considered.

'What you really mean is that she's dead.'

'Good God, child, of course she isn't!'

He lit a cigarette and avoided looking at her. She wore her school uniform, a blue gym slip and white blouse – most unbecoming. But she did not leave the room, which he would have preferred, and when he finally glanced at her she still fixed him with a puzzled frown. He felt obliged to say, 'It was for the best, Eleanor. Your mother was not happy.'

The great revolution of the move kept the child apprehensive and preoccupied, and it wasn't until she had been taken to Ferne Place and then packed off in unseemly haste to boarding school that she asked herself how much she missed her mother. At first she built a sentimental altar in her thoughts. Eleanor made friends easily and, with demands for vows of secrecy to brand-new bosom classmates, described Sara's beauty, fascination and unhappiness. Everybody was deeply interested.

But the subject palled with Eleanor as well as her friends. And besides, as she once remarked when Agnes sympathetically made enquiries, 'She buggered off, didn't she?'

Her mother drifted vaguely into her thoughts as Eleanor wandered out on to the terrace. Now and then, with long intervals, she remembered her. I bet she's lost her looks by now, thought Eleanor. Out on the terrace she threw herself down in a swinging seat and pushed it with her foot. It began to squeak. Accompanied by the hideous row, she sat thinking about Hugo. He had always been thin but now he was positively gaunt. He'd grown that moustache, too, and she didn't like it. What with his pallor and his bones sticking out, she felt rather sorry for him. Eleanor had always looked on Hugo as a sort of cousin. It had been his father John Lawrence who had suggested to Walter Nelson – they belonged to the same London club – that he might consider buying Ferne Place. It had just come up for sale.

Hugo and his sister took a fancy to the little girl when she arrived to live in that over-large mansion. The Lawrences were at Hillier's, an Elizabethan house which had belonged to the family since Henry VIII's time. The young Lawrences invited the Nelson child round and made rather a pet of her. Agnes was a lively girl five years older than Eleanor, but Hugo really *was* old. He impressed Eleanor.

In time he disappeared into the diplomatic service, Eleanor went to the same boarding school as Agnes, and the two girls became friends. Hugo returned from a spell in Madrid when Eleanor was just sixteen. No longer a spider in black stockings given to hanging upside down on sofas, she was almost beautiful. He fell in love with her, which got on her nerves.

Such ages ago, thought Eleanor, making the garden seat screech louder. There was a step on the terrace.

'Good God, what a noise. Luis must see to that tomorrow. Where have you been, Eleanor?'

Her father sat down at a distance from her. Walter Nelson had a heavy face like a Roman consul and thinning white hair, brushed back.

'Did you go round to the Lawrences after lunch?' he asked.

'Yes. After I heard you say Hugo was back from Peru.'

Walter took a cigarette from a gold case and fitted it in a pernickety way into a holder. She wished they could talk comfortably. They never did.

'You should have spoken to me before going.' He sounded displeased; she didn't understand why.

'But Dad—'

He held up his hand to stop her talking. 'Did you see Hugo?'

She was more puzzled still.

'As it happens, I did. He was in the garden. Asleep! I say Dad, he did look gruesome. It must've been jet lag but *you* never go that ghastly colour when you get back from the States.'

'Were you nice to him?'

'Dad!'

'I ask,' he said, sounding more unapproachable than usual, 'because he has had a shock.'

He disliked this. It was necessary, for young Lawrence's father was a friend of Walter's, or as much a friend as anybody in this country. Walter preferred his own compatriots, men in high places. Even the President of the United States knew Walter.

'Did Hugo ever tell you about his housemaster at school?'

Eleanor brightened at the rare feeling that she and her father were having a real conversation. She said yes, of course, Father Edward was a great mate of Hugo's and she'd been introduced to him before Hugo went to South America; she'd thought he was fun.

'Why do you ask, Dad? Have he and Hugo had a row? Hugo told me in one of his letters, I think it was last year, that he saw Father Edward quite often. Doesn't he run a mission or something in Peru?'

'The priest has been murdered.'

Hugo Lawrence would have hated to hear that conversation. He recoiled from Edward's death being spoken about by his family, just as he'd loathed talking to the journalists who turned up in hordes at the embassy in Lima. Least of all could he have borne talking about Edward to the girl who had woken him this afternoon.

He had known Edward Halloran since his first day at public school when, miserable and homesick, he met the priest in a corridor full of boys and suitcases.

'Hello, I recognise you. You're John Lawrence's son. Come and play billiards,' said Edward Halloran.

Dom Edward ruled one of the houses of Hugo's school and was a born teacher, an autocrat and an extrovert. God knew, thought Hugo as he grew up, how Edward followed two of his three monastic vows, poverty and obedience – chastity didn't seem to be a problem. Edward preferred the best cigars, the finest port, and his own way. Hugo was clever and Edward taught and teased him. He made the boy pass examinations as a trainer forces a promising horse to clear hurdles. Hugo shone, went to Oxford and then into the Foreign Office.

When Hugo was posted to Peru, by wonderful chance Edward was also working there. A small mission had been started by the English monks of his order, and Edward had been put in charge.

During his years in Lima, Hugo met Edward whenever their two jobs allowed. They argued and picked over the country's appalling politics. Hugo liked to take the priest out to expensive meals; they were much appreciated. He also gave generous donations to the mission which was impoverished. Sixty-year-old Edward and 30-year-old

Hugo became the closest friends.

The morning that Hugo learned he was to return to England – 'A leg up, my dear chap,' said his boss. 'It looks as if you're to be adviser to the Minister on Latin-American affairs.' – his first thought was that he would lose his friend. He had been worried about the priest lately. At dinner last week Edward talked about a small Maoist group about which Hugo had heard vaguely: the PLFPF, an inflated title for a minor group calling itself the Popular Liberation Front for Peruvian Freedom.

'What a mouthful and it consists of less than twenty men,' said Edward. 'Not a very attractive lot. They came to see me last Sunday, to tell me to pack my bags and get out.'

Hugo looked worried and the priest laughed.

'I said they should cool it. The two who paid me the visit were togged up, of course, like copies of Che Guevara: guns, beards, dirty combat fatigues, ammunition belts. Neither could have been more than 18; they were just boys. I'd have been sorry for them – they looked hungry – but their language was filthy. I told them they had nothing to fear from us. I was very reasonable. 'What did we do?' I asked. 'Only visit the sick and let people use our meeting house.'

'Did they threaten you?'

'Well . . . they waved their guns about. I assured them in my bad Spanish that Juan and I are quite innocuous.'

'Did they believe you?'

'Let us hope so. And now, Hugo, I think I could manage one of those particularly good cigars.'

Learning he would soon leave Peru, Hugo telephoned Edward. The number was out of order. Hugo's secretary checked and was told it was working. During the day Hugo rang six times, to hear over and over again the out-of-order buzz familiar in Lima, where only the telephones of the rich were reliable.

More and more uneasy, Hugo finished his work, took an embassy car and drove across the city to the Barriadas. These were shanty towns which stretched up to the edges of Lima, covering ground where there had once been plains and dry river beds. Now thousands upon thousands of the poor slept here in the open, crowded like herds of animals in a drought. If you had a job, you might own a hut. If you did well, you bought a corrugated-iron roof.

'Our mission is now a positive Claridges,' Edward had said, 'As you are paying, we've bought the best quality iron.'

Driving through the wastes of poverty, Hugo was oppressed; he had never become accustomed to the dreadfulness of this place. The mission house, a glorified hut, stood near the church and presbytery, both of which were actually of brick and stone, built with English money when the mission was founded. The church door was always open. Edward regularly planted bougainvillaeas against the church wall and just as regularly they were stolen.

'How can I blame them, when they sell the bushes for food?'

As Hugo left the car a stab of fear went through him. He saw that the church door was padlocked. He hurried round to the little presbytery. Its door, too, was always kept open: it was shut.

Hugo knocked loudly and shouted in English, 'Edward? Juan?'

A naked child, very thin, padded out from somewhere and stood staring, then disappeared, the pale dust rising round his bare feet.

'Edward? Juan?'

Suddenly Hugo heard a sob. Juan Carreros, Edward's Peruvian missionary, opened the door and rushed out into Hugo's arms.

'Our friend is dead. He is a martyr. A holy martyr.'

Two nights ago the same men had come. They had shouted that Edward was preaching to the Indians and converting them back to Christianity. The priest had no time to say a word, no time to pray. They shot him dead.

Juan and his terrified friends buried him the same night in the waste ground behind the mission house.

'Come and see his grave,' said Juan, tears still streaming down his face.

Two planks had been nailed together in the shape of a cross, with Edward's name in biro and below it in Spanish 'God be with you'. It looked like one of the makeshift graves made during the battle of the Somme.

'I go to my own people, a long way away. I go tonight,' said the missionary. He put both hands on the cross in an embrace.

Such a death, such murder, made shockwaves which crossed the ocean. There were so many people to see and so much to cope with. Hugo's days were occupied with long dubious interviews given by the police, meetings with his seniors at the Embassy, and talking to the droves of foreign journalists – Edward's death had come at a particularly difficult time in the political troubles in Peru.

Edward's Prior at Hugo's old school had to be telephoned, and soon one of Edward's brethren from the English monastery arrived, to be driven under police guard to the now-abandoned mission. Later there was a strangely unreal funeral service; members of the Embassy staff crowded round the poor makeshift grave. Not a single Peruvian peasant, not one poor man or woman to whom Edward had given his love, dared to be there. Plans were made for a marble headstone, and there were serious discussions about the wording to be engraved upon it. Hugo attended every meeting, and afterwards remembered nothing about them.

And there were the letters to be written: to Edward's family, to fellow priests, to boys who had been in Edward's house, and to classy friends in London where Edward had stayed to be spoiled and given the attention of rich Catholics who enjoy the company of clever priests.

Hugo worked fourteen hours a day. His religion mysteriously left him. He never went into Lima's vast cathedral; he never said a prayer. Even his grasp of Spanish faltered. He looked ghastly and he could not sleep.

Sudden death is savage to those who love, but murder has even more terrible elements. The worst part for Hugo was his conviction that he could have prevented it. If not, what was he – what was the Embassy – for? He grieved for Edward selfishly because he had lost him, but he hated himself for doing nothing to protect him. Guilt as well as sorrow were present in his haggard face.

A superstition took hold of him and grew steadily, that when he was back in England the misery would slowly decrease and leave him. Like a man counting the hours before he can take the next two painkillers, Hugo waited. The plane lifted up above the airport and soon the Andes, jagged and arid, rose in the blue distance. Hugo flew further and further away from the dusty spot where his friend lay under the Flanders' field wooden cross. Ahead was the little island in the rain, his family, the rambling old

Sussex house. They would all be part of the cure.

But nothing worked the way he had believed. And when Eleanor left him in the garden he returned to his grief.

Chapter Two

'Is it Eleanor? You can come in, but don't say a word until I finish.'

Head thrust into a basin, Laurette Jacobs was dousing her hair with a jug of black-coloured liquid.

'You're dyeing it!' cried Eleanor before she could stop herself.

There was no reply as Laurette groped for a second jug and poured more dark stuff over her bent head. Finally she gasped, 'That's five and they tell you four. Pass the towel, there's a honey, I bought a black one on purpose.'

Eleanor found a funereal bath towel and placed it in the reaching hand. Her friend straightened up and swathed the towel into a turban. Sombre drops crept down her forehead. She said, 'Hi, let's have a drink,' and fetched a bottle of Martini from the shelf, where it was used to prop up a row of books. Laurette's taste in drinks was looked on as exotic by her fellow students: nobody else drank Martini.

'Aren't you staggered at my wonderful decision to have copper-coloured hair?'

'That stuff looked black to me.'

'The wonders of science. The bottle says: "Do you just long to be a blazing redhead? Make the preppies stare? Hear nothing but wolf whistles?"'

'Laurette, where the hell did you get it?'

'My sister sent it from LA. She's never liked me.'

'But you're a natural blonde.'

'I wouldn't exactly say that. When I'm as God intended, the wolves are mute.'

'Men are mad about you.'

'I'm so glad,' said Laurette, clasping her hands, 'that you're my friend.'

Eleanor was fond of Laurette who was the way she would like to be – cool. Jewish, American, confident, she was reading Medieval English and could recite Chaucer as easily as Eleanor sang the words of pop songs. She suited the times. There was a flavour of the sixties in Oxford still: things were easy-going and optimistic. Undergraduates talked idealistic politics. Thank God, they said, burning joss-sticks in their rooms, the Vietnam war was coming to an end. Their music – you could hear it coming from everywhere – was as optimistic as they were. Laurette was older than most of the undergraduates – 25. She had been married twice, at 17 and 20, and had a certain American glamour. She was recovering from her second divorce, as she informed Eleanor on their first night at Somerville.

'I'm a dedicated marrier. Female Henry VIII. I've only to get into bed with a guy and whoosh, there I am next morning at the altar.'

Eleanor was impressed with her new friend's personality, taste in books, scent (unobtainable except in the States) and quirky clothes. She based her style, she said, on the old movie *Seven Brides for Seven Brothers*. 'If you're twice divorced, you'd just better look like you were born and reared in the prairies.' She had a round face, blue eyes, a sexy figure and a sharp tongue. I'd hate to get on the wrong side of her, thought Eleanor, who up until now hadn't done so.

'Well?' said Laurette, drinking her Martini, 'How's that father of yours?'

'Oh, you know, the same.'

'No, I don't know. I'd like to find out.'

'Come and stay.'

'Suppose I was a success. How would you like me for a stepmother?'

'Laurette, he is 63.'

'And Lee was 24. I need a new angle. Yes, I long to meet your father. So tell about the weekend. Who came to lunch?'

'A fat Labour man Dad seems to like, and the pompous one who's big in industry or something, and the advertising lot as usual, Giles, and the ones my Dad calls his Three Musketeers.'

'Copy, art and TV. Do you think they'd give me a job at Nelson's? Do they need a Chaucer freak? No, I see myself as Mrs Walter Nelson commuting to Washington. I worship politicians. Besides, your father's got all that lovely money.'

She refilled their glasses and continued amiably on the subject of herself.

'How am I going to feel as a redhead?'

'Exactly as you did when you were a blonde.'

'What rubbish you talk, Eleanor. Can a blonde and a redhead feel the same? Blondes open their goo-goo eyes.'

'So what are you doing now?'

'Touché. I must learn to droop them and sort of burn with a hectic intensity. Did you know redheads have a faster metabolism than the rest of us? And they smell different.'

'Nothing you can do about that.'

'Oh can't I? My sister mailed me some new scent to go with the dye. *Sexe-Chataigne.* That's French for sexy redhead.'

'Laurette,' said Eleanor more sharply than usual, 'I did happen to learn French in Switzerland.'

'Oh? I thought you learned Swiss. Now, what else has been happening to me here while you've been gadding about in Sussex.'

She went on talking, scattering her conversation with one-liners. She had her usual relaxing effect on Eleanor, who leaned back and listened and grinned.

Laurette's room was Eleanor's favourite in college. There was a giant coffee-coloured Mexican pot patterned with grotesque dancing figures, and a silk screen embroidered with butterflies – she had brought it back from Hong Kong. On the wall was a plaster cast of Caesar's death mask – 'Did you ever see such a sardonic smile? Imagine *him*' – and a Picasso print of a stout child with an angry expression, sitting in a high chair. 'Don't I know how he feels?' Laurette had fixed a brass hook on her door and hung it with necklaces. Artificial pearls, real jade, real onyx and cheap imitation blue stones. There was always a jug of roses on the window-sill. Laurette had a habit of declaring loudly to any man she was with, 'Nobody in this country gives one a daisy.' Later, 'For me? Now you *are* kind.'

An egotist deeply interested in herself and her own motives, she still remembered the details of everything Eleanor told her. About Walter Nelson, his political connexions, the agency, its clients. She had an American understanding of advertising and taxed Eleanor for her disinterest.

'Fool. Ads are intriguing.'

'So why read Chaucer?'

'He's intriguing too. But coarser.'

She knew about the Lawrence family who lived near

Ferne Place: John Lawrence, his French wife, Eleanor's friend Agnes and the until-now absent Hugo.

Eleanor said, 'I forgot to tell you. Guess who's back from Peru. Hugo. I popped round yesterday to see him. He was in the garden.'

'And?'

'And nothing much. I didn't stay long.'

'Quite right.'

'You mean because he just got back. He looked pretty dire. I thought it was jet lag, but when I got home Dad told me about Hugo's housemaster at school, who was a missionary in Peru later.'

'Dom Edward Halloran.'

'*Laurette!* How did you hear about him?'

'He was killed by the Maoists last month. It was in *The Times.*'

Eleanor was very taken aback.

'Oh hell, I bet Hugo thought I knew too, and was too embarrassed to say anything.'

'He's scarcely likely to think you read *The Times.*'

'Why not?' said Eleanor pettishly.

Laurette did not bother to answer that. The towel round her head gave her the appearance of an idol, and drips had crawled down her forehead like blood.

She looked at Eleanor for a moment or two and then asked, 'So your father told you. Was he very upset for your poor friend?'

'Of course. Dad takes everything to heart.'

'I'm sure.'

Eleanor frowningly thought of the priest whom she had been trying to keep out of her mind. She had never known anyone to whom a tragedy had happened until now. She had never even been to a funeral.

'Hugo did look grim,' she finally said. 'Sort of staring, like a zombie.'

Laurette grimaced. 'That sounds like a depression. When you're in one of those, you look sick. It doesn't do a blind bit of good for people to tell you to pull yourself together. You might as well tell somebody with a heart attack to show a bit of self-control.'

Eleanor looked solemn. 'But you cheer up quite soon, though, don't you?'

'No, Eleanor, you do not. At any rate, I didn't.'

'You?'

'Yeah, I never told you, did I? I got pregnant in Hong Kong and when I told Lee he behaved like a hysteric. Crying jags and imploring me to have an abortion. *He* had to be the child – well, I'd known that when I married him . . . Yet I did so *long* for the one we'd started. But he wore me down in the end. I was too tired to fight any longer. It wasn't such a big deal – I was home in twenty-four hours. But then came the depression, and hence the divorce.'

'I'm so sorry, so sorry.'

'Oh, you needn't be; it's history now. But it was hell while it lasted. When I said I was leaving, Lee kept begging me to stay and sobbing, "I don't understand, I don't understand," and there were the hysterics all over again. Me too. At the airport we both howled like banshees. Back in LA I lived with my sister and we fought like cats. My fault. So I got a job at University and later met this man and we went to bed. He was one of those rich bachelors, you know? Bought me the jade necklaces and took me for a glam holiday to the Great Barrier Reef. But he was so wearing – and picky. When we split he said why didn't I put in for Oxford, since English colleges liked being paid in dollars. So here I am.'

Eleanor was looking at her with such intensity that Laurette had to laugh.

'The reason I've bored you with my saga is because I don't think you should under-estimate what's happened to your friend. You're a cheer-up-quite-soon character. He isn't.'

She stood up, went to the basin and began to unwind the towel. Her previously fair hair was glued to her skull and the colour of liquorice. She looked in the mirror and gave a scream.

'Christ! I must have been mad.'

'But it's still wet,' said Eleanor, who secretly agreed with her.

'I look like a whore.'

'Aren't they usually blonde?'

'So I looked like one before, did I?' said Laurette nastily. She peered at herself more closely. 'The bitch. She sent me the wrong bottle on purpose. She knows I hate black hair.'

Eleanor suggested it might be better when it was dry and hastily picked up the hand dryer. She plugged it in and switched it on, more to stop Laurette from being disagreeable than because she thought it would do any good.

With a face of doom Laurette submitted and Eleanor carefully dried her hair. By the time she had finished her friend's head was covered with glossy red curls.

'Go and look.'

Laurette rushed to the mirror.

'Aren't I cute? I'm so cute!'

She burst into song.

Copper-coloured gal of mine,
I love you 'cos you're so divine,
You will always be my clinging vine,
Copper-coloured gal of mine.

Beaming, she went over to the window and sat down, patting a chair for Eleanor to join her. She poured more Martinis.

Outside was the quadrangle with lawns and old trees and in the distance the chapel building. It was early evening and undergraduates hurried by with their customary burden of books. Young men lingered, propping their bicycles against the wall and tapping on windows, calling out to friends. One couple stood very close under the trees. Sex was in the air.

Laurette said, 'Now let's talk some more about Hugo. What are you going to do about the poor guy?'

'What can I do? You said depression lasts for ages.'

'I said mine did. They pushed Valium down me and a fat lot of good that did. All I got was constipation and a diet of dried apricots and bran. Revolting. What you really need, I suppose, I mean if you *like* Hugo, is to understand him.'

'I don't follow.'

Laurette controlled impatience. Was anybody in the world as young as her companion?

'Eleanor, I am guessing, but maybe he thinks he could have prevented the murder. He's in the diplomatic, for God's sake. And RCs and real atheistic Communists are enemies. My bet is that your friend Hugo is deeply unhappy. When I was, do you know what I kept thinking? The two stupidest words in the language – If Only. Probably Hugo Lawrence is thinking them right now.'

She stood up and began to clear away the bottles of dye, the damp black towel, brush, comb and empty glasses. She returned the Martini to the bookshelf where it was used to prop up *Medieval Monasteries and their Pupils*.

Eleanor fidgeted with her rings.

'I didn't tell you, but I rang him. You know, after Dad

told me. I mean, I couldn't *say* anything, about being
sorry, I just couldn't – so I – well – I invited him to the May
Ball.'

Laurette widened her eyes.

'Did he accept?'

'That's the trouble. He did. I can't go through with it, I
really can't. I've been so worried. What on earth did I do
it for? I can't spend an evening, supposed to be a fun
evening, with someone feeling like Hugo does. I'd be
hopeless with him, honestly I would.'

It was a selfish wail. Laurette only smiled.

'He doesn't have to be in purdah because he's in a
depression, does he? I thought you told me he used to have
a thing about you at one time.'

'Three years ago. I was 16. Anyway, I'm going to the
parties, with Simon and Quentin.'

'And Uncle Tom Cobleigh and all. Of course you can take
Hugo. Show him a good time.'

A silence.

'Maybe he'll cancel,' said Eleanor.

'No, he won't. And don't you ring and put him off,' said
Laurette, interpreting Eleanor's expression.

Laurette had no idea why she was encouraging Eleanor
about Hugo Lawrence. I dare say she'll distract him for a
while, she thought; but what interested her more was that
her friend did not seem particularly happy, so perhaps
taking on somebody else's miseries would distract *her*. It
was sure to be something about that father; when Eleanor
talked about him she sounded like a fan burbling over a
movie star. She was in awe of him, dazzled by him, but
practically never saw him for more than five minutes.
Laurette had formed a low opinion of Walter Nelson and
rather wanted to meet him.

'Take Hugo along,' she said, 'Your good deed for the term. We'll enjoy the May Ball anyway, won't we? I'm told everybody does.'

The May Balls (each college gave one every so often) were legendary. They were also disgracefully expensive and a good many undergraduates couldn't afford the tickets. If you went, you had an evening of costly guilt. Laurette disliked fellow students being kept out because of their lack of cash, but that was as far as her conscience went. She was certainly going herself, and this year, more or less by chance, two colleges were giving theirs on the same night, Somerville and Christ Church.

'Now I've changed myself into a raving beauty, you must leave,' said Laurette, sitting down at her desk. 'I've got twenty pages of an essay to get on with, and *you* ought to be working too, otherwise what's the point of being at Oxford?'

Eleanor wandered away, not cheerful. She thought that yes, she had work to do, and no, she wasn't going to do any. Refusing her friend's advice on another more important matter, she decided she would telephone Hugo. Somehow she must take back the invitation. She needed a really good excuse. But what?

She went down the corridor to the telephone. One of the first-year students, a lively girl called Jill with a loud laugh, was using the telephone. She was feeding in money every now and then and continuing to talk. She leaned against the wall smiling and, with her free hand, winding a finger in her hair. She clearly intended to stay for as long as her money lasted; there were neat piles of silver ranged all along the top of the box.

John and Mathilde Lawrence were pleased when Hugo said

Eleanor had invited him to the May Ball. It was the first time since his return that he had accepted an invitation. Of course they knew how devoted he had been to the priest, whom Mathilde had liked and John Lawrence had not. They expected their son to be very shocked, but they never imagined the extent of his grief or its icy effect. In a polite way, he was unapproachable.

Hugo's sister Agnes was in Burgundy staying with Mathilde's relatives when she heard of the murder on French radio. She knew and admired Edward and, horrified, telephoned to ask her parents to let her know when Hugo was due home. On the day of his return she rang again to speak to him, to say she'd come back next day.

Just arrived and pale as death, Hugo dissuaded her. John Lawrence, handing him the telephone, saw his son's swift change to false casualness when he spoke to his sister. There was a short conversation, and when Hugo rang off he said, 'She agrees that Tante Nicole would be disappointed if she leaves France just yet. After all, she'll be home at the end of the month. She sounded fine,' he added, with the same attempt to sound casual.

In actual fact Agnes had been very distressed. She had twice repeated that she was praying for Father Edward every night, and so must Hugo.

'Tante Nicole has arranged for a Mass to be said at the Cathedral,' she had said. Agnes, thought Hugo, rushed towards prayer like a nurse to an accident.

The Lawrences had been Catholics since before the Reformation. They managed to keep their property in Henry VIII's time and were granted more land by Mary Tudor. They ingeniously kept their heads, and their undeclared allegiance to the old faith, when Elizabeth came glittering to the throne.

Their house, Hillier's, was a rambling old place built on rising ground in the Sussex Weald. It still had a claustrophobic little room up some back stairs, where priests, visiting in peril of their lives, were hidden behind a false wall built to resemble a fireplace.

Among the sprawling families of ten or twelve children born and brought up at Hillier's during past centuries, there were often Lawrences with a vocation, who became priests or nuns. But piety had thinned. John Lawrence had been rather religious as a boy, but it didn't work out that way. He had a lively time at Downside, boxed for the school, and then joined the family firm, Lawrence Brothers, who were fine printers based in Lewes. The company had been founded by John's grandfather and had a certain old-fashioned style.

When war broke out in 1939, John joined the army, fought across the map of Africa, Italy and France, and – he had a reckless courage – was awarded an MC. Just after the Liberation, he fell in love with Mathilde, a dignified young woman inexplicably in love with all things English. He married her.

Mathilde was as French as a woman pointed by Ingres. She had rich black hair, brown eyes and a rounded bosomy figure. She came from an ancient Burgundian family and was the daughter of a count. In the way of some European nobility she actually was the Countess Mathilde but she never used the title, and was put out if it was mentioned.

John Lawrence returned to Lawrence Brothers fine printers until his father's death, when he sold the firm for a good price. He then did what he'd always wanted to do, made an anachronistic life for himself at Hillier's. He hunted, being just able to afford three horses, became a JP, and busied himself with the few tenants who still lived on his estates. He put on some weight, and in his late middle-age, usually in the open air, interested, busy and sturdy, he fairly blossomed.

Hugo's parents were not surprised when he showed little interest in the world of printing. The boy was clever, and with his housemaster forcing him on, did brilliantly at school, shone at Oxford, and as a graduate entrant in the fast stream went into the diplomatic service. His father was proud of him and Mathilde doted on him.

His sister admired him when she was a child and a teenager, but her interest inevitably waned as she grew up. She was studying photography and, more fascinating still, had become a success with young men. Hugo was away in London, Madrid, and later in Peru. Brother and sister could not avoid growing apart.

When Agnes married, Hugo could not even get leave to return for the wedding. By bad luck, it was a time of tricky diplomatic negotiations in Lima and it was not possible for the embassy to spare Hugo for even two or three days. He wrote, he telephoned, he sent some exotic Peruvian silver as his present. Later Agnes affectionately sent a big packet of photographs of the wedding. Looking at them gave him a pang. He wrote again. They remembered each other's birthdays, and forgot each other for weeks on end.

It was exactly like Agnes to offer to come back from France when Hugo arrived home after Edward's death. His refusal to her was automatic. His sister was too fond, too imaginative and understanding, and much too tender. His father's English reserve, his mother's embarrassment, were preferable.

Hugo was thinking vaguely about Agnes as he drove to Oxford. She was like summer, and every tree and hedge, every flower and weed, was burgeoning this evening. The colour was a pure fresh yellowish green; it was the first week in June. The May Balls were always held in June, a joke so old that nobody made it any more.

Hugo was glad of the drive and took side roads to make the journey longer. Heavy roses hung over garden walls and now and then he passed a flint church which had stood in its place for a thousand years. At the top of a familiar high street of a little country town, he glanced up at the clock on the town hall. It had stopped at half past two when he was at school, and nobody had mended it yet.

Why was he going to the party this evening? He despised himself for accepting. What sort of partner was he for a girl like Eleanor? However much he made the effort, his depression would show sooner or later. He knew he was dreary company, was ashamed of it and couldn't change. Yet, knowing that, he hadn't been able to stop himself from saying yes when Eleanor telephoned. She had sounded so carefree. And he'd been in love with her once when she was scarcely an adult. When he had seen her in the garden in that vivid dress, a momentary sensation very like the old longing had stirred his heart. She had reminded him of the rose in Herbert's poem. 'Sweet rose, whose hue angrie and brave Bids the rash gazer wipe his eye . . .'

But he thought – I shall bore her. I will stay for a while and then I must think of an excuse and drive home, so that she can enjoy herself without being saddled with me.

Oxford was *en fête*, undergraduates everywhere. They walked in groups arm in arm or balanced on bicycles, their baskets crammed with bottles of champagne. One girl carried an enormous bunch of gas balloons. The girls all wore long dresses which billowed as they walked; the young men wore dinner jackets. Cars had to crawl because everybody, hand in hand or arm in arm, wandered in the centre of the road.

Eleanor had posted his tickets. 'I'm madly extravagant, I've bought us tickets for *both*!' she had scrawled, and certainly the tickets were so costly that Hugo determined to pay for them. He had rung her at Somerville, getting her with difficulty, to ask where they were to meet.

'Oh, I dunno. Where do you think?'

'Shall I meet you at the porter's lodge? Or would you prefer the lounge at the Randolph?'

'Wait a sec. I know. Try under the trees in our quad.'

Hugo, the diplomat accustomed to appointments of exact place and time, asked uncertainly if that would be all right.

'It'll be okay, sevenish or later. If I'm not around you'll find your instructions on a tree,' was the blithe reply.

Walking across the quadrangle, Hugo saw a number of people sitting on the grass under trees threaded with lights. He felt self-conscious as he approached them. Here was a world he had belonged to once, but he had forgotten its laws and could not speak a word of its language. He was not surprised to see no sign of Eleanor.

As he came up a girl offered him a slice of cake, and somebody shouted,

'Don't touch it. It's an aphrodisiac.'

'I'm looking for Eleanor Nelson,' he said, thinking how absurd he sounded, 'You don't happen to know . . .?'

'Aha. Hugo Lawrence,' said an American voice above his head. Looking up, he saw a girl sitting in the higher branches of a tree. Her long emerald-coloured dress, edged with a fringe, hung down like a silk shawl.

'Eleanor left a message for you,' she said, pointing to the trunk of the tree. A prop dagger, silver-handled, skewered a piece of paper. It read: 'The Riverside Caff. If I'm not there, why not try the river? Not drowning but waving. E.XX'

'Silly, isn't she?' said the girl in the tree, who had a mop of red curls. She peered down at him with a grin. 'We told her to hang about but she said if you didn't show by seven she guessed you'd changed your mind. Try the Riverside. She'll be there.'

'Swimming?' said Hugo, with an attempt at a smile.

'Don't you believe it. She's wearing her Balmain and nobody's going to get her to take *that* off. Not yet, anyway.'

When he left them, Hugo wondered why he was bothering to look for Eleanor whom he would probably never find. The whims of the young were tiresome. But Mathilde would be only too pleased if he simply drove back home. His mother was a great one for being wise afterwards and would say, 'I keep telling you, darling, that you need more rest.' Rest. He had scarcely slept last night and when he did, his dreams were terrible.

He drove down the Banbury Road, turned into a leafy side road and drew up further on in a lane crammed with cars. He could hear music from a gimcrack building by the river; it had once been a boat-house. It was smarter than when he had been at Oxford, and larger too. Trestle tables were set out in front of the barn-style restaurant, and crowds of the young sat at them, drinking and talking at once. As he arrived, he was conscious that the music was deafening and that everybody had to yell.

Looking uncertainly along the tables, he had no hope of finding Eleanor. He turned, about to go, when a girl in white sprang out from somewhere and came running.

'Hooray. I thought you'd chucked.'

'I'm so sorry to be late.'

'The thing is you're here. You found my *As You Like It*

message. Wasn't it a good idea? Come and meet the gang.'

Eleanor was buzzed up, excited, stimulated by the noise and company, and in a mood of wild gaiety which can be the result of having recently been distressed. She had dressed for the party, looked at herself with satisfaction in the mirror, and then in an impulsive happy way had telephoned her father. She wanted to hear his voice, and tell him about her dress; he had briefly said he liked it when she'd worn it to an advertising ball last month.

'Yes?' he said.

The conversation of three sentences made her want to cry. He said nothing unkind. He was in a hurry.

She dragged Hugo over to a table crammed with people and gabbled introductions: Donna and John, the Gould twins, Nick and Josh, and that's Angie over there. They raised their glasses, and made companionable room for him on the bench, already squashed. The noise and the euphoria of the evening swept over Hugo like an avalanche.

Eleanor was surprised that she was so glad to see Hugo. He was so tall and thin and old and she liked his seriousness – she thought it had style. She forgot promises to other friends, sat on the few remaining inches of the bench next to Hugo and would have tumbled off if he hadn't put his arm round her waist and saved her. She gave him a wink.

When the champagne ran out, everybody drank mead which was oversweet and sticky. Hugo, pretending to enjoy it, left most of his. Sitting with noisy drunk people much younger than he was, he would have felt uncomfortably out of place if it hadn't been for Eleanor who smiled at him in her daring dizzy way, and touched his hand.

The meal ended and Eleanor's friends voted to go on the river: somebody had booked two punts. Half a dozen people piled into one shallow craft, the second was

boarded. Both punts rocked dangerously as the girls stepped in, supported by reaching hands. Eleanor stood at the water's edge, her arm linked with Hugo's.

'You wait,' she said, 'Angie will fall in. She always does.'

The first punt swung out midstream and a moment later there was a scream and a splash. Was she pushed or had she fallen? Two men jumped in and dragged the girl, gasping and dripping, back into the boat. Her long blonde hair was stuck to her head, her blue dress to her body. Everybody cheered.

'No swimming for me,' said Eleanor, as the punts slowly moved down river, 'Christ Church next?'

May Balls. Hugo had forgotten them. The trees with their necklaces of lights, the figures sitting on the rims of fountains, the shifting crowds across lawns which stretched into infinity. On long tables laid with white cloths was the food conjured in German fairy stories: elaborate cakes, pyramids of strawberries. Jugglers moved about, their glittering bottles spinning in the air. Barefoot on the grass, an acting company was playing a scene from *The Tempest*. A pop group from London, it was Aeroplane, was giving its wildest numbers to rapt approval. And under a huge catalpa tree was a figure Hugo recognised with a lurch of the heart – an old black guitarist playing the Blues, his sweet face like crumpled leather.

Hours later, Hugo and Eleanor walked back to Somerville. In the quadrangle people were dancing on the grass to a tape recorder.

'Shall we?' said Eleanor, swaying to the beat.

She faced him, moving close, then out of reach. The fragile dress made her look like a ghost. Hugo had danced a good deal – at Embassy parties with rich, sometimes elderly, Peruvian wives; the dances were usually respect-

able versions of the South American samba. Dancing with
Eleanor was as far from those stylised movements as sex
from a game of dominoes.

It was very late and the party at last began to break up;
now and then there was a noise of smashed glass. The music
paused and somebody argued about changing the tape.
Eleanor and Hugo stopped dancing and just then a furious
girl rushed by, almost knocking Eleanor over. A boy behind
her shouted, 'Clare, don't be an idiot, come back!'

'Go to hell.'

The girl disappeared into the college, the boy in pursuit.

Eleanor grimaced.

'A row.'

'Parties often end like that.'

'I thought they ended in bed.'

'That too.'

It was as she looked at him and he smiled back at her that
Eleanor knew they were going to make love. She had begun
the evening feeling so hurt, had rushed at the party with her
arms flung out, and here was a man whom she *knew* saw
nobody, nobody but herself. She came close and pressed
against him and he trembled. He stared down at her pale
face and when he spoke his voice sounded blurred.

'What can we do?'

People dying must look like that, thought the girl.

'Let's go back to my room.'

'Can we—'

'Nobody will notice.'

She took his hand, it was cold, and they went into the
college. The corridor was deserted; a yellow rose lay on the
floor beside four empty champagne bottles. Every door was
shut. The music in the quadrangle started up again.
Eleanor unlocked her door and pulled him into the dark

room. She stripped off her dress and ran naked into his arms. And saw, as they embraced, that same strange expression of pain.

It was broad day when Hugo climbed from the bed and stood looking at her. Her hair was spread across the pillow, one leg and part of her bottom were uncovered: she slept as deeply as a child. He wanted her again but could not bear to wake her, and begun to dress very quietly. Then he sat down at the desk and wrote a letter, glancing over his shoulder at her now and then. She didn't stir. Propping the letter against some books he crept out of the room.

Last evening Eleanor had taken him through a back gate into the college; he made his way towards it, walking fast across the quadrangle, down a passage and past further buildings, wondering nervously if he would meet a don or a porter. There was nobody. When he was out in the street it was deserted, littered. The city lay in a stupor. The only sound came from the birds singing in the lime trees and when he started his car the noise of the engine was a shock.

Her breathing steady and gentle, Eleanor slept through the chimes of all the clocks of Oxford. The college woke, there were voices and the slam of doors. She slept on. The only reason she woke at last was that somebody nearby began to practise the drums. She lay sleepily listening to the beat until there was an angry knock at the door and a voice called, 'Rachel! How many times must I tell you that *we will not have that noise*.'

Eleanor yawned and stretched. Hugo must have left hours ago. Was he worried that he might be spotted? His conventional ways touched her, she liked him for them. He was so different from Oxford friends. She lay and remembered him physically, and smiled.

Her previous ventures into sex had scarcely been love affairs. Her first had been a conscious decision that she might as well get it over with. She liked Michael Matheson, a good dancer, a great chatter, rather ugly, good natured and no fool. He made it obvious that he was attracted, and after a party proved expert and enthusiastic at sex. Eleanor thought it interesting. But he did not chase after her later and Eleanor was annoyed. I was a virgin, wasn't I? Doesn't he realise how important that is? But Michael bounded away like a cheerful dog, waved chummily at her from across the street, and wounded her vanity. She had not fallen for *him*, but she wanted her own effect to be strong. She waited for him to telephone and was astonished that he never did.

Weeks later Raymond White had, as she said to Laurette, hove into view. He was generous and good company, had ginger hair and an expensive car. After supper at the Randolph, Eleanor found herself in bed again. Raymond lacked Michael's skill and sex was over almost at once. It was embarrassing and he apologised. Eleanor behaved well and was told she was wonderful. Unsatisfied, she still felt sure that this time, this man, must fall. Not a bit of it. She did not hear from Raymond again. When she heard the two stories, Laurette raised an eyebrow.

'I don't get it. Lots of guys lust after you. What about the one who writes the poems? And the boy at St Johns who left bluebells in a bucket outside your door? So what do you do? Shack up first with one guy and then another who merely fancy you after a good meal. Did you think one night of sex with you was going to bowl them flat?'

'I thought it worked that way.'

'If the woman happens to be you. My poor friend,

nobody is irresistible. Even you. Even me. Why did you want them to fall?'

'They owed it to me.'

Laurette burst out laughing.

Eleanor did not admit to Laurette that she was ashamed of herself. Yet if Michael or Raymond, preferably both, had fallen in love with her, it would have been different. Now she lay in the rumpled sheets smelling of sex and St Laurent and thought lazily how different last night had been. She had enjoyed it so. She liked Hugo so. And she had discovered at last that sex really was delicious.

She reached for the clock by her bed and sat up suddenly. Four o'clock. She had slept half the day away. Then looking across the room she saw his letter. Still naked, she padded across to get it.

Outside the quadrangle were the usual companionable noises, footsteps, the sounds of people coming and going in a busy, and in many ways a happy, sort of world. Eleanor tore open the envelope. And all her lazy bliss drained away.

'Of course you must have guessed how deeply I cared for you before I went to Peru, but, dear one, you weren't ready then, *of course*. I never forgot you when I was away. You were always in my imagination and my heart's longing. And now ... things have been sad for me, darling darling Eleanor, but they won't be any more.'

Oh God, she thought, it's a love letter. She felt trapped. The very thing she had wanted in other men scared her silly. She looked at it with a sort of horror. She came to the P.S.

'I have to go to London and could be away, complications and work, for nearly a week. I'll ring, dearest. I long to hear your voice. Your slave, H.'

Nearly a week. A respite.

She dragged on some jeans and a T-shirt and rushed out into the corridor to Laurette.

The door of her friend's room was wide open, and as Eleanor went in she saw a gaping wardrobe and a full paper basket out of which some dead roses wrapped in manuscript forlornly peered. On the mirror a large piece of drawing paper had been cellotaped, the message printed in bold felt-tip:

To anyone who wants me and I hope you-all do. Gone to LA in a rush. What a time to leave Oxford! Cable from family. Somebody *else* getting married. Amazing.
Back Michaelmas term,
Laurette

'As you see, I'm off,' said the author of the announcement unnecessarily as she stuffed shirts into an orange and purple zip bag shaped like a sausage. 'Wouldn't my sister just choose today to demand I go home? She's read my stars. "Close relatives suffering from hangovers." She only likes me when I can't put one foot in front of the other. And not even then.'

She looked up from her packing.

'You look fragile too. You okay?'

'Sort of.'

Zipping the sausage with difficulty, Laurette threw it on the bed to join an assortment of bright nylon luggage, books strapped together, make-up cases and an international collection of hats. She straightened up. 'So how was everything?' she enquired. Eleanor gave a loud sigh.

Laurette was white in the face from lack of sleep, had drunk too much champagne, been made love to by a boy

whose name she had forgotten and was furious at going
to Los Angeles to an unending wedding thrash. But she
couldn't resist news.

'Tell Momma. What happened?'

'You mean with Hugo.'

'Who else? I talked to him in the quad when he was
looking for you. Very straight up and down, isn't he? But
sure knows how to wear a dinner suit. How did it all go?'

Eleanor fretfully shoved the luggage aside and sat down
on the bed.

'We made love.'

'No big deal. Wasn't he any good?'

'Oh yes. Great. Really great.' Eleanor paused and then
went on, 'Don't you hate women who go round saying
"lovely sex last night" as if you're supposed to be envious.'

'Yeah. But in this case—'

'He was wonderful. Honestly.'

'So?'

Eleanor gave a louder sigh. 'Then,' she said, 'there are
the women who swear every man in sight has fallen in love
with them.'

'Aha.'

'I'm not like that, am I? You know what a flop I was with
Mike, and as for Raymond – but this time, it sounds stupid
but I truly think Hugo's fallen for me again. I didn't like it
when he did it the first time.'

'Woman, you were sixteen.'

'I know, but *could* it happen – he was only with me a few
hours!'

'It can take less than that. Look at Dante. One quick
oeuillade at Beatrice by the Ponte Vecchio and

Again mine eyes were fix'd on Beatrice;

And, with my eyes, my soul that in her looks
Found all contentment.'

'Oh, do shut up. I'm talking about a real person.'
'And what is Dante, pray? An old reprobate if you ask
me. Do you realise that Beatrice was eight years old?'
'Laurette, have mercy. Just read this.'
Laurette's round eyes positively shone with interest.
There was a considerable pause.
'Well?'
'Hold everything. I need to read it again.'
Eleanor fidgeted until at last Laurette handed the letter
back.
'I fear you're right, that's a 22-carat love letter. Holy
cow, I always got the impression listening to you that he was
inhibited. He certainly looked it when I talked to him last
night. Not when he writes, though. Well . . . the sex bit was
good anyway, wasn't it?'
'Yes it was, but what's that got to do with it? Am I going
to spend the entire summer feeling a bitch because I shall
upset him? He's utterly miserable over Father Edward and
now what with our love-making—'
'Which you say you both enjoyed.'
'That's the *point*. I wouldn't dare do it again.'
'Why ever not?'
Eleanor gave a shocked laugh.
'Because I am not in love with him, and when he realises
it he will be more unhappy still.'
'But you won't be around, will you?' said Laurette, with
simple logic. 'I thought you and your rich parent were off
to Cap Ferrat.'
'And who do you suppose Dad will invite to join us? It is
sod's law.'

'I don't swear the way you do, Eleanor. I realise it is trendy, but it doesn't suit my clean American college girl image. So go see your father and stop him asking Hugo, for Pete's sake.'

'How can I possibly march up and ask Dad that?'

Laurette's eyes were straying towards her packing.

'I've no idea. You just try.'

Chapter Three

'Eleanor? It's Agnes. Luis said you'd be back today. Can I persuade you to come and have some tea this afternoon?'

Eleanor, sounding pleased as she accepted, asked herself exactly what the call meant. Did Agnes just want to see her? Or had Hugo confided to his sister how he felt, and was she being asked round – horrid thought – to welcome Eleanor metaphorically into the family?

For the twentieth time since she had found Hugo's letter, Eleanor wished, oh how she wished, that they had not been to bed together. Sex faded. Complications multiplied.

There was an age difference between the two girls of over five years, and although they'd been to the same school, they had only seen each other to wave at a distance. Eleanor had been very impressed by the so-much-older Agnes then. But the space between them had diminished and they were now contemporaries, although Agnes, married and 25, was inclined to be a little motherly.

Last year when Eleanor had been at finishing school in Montreux, Agnes wrote saying she was engaged. She begged Eleanor to get permission from her father and the school to come home for the wedding. 'I do so want you to be bridesmaid. There's a big political shake-up in Peru which means Hugo can't come. I couldn't bear it if *you* aren't here either!'

Eleanor's telegram said 'Just try and stop me.'

The wedding at Hillier's was a big, sunny, country affair, even Walter Nelson was present; Eleanor was the life and soul of the party. Eleanor thought Agnes's husband, David Lyttelton, was from another era. Handsome, yes, but his Senior Service good manner amazed her and he seemed to think it necessary to laugh at everything she said. As for the bride, *she* was a soul in bliss.

David had recently been posted to Singapore where, it seemed, at present Agnes would not be joining him. Ordinarily Eleanor would have jumped at the chance of seeing Agnes, but today she felt twitchy as she drove to Hillier's. She found Agnes in the garden, sitting by the old hammock which John Lawrence fixed, every summer, between two sturdy cherry trees.

'Look, your favourite seat. But be careful getting into it,' said Agnes, laughing. Last year Eleanor had tumbled out on to her bottom with agonising results. Agnes looked very elegant and summery, dressed in her usual Laura Ashley gear, a fashion she had adopted the moment it began: long cotton skirts, sashes, high stitched necks. It was up-to-the-moment to look like that, but Eleanor resisted it.

Agnes's paradox was that despite the appearance of a Victorian miss whom Dickens would have canonised, she was intellectually as bright as her brother. Once during a school holiday when Eleanor was stuck over an essay, Agnes had written it for her. It had been too clever, and the following term the English mistress remarked sarcastically, 'Eleanor, this does not read like you. I wonder why?'

'My parents are out for the day. Tea in Brighton and then a concert.'

'Why didn't you go? You love concerts.'

'It's Beethoven. He's like those paintings of God the Father on church ceilings. You know the sort of thing.'

Eleanor didn't.

'So here you are. I am glad to see you,' said Agnes, with one of her blissful smiles. She was small, five foot two to Eleanor's five foot seven. Her nose was short and straight, her colour naturally rosy, you would have thought from rouge, and her hair worn to her shoulders curled naturally. The Ashley dress was blue and white with frills.

'Be impressed, Eleanor. Look at my sewing.'

She fished some canvas and skeins of coloured wool from her shoulder bag and laid them out on her lap.

'What are you making? It looks most odd.'

'It's a pew kneeler. I did two in France and this is my third. Father John wants them by the weekend.'

'Aggie, you are turning into a caricature.'

Agnes made a clucking noise and started to sew. Eleanor swung the hammock, glancing at her covertly. She decided there was nothing to worry about and felt brave enough to say, 'Where's your brother? I thought he might be here too.'

'Still in London with the FO. It was kind of you to ask him to the May Ball, Eleanor. It really cheered him up. When he rang this morning he specially asked me to give you his love.'

'Give him mine.'

Agnes bent over the hideous piece of khaki and scarlet embroidery.

'You know about Father Edward, of course.'

'Wasn't it terrible? Almost impossible to believe. I mean, we've never known anybody who was *murdered*.'

'I'm sure he is a saint. He died because he was a Catholic

and that means he is a martyr for his faith. Oh Eleanor, you must have seen how upset Hugo was, when he came to see you in Oxford. He's taken it so to heart.'

Eleanor murmured, 'Yes, it was awful.' She was in a quandary, remembering Hugo and herself dancing under the trees . . . and later in bed.

'Of course, we know in the family that he'll recover, but it's hard to watch and not be able to help,' said Agnes. She paused while she went on sewing. She pulled the thread through the canvas to make it very taut, with a noise like the string of an instrument.

'But I didn't ask you here to tea to share my worry about my poor brother,' she said after a while. 'I wanted to see you rather selfishly really. To tell you my big news. It's settled about me going to Paris.'

'For a holiday?'

'Not a holiday, Eleanor. For six months.'

'Aggie!'

'I didn't tell you before because it looked as if it mightn't come off. That was why I went to Montbard to see the family. They've managed to get me onto a photographic course which is part of the art department at the Sorbonne. Isn't it great? They don't take foreigners but uncle Jean-Claude told them I was "almost French",' Agnes said, laughing, 'and they sniffily agreed to accept me. And more lovely still, my cousin Didier was studying in Paris last year, and he knows a flat near the Porte de la Chapelle. One room and a teeny kitchen and bathroom – we can *just* afford it. Paris! Imagine. I cabled David and he's so pleased. He hates it when he has to be away and I'm not doing anything worthwhile,' finished Agnes piously.

'I'm pea green.'

'You can't be,' said Agnes, beginning on what looked like

a yellow tongue in the centre of a scarlet blob. 'You were in Switzerland all last year.'

'But Paris is better. Wish I could stay in your flat with you and lark around.'

'And give up Oxford?'

'I suppose there is that,' conceded Eleanor. Now that her worries over visiting Agnes were unfounded, she was expansive. 'Oxford is pretty good. I'm learning quite a bit,' she said, untruthfully, 'and making friends,' truthfully. 'Anyway, my dad wouldn't want me abroad again. You know how he prefers me to be at home.'

Agnes went on sewing, remarking that she would be back from France now and then, and they could meet. Eleanor thought her friend was not as cast down by the coming separation as she should be. She felt impelled to paint a glowing picture of her own summer to come.

'Dad's taken the yacht again. We are both looking forward to it.'

Agnes gave a friendly murmur. She felt the familiar pain of pity. Eleanor's part-orphan state never ceased to strike at her heart. Mrs Nelson might as well be dead for all the mention ever made about her. Her daughter did not have a single photograph. She'd once said that her mother had been pretty, 'with lots of French scent'. That had been the total description.

For years, thought Agnes, Eleanor has been a child with virtually no parents. Nobody to read to her in bed, admire or be cross about school reports, come to prize-givings, lecture her, scold her – or love her. Agnes had had a steady father, a concerned mother, a loving, if absent, brother. She marvelled at Eleanor's life. Walter Nelson had dumped his daughter: at boarding school, at Hillier's, in Switzerland, at Oxford. His answer to everything was money, and the fact that Eleanor loved him so was pathetic. Sometimes Agnes could scarcely bear it.

The only time his daughter was with him for any length of time was every summer at Cap Ferrat, and that was because he invited a lot of useful people – VIPs, advertising colleagues – to spend weeks on the yacht which he hired. Eleanor went along as one of the crowd.

The Lawrences had stayed on the *Marie Cristine* three or four times, but Mathilde never enjoyed it. This year she had put her foot down.

'The fact is, John, I do not wish another stay on that yacht with Walter talking politics in his bathing trunks.'

'I thought you loved the south of France.'

'I prefer La Grande Bourgogne.'

'But you like the swimming.'

'This year we will swim in the Armançon,' said Mathilde, knowing very well that in August it shrank to a 12-centimetre-deep trickle.

Agnes glanced at Eleanor now. The pause had been interrupted by wasps and her friend was flapping uselessly at one which had taken a fancy to her.

'I know I shan't be around,' she said, 'but when you are home from Cap Ferrat there will be Hugo. He always *loves* to see you, Eleanor.'

Whenever Eleanor turned her car into the drive of Ferne Place she put her foot down, accelerated and stopped with a screech of brakes. Luis then appeared before she had time to open the car door. They greeted each other with pleasant smiles. Luis and Maria, his plump wife, had been with the Nelsons for a long and settled time. Walter relied upon them. The Spaniards, for their part, lived their own life in their part of the house, and were saving for the day when they could go back to Bilbao and buy their own house. In the past, young upper-class girls had wept on their maids' broad bosoms, and young men confided in elderly butlers or valets. Those servants were shadows now. Luis and Maria worked for money. Yet Eleanor still sensed allies.

Luis was small and neat as a Spanish dancer. He greeted her with a friendly, 'You were asking when Mr Nelson would be back? He's in the library now.'

'Anybody with him?'

'He is alone. I haven't heard the telephone for a while.'

'You mean for the last five minutes,' said Eleanor, but she didn't smile. She looked doubtful and he noticed it. They went into the house, he disappeared towards the kitchen, thinking, as Agnes often did, that Walter Nelson was a bad father. Luis Marcos had a deeply sentimental attitude towards his own parents whose meagre life he had left without a backward look. To Maria and to Spanish friends who worked locally, he spoke of his parents with emotion, 'My mother is a holy angel. My father is good as a little bit of bread.'

Eleanor knocked and put her head round the library door.

Walter was sitting in a green leather chair with wings and a high back. It was enormous, and when moved as heavy as lead. He looked up.

'Hi, Dad, I'm back,' she said, sitting down opposite him.

'So I see. How is Oxford?'

'Fine. One of my tutors said my essay on Dean Swift was quite promising.'

'Good,' said Walter. He was too practised at dealing with people for his eye to return to the document on his lap (on the fascinating matter of the implications of transatlantic trade). But he wanted to and Eleanor knew he did.

'I must show you the essay,' she said.

'I'd like that.'

'Perhaps I've inherited your brains after all, Dad.'

Just then, wearing one of those diaphanous Indian-looking dresses, her thick hair catching the sun, her body in an awkward–graceful hunch on the sofa, she strongly resembled Sara. He wished she would go.

'Actually I came to ask something. Who'll be with us on the *Marie Cristine*?'

'The usual. Tommy Thompson with Audrey.'

Eleanor liked Tommy Thompson, a marketing man, physically rather repulsive, with lank hair and a suet-coloured face, but ten times more alive than anybody else in a room. His jokes were nearly as good as Laurette's.

'I've made a bet with myself that you ask the Three Musketeers,' she said, wanting to please. She was not very interested in them: Dennis who chain-smoked and talked about advertising like a converted Catholic about religion, Greville who behaved like a knowing Tory MP and Nick Dalling who worried and had stomach ulcers. They were familiar figures in her life, and so were their wives. Not friends.

'What about the Lawrences?' she cautiously asked.

Her father smoked for a moment or two.

'They've cried off. Apparently Mathilde has to go to Montbard for some family shindig. It's a damned nuisance, I have things I want to talk about with John.'

Eleanor's spirits soared.

'But Hugo isn't going to France with them, and I thought a week or two on the *Marie Cristine* would do him a power of good,' said Walter, who liked men in the diplomatic. Her spirits thudded back to her boots. But she got her wits together and said casually, 'Dad. Would you mind very much if you didn't ask Hugo?'

Her father looked straight at her.

'What do you mean?'

She was very nervous. She never asked him such favours but simply floated along in his wake, a featherlight craft at the end of a rope. Over and over again she tried to crawl out of her little boat and scramble aboard the great ship surging ahead. Nobody gave her a hand, and back she toppled.

In as light a voice as she could manage, she said, 'I don't want to bore you with details, but do you remember I asked Hugo to the May Ball? I mentioned it to you when I telephoned that evening. Well, it was fun. But . . . I'm sure you knew that Hugo fell for me before he was posted to Peru.'

'What nonsense is this, Eleanor?'

'Dad. It isn't. The trouble is Hugo has fallen for me again. You'll say this is just a lot of stuff, but I had a letter from him. It was serious. I really would hate to spend my hols on the *Marie Cristine* dodging Hugo, or being forced to be pleasant while he went on and on about the way he feels.'

Walter studied her for what was an unusually long time: a good minute. Finally he said, 'Very well. If you don't wish him to come there is no reason why he should.'

She jumped up, ran over and kissed his unresponsive cheek.

With a quick 'Thanks, Dad, thanks,' she escaped.

The sum of August grew fiercer every day and the crowds in Juan and Antibes thicker. Pop music poured down streets filled with boutiques called Tick-Tack or Gorilla, displaying rails of T-shirts bright as flags and windows full of swimsuits. Enormous motorbikes parked across the

pavements forced pedestrians to walk in the road. And at
the end of every street and across every square was the
blinding sea.

Eleanor lay on the deck of the *Marie Cristine* pretending
to sleep. Her skin was shiny with sun-oil which smelled of
coconut. She wore a swimsuit with strings down the back
like the strings of a harp but had pushed them aside, and
her back was a smooth even brown. Eyes closed, she could
hear Dennis's voice and the cackle of Tommy Thompson's
jokes.

The South of France in high summer was a good place to
be if you were rich enough to live on a yacht, avoiding the
surging crowds and waited on as the daughter of the host.
Eleanor loved the weeks spent here with her father,
although he paid little attention to her.

Once, just once, it had been different. Two summers ago
on the yacht, she had woken at four one morning. An idea
came to her, wouldn't it be fun to swim while it was still
dark. She crept up on deck barefoot. The night was almost
over, the hush broken only by the yacht's faint creaking.
There was not a soul about. Along the horizon a band of
yellow shaded into red – the very beginning of the dawn.

'Eleanor?'

It was her father in swimming trunks.

'Dad! You've had the same idea.'

The ship's ladder had been put over the side, she
wondered if he had ordered it. It would be like him. They
slipped in silence into the water which was deep and calm
and wondrously cold.

A great sweep of happiness came to Eleanor as they swam
in a sea-world empty of human beings. If only the swim
could go on for ever. Her father didn't speak to her but he
was there quite close, and once when she dived and bobbed

up beside him, he smiled. At last he said, 'Better go in,' and they swam together back to the yacht, climbing back on deck, dripping and chilled.

After that Eleanor had woken before dawn every morning and gone up on deck in her swimsuit. He never appeared again.

Of course, Walter was always around, presiding at drinks on deck, meals on the yacht, dinners on shore, host to his guests. He was hospitable and urbane. But, 'Ah, Eleanor, there you are,' was the sum total of anything he ever said to her.

The days on the *Marie Cristine* and on shore were sociable. Walter's friends were ferried in the small motor launch to lunch or to dine at St Jean Cap Ferrat. Eleanor had a new admirer, Jean-Loup, who raced cars and taught her to water-ski; he drove her to Monte Carlo in the evenings and they danced. The weeks in France were an idyll – Eleanor always looked forward to them, to the hope of another swim with Walter, to the fun and luxury of the south.

But now, lying with her cheek against the mattress and seeming as relaxed as any sunbather in the south, she was filled with fear.

Last night the *Marie Cristine* party had dined at a beachside restaurant in St Jean, and when they were walking back to the quay, Eleanor saw a door with a square brass plate by the bell. On the pretext of admiring a shrub, she went over to look at the plate. It said *Docteur Anselme Césaire.*

She rehearsed her plan for the twentieth time. Jean-Loup was away until tomorrow but nobody except Eleanor knew that. Walter and his friends were not much interested in the flashy young man who in his turn was only flashily polite to them. She'd told her father she was meeting Jean-Loup this afternoon.

Luncheon was unbearably long. Everybody else had swum and sunbathed and was in the mood for talk and drink about politics and advertising. The talk never seemed to end. Pretending to listen, Eleanor ate nothing, but the rest of the party were too busy enjoying themselves to notice. At last the meal and coffee were over, and there was a general chorus that what was needed was a siesta.

A big Italian sailor, Pruccoli, was in charge of ferrying the visitors ashore. Eleanor had already fixed it with him to take her that afternoon to St Jean. When the yacht cleared of people, and the afternoon lull descended, she went to find Pruccoli. He was waiting, the motor launch lowered and gently bobbing. He descended the ladder and put out a huge hand to steady her, started the engine and they set off across the short expanse of blue water.

'Could you come back to collect me at the quay in two hours?'

'No problem.'

Even if she was lucky enough to get an appointment, she would be certain to be kept waiting.

'I think I can make it by five, but it might be later.'

'M'selle.'

'So that's all right, is it?'

'No problem,' repeated Pruccoli, steering with a hand which held the butt of a cigarette.

He delivered her to the steps of the quay and as she thanked him, thinking she'd have good news by then, she gave a sudden heart-rending smile. The look he gave her was strange, almost fatherly. He nodded and set off back towards the yacht.

Eleanor made her way down the waterfront; the long midday meal had not ended and customers still lingered under the vines, as she often had with Jean-Loup. Lunch in the south went on for ever. The afternoon was lazy and very hot and the morning glory, high on a fence, had already turned from deep blue to purple. A few racing yachts flickered on the horizon.

Keeping in the shade she turned into a steep side-street. The house she had seen last night, painted white with green shutters, was soon in view. When she rang, the door was opened by a woman straight from a TV mini-series. She had neat hair dyed blonde and a starched white overall; she wore white stockings and white shoes.

Eleanor explained that she was a visitor, and apologised for being unable to make an appointment. The lady, like Pruccoli, said something about there being no problem and showed her into a waiting room. There was only one other patient, a man reading the *Nice Matin*. Eleanor sat on a reproduction Louis XV chair, its cushion patterned with the fleur-de-lis. She tried to relax.

But time crawled. She felt more and more nervous and at one moment the man with the newspaper put it down and gave her a single piercing glance. He had black eyes. For some reason the look made her feel worse and she was glad when the receptionist came to fetch him.

How quiet the house was; she had become used to the noises on the yacht, muffled voices from the crew, laughter from friends on deck, the chattering of a French radio, the burring of a portable telephone, the slam of cabin doors. And the creaking, the slapping waves, all the soothing sounds of living at sea. At last she heard voices which by their tone seemed to be goodbyes.

'The doctor will see you now, Mademoiselle,' said the

receptionist, coming into the room again.

Matching her pristine appearance, the surgery into which the receptionist took Eleanor positively glared. Glittering chrome and formica everywhere, the place even smelled new. The owner of this glory was in a white overall with short sleeves and was fortyish, fair-haired, with the face of an ingenuous boy.

He shook her hand kindly. Would Mademoiselle take a seat by his desk? And would she give him, please, her name, age and address?

Then, encouragingly, 'And why have you visited me?'

Eleanor said she had missed two periods – she was sure she was making a fuss about nothing. Perhaps she was anaemic, she added, unaware that her explanation had been used by women for hundreds of years.

He nodded and asked her to go behind the screen, please, and put on the robe she would find on the hook.

The screen was dazzlingly white, the gown starched and scratchy, fastened at the back with tape.

Eleanor's experience of doctors was slight. There had been the time a thorn had festered in her finger, and a mild bout of chicken-pox at school. She had never been given an internal examination and grimaced, but the doctor was gentle and it was soon over.

Would she dress, please, and join him?

She pulled on her bright orange and yellow sundress, and fixed the thin straps of her sandals. Her heartbeat suffocated her. When she came out from behind the screen, he was back at his desk and gave a little hospitable gesture to the chair where she had sat a few minutes ago.

He looked at her, unconcerned.

'There is no doubt about it, Mademoiselle – my excuses, I should say Madame. You are *enceinte*.'

*

Climbing the vertiginous ladder to the deck Eleanor found herself face to face with Tommy Thompson, a bulging figure in white trousers and a T-shirt lettered 'Cannes Film Festival' surrounded by bursting red and blue fireworks. He held a glass in the easy way that a tennis player holds a racquet.

'And where have you been all afternoon? Don't tell me, I shall only get jealous.'

She managed a laugh and in a voice meant to be flip told him not to be a fool.

'No good trying to fob me off, I've got eyes like a hawk. I know when a girl's . . . mmmmm . . . what will you pay me not to split to your father?'

She could take no more and fled down the companionway followed by laughter.

Safe in her cabin she locked the door and sat down at her dressing table. Pregnant. I am pregnant. I can't be. I am sure he is wrong. After all, he isn't a Harley Street specialist, he's only a doctor in a little French town. I must get a second opinion. It was a phrase she had once heard Agnes's father use; yes, she thought, I need a second opinion. But she knew very well that Dr Césaire had made no mistake.

She had lied to Hugo before they made love, saying she was on the pill. She had said the same to the two other men with whom she had been to bed. When she'd told Laurette that, Laurette had declared that she was an idiot and must go on the pill at once.

'I don't want to, it's so calculating,' Eleanor answered, irritated. 'It isn't spontaneous. I just don't see myself that way.'

'Brother,' was all Laurette had replied.

Eleanor always brought a small gilt-framed calendar with her on holiday and kept it on her dressing table. She ringed the date of their return in red. She liked to relish the time spent with her father; the only trouble was how fast the days went. Now she picked up the calendar and counted. There were eight long days before she was back in England.

Yesterday evening, Tommy Thompson's wife Audrey, in the sort of conversation Eleanor loathed, had been talking about childbirth.

'It seems incredible, Eleanor, but I took *ages* to get pregnant with Mandy. Poor old Tommy got so bored with me bursting into tears every month; it was nearly three years before I finally conceived, and Mandy made her presence felt, bless her.' A complacent laugh.

Three years! thought Eleanor. All it took me was one single night of sex and I've already forgotten what Hugo was like.

She stared at herself with dull curiosity, wondering why she did not look changed. And just then a girl, a ghost, appeared unbidden in her thoughts.

Felicity Silver had been in the same senior class as Eleanor at school, and during their last term had mysteriously disappeared a few weeks before A levels. At evening Assembly Mother Superior had explained her absence.

'You will all have noticed that poor Felicity has left. She had to be taken home last night; she was suddenly and quite seriously ill. The doctor fears pneumonia. I want you girls to pray for her.'

Eleanor and her friends were fascinated and impressed at the idea that one of their class could actually be near death. They repeated to each other that she had not *looked* ill. It was all very strange. They trooped up in chapel to light candles for her; somebody suggested a novena.

It was months after Eleanor had left school that she was invited to a party given by one of her old classmates who told her, swearing her to secrecy, that Felicity Silver had had an abortion. 'I've asked her to the party. We must be specially nice to her.' Eleanor was horrified at what had happened to the girl. When she arrived at the party, there was Felicity on the other side of the room; she was stones thinner and looked years older. Is that what will happen to me when I get back to normal? thought Eleanor, seeing herself again in the glass. Getting back to normal was all she had in mind.

Chapter Four

As Hugo Lawrence walked down Buckingham Street on a chilly day at the end of August, he knew his grief over Father Edward was fading. He did not want it to happen, yet could not stop it. It wasn't that he loved his friend less but recent events had proved distracting. Edward's face, brilliant with life – the bony cheekbones, reddened skin and harsh laugh – was growing less importunate. The priest had begun to leave him. That in itself was sad, but there was another reason for Hugo not to be happy. When it came into his mind he pushed it uneasily away. He concentrated instead on considering the lengthy meeting at the Foreign Office this afternoon.

His leave was over and it was time, his masters informed him, that he took up the reins again, this time based in London. His new post and duties were described. His superb Spanish and his knowledge and affection for the country he had served 'was going to prove invaluable to the Minister'. More compliments followed. His reputation, they said, was high and the work he had done in Peru impressive.

Hugo sat listening to all this and only occasionally asking a question. He was quietly attentive. His seniors knew a useful man when they saw one, and they approved of him.

There was nothing of even minor importance that did not make its way into FO files, and they also knew all about the murder of Edward Halloran. They were aware that the priest and Hugo had known each other for years, that he'd been Hugo's housemaster at his Catholic public school, that the two men had been close friends, and that the priest had been running a small mission in the slums of the Barriadas; also that some gimcrack cell of Maoists had shot him dead. But Halloran's murder was nothing to do with Lawrence's future work.

The Foreign Office disliked and avoided anything to do with emotion – gravel in a finely-tuned machine. Men in the Service had ruined their careers because of it: anger or love or despair had damaged their judgement and affected their actions. What was needed at all times, and most of all when things went badly, was a cool head. Despite the recent tragedy, it was clear that Hugo had this.

Great slow-moving clouds hid the sun as Hugo walked down the street towards Saville Mansions, the apartments where a colleague in the FO had a pleasant and convenient flat. He was abroad at present, and had written to tell Hugo he might borrow the flat whenever he needed to spend a night or two in London. 'Glad to have it used, and it's handily near the Savoy,' his friend had written.

The apartments had been built in 1880, were elaborate and solid, little changed from Victorian times. Bankers had flats there, and the more distinguished journalists. The porters were ex-sergeant majors, and Hugo was given a smart salute as he went through the double glass doors.

He took the lift to the third floor and opened the flat door with his latchkey. An evening of solitude lay ahead. It was a good opportunity to work on the detailed report he had to submit on Lima, and to tackle more of the many letters from Peruvian friends. He must also telephone his mother, whom he guessed would be waiting to hear from him. To be alone meant freedom, for a while, from Mathilde's affection. Love of that kind was what he felt he needed least.

Entering the flat, he frowned. What tricks the mind plays, he thought as he walked into the sitting room. He had actually imagined a tang of scent.

He gave a violent start.

Silhouetted against a view of the distant river was the last person in the world he expected to see.

'Eleanor!'

'Hi. I say, I did give you a fright. Sorry. Didn't the porter tell you he let me in?'

'But – but what – I thought you were in the South of France.'

'Back last night. I wanted to see you.'

His thoughts were in a turmoil, for here was the reason for that other misery in his mind.

He could scarcely bear to look at her.

The night they had made love had been the only time Hugo had been happy since Edward died. Like an idiot he had fallen in love with her again, and like a double idiot had believed that this time his love was returned. He had rung her time and again without success, at Oxford and later at Ferne Place. Then, told by Luis that the Nelsons had left for Cap Ferrat, he had written to her twice. She had not answered.

'May I get you a drink?' was all he said.

'Have you any tonic?'

'Nothing stronger?'

He moved to a table where there was an array of bottles. Eleanor remarked brightly that she seemed to have gone off drink. She pleated the brilliant folds of her yellow dress.

This is going to be tough, she thought, so I'd better get it over.

He passed her a glass without a smile, and sat down facing her, apparently waiting for her to speak. Why did I go to bed with you? she wondered. You aren't really my type. You remind me of those guardees who chase after Laurette: you're conventional and sort of muffled. You could have come straight from Buckingham Palace. Why *did* we go to bed? I suppose I was drunk.

But she hadn't been. Not really.

She disliked the tonic and had chosen the drink on purpose for that reason. It was worse because he had added ice and lemon. She gulped some of it down.

'Hugo, I have something to tell you.'

'Please don't. I know what it is and please don't.'

'What *are* you talking about?'

'You know perfectly well. I don't want you making excuses about why you haven't been in touch. You prefer not to see me – fine. I'm sorry I wrote as I did. Forget it. But no excuses, please.'

His voice was slightly strangled, his face tense. Eleanor never thought deeply about the effect of what she did on other people, although Walter's effect on *her* was often in her mind. Now she saw how much she had hurt Hugo, and was shocked. I'm a selfish bitch; oh well, I'm getting my come-uppance.

'It isn't about that. I know I didn't ring back when you called me at home; I meant to, truly. But then Dad heard the yacht was going to be ready a week early, somebody else cancelled, so we left in a rush. I am not making excuses,' she went on quickly, seeing that he was going to interrupt, 'I know I should have rung. Or answered your letters. But somehow I've never been any good at letters – I do scribble a postcard sometimes when I'm feeling okay. But at present I'm not. Feeling okay, I mean.'

The words hung about. She gave him a helpless look.

She has fallen in love with somebody else, he thought. Why doesn't she go? Her scent was strong in the room; it was the same scent which had impregnated her hair and skin when they made love. His body remembered her, and a moment of sad desire went through him.

She licked her lips.

'Hugo. I am pregnant.'

If she had levitated like a medieval saint and floated up to the ceiling he could not have been more astounded. He stared like a man faced with a sight his senses could not credit.

'*What?*'

'Two months. I saw a doctor at Cap Ferrat.'

She astonishingly added, 'I'm sorry.'

'But—'

'I must have been crazy. I told you I was on the pill but I wasn't. I have never taken it. And it couldn't be anybody but you,' she added with careful politeness. 'Because I haven't been to bed with anyone else for months. So there we are.'

He came across to her and threw himself on his knees. She felt weak and weepy when he did that; no man had ever knelt to her before. He took her hands and said in a voice filled with sweetness.

'My poor love. My poor darling. We will do it right away.'

The look Eleanor gave him was quite blank and he went on, the words tumbling out, 'We'll get married. Just as quickly as we can. Of course I could get a special licence. It would be wonderful to do it like that, to have you to myself, to be married this week – maybe in two or three days – but I'm afraid your father and my parents would be upset, wouldn't they?'

She was, for a moment, speechless. It was worse than she had imagined.

She burst out clumsily,

'But I don't want to get married. I am going to have an abortion.'

He remained on his knees, speaking to her in the same gentle voice. He understood that she was frightened, it had been a shock for her, but everything was going to be all right – he promised, he promised. He put up his hand and touched her hair. The sun which had been hidden came out from behind a cloud, a sun of the beginnings of autumn, and drenched the yellow-clad figure with light. She was a vision in stained glass, a saint, a seraph.

The saint violently shook her head.

'Do stand up. I can't talk sensibly with you kneeling down like that. Look, Hugo, I'm sorry, sorry, sorry. It is all my fault for getting us into this awful mess. I admit it. What more can I say except that it was ghastly carelessness and stupidity? But I am not going to make things worse by marrying you and having this baby. I'd have to leave Oxford. For God's sake, my life's just begun, I'm nineteen! What do I want with a *baby*? I can't marry you, it's impossible. I came here to tell you...' after the burst of energy her voice faltered, 'because I don't think I can go through what's going to happen without a bit of moral support.'

As she looked at him, suddenly timid, he got to his feet, automatically brushing the knees of his trousers.

'I refuse to allow you to have an abortion. You are going to marry me.'

*

Eleanor kept crying while she drove back to Sussex. She knew that she must concentrate on the road, but tears would keep pouring down her face. At the traffic lights in Roehampton Lane she saw a middle-aged driver, in the adjoining queue, staring at her through the car window. She rubbed the tears away with the back of her hand. But as she drove on, they started again and every now and then she gave a shuddering sob.

She had rushed out of Hugo's flat refusing his entreaty that she should have dinner with him, just as she'd refused to listen to his arguments, his kindness, and later to his anger. At last he accepted that at present nothing he said was having any effect.

'Very well. We must talk later. But at least let me drive you home; you're in no state to do that journey alone.'

They had gone down in the lift together, and were standing in the small private gardens of the flat where her car was parked.

'I'm perfectly capable of driving. You are the one who is upsetting me. Just leave me alone.'

Hugo opened the car door for her and was about to speak again when Eleanor slammed it shut and drove off. She began to cry at once, a danger to other drivers.

She had really believed he would help her. During the last – to her, unending – week on the *Marie Cristine*, on the flight home, back at Ferne Place, she had clung to that. Nothing was so bad if there was another person who was on your side. And when he'd come into the flat – after he had got over the surprise of seeing her – she was sure there had been a sort of longing in his face. But nothing had gone right. He had said over and over again that he refused to allow her to have an abortion. How could he refuse such a thing? What rights had he? When she had said that, he had become so bitter. She had scarcely recognised, in his harsh voice and furious eyes, the tender man who a few minutes before had begged her to marry him.

Eleanor had become as angry as he. He had to be the one to see her through, it was only fair. She needed somebody who loved her to stand by her, not only for the comfort of his being there, but somehow to give her back her shattered self-confidence. She hated him for letting her down. Was that supposed to be love? Miserable, angry, and in her mind deserted, she was still realistic enough to know that she couldn't manage alone. She must have somebody beside her, and it was now Hugo's fault that she would be forced to go to her father. And that was the worst thing of all. Had Hugo helped, Walter need never have known.

She cared for her father more than for anybody in the world, and had always longed for his good opinion. Now and again she thought she saw glimmers, or believed that she did. In her heart there constantly sprang the thought, strong as a plant renewing itself every single spring, that one day they would – they must – be closer. And now this.

As she turned into the drive of Ferne Place she forgot to accelerate and then slam on the brakes, so Luis did not hear her arrive. She went into the house more quietly than usual, conscious of her swollen eyes. Up in her room she washed in cold water, pressed a flannel to her eyes and made up her face. But she couldn't conceal so much weeping: her face was blotched and her eyes narrow.

As she came down the stairs, she heard a guffaw coming from the open door of the library. Oh God, she thought.

She looked into the room. Tommy Thompson and her father were sitting together at the desk, and as they turned to see who had come in, they were both smiling.

'Eleanor,' said her father. The usual greeting.

'Here's the lovely daughter of the house who can't keep away from me,' said Tommy.

'I'm sorry to interrupt. Dad, could I have a word when you and Tommy have finished.'

'Want me to pop into the garden for five minutes?' asked Tommy, always obliging.

'Of course not. I'll wait until you're through.'

'Your girl wants a long chinwag, Walter,' said Tommy, with a music-hall wink. He never bothered to hide his admiration for his boss's irresistible daughter. He hoped it would please Walter. Everything Tommy did was for a purpose, unless he happened to be drunk.

'Yes. A chinwag,' quoted Eleanor.

'I don't expect we'll take more than an hour,' said Walter, plainly showing he thought her a nuisance. His eyesight was not as good as Tommy's and he did not see that she had been crying. But Tommy's sharp eyes missed nothing.

Eleanor thanked him and left them.

An hour. She didn't know how she was going to bear a whole hour of waiting. She was in the drawing room, staring out at nothing, when Luis appeared. He asked if he could bring her some tea.

'No, Luis. Thanks. Nothing,' she said without turning round. Something in the way she stood, something in her voice, made the Spaniard give her a look of concern.

She wandered out into the garden and went into the tennis court. A stray ball was lying on the ground, she picked it up and threw it against the nets draped on the court's four sides. The ball fell weakly back at her feet and she threw it again. She said aloud, rehearsing, 'Dad. I'm afraid I'm pregnant. So I need an abortion.'

What a word, it made her shudder. Yet it was used to describe something else, she had heard advertising people say that a business plan had been aborted. She still thought it sounded horrible. Termination was better. She tried to imagine how her father would look when she told him. His face strangely eluded her, and she was in such a state of nervous anticipation that she could not even remember the sound of his voice. She walked, dragging her feet, from the tennis court into the rose garden; some of the bushes were grey with mildew and the roses had withered in the bud.

At last the time was up and looking towards the terrace, she saw her father coming out through the French windows. With the great elaborate stone house at his back, his broad-shouldered figure was like that of an aristocrat in a boastful eighteenth-century painting; he only needed the company of some kind of hunting dog. Faintly on the air came the purr of a car. Tommy was on his way back to London.

She felt self-conscious as she walked up to her father. He had been watching her – or she thought he had. Actually, he scarcely noticed the girl coming towards him, his mind was teeming with plans. His life was of absorbing interest to him, and he sat at it like a chess player who spends every waking hour deciding his next move. Eleanor was always an interruption. But since she had asked to see him, he made an effort.

'Well, Eleanor? Ask Luis to bring us some tea in the drawing room.'

Eleanor poured out, and there was a pause while Walter drank his tea. The formal room where they were sitting had a curious non-effect. There was nothing beautiful in it, and certainly nothing ugly. It was the work of an interior decorator and that was how it looked. There was no inherited piece of porcelain, no amateurish water-colour left to Eleanor by a doting aunt, no silver cups from school, no vast Benares bowl sent home by some relative long ago in the lost Colonies, and kept because Walter had loved the man or woman who had thought of him. The room was spotlessly clean, polished, and its statement was money. Eleanor sat in a low chintzy chair and waited until her father asked for his second cup.

Then she jumped in at the deep end. Her voice sounded slightly hoarse.

'I want to talk to you about something, Dad. Will you promise not to be angry?'

It was a bad start. He put his cup down carefully and looked at her with an expressionless face. Eleanor forced herself to go on, feeling the awful thudding of her heart.

'I hate involving you, it's all my own stupid stupid fault but I do need you, Dad. I can't manage on my own. The fact is – I am pregnant.'

'What did you say?'

Floundering, she said wildly, 'Don't be angry, I couldn't bear it if you were angry. I know it just proves I am an irresponsible fool and I am. Such a fool. I saw a doctor in France—'

'You did *what?*'

All his reaction seemed to be was in harsh questions and she fought back a desire to burst into hysterical crying.

'I saw a doctor in St Jean, to make sure. I'd been getting into a panic, not sleeping, and I had to know. He said there was no doubt. I'm two months gone now. The thing is we've got to do it right away, every day matters. Dad, can we go to London tomorrow and get it fixed, the – the termination, I mean? You will help me, won't you?'

Her eyes swam. She was like a creature trapped in a net, as an owl had been once in the tennis nets. You couldn't be sure, the gardener had said, that when it was freed it wouldn't die of fright. He made an unconscious movement backwards in his chair. When he spoke, his voice was perfectly calm.

'You have not told me who is the father.'

'Hugo.'

'Hugo *Lawrence*?'

The stress bewildered her. Did they know a dozen men with the same first name?

'I asked him to the May Ball and—'

'That's enough.'

She did not know what to do next. She did not know what *he* would do and she swung between the certainty of her love for him and the fear of his stony face.

'Hugo doesn't want me to have an abor— termination. He said we've got to marry. Imagine these days having to marry because you get pregnant, it's ridiculous. I don't want to marry him, Dad, I don't want to marry anybody and he was so furious with me when I refused.'

Her voice trailed away. She fixed her eyes on him like the trapped bird. He thinned his lips in a characteristic way he had and was just about to speak when the telephone rang.

Did she imagine he would not answer it? Or call out to Luis to say he was not at home? He picked it up at once, and she saw his face totally change.

'Dexter? Why yes, I got it this morning, I'm right in the middle of it now. Very promising. Yes, it's exactly what we thought they'd offer—'

He paused, listening and smiling.

'That will be the punchline. I agree.'

He chuckled.

The conversation went on and Eleanor sat as if skewered to the back of her chair. The talk was full of approval, old

American catch-phrases, suggestions for angles, approaches, strategies, yet you could not tell, as you listened, what on earth they were talking about. At last it ended, after Walter had arranged to meet whoever it was in New York in two days' time.

When he put back the telephone she watched with an awful fascination the good humour drain away from his face which turned back into stone.

She couldn't stop saying, *'Dad?'*

When he answered, he sounded like a man giving an employee notice.

'You will have to sort this out for yourself. You are an adult now. It has to be your decision.'

He added after a moment, 'Send the bills to me.'

At the time Eleanor was waiting to see her father, Mathilde Lawrence was also in a garden. There was no trace of mildew on her roses which she knew, bush by bush. But she scarcely paid any attention to them this evening while she waited for her son.

Hugo had been in London for days, spending time at the Foreign Office, seeing one or two old friends and on one evening actually dining – it surprised his mother that he had felt strong enough – with one of the priests from his old school. Perhaps he had made a special effort to overcome his grief that night, or at any rate to conceal it. Or perhaps he was beginning to recover at last. Hope grew in Mathilde's heart, no matter how much French realism tried to prevent it.

Agnes had departed for Paris two weeks ago. Mathilde missed her. There had been something comforting about her daughter at home messing about with that photography of hers. Mathilde could never treat the singular choice of career very seriously, particularly now that Agnes was a married woman. It was Agnes's father who liked to climb the ladder to the dark room. He admired the photographs which Agnes enlarged and cropped, and often somehow distorted. Mathilde didn't get the point of them. What *she* admired was the sort of girl Agnes had turned out to be. In a curious way, although she was Agnes's mother, she looked up to her. For a woman of strong character, Mathilde was sometimes as naive as a child and she liked to turn to her daughter when things were difficult. Agnes was so sensible. She even managed to turn some of Mathilde's worries into a joke. Mathilde did not laugh at the joke, but it relieved her mind.

She wished Agnes was still here. She never seemed to mind when her mother went on at length about her brother, she was never jealous but fair and very perceptive. Without admitting it to herself, Mathilde knew that Agnes wasn't hurt because of her partiality for her son. She knew Mathilde was at the mercy of that love.

Longing to see him all day, when at last his tall spare figure came down the steps into the rose garden, Mathilde scarcely managed a smile. She allowed Hugo to kiss her and did not kiss him back.

'Well, Mother? Shall we sit by the lake?'

'Hello, Hugo. There'll be clouds of mosquitoes.'

'Then I will fetch your citronella.'

Mathilde protested that he had only just arrived, but he said it would not take a moment, and went quickly back to the house. He returned very soon with the miniature bottle; she carefully anointed her wrists, cheeks, neck and forehead. She offered the bottle to him.

'Thanks, but perhaps I'll risk the British specimens. Peruvian mosquitoes are twice the size and ten times as vicious. I expect I'm immune by now.'

They went through a wrought-iron gate and crossed a stretch of grass, newly mown, down to the verge of a lake fed by a tributary of the Ouse.

An army of Canada geese swam by, brown and black and white. Foreigners and strangers. Hugo sat and watched them.

'Do you feed them?' he asked.

'Goodness, no. They come and they go,' said Mathilde indifferently. Years ago, to Agnes's horror, she had suggested killing one of the geese and roasting it for dinner.

She waited patiently for Hugo to tell her how things had gone in London, and when he said nothing, asked tentatively, 'And how was the meeting. It went well?'

'Apparently. I was officially told that I am to be adviser to the Minister.'

'Hugo, you must be very pleased!'

He did not look it. He said he supposed so. She simply could not understand his sombre manner or set looks.

'What is it? Something is wrong,' she said and looked at him with anxiety.

Hugo hesitated. He was with somebody who loved him deeply and just then he felt he must speak or he would burst. For once, he didn't stop to think – he was only conscious of longing to confide how unhappy he was.

'It's nothing to do with my work, Mother, and everything to do with me. Eleanor came to see me this afternoon at Saville Mansions. To tell me—' he took a breath, 'to tell me she's expecting a child and that I am the father.'

He looked at her. And could scarcely believe the expression on her face.

'*My dear boy, how wonderful!*'

'Mother, you really are extraordinary.'

'Am I? Why?' She was radiant. 'I am so happy for you. When are you to be married?'

His heart turned over to see his Catholic mother, so narrow and conservative, so pious and rigid, sweep away her every prejudice. But such happiness couldn't last. When he told her what Eleanor wanted to do, she was angry and disgusted.

'What you're saying is loathsome. It is murder.'

'I'm afraid that's not how women think now.'

'I don't care what they think. Only a few years ago, it was a crime.'

She began to rail against Eleanor. Hugo could scarcely bear to listen as she repeated every single thing *he* had said and still felt. There was not a word Mathilde spoke which did not reverberate and hurt him. In the end she ran out of steam and took his silence for reproach and disagreement. She said, 'I forbid you to tell your sister.'

'I had no intention of doing so,' exclaimed Hugo, speaking more unkindly than he meant to do.

'And your father?' Mathilde wasn't unkind. She was ice-cold.

'I don't know. I'll think about it.'

Without another word she stood up and left him, walking slowly up the grassy slopes towards the house.

When she had gone, his guilt about her also left him. He sat very still. He stared at the water, ruffled by an evening wind, and tried to get back his sense of proportion. He was not very experienced with women and at 31 had fallen into love like a man accidentally involved in a vicious fight. He was pitched here and there, expecting to be knocked unconscious. He thought of the desperate girl who had flung him off a few hours ago. Their sex came back to him – she had wanted him *then*. Despising himself for his anguish, he still reeled: first Edward, now Eleanor. Mother has gone to her room to pray, I suppose. She is lucky, he thought. And suddenly he remembered a dinner at Lima with Edward not so long ago, and how the priest had laughed when Hugo told him he'd had doubts about religion.

'Everybody has, what about St John of the Cross? But do you know what that old rogue Picasso said? "How can I be sure there isn't something in it."'

Chapter Five

Chestnut leaves crunched under her feet as Eleanor walked through the gardens of the Louvre. Summer had been very hot and although it was not yet September, many of the trees were already shedding. The leaves were brown and curled and breaking into dust. Paris was dusty too. The streets were crowded with tourists, the smarter shops and restaurants still closed. The city had a draggy feel about it, and the river boats which went down the Seine reverberated with four-language commentaries on the death of Marie Antoinette.

The boulevards and elaborate buildings, the flags unmoving in the still air, the dawdling tourists leaning over bridges, meant nothing to Eleanor. She had first come to Paris when she was sixteen, for a memorable week with the Lawrences and Agnes, to meet and celebrate the twenty-fifth wedding anniversary of Mathilde's sister Nicole. Being with real French people, Eleanor had felt proud; the city dazzled her. Since then she had visited Paris twice with friends from her finishing school. All the girls thought the city exciting.

But now she was indifferent to its over-praised beauty. Like a bored small boy, she kicked up the leaves as she walked. Her shoes were soon filthy. Now and then she looked at her watch.

Her decision to come to France had been sudden and violent. Up in her room in Ferne Place, there had been a few minutes when she simply could not grasp what had happened. That her father would not help her. He took no responsibility for her. All he had said was that he would pay.

She had loved him for so long. She had rested in a way on that love; she had believed in him. Hunched like a woman trying to recover from a kick in the stomach, she let excuses, the lovely slaves, cluster round her. He had not meant it. The telephone call had interrupted. It wasn't his fault that he didn't understand how awful she felt. But the slaves began to fade into the air one by one, and all she was left with in the end was the fact.

Her instinct was to run, to get out of the house and out of the country as if her father's attitude would somehow poison her. She sat deciding what to do, and when she had made up her mind the pain very slightly lessened.

She went to a table and wrote on a sheet of paper, '*I will be back when things are fixed. E.*'

It was crude but she felt crude. She was no longer tender to her unfeeling father. Downstairs the old house was quiet, there was no sign, thank God, of Walter. Eleanor found Luis in the pantry cleaning the silver, and gave him the envelope.

'Luis, will you give this to my father in the morning? Not tonight. Tomorrow.'

He took it without asking a question. She had left a zip bag in the hall and he followed her with it out to the car and put it in the boot. She did not say where she was going or for how long, something she'd always done until now, often with jokes to make him laugh. As the car drove away into the dark he stood and watched the rear light until it vanished, his Spanish face sorrowful.

Eleanor spent the night in an expensive characterless hotel in Sloane Street. She actually managed to sleep for a few hours. By midday she was on a Paris flight.

At last it was six o'clock, the hour which she had calculated Agnes would be home. She took a taxi from a row waiting at the corner of the Rue de Rivoli.

She looked out of the window indifferently, thinking how the ranks of her friends and supporters had thinned almost to nothing. Her father had rejected her. Hugo didn't – couldn't – understand how she felt. Laurette, the real person to help her in this crisis, was in Los Angeles.

She had given the taxi Agnes's address, and now vaguely noticed that he did not set off towards the Etoile or the Avenue Montaigne, but was driving along boulevards which grew steadily more shabby, until the taxi was in a district of drab apartment buildings and an overhead railway. They passed an enormous church like an abandoned army fort, with a dusty statue of Joan of Arc, hands clasped round a flag, outside it. Many of the streets were under repair and the driver, muttering to himself, had to take complicated diversions.

At last he turned into a poor-looking street. The shops sold horsemeat or mended bicycles. He drew to a stop at a corner by a small restaurant called *Chez Les Pêcheurs*. There was a side door.

'Twenty-one, Rue des Roses,' he said laconically.

Eleanor thanked him, paid him and added much too large a tip.

He actually managed a smile and said 'Merci, Mademoiselle' with a certain surprise. Parisian women gave tips so small that only his good sense prevented him from shoving the money back at them.

The door of No. 21 was peeling, and beside a row of bells were cards in small brass frames blackened with age. One card was noticeably new.

'Lyttelton. Mme David. 2ième étage.'

Eleanor rang.

A waiter came out of *Chez Les Pêcheurs*, gave her a look of interest and began to put bunches of plastic seaweed along the counter in front of the restaurant. He disappeared, returning with a basket of slippery grey and white soles. Fish and seaweed were artistically arranged, with lemons dotted here and there. Eleanor rang the bell again – twice. The door stayed shut.

What was she going to do if her friend was not here? It had been impossible to ring in advance. Agnes had told her weeks ago before leaving that the Paris flat would have no telephone. Controlling panic, Eleanor pressed the bell again for a long time. She had given up hope when the door suddenly opened.

Agnes burst into an astonished laugh. *'Eleanor!* Why didn't you tell me? When I heard the bell I was sure it was one of the schoolboys – they drive us all mad. Where have you sprung from? Oh, what fun!'

The non-stop welcome continued as she led Eleanor up the uncarpeted stair. On the second landing, Agnes opened a door. 'This is my new home.'

The room faced buildings on the other side of the street and was large and dark. Eleanor slithered on the thin cotton mat which half covered a polished floor. Agnes's clothes hung on three old-fashioned stands of the kind used in French cafés, her straw hats were balanced on top. Books were everywhere. On the window-sills and on the tables, on the floor with bricks as bookends, and on the bed which was covered with an embroidered shawl. Four or five of Agnes's photographs, much enlarged, were blue-tacked on the wall: a gardener with a wheelbarrow, two Canada geese alighting on the lake at Hillier's, her father – his face hidden by a hat tipped over his eyes, and photographs of flowers.

'Sit down, sit down. It's lovely to see you. Why, I can't believe you are actually here. I'll make the tea.'

Agnes always made tea.

She went into a kitchen the size of a cupboard. Her mother's French order and discipline had clearly been left behind in Sussex – the kitchen was piled with dirty dishes and most of the saucepans had overflowed on to the floor. She called out, 'Mum insisted that I brought my own Earl Grey. She was quite right, most French tea is undrinkable. I suppose you and Mr Nelson are staying in glory at the Crillon?'

She came back with a tray on which were two mugs, a loaf and a pot of jam. The meal had a Dostoevskian air. She poured out and sat down, looking at Eleanor with friendly love. Something in Agnes's face, perhaps an accident of its shape, the arcs of cheek, chin, mouth, gave it a quality of tranquillity. Even looking at her made you feel peaceful.

Eleanor thought, bloody hell, how many more people do I have to depress? First Hugo starting so happy and finishing so angry and then Dad – but she shied away from remembering her father.

She took it at a run. 'Oh Aggie, I feel awful telling you of all people, but I'm pregnant.'

Agnes's cheeks flooded with scarlet. 'Is it Hugo?'

Hating herself for her friend's red and stricken face, Eleanor was suddenly angry. 'Of course it is.'

'I'm sorry. Of course it is,' repeated Agnes, still stunned. 'I didn't know you and he—'

'Only at the May Ball. Just that once. Imagine, *just that once.*'

'Have you told him?'

'He wants to marry me,' said Eleanor with a savage shrug.

Agnes had partly recovered; the colour had left her face. She looked grave. She made out that her brother's solution was not why Eleanor was here.

'Couldn't you? Shouldn't you?'

'For Christ's sake, Aggie, I don't want to marry anybody. Sorry, I am *sorry* and I am a bitch even coming here, but I'm desperate. I need an abortion.'

Agnes floundered. 'And my brother—?'

'Made a hell of a scene. About us getting married, I mean. He told me he wouldn't allow the abortion. It was awful. I'm sorry,' repeated Eleanor. She looked at her friend, waiting for questions, reactions, but when Agnes only sat, gazing at her with unspeaking sympathy, she forced herself to go on.

'I know it would be simpler to get it done in London but I, well, I just can't go through it alone. I've told you how it is with Hugo, and as for Dad, well, quite honestly, he prefers not to know. He thinks I'm old enough to get on with my own life, or make a mess of it as I seem to be doing.'

There was a pathetic trace of the old swagger.

'So I thought I could get the op. done here. Quickly, then I can forget all about it. Dad won't give me moral support, Aggie, and I sort of hoped perhaps you would. I'd so much rather it was you.'

Agnes was appalled. She knew nothing about abortions. Did Eleanor?

'Is the op. – is it possible?' she hesitatingly asked, after a marked pause.

'Anything's possible if you pay enough,' said Eleanor, sounding like her father. Then not sounding like him at all. 'I know I never should have come to you.'

'Of course you should! I'm glad to have you. It's only worrying because I don't know anybody in Paris. I can't ask the relations in Montbard, of course. They'd – well – I couldn't. And at present I'm still such a foreigner here. Oh Eleanor, what can we do?'

Eleanor did not reply. She absently took a chunk of bread and spread it with black cherry jam but did not eat it. Agnes drank her tea. She knew her friend's appearance as well as she knew her own in the looking glass, and she saw now that Eleanor was subtly, strangely changed. It was as if a cloth had been thrown over an electric light and it gave Agnes a pain in her heart to see Eleanor dimmed. She couldn't think how to help her. *She* would never have gone through an abortion, she only hoped and prayed for a baby of David's when the time came. Somewhere in Agnes was a reverence and a terror of the beginnings of life. But she did not judge Eleanor for a moment; although the child was her brother's, her own blood and to think of it was excruciating. Eleanor had a right to make up her own mind.

A thought struck her.

'Does your father know where you are?'

'No.'

'Did you tell anybody? Leave a note?'

'I just wrote I'd be back.'

'Why didn't you tell him where you'd gone, Eleanor?'

'I need a free hand.'

'But won't he be worried?'

Eleanor wanted him to be. Longed for him to be. Knew he wouldn't be.

'I'll be back later. I'm on my own now.'

Agnes looked at her fixedly.

'No, Eleanor. You are not.'

Two days went by, while Agnes wrestled with the dreadful problem which had arrived with Eleanor at 21 Rue des Roses.

She considered her fellow students on the photographic course; young men and girls to whom she occasionally talked in the canteen. They were cliquey, and when she struck up a conversation, patronisingly polite because she was a foreigner. It had been no use mentioning that she was in actual fact half French, she knew very well that that fact would have made them condescend more; she heard her own English accent with shame. Would they help her? Of course not, and she could never ask them. When she reflected upon her own situation, she saw there was not a single acquaintance in Paris who even knew where she lived.

By the evening of Eleanor's second day, Agnes had a new worry, her friend had begun to be violently sick. That could be usual enough, but what was troubling was that Eleanor had the appearance of somebody with bad flu. She was listless and silent, ate nothing and stayed in Agnes's bed most of the day. When she did get up to dress in time for Agnes's return, she look plainly ill.

Agnes arrived home from her classes determined to be cheerful.

'Could you manage just a little supper?'

'I don't think so, Aggie. Sorry.'

Eleanor was a ghastly white.

Agnes took her hands. And gave a sigh.

'Look, shouldn't we be sensible and ring your father?'

'No. He told me I must sort this out for myself. He *told* me.'

There was misery in the voice and the poor pale face.

Agnes thought longingly of England, of Walter Nelson's authority, he was the man who *should* take this heavy burden. For the first time since she had come to France, she felt the heartlessness of an unknown city. She paused, and her silence was too much for Eleanor who apparently read her thoughts.

'You've got to promise you won't ring him.'

'But Eleanor, you really are ill. And he doesn't even know where you are.'

'I don't want to talk about him.'

'But—'

'Unless you promise, I shall leave,' said Eleanor and actually stood up, looking as if she was going to faint. 'I shall go now.'

Agnes pushed her back into the chair, noticing with pity her friend's squashed dress, her beautiful hair lank and lifeless.

'Okay, okay, I won't ring. But for heaven's sake get undressed and go to bed. It's the best place for you.'

Neither of them slept much during the long slow hours of the night. They didn't speak to each other, though each knew the other was awake. Agnes thought of her husband with love and longing. Yet David would never have approved of what she was trying to do for Eleanor. Nor would her parents. Nobody in her family would. She was glad when the early Parisian traffic began its cheerful noise and there was daylight round the edges of the curtains.

Before leaving she coaxed Eleanor to drink some weak tea. Eleanor sipped and left it. Suddenly she caught Agnes's arm. 'Try and think, Aggie. Oh, please.'

When the door closed, Eleanor lay wondering how to get through the day which seemed longer than the night gone by, and so much lonelier. She imagined Agnes going out into the street and catching her bus, arriving at class, talking to other students – and feeling well. The idea of health and normal life had become totally unreal to Eleanor now, it was a phantom lake seen by a traveller tortured by thirst. She wondered if she would feel less sick if she did not lie flat.

The course today was long-winded and curiously boring. Agnes had perfected a good many techniques in her dark room at Hillier's, and today's lectures told her nothing she didn't already know. Her attention wandered, and she kept thinking about Eleanor. At lunch in the canteen, she studied her companions casually and decided she was right about them. There wasn't one she could ask to give her the name of a doctor. It would embarrass them and probably they wouldn't wish to recommend their doctors to a foreigner they knew nothing about. Talkative, wearing inevitable jeans, laughing over private jokes, they were unapproachable.

When class finished at last, she was tired. She walked home slowly from the bus stop, thinking about her honourable promise. It had cut her off from telephoning Walter Nelson; her own husband was on the other side of the world, and Eleanor obviously meant her not to get in touch with the Lawrences either. It came to Agnes as strange to think that here at present, apart from one sick girl, she did not have a single friend.

At *Chez Les Pêcheurs*, Marcel, in his usual long starched apron, was shovelling oysters out of a barrel to heap them on his stall. He called a cheery good-evening.

'What did they teach you today, Madame? How to photograph politicians so that we will believe them?'

She paused for a chat and he looked pleased. They talked for a while about photography, and then she said, 'You didn't happen to notice my friend who arrived here the other evening?'

'Evidently. Another *belle Anglaise*.'

'Yes, she is rather *belle*,' agreed Agnes, thinking of Eleanor's lost beauty with sadness. 'The trouble is that since she arrived to stay with me, she has not been well. Marcel, I have a problem – no doctor. I am only a foreigner, and I simply don't know what to do—'

He was sympathetic, reactive and more than anything, delighted that she had confided in him.

He knew an excellent doctor who attended his whole family, parents, brothers, young sister. He assured her that Madame could rely on the man.

'Is the matter of your friend's illness urgent? Unfortunately I will have to get his address from my home tonight. You see, he is called Lebrun, and there are hundreds of Lebruns in the Annuaire.'

'Like Smiths in our telephone directories.'

At the mention of the name Smith, Marcel exclaimed 'most comical', and burst into a roar of laughter. Agnes hastily said it was so kind of him, that it was not urgent, and to have the doctor's address tomorrow morning would be fine.

'You shall have it the moment I arrive,' said the waiter. 'Or of course I could get a bus back with it tonight.'

Agnes refused at once; she knew the restaurant did not close until nearly midnight. What she did not know, and it would have deeply touched her, was that Marcel lived miles away in the suburbs of Pierrefitte.

When she thanked him, he gave the mysterious French reply, 'It is I who should thank you.'

Going into the flat, Agnes found Eleanor lying in a chair asleep. She put down her books and shopping very quietly, and stood looking at her. Oh God, she really is ill. It is terrible that her father doesn't know. She ought to be flown home at once instead of staying here trying to get rid of the child and perhaps getting worse. Eleanor lay so still. What would poor Hugo think if he saw her now? thought Agnes. But if I rang him, it would only upset her so, I'm sure she would run away.

Superstitiously believing in the healing power of sleep, Agnes crept about the apartment. But she made an inadvertent noise with a cupboard door and Eleanor opened her eyes.

'You're back.'

'How's it been?'

'Sick rather a lot, off and on.'

Agnes sat down and took her hand which was damply cold.

'I've got some news. You know Marcel, my waiter friend at *Chez Les Pêcheurs* downstairs? He saw you when you arrived. I spoke to him just now, and he's going to give us the address of his family doctor. Isn't that good?'

'A *waiter*,' said Eleanor pettishly.

Agnes was shocked. 'A waiter can have as good a doctor as some fat cat in advertising.'

'I suppose so.'

'I know so. We must get an appointment as soon as possible and I shall come with you.'

'Guardian angel,' said Eleanor, self-conscious at her own ingratitude and feeling foolish as well as sick.

The next morning Agnes found a letter had been pushed under the door. It was scrawled on the back of a restaurant bill, with the address and telephone number of a Dr Jean-Pierre Lebrun, plus a bold '*Bonne Santé!*' and Marcel's flourishing and illegible signature.

After breakfast eaten by Agnes and refused by Eleanor, Agnes went to the telephone down the street. *Chez Les Pêcheurs* had a public telephone, but the restaurant was not yet open and although Marcel would willingly have let her in, Agnes preferred not to have his proprietary eye on her.

When she rang the doctor, she managed to be given an appointment at midday. A woman's voice, hard as nails, said she was very fortunate that there was a cancellation, and she must be 'on the point of punctuality as the doctor is very very busy'.

Agnes cravenly thanked her.

Back in the flat she helped a weak and queasy Eleanor to dress, brushed her thick hair and suggested a little make-up.

'What's the point?'

Eleanor said nothing more until they were in the taxi when she suddenly asked, 'Suppose I'm sick again.'

'Do you feel it coming on?'

'Not yet.'

'Don't worry. I've brought a towel and a huge box of tissues in my shoulder bag.'

'Oh Aggie.'

The doctor's address was somewhere off the Place Blanche and Eleanor, taking in the sleazy district with a sense of doom, thought – so much for going to a waiter's doctor. On shabby boards over strip-tease clubs were the words, '*Sexe! Sexe!! Sexe!!!*' Flyblown cinemas advertised '*Les Nouveaux Filmes Pornos*'. But the old days of Paris as the naughty city, symbolised by the poster of a girl with big naked breasts and feathers on her bottom were fast fading. There was an air of desperation about the exclamation marks. '*Erotica!*' '*Les Girls!*' And nobody seemed to be going into the clubs and cramped cinemas.

The street was steep and sloped down towards the Gare St Lazare; many of the ancient buildings had been demolished. Sparkling new blocks of flats rose up where there had once been brothels, and the taxi stopped at one of these buildings, faced with creamy marble, 'Les Résidences de St Luc'. The double doors opened by ray into a huge thickly-carpeted entrance hall. The place fairly shimmered.

The doctor's receptionist was as hard as her voice, gave Agnes and Eleanor (as foreigners) a look of contempt, and showed them into a large, smart and crowded waiting room. Agnes counted eight other patients. She and Eleanor huddled together in a corner in silence. It annoyed Agnes that they were being stared out. She had not yet realised that what Parisians were curious about were her Laura Ashley dresses.

At first Eleanor was merely relieved that she hadn't been brought to a dirty back-street surgery. Later she had to concentrate on not being sick.

Her turn came at last and Agnes gave her hand a painful squeeze. Eleanor was taken down a corridor into a smallish consulting room.

One night of sex, she thought, and already two doctors. Was it worth it? Like hell it was.

Unlike the doctor at Cap Ferrat, Jean-Pierre Lebrun was old. Tall and high-shouldered, he had crinkled yellowish grey hair and a prissy look. Her heart sank. How could she tell this foreigner what she had come for?

When she had sat down, he asked her the usual questions: her name, her address, her age. Eleanor said she was 21, something which Agnes had suggested, 'just in case'. The doctor wrote down the details and then asked if she had had any illnesses. No, she said.

'And so?'

'I am expecting a child.'

'Felicitations, Madame. You will wish to make the necessary arrangements, is that it? I attend a very pleasant clinic, *Les Lilas*, not far from here.'

'I am not married. I wish for an abortion.'

She had looked up the word in Agnes's dictionary.

He pursed his lips, picked up his fountain pen and studied it for a moment or two.

'Why have you come to me?'

Eleanor was beyond being nervous.

'I'm English. I do not know anybody in Paris.'

'You are aware that it is against the law in France?'

She did not answer.

'In your own country, however, such matters can be arranged. Go home, Mademoiselle.'

'I cannot.'

'Why?'

'I ran from home.'

'The child's father, I take it, wishes for no part in this.'

'Yes, he does,' said Eleanor, stung.

'But does not care for you?'

For the life of her she couldn't think of the French words for such subtleties as 'he's devoted' or 'he's very fond'. She blurted out, 'He loves me and wants to marry me.'

'But you dislike him.'

'Of course not. He is an old friend of my family.'

The doctor's face wore a look of martyred patience.

'And of yours?'

'I suppose so.'

'But no love on your part, evidently. How many weeks do you calculate?'

Eleanor told him.

'You are most exact.'

'It was the only time I made love.' I should have said 'had sex' she thought.

'What do your parents make of all this?'

'That I must decide for myself.'

He regarded her steadily with his lined sensible face.

'Mademoiselle, I cannot do anything for you. French doctors do not perform such operations. There is talk of changing the law, but it is still merely talk. I fear you must return to England to solve your problem—' still looking at her, 'one way or the other. Think about it with the right seriousness. You appear healthy and intelligent. How did you happen to become pregnant?'

'I did nothing to prevent it.'

'Foolish. Very foolish. You will of course take precautions in the future.'

She disliked him and did not answer.

'You will understand that it is my duty to ask you to reconsider your decision. You seem set against the marriage.'

'Doctor, I am nineteen.'

She did not notice the slip. A wave of nausea came over her.

'The basin is over here.'

He took her arm, accompanied her, held her head while she vomited, then passed her a clean towel and a glass of water, and ran the tap. He led her back to her chair, and sat down himself at the desk.

Eleanor waited, conscious only that the sickness had gone for the moment and feeling dumbly grateful.

'There is one more thing,' he resumed. 'If, in your country, you go through with the operation, afterwards there is sometimes, I do not say always or even very often, the matter of a nervous depression.'

Out of the blue, forgotten until this moment, came the memory of Laurette.

He studied his fountain pen again.

'Nature has begun the creative process in you. If the body refuses to accept it and brings it to a stop, who can measure precisely what happens to the hormones – to the mental as well as the physical state? Even,' he added disparagingly, 'to the heart. I am not in a position to reassure you as to how you will react, Mademoiselle. For the body it is a brief matter and soon over. But for the mind, who can say? You must decide what you will do. But not in France. Not here with me. In the meantime I will give a little advice about how to cope with the sickness.'

'You'd better take a taxi and get to your class.'

'But Eleanor, what happened?'

'He won't do it. I can't talk now. You'll be in time for lunch and the afternoon lectures if you hurry,' said Eleanor. They walked to a rank on the corner.

'The doctor said if I have small sips of water and eat bits of dry toast it may stop the sickness slightly. I'm going to a café now. But Aggie, *you please go.*'

She more or less shoved Agnes into a taxi, went into a café and sat sipping a glass of Evian and eating tiny fragments of what the waiter called grilled bread. Leaving the place she turned into a broad unsmart boulevard where crowds, like pigeons pecking scattered grain, were milling about in a street market. The shouts of the stallholders, the strong smell of fruit and the stink of exhaust, the teeming people who jostled her in their eagerness to get to mounds of oranges and piles of cheap nylon sheets, made her dizzy. She was swept along like a straw in a flooding gutter. At last catching sight of a Métro entrance, she managed to make her way through the press of shoppers and go down the steps.

The dull morning had cleared, the sky was streaked with blue when she went into the Luxembourg Gardens. She walked as far as the terraces of the palace, where the row of statues stood, a company of French queens with expressionless stone faces. Eleanor stood looking up at them. And over their shoulders she saw stretching ahead of her among the formal gardens, her whole unanswered future.

She had come here for nothing but Agnes's kind and useless company, her fate was to be in London after all. She sat down rather suddenly on a bench. The prospect of what was going to happen began to frighten her. She had never had an operation in her life. What would it be like? Would it be very painful? Would she feel very weak and ill afterwards? Would they keep her in hospital a day, two days? She had asked the doctor nothing. Much worse, how would she react when it was over? She remembered Laurette's words, 'We fought like cats . . . I was hell to live with.'

Lebrun was old and French, a man used to laying down the law, and even he admitted he did not know how the abortion was going to affect her. The question surrounded her. It was everywhere, in the pitiless stone statues, in the gardens, in the air, in the grass under her feet. After it's over I could be completely changed, and never be quite the same again.

Compared to the din of the street market, the gardens should have been quiet, but they were not. They were full of another sort of noise, chattering voices of mothers and shouts from children who hopped about like sparrows.

Eleanor did not like children. Young herself, she found

them boring and never knew what to say to them. If any of Walter's acquaintances came to Ferne Place with their children, Eleanor only pretended an interest in them, and escaped as soon as possible.

Hearing a soft monotonous sound she looked up to see a small boy nearby. He was sweeping the path with a stick, making parallel lines in the gravel. He worked very intently, his face hidden as he bent down, a lock of mousy hair falling in a crescent. While she watched him, Eleanor saw a woman with a pram sauntering towards her; she sat down on the same bench. Then the woman lifted a baby out of the pram and tenderly unwrapped him from a shawl. If she starts to breast feed, I know I shall be sick again, thought Eleanor and stood up.

She walked away among the trees. The thought came to her at last that inside her was a human creature as filled with future life as a bulb with next season's hyacinths. She intended to slam the door of being in its unformed face when a man in the guise of a god cut the new life out of her. She shuddered.

Something hit her feet.

It was a shiny ball patterned with blue dolphins which a girl of about 5 had thrown at her. Eleanor bent down, picked it up and threw it back. The child scrabbled after it, clasped it to her chest with two plump arms and energetically threw it back harder, hitting Eleanor's feet. She laughed out loud. Her fair hair was tied up in a pony tail with a red bow and she wore a white blouse and a frilly red skirt. When Eleanor leaned down again to bowl the ball back towards her, the child made her mouth into an 'O' of expectancy.

Eleanor threw the ball and fled.

*

Marcel saw Agnes the moment she came round the corner, wiped his hands on his apron and came over. What a day, wasn't it? Perfection. Had they managed to see the doctor? Had he diagnosed what was wrong with her poor friend? He did trust that Lebrun had been of use.

Agnes said a few grateful lies about the doctor's kindness. Marcel appeared sceptical.

'Now, you surprise me. I had meant to warn you that Lebrun is an old tomato. I did not hesitate to recommend him, his reputation is good and they say his practice grows all the time. His clinic, also, very smart. But are you sure your friend actually liked him?'

Agnes, wishing she had held her tongue, said yes, yes, very much.

'Incredible. Good news, of course, but to me, incredible. For the antibiotics he is your man, but for the benevolent heart – I would never say so. Take my mother,' added Marcel, warming to his subject while the girl stood longing to get away. 'Madame, he told her, your entire weight of 85 kilos presses upon your unfortunate feet. Can you blame those feet if they grumble? If they complain? The solution is diet, Madame. Diet, and again diet. He gave her sheets and sheets of commands. She was very angry,' he finished, laughing. 'She said he planned to starve her to death.'

Joining in the laugh, repeating her thanks, Agnes managed to get into the building.

Since the moment she had taken the taxi this morning she had been worrying about Eleanor – and thinking about Hugo. She had scarcely managed to concentrate on her work all day long. Was Eleanor going into the clinic at once? Would she have already left the apartment? New and alarming ideas had come to Agnes. Suppose Walter Nelson had decided to put Interpol on to finding his missing daughter; it was just the sort of thing that a man as busy and cold and rich as he might do. The police could be waiting upstairs even now. Suppose Eleanor had not already gone – how shattered she would be to be faced with the police. Then there was the thought that Walter Nelson would be angry with *her* for sheltering Eleanor, and her own parents who would not understand, even David might think . . . and there was Hugo. She went sadly up to the second floor.

Eleanor, a slight colour in previously green cheeks, was sitting propped up in bed, sipping some water.

Agnes's books dropped to the floor.

'Oh Eleanor, I have been so worried! How are you? What happened? You actually look a little better.'

'I am. The doctor recommended water and small bits of dry toast. It sounds ridiculous but it seems to work. He also said something about keeping calm.'

'I'm so glad—'

The look Eleanor gave her was cold. Agnes recovered her possessions, turned to put them on a shelf and with her back to Eleanor said, 'So what is the answer?'

'Oh, apparently he's got a clinic somewhere near his consulting rooms. I bet it costs a bomb. He indicated that I could have the baby there.'

'What do you mean?'

'Nothing. That's what he said. When I told him I didn't – you know – when I said what I *did* want, he was nasty. In a detached sort of way.'

Eleanor could not blind herself to her friend's solemn earnestness, but she felt raw.

'You mean the doctor would not agree to help you?'

'Flatly refused. It's against the law still in France. He was quite unpleasant, really. Kept telling me to go back to England.'

'Because it's legal there.'

'Yes. It is legal,' said Eleanor with infinite dreariness.

'Did you come straight home?'

Eleanor felt the weight of the question and replied sharply, 'As a matter of fact, I didn't. I went into the Luxembourg Gardens. Then I walked to a travel agent's. My flight is at ten tomorrow.'

Agnes gave a low sigh. The sound was expressive of the sense that she could not make her friend out. At least, thought Agnes, she looks better and the lethargy seems to have gone.

Part of Agnes, the old-fashioned near-religious side, began to wonder if Eleanor appeared angry because the doctor had failed her, or because she was having second thoughts.

She didn't dare to ask.

'I'll come with you to the airport.'

'Of course you won't. I'll get a cab. Now I am going to take you out for a meal, you'll be surprised to hear. Howsabout *Chez Les Pêcheurs*?'

It was in keeping with the whole thing that it rained heavily when Eleanor left Paris. The golden day in the Luxembourg Gardens had vanished. It looked as if it had not stopped pouring for months, and when the plane was airborne it was some time before it finally emerged out of the great dark barriers of cloud. Last night Eleanor had slept badly, and had woken three or four times to envy Agnes's steady breathing. Now I'm off her hands she can sleep, she thought. When morning had come, she had asked Agnes to telephone the Connaught Hotel and book a room.

'Couldn't you use the restaurant telephone? Marcel's your mate, surely he'll let you. I hate you having to go out into the street and I do feel a bit flaked out.'

'Of course I'll go,' said Agnes, eager to do anything to help, 'And Marcel will let me in. I'll ring at once. Shall I book you in the name of Lawrence? I expect you'll prefer to be on your own for a little.'

'You mean in case my Dad—'

Eleanor looked so upset that Agnes wanted to throw her arms round her. But again didn't dare.

Why do I want to hide? thought Eleanor, lying back in her seat in the noisy plane – from my father, from Hugo ... She knew that she desperately needed solitude and that Harley Street was close to the hotel. She refused to think further than that.

Down came the plane through the impenetrable clouds, back into rain which beat against the portholes. The travellers loosened their seat belts, the stewardesses adjusted their smiles. The passengers were herded into a little bus which set off through the rain to the airport's arrival buildings.

There was no need for Eleanor to join the crowds which stood waiting for their luggage to come rocketing down the chute. She only had one zip bag which had been treated as hand luggage. I must find the taxi queue, she thought. Indifferent to any kind of hurry, solitary, tired, she began to drift towards an Exit sign.

A voice said, 'There you are.'

She gave a start.

Hugo was walking towards her. And at once she knew why.

'Hello, Hugo. What are you doing here?'

'Agnes rang.'

'Of course she did. Very kind and silly of her. It was also kind of you to drag all the way out here to meet me, but pretty pointless. I am quite okay.'

'She said you have been ill.'

Eleanor shrugged.

Hugo said nothing and began to walk beside her. Acres of shining floor stretched round them, crossed and recrossed by all the travellers in the world. Before she could stop him, he took the bag from her hand.

'I've brought the car. I'll drive you back to London.'

Eleanor froze.

'Hugo. I'm sorry if I sound rude, but please leave me alone. That's all I want, just to be on my own at present. I was mad to go and dump myself on Aggie, although she was so good to me. I realise now that this is something I've got to work out for myself. And by myself.'

He stood looking down at her, and just then when she least expected it, her own fear and self-absorption left her. She looked instead at the haggard face and the dark marks under his eyes. Seeing him and not herself, she was afraid she was going to cry.

He said pitifully, 'Dear Eleanor. Marry me.'

And then she did begin to weep. 'I don't know, Hugo, I don't know,' she said, sobbing.

PART TWO

1978–9

Chapter Six

The answering machine – a rare device and typical of Laurette to have one – said matily, 'I'm out right now but back any time. Do, oh do, call me again.'

Damn, thought Eleanor. She had deliberately put off ringing Laurette until Hugo was safely out of the house. She disliked using the telephone when he was around. It was an instinct with her; once she had mentioned it to his sister Agnes who had chuckled, 'I believe all men are the same. You should just see my French uncle at Montbard. If anybody's rash enough to use his blessed telephone, he stands over them throughout their conversation, jumping up and down.' Hugo was not as uninhibited as that, but he still sent out waves.

It was fresh summer in London, the dog days had not yet arrived. The sky was pure, and people had begun to appear in light clothes: T-shirts with messages, white shirts with the sleeves rolled up. Less clothes were a kind of freedom. Today, thought Eleanor, contained some freedom for her too. Her Spanish help, Mirrén, had arrived to do the house, and Eleanor's daughter Joanna, four and a half, was at nursery school until mid-afternoon. It was just the day and just the weather to see Laurette.

She and her American friend were not far from each

other in actual miles: Eleanor in the small news house Hugo
had bought when they married, and Laurette in a mansion
flat in Swiss Cottage. But weeks went by and they did not
meet. Eleanor found that she missed her. Laurette
impressed and amused her, and led the kind of life which
she might have done if Joanna had not been so determined
to survive.

Eleanor picked up her date-book and was brooding
through her appointments – there were two evenings when
Hugo had invited Foreign Office friends to dinner which
meant Eleanor's unfavourite task of cooking, when the
telephone rang.

'Is that my one friend?'

'Laurette! You got my message very quickly.'

'Ah. That's because I have a relationship with my
ansaphone. Are we seeing each other? I am dying for us to
meet.'

'I suppose today's impossible?'

'Today? Don't see why not. I don't have to be at the
House until four. My boss is at his constituency and when
he gets back he'll have lost every piece of paper in sight. He
uses his car like some crazy filing system . . . I shall need all
my strength. You're just the one I need until then. Where
shall we lunch?'

'Here. We'll have cheese and apples.'

Laurette chuckled. Together and apart, they never
stopped slimming. 'No, no,' she said, 'You must come to the
A.W.A. You know. The Artists' and Writers' Association,
it's in Half Moon Street. You've been with me before. They
do a cold soufflé, only 62 calories. Lunch is on me. My boss
had a fit of madness and gave me a rise.'

When they rang off, Eleanor looked forward to her date.
Her life was startlingly changed from the days when she had

been Laurette's impulsive neighbour at Somerville. She had married Hugo. His parents – well, his father, but not the French mother – had welcomed her. Walter had said nothing, but had given her an enormous cheque at the reception after the wedding. Eleanor, kissing him, felt no gratitude. The size of the gift indicated that he was buying her off.

The most radiant face at the church had been Agnes's. She had flown back from Paris to be matron of honour, and when she had handed the bride her bouquet after Eleanor signed the register, she gave Eleanor a look filled with unshakeable faith in happy-ever-after.

If Eleanor did not see Laurette much, she scarcely saw Agnes at all. It was months and months, once over a year, before they managed to meet. David Lyttelton had been stationed in Singapore when their first child, Emily, was born, some time after Joanna. Agnes was a faithful correspondent and wrote often, but although Eleanor replied, her letters were dull and read like those of a dutiful child.

The Lytteltons returned from the Far East and came to live in Plymouth, managing to get to Sussex sometimes to see Agnes's parents. Hugo and Eleanor arranged to visit at the same time and the old house bulged. Mathilde, busy, happy, trotted about on high heels looking after a big family: a beloved son and a dear daughter; David, whom she liked, and Eleanor to whom she was invariably cool. The little girls were a success, and Mathilde and John Lawrence spoiled them.

Eleanor found Agnes's husband somehow difficult to know. She never quite connected with him. Although not unfriendly, he was reserved and not easy to talk to. And it was odd that with a clever wife like Agnes, he was more at ease with men than with women. He was devoted to his wife and clearly admired her very much. He was protective towards her; she had only to put her nose into a room for David to spring to his feet. His good manners were a positive poem. So, when Eleanor thought about it, were Hugo's. But the two men were different. Hugo was bookish, David a man for action. Hugo smiled when amused. The usually quiet David burst out laughing, a rat-tat-tat like machine-gun fire. The loud cheerful sound could be heard from any room where he, Hugo and John Lawrence were together, comfortable because they were by themselves. What went on behind David Lyttelton's pleasant rather boyish face and blue eyes? Eleanor never found out.

'Nobody can be so all of a piece, can they?' she said once to Hugo after a weekend at Hillier's.

'David's strong.'

'You mean physically. I can see that.'

'No, darling, I mean his nature. He's very tough. I wouldn't like to cross him and Agnes told me he has a terrible temper.'

It piqued Eleanor that Agnes had never said that to her. But even the temper she'd never seen did not explain Agnes's husband. He was a mystery. Perhaps in dangerous times he would have been a hero? DFC, that sort of thing. Eleanor imagined him guiding his ship through ice floes, obsessed in the pursuit of an enemy submarine. She'd seen a movie which had a situation like that. Was David perhaps a hero? They were supposed to be odd.

Hugo and Eleanor were comfortably settled in their mews house, five minutes' walk from Sloane Street – 27 Leveaux Mews. It has been Eleanor's choice. At the time when he was coping with a girl in a state of acute misery, Hugo would have given her anything she asked. He was afraid she would break her promise and try to get rid of the baby again. He spoiled her as if *she* were the child, and when she took a fancy to the little house, he agreed at once.

It was a cottage made from two stables where, in the days of Queen Victoria, the ostlers lived, their horses shifting and clattering below, men and animals conveniently close to the mansions of Chester and Eton Square. The place had been ingeniously converted, with a neat staircase and low ceilings and pretty latticed windows. What attracted the pregnant Eleanor – alarmed at the very idea of her own home – had been that it was ready. Freshly decorated and smart, nothing needing to be done to the doll-like house. Eleanor wanted it because she did not have to think, and Hugo wanted it because he wanted her.

Now, with a daughter growing taller every month and the duty of entertaining for Hugo, Eleanor knew Leveaux Mews would soon be too small.

Mirrén, the Spanish girl who came in to help on three mornings a week, was on her knees cleaning the cooker. She had a flawless face and black hair pinned on top of her head in a twist like a Toulouse-Lautrec dancer. She turned to give her employer a smile indicating the job she'd taken on this morning wasn't as bad as it looked.

'Mirrén, I'm going out to lunch and there's a big parcel of books Mr Lawrence has ordered, it's being delivered early this afternoon. Can you possibly stay?'

'I like,' said Mirrén. So she did, for the extra pay.

'It's very kind of you.'

'Is nothing. I like,' repeated Mirrén.

Eleanor knew her luck in having the Spanish girls to help her. They never lasted long, arriving in London to learn the language, going to their classes loaded with volumes of George Orwell, and returning soon to Spain with their certificates and their hopes. To Eleanor they were like roses. You bought and admired them and lo, only too soon, off you had to go to the flower shop for more. The shop in question was a Spanish convent where the girls roosted before finding temporary jobs.

Free from the duties of mother and home, Eleanor set off to walk to Mayfair.

She was not as beautiful as she had been at nineteen. Insouciance, confidence and mischief were gone. But the wistfulness which had been an undertone in her personality, caused by her father, was there still. She was cheerful rather than happy. People were often surprised to learn that she had a daughter of nearly five, and would exclaim, 'It's impossible, you look so young!'

She did not feel that she was.

Today she wore a white dress like an Edwardian sailor-suit, with a big collar and navy ribbons. Her coppery hair was cut rather short and Hugo's wedding present, real pearl earrings, shook as she walked. One or two men looked at her with interest as she went by, but Eleanor never noticed.

Half Moon Street was covered in dust and so was the building occupied by the Writers' and Artists' Association. It was the house where, rumour had it, Lord Byron had taken boxing lessons. The story was probably untrue but, repeated from generation to generation, had become true. Whether Byron had visited it or not, it was still a graceful eighteenth-century mansion which survived the demolition and dirt spreading across London. Eleanor had to pick her way over planks, sacks of cement and muddy ropes before arriving at the front door.

With American courtesy, Laurette was waiting in the hall.

'Hi. I'm here to sign you in. You're so punctual, Eleanor;

the politeness of kings. Did you know it was Louis XVIII who said that? The fat one.'

She took Eleanor up a curving stair, its wrought iron bannisters in a design of lilies. The walls were hung with many portraits. It seemed to Eleanor, meeting painted eyes, that the sitters had decided how they wanted you to see them; the choice was wide. There were dreamers and businessmen, romantic youths with flying hair, beauties, suffragettes, grave thinkers and grandmothers.

In what was called the Green Drawing Room – a very large room set about with sofas, easy chairs and little tables, a good many people were talking and drinking. There was a low pleasant buzz. Laurette took her to a table where two glasses were already set out.

'Cold soufflé on its way. Let's drink to my rise, and then you must tell me everything about yourself.'

Unlike Eleanor, Laurette had not changed. She did not look a day older than when she'd served Martinis to Eleanor in her college room. Her clothes had always been eccentric and expensive and today she wore a loose fitting suit, baggy trousers, the influence very Japanese, with a Lauren cowboy hat for good measure and a Navajo Indian belt. Her passion was still for semi-precious stones and she had two or three long necklaces of amber and agate.

A remarkable memory and a lot of push had landed her a post as researcher in the House of Commons; she worked for a Conservative MP who was not particularly distinguished but had money. His photograph appeared now and again in the newspapers and Hugo had wondered aloud to Eleanor if that had been with Laurette's help. 'Your friend, I imagine, knows her way round Fleet Street.'

'So how is Hugo?' enquired Laurette, pushing the ten-gallon hat on to the back of her head. 'I saw him on the terrace the other day, having tea with some old character from the FO. He looked worried.'

'He always does.' Eleanor was unsure whether she was defending him or not. 'It's the shape of his face.'

'A nice shape. So how is the dear man?'

'Busy. That trouble in Costa Rica.'

Laurette nodded. 'And Peru and Argentina, come to that. A lot of places over there are in a mess.'

'He chose a tricky career when he specialised in South America,' said Eleanor rather seriously.

'I don't think guys choose the country they specialise in, Eleanor. They sort of get landed.'

Eleanor agreed and sipped her white wine, looking about. Laurette looked at her. It was not only men in the diplomatic who got landed, she thought, it had happened to Eleanor – landed with Hugo Lawrence. Laurette knew Eleanor had never been in love with him and because she'd taken no precautions on the night of the May Ball there had been a shotgun wedding. Laurette had come back from Los Angeles too late to see Eleanor married; she'd sent a showy wedding present and held her disapproving tongue.

Now it seemed as if Eleanor was having a dull time. Considering she was five years younger than Laurette and quite sexy looking, what had she got? A daughter, doubtless quite fun if you liked kids, but Laurette, after the long-ago and miserable abortion, now didn't like them at all, and a husband who might be stylish but who stood on the terrace looking as if he had toothache.

'What have you been doing with your life?' she enquired, 'Fill me in.'

'Not much,' said Eleanor. 'Not a lot. And don't be afraid I shall bore on about Joanna. I made a resolution on my way here that I wouldn't mention her.'

'Why not? I'd be interested.'

Eleanor laughed. 'Don't lie. Tell me about *your* life, Laurette. You know I enjoy your stories. How about your boss?'

'Charley is a nervous wreck. He's one of those muddlers. He loses and forgets things, and then gets round everybody to help, even me. Bags of charm but not ambitious enough for my taste. He's a softy. But he sure likes a good time. You should see him every morning going through his invites. Barges into his secretary's room to collect them, then picks up the pile and holds it in his hand like a woman with a fan. Finally, reads them aloud to us, one by one.'

'I suppose they're the same as Hugo's. Political do's.'

'They should be, shouldn't they? Most are miles from the job dear Charley is supposed to be getting on with. Dress shows, book launches, foreign film promotions, advertising freebees. What Charley enjoys is the being wanted. He behaves like a beauty besieged. "So difficult having to spread oneself so thin."'

Laurette had an unsuccessful try at an English accent.

'Lucy panders to him because she's in love. Very off-putting if you go into his office and they're together – hot with sex.'

'Him?'

'No, her. She lusts after poor old Charley and all he does is decide if it will be the Italian dress show or the blue Swedish film.'

'You lead a wonderful life,' said Eleanor teasingly.

'Don't I, though? Now I'll tell you something much more interesting – about my new man. He works at a German university, Bayreuth, and he's over in London right now. Short and fair and heavenly. Do you know what he said to me yesterday? "What are you doing every night this week?"'

The phrase stayed in Eleanor's mind after she and Laurette had said goodbye. She envied her: for her career, for such masculine admiration, even for a man who could say such a thing.

Still musing, she arrived at Joanna's school. Hugo had made a joke about the school, he said the only subject they taught was which expensive toy from Harrods to ask for next. A few mothers and far more nannies were waiting on the steps of the Pont Street house. Eleanor knew one or two of the mothers but not a single nanny. Appalling snobs, arrayed in sober grey, they formed an exclusive gossiping clique. They did not conceal their opinion that mothers shouldn't be there at all to collect their children. A mother should be out, having tea at the Ritz.

The double doors of the school opened and the children in green checked dresses or green corduroy shorts surged down the steps. Their satchels were full of wild and incomprehensible drawings destined to be waved at nannies and parents to earn exaggerated praise. Some of the pupils rocketed out still full of energy, others were more sedate, some held hands. One or two of the boys showed off. Eleanor's daughter arrived, hopping. She had inherited her mother's freckles, but her hair was brownish and curled all over her head like Shirley Temple's, giving her a deceptively angelic look. Walking beside Eleanor she said, 'I got six for drawing. Abigail's was worser and had a blodge, but she got seven. Lunch was yukky – why can't I take sandwiches? Can I have Hannah and Mary-Beth to tea?'

After Mirrén had left, taking her comforting presence from the cottage, Eleanor gave Joanna some tea, admired the drawings, allowed a rationed half hour of Children's TV and then took Joanna off for her bath. She felt, remembering Laurette, somewhat over-domestic. Other women had dazzling jobs. When she went to Ferne Place, for instance, she had noticed that Walter's Three Musketeers had changed, one was now a woman. A Musketrice, Hugo said.

It grated on Eleanor, much as she adored her pretty, demanding daughter, that she was trapped. She had walked into the trap with her eyes open, but that did not make it less constricting. To be a wife-and-mother, the words tied as if by the umbilical cord, was looked on now in the late seventies as an anachronism. American opinion had crossed the sea.

'Can I have a kiss and cuddle?' said Joanna and nearly throttled her.

Hugo was late that evening. The day had been warm but as evening drew in it became unexpectedly hot. The cottage windows were not big enough and when Joanna was asleep, Eleanor crept round propping open every door. Supper was cold, thank heaven, and there were no visitors. She had nothing to do.

It was quiet in the mews. Now and then a car drove by, slowing down as it went through the archway. There was the sound of footsteps on the cobbles and once she heard a girl laugh.

She felt inexplicably sad. The world was a terrible and tragic place and her part in it was little enough. People had discussed that this morning on the radio. She did not find it comforting to see herself as a minute dot in the enormous and mysterious universe. She could not grasp the loss, grief, starvation, poverty and war. The world was too big. She remembered an elderly mistress at school saying to Agnes and herself, 'I believe God meant us to be happy.'

When Hugo drove into the mews and let himself into the

house, he called out as usual, 'Eleanor?'

There was no reply. A spell of absolute silence. Surprised, he called again from the foot of the stairs, 'Eleanor?'

Still no voice answered and he went up to the sitting room faster than usual. The door was open and as he came in he saw her. She was deeply asleep, her Rossetti hair fanned out on a cushion, her dress creased. At the sight of the still figure, he gave a tender smile. In his daughter's room, Joanna was also dead to the world, one arm flung out and her mouth open. A smell of peppermint filled the room; she had been eating sweets in bed again.

Going back to his sleeping wife, he sat down and stretched his long legs. Silence came lapping up like a slow incoming tide, and after the long day of talk, quiet was a balm. He, too, closed his eyes.

When sleep took away the intelligence and awareness of his face, he looked worn for a man scarcely 37. He had always been thin but it was not a thinness which made for grace. He was high-shouldered. A swathe of dark hair fell in a crescent across his forehead and its anxieties. Awake, he was clever and worried and kind. When he smiled, it was a reward.

Into the long pause, the telephone rang. They both woke with a start.

'Hugo, you're back.'

'Only a while ago,' he said, picking up the telephone.

She yawned and lazily stretched, but as she glanced at him, the sensuous movement stopped.

'Luis? Yes, she's here. I see. . .' Listening. 'Of course. I'll ring back right away. Goodbye for the moment.'

Eleanor burst out as she replaced the telephone, 'Something awful's happened to Dad!'

He said carefully, 'Nothing serious. Walter had a little heart attack—'

'He's dying!'

'Calm down, Eleanor, he is *not* dying. You really mustn't get into such a state. Apparently he was taken ill this afternoon—' Hugo realised too late that he should have used milder words.

'This afternoon! Why didn't Luis ring at once?'

'My darling, just listen. Let me tell you what Luis just told me. Your father was okay when he got back from London but then he became ill and Luis sent for the doctor who examined him and gave him something. He's asleep. A more thorough examination has been fixed for tomorrow. The reason Luis couldn't ring you earlier was that Walter asked him not to. Didn't want you bothered, apparently.'

She was about to burst out again, and he added calmly, 'In any case Luis was kept busy by your father who gave him a string of international calls to make. Luis rang us just now from the local pub.'

'My God!'

'Eleanor, don't shout. He went out to make the call because Walter said we weren't to be told and Luis decided, quite rightly, that we should be. You are to stop being hysterical or you'll be useless when you go down to be with Walter. Now be quiet, while I think.'

Hugo's sharp voice and obvious disapproval worked. Neither she nor he had turned on the lights; the room was barely lit by street lamps in the mews. She switched on a table lamp. Hugo was at the window, standing with his back to her. He turned round.

'This is what we will do. Of course you want to go to Ferne Place. We'll take no notice of your father's ban; when people get ill they often say things like that. But you certainly don't want Jo with you, so I'll ring Agnes in Plymouth. She'll be glad to have her.'

'But—'

'No buts. Jo doesn't have to go to school, even if she does enjoy it. She'll be no trouble with Agnes, who is always wanting her to go and stay. And Jo is mad about Emily, so that'll work well. I'll ring Agnes at once.'

He did not wait for Eleanor to agree but went into the bedroom to telephone, shutting the door. He often did that.

Later he came back to say Agnes was only too pleased to have the little girl, and that he'd take Joanna down to Plymouth tomorrow morning. There was a train at half past nine, the Cornish Express.

'I can be back in London easily by tomorrow night.'

Eleanor let him take over. She went to bed early and slept badly. Once, waking and turning towards him, she saw that he was wide awake. He put his arms round her and pulled her to him, making a soft sweet noise.

Thanks to Hugo things went as smoothly as a Rolls-Royce engine. He rang the Spanish convent very early, 'Nuns wake at dawn,' and got hold of Mirrén who arrived before breakfast to pack and jolly the little girl out of her loud complaints, 'Why do I *have* to go?'

Hugo had made up his mind that Eleanor needed Mirrén's help. She was too miserable and anxious to cope either with a crying daughter or the simple task of packing Joanna's suitcase. Mirrén even cooked breakfast and forced the little girl to eat something while Hugo telephoned for a taxi.

When Eleanor came out into the mews to see them off, Joanna was scowling from the taxi window. Hugo had fetched his own car and parked it at the door; he gave her the keys.

'I'll ring you tonight, sweetheart. I know Walter will pick up; he's as strong as an ox. I'll be down at the weekend.'

Joanna gave her a hug and a sob, and Eleanor turned to embrace Hugo. Her arms were as tightly round him as if they were parting in time of war.

She drove out of London, all her thoughts on her father. She had rung Ferne Place before leaving, but Luis reported no news. The doctor had come again, and had left; her father was asleep, and must be kept completely quiet. Luis sounded calm. But Eleanor remembered that her friend, the dignified Spaniard who had been part of her life since she was a child, had been forced to go to the pub to let her know her own father was ill. Had Walter really wanted to prevent her being told? Hugo said it was because he hadn't wanted them to worry. She scarcely believed it.

Since the time when Walter had not lifted a hand to help her when she was desperate to have an abortion, her feelings for him were ambivalent. She believed he probably did not love her. But nothing was as simple as that. Feelings moved and changed, lightened and darkened, filled out or reduced. Walter was no longer in the centre of her life: the man who was her next of kin, who sent her off to school or university but who was *there*, his American presence and broad shoulders filling the house and the calendar. Marrying Hugo had meant losing her thirst for Walter's love. Disillusionment in him had helped. But you did not stop loving people because you found them out, just as you did not stop hope of love when there was little point in it. Driving through the speckled light and shade of Balcombe woods, Eleanor still hoped.

It felt odd to turn into the drive of Ferne Place. She and Hugo and Joanna did come down sometimes, usually because Hugo insisted. Eleanor found the visits unsettling.

She knew Walter might – perhaps – have been interested if Joanna had been a boy. Hugo disagreed, saying how proud Walter was of his granddaughter. What he meant was that Walter asked Joanna the automatic questions grown-ups ask children whom they don't know.

'How's school?'

'What have you got there?'

Joanna was too shy to answer and Walter would give a sort of laugh while Hugo, a diplomat in his bones, looked approving. He enjoyed staying at Ferne Place, and always combined the weekends with seeing his own family at Hillier's. Without husband or daughter, Eleanor drove up to the old house as if back into girlhood.

Luis came out before she put on the brakes.

'Luis.'

'Mrs Lawrence.'

The small man was exactly the same, dark and neat. He took her hand and pressed it, and the rare gesture brought tears to her eyes. They stood for a moment outside the house which was hung with the grapes of flowering wisteria like a sentimental painting.

'Is he really bad?'

'I don't know, Mrs Lawrence. Perhaps a little bit bad.'

'Were you with him?'

'Maria and I heard a noise. A fall. We found him in the study on the floor; he could not get up. But he is better, the doctor said, and will be glad to see you.'

'Oh. I hope so.'

The house was full of sunshine. When Luis took her bags upstairs she stood for a moment not knowing where to go. The door of the study was wide open and a voice called, 'Is that Eleanor?'

Giles Burnett, her father's partner and perhaps his only

friend, came out to give her a kiss. He was quite matter of fact. 'Luis has just made coffee. Come and have a cup with me.'

The manner and voice were not deliberately used to calm her down. Giles would have behaved in the same way on the *Titanic*. He settled her beside him, poured the coffee, asked after Joanna and Hugo, and smiled and nodded. Eleanor was not sure whether to be glad or maddened by this and cut through it by blurting out, 'Giles, is my father going to die?'

He had been expecting the question, and answered in a manner not unlike a priest's. His nature was old-fashioned, shrewd, dryly humorous and charitable. It was the anti-thesis of the way he looked, which was rather like one of the long narrow animals of the hedgerows and English woods: a stoat, a weasel. His features were thrust forward, his nose long and his eyes set flat in his head like silverish stones. He was handsome in a way, his hair, like his eyes, a greyish silver. He remarked that he had talked to the doctor.

'We won't know how it is with Walter for a day or two.'

'Oh Giles.'

Compassion filled the narrow eyes.

'My dear child, you have to be your brave self, you know. Very positive. I'm sure you won't find that difficult.'

'But I'm scared. Ever since last night I keep having a — a feeling—'

'We're not going to have the bit about feminine intuition, are we, Eleanor? In my experience it can be counted upon to be wrong every time,' he said. She gave a weak smile.

The room, warmed by the morning sun, smelled of polished furniture and leather, of Walter's cigars, and a particular smell which came from new books. Walter's shelves were filled with books and whenever she came into the study, she noticed a number more. They lined the room, their shiny jackets vivid or white, many as stout as dictionaries, most of them brand-new. Her father had got into the habit of buying books, mostly on the subject of American politics: *The Modern Corporation and Private Property*, *Governing the United States*, *The Pentagon Papers*. The titles did not interest Eleanor and once, idly taking down a book to flip through it, it was clear from the way some of the pages were stuck together that her father had never opened it.

'Have you seen him yet, Giles?'

'Only for a minute or two. The doctor said I mustn't stay. But Walter wanted me to.'

Eleanor looked at him and said nothing. Outside the windows the tended garden basked. The lawns were shaved as close as the nape of a soldier's neck, hedges clipped, not a weed dared pop up across the beautiful Cotswold stone of the terrace. Roses obediently flowered, crimson and yellow, orange and white; a summer day in blossom. Eleanor wondered what it held for her, and Giles wondered too. Walter had no experience of being ill. Did it, Giles asked himself, need a special sort of skill; and who amongst us was up to it?

The telephone rang all day. Luis had removed one of the instruments which was in his employer's bedroom; there were six around the house. Giles took the calls, all of them to do with Walter's American interests, nothing to do with Nelson's advertising agency. After lunch with Eleanor, he spent the day at Walter's desk, fielding the calls. Even during the meal, the telephone had interrupted.

Eleanor was at a loose end. She and Giles both agreed she shouldn't go to her father before they checked with the doctor. Luis told them Walter was still asleep.

Leaving Giles occupied with those non-stop telephone calls, she went out into the garden. The beauty of the day, the scent of roses, the dazzling sunshine, made her feel worse. When she saw Giles beckoning her from the terrace, she ran.

'The doctor's arrived, Eleanor. He wants a word.'

'Surely he'll let me see Dad now!'

Christopher Wilkinson, tall and grizzled, had attended the Nelsons as far back as the time when Eleanor, aged twelve, had had the chicken-pox. He was soon to retire, and had about him something people used to believe was a doctor's power. He never hurried, thought nothing of spending half an hour talking to a patient about the most unimportant little worry, aimed to send any man or woman away feeling better, perhaps only by giving them obvious and comfortable advice. He was out of date, like the cut of his dark suit and his little jokes.

He was standing in the drawing room by the fireplace which Luis, every summer, filled with beech leaves.

'There you are, Eleanor. Luis said you came from London this morning.'

'I came at once. I can nurse him.'

'I don't think you can, my dear, but that's the spirit. Come and sit down.'

'You're going to give me bad news.'

'You look a wee bit tired. Come along now.'

She sat down beside him. All the upholstered furniture in the Nelson house was filled with the finest feathers, and she sank into cushions as if into a great bowl of thistledown.

'How strong do you feel, Eleanor?'

'He's dying!'

'No, I wouldn't say that. But he is very ill and he could decide to leave us. He'll either pull through within the next

forty-eight hours or he will go. You will have to be strong,'
he said, sounding like Giles.

She was aghast.

'Shouldn't he be in hospital?'

'Yes. He won't go.'

'*What do you mean*?'

'Eleanor, a patient who is in his right mind, and your
father is completely in control not only of his mind but of
his life, has a perfect right to refuse hospital. He informed
me that he detests the idea, and refuses to be moved. He
said that I could hire a nurse, or get necessary equipment
and whatever is needed. But that he will not leave Ferne
Place. As a matter of fact, I'm content with that. The more
he stays still the better, and I've engaged a first-class nurse
who has worked with me before. She's just arrived, by the
way. So, Walter has made up his mind, and you and I, and
Giles Burnett, and the world of advertising will just have to
accept it. You see,' finished Wilkinson, studying her
thoughtfully, 'I'm providing what your father calls the
doings, while you—'

'And Giles.'

'No, not Giles. The less business is brought into the
sickroom the better. Your father must not be disturbed or
worried. He needs all his energy to fight this. You are his
only relative, that's right, isn't it?'

'His parents in America both died. Yes, there's only me.'

'I gathered as much. You must be in evidence. Go in and
see him. Sit by his bed. Be there.'

'Of course!'

'Good work.' He stood up, with a glance of approval at
her, like a schoolmaster with a clever pupil.

When the doctor had left, Giles appeared and said the
nurse was waiting to see Eleanor.

She was young, dark, pretty and with more freckles than either Eleanor or Joanna. Eleanor was glad of her good looks; Walter had a disgraceful dislike of plain women. Her name, she said, was Jill. She sounded as relaxed as if she had just arrived for tennis.

'Would you like to pop up now for a bit, Mrs Lawrence?'

'Nurse—'

'Do call me Jill. I'm not mad on the Nurse title, are you?'

'My name's Eleanor.'

'That's a nice name. So, Eleanor, would you like to go up and see him? Don't stay long. He is awake and not too comfortable. I have given him an injection, and he should be asleep again soon. You've got about ten minutes. Good luck,' added Jill.

Eleanor hurried up the stairs. The whole house was washed in sunlight, every window, many of them tall and fine, was open and all summer flooded in. She went down a panelled passage, its vivid blue carpet like a strip of sky, to her father's bedroom. She pushed open the door.

She had only once before in her life been into this room. It was when Walter had been abroad, and a longing had come over Eleanor to see if he kept a photograph of herself. There had been none.

Her father lay in a large double bed with a dark, carved oak bedback; it had originally been part of a four poster. The pillows were piled high. He lay with his eyes shut, his face not grey but pink. His hair had been carefully brushed; his silk pyjamas were pristine. The sheet had been folded by a hand so skilful that the band in front of him did not have a single ruck or crease.

Eleanor's heart stifled her. She pulled a chair towards the bed; it made a swishing noise across the carpet and he opened his eyes.

'Dad.'

He said in a normal voice, slightly weakened, 'What are you doing here?'

'Just on a visit,' she managed, to the accompaniment of her hammering heart. He continued to look at her. Her hair flamed in the sunny room, her white blouse dazzled. She was a Rossetti damsel too bright for his eyes; he narrowed them.

'Is Hugo here? And the child?'

'Do you want to see them, Dad?'

'Not particularly,' he said, dry as dry.

'Then you don't have to.'

'But are they here?' You could never put Walter off without a complete explanation.

'There's only me. Hugo's working in London and Jo has gone to stay with Agnes.'

No reply. It occurred to Eleanor, very late, that the room was too glaring and so was she. She went over to draw the curtains across one of the windows, but it was the wrong one. It put a different part of the big room into shadow and Walter's bed was still in the light. He said tetchily, 'There are Venetian blinds. Call the nurse.'

'But I can easily—'

'Do as I say.'

She went to the door and called and by some magic, Jill who had not been in sight, appeared from an empty bedroom. She fixed the blinds in silence, gave Eleanor a glance of encouragement and went out again.

With the room now in tiger stripes, Walter was less troubled by the blazing vision of his daughter. He closed his eyes just the same. She returned to her chair, and to hope.

The silence which followed filled up with strangely loud bird-song coming through the open windows. There were no house sounds. Ferne Place could be completely empty except for Dad and me, she thought, thank God it isn't. Glad that his eyes were shut, she looked at him earnestly, even reverently, with a flood of love as strong as sunshine. Why did it take illness to release emotion like this? She looked tenderly and passionately at the old face, once handsome but always since she could remember with the same set expression – to her.

She had been to an exhibition at Greenwich once; there were treasures saved from old, old ships, and the faces of the garishly painted figureheads which had braved the oceans were like Walter's. Roughly carved by the hands of inferior carpenters using coarse wood, the figures had jutting noses and harshly angled chins. She had never had the chance to stare, hungry and uninterrupted, at her father's face until now. His eyelashes were short and pale. Grey hair in little tufts grew out of his ears. Why hadn't the expensive barber in Jermyn Street clipped those? They were ugly. Walter had never been vain. He was dignified, strong, fixed and never not fiercely ambitious. But physically he was unaware of his looks, demanding only that his expensive clothes should fit well, and that his ties were of the style you did not notice.

She was leaning forward, straining to anatomise him, when he opened his eyes again.

She blushed.

When he spoke, his voice was weaker. 'You'd better go.'

'You want to sleep, Dad?'

'Probably. Leave me in any case.'

'Of course. I'll come back.'

He did not answer that, but stared into space for a while. Then, with all his coldness, 'I have a great deal to think about.'

'Of course,' she said again.

Jill was brisking along towards the sickroom as Eleanor came out. Her energetic walk, her practical air, comforted Eleanor. Nobody could be like that if they thought—'

'You're out rather soon. Everything okay?'

'Yes.'

Jill gave her a quick look.

'I'll come and get you when he wants another little chat.'

Eleanor couldn't settle and trailed down to the kitchen to talk to Luis's plump little wife, Maria. The Spanish woman, though in her late twenties, had no children as yet and a passionate adoration of Joanna, who on the family's not very frequent visits to Ferne Place, spent her time in the kitchen being spoiled to death. Today Maria, muttering sympathetic sentences half in Spanish and half in English, asked for news of the little girl. Eleanor lingered and they talked. Maria was cooking: scones, apple tarts, home-made pâté. She seemed to expect scores of visitors. Funeral baked meats? At the thought Eleanor grew nervous and after a while, murmuring an excuse, left Maria and went to the library.

Giles was replacing the telephone.

'New York again,' he said, with a sigh. 'Some senator or other talking about the problem of getting re-elected. I'm sure he thought I work with Walter on his American projects. Apparently your father was due at a meeting in New York tomorrow morning.'

Eleanor was struck and uneasy.

'What did you say?'

'That Walter isn't well. The man didn't mind that too much, anybody can be indisposed. But when he asked to speak to Walter and I said he couldn't at present, I'm afraid he got ratty.'

'Why was he ratty?' she asked, using the curious word.

'Perhaps rattled would be more accurate. It was quite difficult. I expect you know, Eleanor, that neither the agency nor I myself have anything to do with Walter's politicking in the States. I scarcely know what he's up to, but he's involved, apparently, in a number of councils, trade conventions and so on. He gets himself into business which is nothing to do with Nelson's. I'm no use at coping with that side of his work.'

Eleanor sat down, hugging her shoulders. After a while she said, her voice hoarse, 'He always makes everything happen the way he wants. He can't die. He mustn't.'

'My dear child, I am sure he'll pull through.'

'No, you're not, Giles. You think there's no hope. And Dr Wilkinson practically said—'

'Doctors get things wrong too often for my liking, Eleanor.'

'I want to believe you. I don't believe you.'

The telephone rang again.

The sun flooded through the south-facing windows until it was the turn of the western casements to wink and sparkle. Luis brought tea and Giles and Eleanor were briefly joined by Nurse Jill, bright as the afternoon. She made Giles laugh once or twice. Eleanor despised herself for not behaving well. She knew how much they wanted her to. But all she could think was that she must see her father again and that minute by minute the time was going. Jill left them, but did not come back to fetch her.

Eleanor waited until early evening. Then she could bear it no longer and went upstairs again, down the long blue corridor. Her father's door was ajar, and when she put her head in, the nurse sitting on the opposite side of the bed saw her at once. Walter was sleeping.

Jill beckoned, standing up and moving as silently as a leaf, went to Eleanor. She whispered, 'I'm glad you came. I've been hoping you would. I prefer not to leave him and I was certain you'd come for a chance of a word when he wakes.'

'Will he wake?'

'Quite soon, I'm sure. I know those particular pills and they're due to wear off about now. His pulse is uneven but I think I could leave you with him for a little. Is that what you want?'

The sentences were so low as to be well-nigh inaudible, breathed first into Eleanor's ear and then in turn to Jill's.

'You want to stay, don't you?'

'But ought you to be here too?' whispered Eleanor, longing for her to say no.

'I'll leave you for a few minutes. Okay? Five minutes,' said Jill in less than a breath.

She gave Eleanor her almost inhumanly kind smile and crept out.

Eleanor went to the bed. Here at last was the longed-for, refused, ached-for, prayed-for, rejected and still believed-in chance to reach her father's heart. She no longer thought that the old man was dying. Only love obsessed her as it had done all her life since her mother had gone. She sat down in Jill's chair, pulling it closer to the bed.

It was as if *her* heart expanded, grew larger in her breast, filled up with beautiful and blessed emotions of daughterly love and faith, as she sat so near him and he lay so rosy and still and, in a strange kind of way, so good. He looked noble. And she thought now that this was the father who had swum with her that time, who, when they came out of the sea and climbed on board, had smiled. That was all she remembered as she sat close. He breathed so quietly that she couldn't hear him.

At last his eyelashes fluttered and he opened his eyes.

In his misted view, half drugged, half sleep-slurred, he saw a beautiful face framed in reddish gold hair, all earnestness and devotion.

'I thought – I said – you should go.'

'I did, Dad. I've been away hours. It's late afternoon and I came to see you this morning.'

Although she spoke quietly, the life and energy in her voice made him grimace as if in pain.

'What's the matter? Shall I get the nurse?' She spoke more loudly in alarm.

'Nothing. Don't get her. Nothing.'

'You're going to be better, Dad. I *know* it.'

She leaned over and took his cold hand.

He did not react, gave no answering pressure. He simply lay and looked at her.

'Dad.'

He did not answer but she knew he was listening.

'I love you,' she heard herself say in a strangled voice.

Such a look he gave her. It was filled with irony.

Tears came into her eyes. She leaned forward, the bright hair falling across her face and tears spilling as she stammered, 'I do, I do, I always have. You've got to get better. For me and – and Giles and your friends – and Hugo and Jo. We need you, Dad, me most of all. I do love you,' she repeated, her eyes swimming. She bent and kissed his hand, the tears falling wetly on his freckled skin. She felt his hand move. He was trying to take it away and said, speaking with difficulty, 'You had better go.'

'Whatever you say, Dad. Whatever you say.'

She was scarcely conscious of her words, only of what she wanted to do. She bent towards him and leaning down, pressed her lips on his cheek.

He turned his face weakly away.

Even Eleanor far gone in sorrow and with a bursting heart saw the feeble gesture for what it meant, and gasping, 'Sorry, sorry,' ran out of the room.

Walter died late that night. Giles was there, and the nurse. Eleanor had sobbed herself to sleep and when Giles, at the end, gripped his old friend's hand and said he would fetch her, Walter managed a 'No, no, no, no, no,' as final as Lear's five nevers.

Chapter Seven

'So they've decided I'm to be Second Secretary.'
'*In Brazil!*'

He laughed at her expression.

'Does it sound hideously far away, Eleanor? I'm sure we'll enjoy it. You remember Bob Johnson worked in Brazil for two or three years. He says Rio is spectacular.'

Hugo spoke in his usual easy manner but had not been looking forward to breaking the news. He knew it would be a shock.

They were breakfasting late. It was Sunday, and Hugo had decided two days ago that this would be the right time to tell Eleanor that they would soon be leaving London. By the end of the day she would have become slightly used to the idea – which was a bombshell he himself had been expecting for months.

It was late into the autumn, wet and chill, and nearly four months had gone by since Walter Nelson's death. Hugo had been anxious about Eleanor; her recovery was slow. She had not told him but he guessed that at the end her father must have rejected her, and his heart ached when he had looked at her stricken face that day. He had never made Walter Nelson out, but knew him to be a cold man. How could he have been cold to an only child and such a beguiling one? Hugo sometimes remembered that Eleanor's mother had left Walter. It seemed a curious revenge.

On that first morning at Ferne Place after her father's death, Hugo had driven down to find his wife unable to speak without sobbing, and when she did manage to bring out a sentence it scarcely made sense. It was the good-looking nurse who said, 'Perhaps you could leave her to me for a bit?' and dragged Eleanor out of the house for a walk across the fields. The nurse had been practical as well as pretty, and curiously in command; what had she said to her? Hugo never knew but the Eleanor who returned home after more than two hours was at least rational.

A look of shock, a recurring melancholy, remained. When he was told that his posting was confirmed and he'd be working once again in South America, but this time in Brazil, Hugo had been relieved. Now he said in his concerned way, 'It's what you need, darling. A total change of scene. Literally another world. It will help you recover.'

'Hugo, I'm not ill.'

He didn't answer, a habit which sometimes annoyed her, but remarked that there were a great many things to be done, and the toughest was breaking the news to Joanna that she must leave her school. She enjoyed it so much, and had at least half a dozen friends.

'Will you tell her? Or shall I?'

'Of course I will,' said Eleanor, frowning. She didn't like to admit that Joanna's temperament sometimes unnerved her. Where did the child get her love of drama, her high spirits?

The following day Hugo dropped Joanna at school, the dread subject had not yet been broached, and Eleanor, alone, faced her own feelings of alarm and dismay. She

needed to talk, to be reassured, but was too proud to turn
to Hugo. He had supported her with all his strength when
Walter died. She couldn't be so stupid as to go sobbing to
him again. She sat for a while, wondering who would – at
least – comfort her slightly, and telephoned the House of
Commons. In a surprisingly short time she was put through
to the Library.

'Laurette Jacobs speaking. Who is this?'

'Me. Eleanor.'

'That's a nice surprise. What can I do for you this
depressingly wet day?'

'Is it raining? I hadn't noticed.'

'Observation has never been your strong point. It's cats
and dogs out there. Why have you called? Don't think I'm
not delighted, but is there a reason?'

'I want to see you.'

'Oh good. Any chance of lunch today?' Laurette's
hospitality suggested that this time Eleanor should come to
the House. 'They do a mean ham sandwich in a crazy sort
of Gothic bar. You'll like it. Also there's a hot debate on
unemployment – which is up to well over a million! With
Labour not even having a majority – poor old them – any
debate at present really *is* hot. We'll have the place to
ourselves. Want to bring your daughter?'

'No, thank you. Jo's at school, and anyway surely in
Parliament . . .'

'MPs often appear with broods of kids. Quite the day
nursery, specially at Christmas before they drag them off to
pantomimes. Why do they bother when there's one right
here? See you at 12.30.'

Eleanor had never met Laurette before in what her
friend called her place of work. She arrived in a taxi
and, shaking a dripping umbrella, came into a vast

high-ceilinged echoing hall haunted by statues. There was
no sign of Laurette, and all she saw were crowds of men
hobnobbing or hurrying. Eleanor, somewhat lost, stood
staring fixedly up at a marble Disraeli when Laurette
appeared. She wore a tweed jacket with black velvet lapels,
a green satin blouse and long sleek pants. She was still
redheaded, her hair a mass of curls.

'Good to see you; it's been too long. Let me lead you away
from this monkey house.'

Eleanor was bustled down corridors hung with paintings
– Kings, Queens and a good many commoners on their
knees – like those in an old-fashioned storybook. Statues
stood in every corner. Laurette finally took Eleanor into a
bar with latticed windows which overlooked the grey river
on a grey day. There was a table by the window with
'reserved' on it, drinks and a silver-covered dish.

'To us,' said Laurette, as they picked up their glasses.

Eleanor blurted out, 'Hugo's been posted. We're going to
Brazil in less than a month.'

'Leaping lizards!' Laurette contrived to look fascinated
and stimulated at the same time. 'Fun, surely?'

'Will it be?'

'You're not telling me you're not delighted.'

Eleanor said doubtfully that Hugo thought the move
would be good for her and Laurette nodded without
sympathy. In the past she'd been intrigued by the idea of
Eleanor's rich and successful father and had managed to
get Eleanor to introduce them. But Walter had been one
of her rare failures, although she had determinedly
sparkled at him. When he died, she wrote her friend an
intelligent letter of sympathy and that was that. She
considered people shouldn't wallow. She herself wallowed
a great deal if things went badly but never allowed the

luxury to be acceptable in her friends.

'You'll have a fantastic time. The Latin-American thing is exciting. Dangerous, of course, but exciting. I only wish I could get to Brazil or Argentina. Have you read any of their history?'

Luckily for Eleanor, Laurette did not continue; one or two of Hugo's friends would have talked about Brazil for hours. All she did say was, 'You realise it's the fifth largest country in the world.'

'You're so American.'

'Sure am. Honestly, Eleanor, I don't know what more you could want. Brazil's a legend: the amazing scenery, huge jungles and waterfalls, that Carnival! And the people, all different races mixed up and apparently terrific, warm and friendly and sexy. God, I sound like a brochure.'

'You sound good to me.'

Laurette continued to encourage her to look forward to Brazil, adding that there was the merry fact of being in the diplomatic abroad. She and Hugo would live in luxury, that couldn't be bad, could it?

'Hugo says it isn't like that any more – economies.'

'Your husband was born to do his job: sounding the note of caution.'

Having covered Eleanor's future, Laurette now settled down to talk about her own affairs.

'Or to be precise, a new affair. Guess who? My boss.'

'But you said last time that it was his secretary who . . .'

'Yes. Poor Lucy. She was in a bad way. She had to go. Now we have the professional woman, fortyish, sterner stuff, good for Charley's image. Shall I tell you about him?'

Of course she did. Charles Westrow was upper-class, heavily married, moneyed and wonderfully old. He would never see fifty again. He had two daughters at Cheltenham Ladies' College ('Can you beat it?') and a long-suffering wife from the Shires.

'Poor her.'

'I don't see why. Charley would never leave her, and he is much safer with me than Lucy; she would have sobbed him into the grave. The wife is a loyal political spouse; you know, gives teas. She used to like me.'

'And now?'

'What do you think?'

'Yes,' said Eleanor, 'I don't think I'd be too keen on you as a rival.'

The big Gothic room was filling up; apparently the excitement in the House had subsided. Men in dark suits, many with ties which sprouted flowers, gathered in loud talking groups. Few women were present, and the ones who were around noticeably lacked Laurette's glamour. Now and again a man looked over at Laurette, gave her a salute or even, once, a wink. Laurette responded with pleasure.

She was strong and lively and somehow pitiless and she comforted Eleanor who had had, ever since the first time they met, the surprise of being liked by her. Time went fast and Eleanor said that she must go.

'Must you? I could always work late. Let's have more coffee.'

'I wish I could stay. But I must collect Jo from school.'

'Maternity, maternity,' mocked Laurette, waving to an elderly waitress and signing the bill. They walked back down corridors looked down at indifferently by Gladstone and Peel.

'So,' said Laurette in the entrance hall, 'I'm going to lose you to the Land without Limit.'

'Who called Brazil that?'

'Some guy. That's what I want to be called: Laurette –
Woman without Limit.'

'Conceited *and* American,' said Eleanor, laughing as
they kissed goodbye.

There was too much to do. Long telephone calls to Agnes
who took the news with annoying calmness. But Eleanor
was not the only one with departures in mind: Agnes was
due to follow David soon to Singapore. Eleanor, said her
sister-in-law, would have a wonderful time. In the tones of
Agnes's voice, Eleanor recognised the Service wife's philo-
sophical outlook at being shifted all over the globe. *She* had
none of that and was as disturbed as she was busy. The
cottage was to be let furnished; Hugo did not want them to
lose their London home and his posting was fixed, at any
rate at present, for only two years.

If Eleanor was unsettled, Joanna was downright upset at
having to leave London, lose her friends and give up her
school. When she was told the news she rushed to her room,
threw herself on the bed and wouldn't budge. It was very
difficult to shift her: she was sturdy and strongly-built.
Mirrén, sad to lose the family, begged. Eleanor, worn out,
scolded. At last Joanna lifted an exquisite tear-smeared
face, mouth trembling, and wailed, 'I'm so miserable.'

It was Mathilde who came to the rescue. She was fond of
Agnes's Emily and Nicole, but was not too sure about
Joanna who invariably wanted to sit on the floor or stay up
for dinner. Mathilde liked her rules kept. But when the
family arrived at Hillier's for a farewell weekend, Hugo
confided in her that Joanna was very upset by going away.
Mathilde listened gravely.

During tea, an elaborate Hillier's meal and the only one
Joanna enjoyed, Mathilde produced a faded exercise book.

Joanna, she said, must draw the animals, birds, reptiles and insects native to Brazil. Each drawing above the first dozen would earn twenty pence.

'But I do not think you will manage very many.'

Joanna's eyes gleamed.

Mathilde would have made a good teacher. She found the child an old and magnificently illustrated Larousse. She drove her to Brighton, Joanna much impressed at a journey entirely on her account. They went together to the natural history museum, and Mathilde bought her a chart – Wild Life in the South-American Continent. Painting black vultures, butterflies, green tree frogs and humpless woolly llamas, Joanna grew positively cheerful.

But when not with the child, Mathilde was sad. Her son was going away again, this time even further than when he had been posted to Peru. John Lawrence understood her fond heart. He did not sympathise in words, he believed actions spoke louder, and paid more attention to her, and took her out more. She was always in his thoughts.

He himself was pleased about his son's new job. The Lawrences, until Hugo, had been Army people. To be sent across the world, to have life fractured and re-made somewhere far off was to be expected. He and Hugo shared a bottle of champagne.

'Second Secretary,' he said, toasting him.

'It's an automatic step, Father.'

'Up the ladder, though. More responsibility.'

'Yes. Quite a bit of that.'

Lawrence's weatherbeaten still-handsome face creased into a smile. 'You sound as if you don't dislike the prospect.'

Neither mentioned money. Walter would have done. Eleanor had done.

'I'm afraid your mother's a wee bit down about you going,' confided Lawrence as he refilled the glasses. 'As you know, David and Aggie aren't off to Singapore just yet fortunately. I'm going to ask Aggie to come and stay after you've left. Later I shall take Mathilde to Montbard. Seeing her French relatives and privately telling me they've all got old and dull does her a power of good.'

Hugo was at home with his father. They loved each other in the same speechless way. Intuitive about women, they were still half mystified by them. Needing them, they scarcely knew it. In the old despised days of the past they would have called their wives 'the little woman'.

Despite not much liking Mathilde and aware the feeling was returned, Eleanor enjoyed her time at Hillier's. It was a treat to have Joanna consulting Mathilde or being taken on country walks with John Lawrence. Eleanor decided that she now had the chance to drive over to Ferne Place. Luis and Maria were still there. When she telephoned them, they sounded so pleased to hear her voice. She had made no decision about the house; Giles and the solicitors had advised her to let the matter rest for the time being.

Before she drove to her old home, she rang Giles.

'I'm glad you telephoned, Eleanor. Luis has been on to me: a thoroughly reliable man. He tells me they plan to return to Spain soon. They have saved quite a bit,' he added approvingly.

Eleanor mentioned that she was driving over to Ferne Place to see them. 'I realised they'd be going one of these days,' she said. 'This will be a chance to say goodbye and thank them.'

'Good idea.'

A pause.

'Eleanor, there are matters we must discuss now time is

getting short. Would you like me to come and meet you at the house?'

She accepted almost too fast.

She was at sea about everything to do with her father: the great empty house with Walter's possessions in every room; the agency, half of which they told her now belonged to her. She had been too sad to think about any of that. She could only think of Walter, and those thoughts were useless.

It was cold and dull as she turned into the familiar drive leading down to the house. There it was: grey, elaborate, formal, impressive, the place where he had died. She was surprised not to feel a single stab of pain.

Luis appeared. But there were no bags to swing from the car.

'Luis, I am so very glad to see you.'

'It is good. You look well, Mrs Lawrence. Maria has made tea in the kitchen. Will you come?'

'Yes, please.'

She preceded him into her own house and the pain she had wanted came then. The door of the library across the hall was open and there was her father's green chair.

The kitchen was warm and Maria positively bloomed as she ran over to kiss her. It was only then, seeing her even more plump and rounded, that Eleanor realised she was pregnant.

Maria interpreted the look. 'Yes, I am having a baby. It will be born in Spain. I am very old – twenty-eight already.'

Eleanor hid a smile. To Maria, it was more normal to have babies at seventeen and eighteen.

She congratulated Maria, who looked shy. So did Luis. They sat down for one of Maria's hospitable teas and the

Spaniards told her about their house in Bilbao. All the years they had worked here, it seemed, they had been paying at long distance for a house which had been gradually built for them, watched over by Luis's family. Photographs spilled across the kitchen table like playing cards. The house was white, square and quite large.

'The roof, you see? A terrace for the washing to dry.'

'That will be a garden. Luis must do it all.'

'I must learn, never have I grown things,' Luis said. While they were talking the front door bell rang.

'It is Mr Burnett. He telephoned,' said Luis, putting on his jacket.

'Yes, I knew he was coming, but I hoped he'd be late.'

'Mrs Lawrence. He never is.'

When Luis had left the kitchen, Maria put her plump face on her hands, her elbows on the table.

'You do not think us unkind? To be excited to leave where we have been so happy?'

'Of course not, Maria! And it will be wonderful to have your own home.'

It gave Eleanor a little ache in her heart to hear Maria talk like that about working for her father. He had treated them well. He did the same with everybody he employed. He had deliberately overpaid them. But what else had he given them? Yet they'd loved him, and so had she.

'Dear Mr Nelson,' said Maria with a sigh. 'We miss him very much.'

Giles was standing at one of the tall windows which overlooked the terrace, staring out at the rain. He turned when he heard her come in, a slight figure in a pale greenish dress.

'It was kind of you to come, Giles.'

A day of kisses.

When they sat down, Giles unthinkingly took his old partner's chair, leaning back, dark suit against dull emerald. His hair reminded Eleanor of a badger's, there was a swathe of pale grey which ran down the centre of the darker hue, exaggerating his long face and prominent nose.

'You look a little better, Eleanor.'

There was an improvement from the ravaged figure at the funeral. He'd had a pretty good idea how much she had suffered. He had known Walter better than anybody, even Walter's only child.

'Do you feel strong enough to talk a little business?' he asked in a rallying tone.

Giles had considered a good deal about where this conversation might lead, but without much idea: he had no children and the younger generation, particularly women, were not easy to understand. He had a soft spot for even the silliest young girls. He couldn't miss the fact that women were rising in power nowadays, taking their place in business as in everything else. There were some formidable women at Nelson's as well as some silly ones. Stupid men he had no time for; Nelson's couldn't afford them.

He did not underrate Walter's daughter: he thought her reasonably intelligent and as naive about business as a bird who has not yet learned to fly. Yet a big slice of Nelson's was hers. She was going to be wealthy and her voice mattered.

'I wonder if you'd like to take a look at some recent figures,' he said, opening his brief case.

The suggestion was preposterous. Some women, certainly Laurette, would have had a go. But Eleanor was unsettled and anxious and still grieving and what he said was absurd.

'Giles, don't make fun of me.'

'My dear child, I am not!'

He was used to her treating him as an elderly godfather

to young goddaughter, family confidant and friend. He was offended.

'You know perfectly well I couldn't make head or tail of the figures. I realise the impressive amount Dad left, but how can I be involved in his business? It's yours.'

'No, Eleanor, over half belongs to you.'

'I don't mean I'm dumping my share in your lap,' she said, with what he considered a shocking flippancy.

He looked down his long nose while she sighed and fidgeted. When he said nothing, still disapprovingly, she said, 'What do I know about Dad's business? Not a thing.'

'But you grew up—'

'Have a heart. I grew up hearing people nattering on about advertising, and telephones ringing, and the agency people staying on the *Marie Cristine*. I don't even understand which is a good ad and which is a flop. I scarcely,' she continued, shocking him more, 'look at them. Anyway, Hugo said I can sign a power of attorney in your favour, so that you can act for me while I'm in Brazil. He says you can fix it with the lawyers. Is that okay?'

'This is a serious decision, Eleanor.'

Demurring, he accepted. Disagreeing, he agreed. Protesting, he was pleased. But wise enough not to look it. He turned the conversation to Nelson's in a way he hoped would interest her, describing an account recently captured from J. Walter Thompson's which had been 'entirely due to the high quality of our creative work'.

How often Eleanor had heard Walter's glib phrase. It only needed a florid reference to the Three Musketeers. Giles went on to talk about another account, an international product for which Nelson's was in competition with three other agencies.

'You'll get it.' Eleanor's loyalty was automatic. 'Dad

always said Nelson's is the real top notcher.'

Oh, did he, thought Giles, remembering that Walter had ceased to be truly involved with Nelson's for what seemed a long time. What exactly had he been doing? He had flown to the States and back on Concorde, he had talked to senators, he had once even been entertained in the White House. Occasionally he'd spoken to Giles about this or that high-up American, indicating that there 'might be something big in this for the agency'.

It had never materialised. After Walter's death, Giles had the difficult task of sorting through his papers. There were folders of letters, thick documents of research, reports, recommendations. Senators and representatives, apparently, were all keen on the best way to use advertising in their drives to get re-elected. Giles recalled the senator who had spoken to him on the telephone when Walter was lying upstairs on his death-bed.

In his office late at night on the day after the funeral, Giles had spread every piece of paper belonging to Walter across his desk, and studied them one by one. It had been an eerie experience. All that ponderous writing, and nothing concrete, nothing to be continued or cancelled. What lay in front of him, inches deep, was so much stuff.

The talk between Giles and Eleanor had now languished, and she fidgeted like a tired child. Talk about her father oppressed her; so did this house and this room. How Walter would detest to hear his business discussed *with her*.

Luis, with an instinct for good timing, tapped on the door and came in with a tray, glasses and a bottle of champagne.

'I thought, Mrs Lawrence, you and Mr Burnett might like to drink to your *buen viaja*.'

They were both glad of the interruption. Luis opened the bottle, poured the wine and left them. Giles looked at the label, recognising the vintage; Walter's best, saved in the past for clients.

There was a pause. Eleanor sat with her legs tucked under her full skirt, leaning back to look out vaguely at the rain making patterns on the window. She was trying to resist Walter's cold presence which had come into the room.

'There's something else I think we should talk about, Eleanor,' said Giles, interrupting her thoughts. He waited for a moment and then came out with, 'As a matter of interest, has it struck you that your mother is living in Brazil?'

Eleanor absolutely stared.

'That's where she went after she and your father parted.'

'But it doesn't mean she's there now. She may be dead,' she said, eyes still large.

'No, Eleanor. Very much alive.'

'How do you know?'

'Christmas cards every year. With scraps of news scrawled inside them. Dreadful handwriting, it takes Mary half an hour to decipher it.'

She was struck and silent. Finally she said perversely, 'Brazil's the fifth largest country in the world.'

He gave a short laugh.

'Guide books. So it is, enormous. Your mother lives in Rio de Janeiro.'

No reply to that.

'Eleanor?'

'Yes?'

'Do you understand why I am telling you this?'

He thought her tiresome and had stopped being sorry for her. She had a wary look which he couldn't understand. He rubbed his chin. My trouble is that I'm too reasonable, he thought – the old friend; the right hand you can rely on; what is worse, the do-gooder. Why not do good, for God's sake? This difficult young female thinks of herself as an orphan and she's no such thing.

'Your mother was delightful,' he went on ruminatively, 'I knew her well at one time. You never saw anybody so beautiful. Funny and lively and glorious to look at. Your father was crazy about her. He was so in love that he almost battered down her doors, if you know what I mean. Simply refused to take no for an answer. He took her by storm. I imagine she didn't want to marry him at first, but later she was affected, as most women would have been, by that campaign of his. It was a mistake. She never fitted in and he made her unhappy. It's strange now, when I remember how it was when he met her first: so in love he was out of his senses.'

Eleanor looked incredulous.

'I remember being astonished when she accepted him,' Giles added after a short silence.

'And were you surprised when she buggered off?' said Eleanor.

He looked, for a moment, quite angry. 'I knew she was not happy, although in the later years of the marriage, I did not see much of her. Always out. I suppose that's how she met the Brazilian she married later. Marquez, his name was. Sara probably hadn't got the courage to face up to Walter and say she was going. He was her slave, but I sometimes thought he rather alarmed her. All I knew was that he told me she'd gone. He looked very ill. And never spoke about her to me again.'

Eleanor listened.

The ghost in the room had not gone.

'Poor pretty thing,' Giles said, smiling at a spirit *he* had conjured. He roused himself. 'So you will have the chance to look her up, won't you? Here is the address.'

He handed her a folded piece of paper.

Eleanor thanked him, looked about for her shoulder bag and pushed the paper into it.

Giles stood up.

'Keep it safe. It would be a pity to lose your mother a second time.'

Chapter Eight

After a pause at Rio too short for passengers to get out and stretch their legs, they at last touched down in Brasilia. Eleanor came out into the echoing acres of the arrival lounge, saw Hugo and could have cried with relief. The journey had been over twelve hours and an ordeal — she'd never travelled before on so long a journey in a plane with Joanna. The little girl had grown steadily more fretful, exhausting and exhausted. The sight of Hugo, pale suit, panama hat, looking as if he had lived here for years, was a wonder.

'Dads, Dads,' moaned Joanna, climbing and clinging.

Kissing her, he looked over her curly head in enquiry. Eleanor gave a somewhat helpless shrug.

'Come along, you must both be so tired,' he said, bustling them. Out in the sun, the glare was like a blow on the skull.

'It's too hot,' wailed Joanna.

'You'll soon be in the swimming pool.' Her father shovelled her into a large waiting car.

The Brazilian driver set off smoothly into the early morning dazzle, on to the hugest motorway Eleanor had ever seen. Cars in every direction, glittering.

Hugo pressed her hand.

'So good to have you both here. How I've missed you.'

150

She squeezed his hand in return. 'So have I. So have I.'
Then adding, 'How has it been here?'

'Busy.'

As if he would say anything else, thought Eleanor,
affectionate and irritated. She turned to look out through
the car window at the motorway which took twelve cars
abreast and apparently stretched to infinity. Peering across
the bonnets of cars she made out broad carpets of flowers
planted on both sides of the highway; horticultural public
relations.

Set back at a distance from the pitiless traffic was row
upon row of buildings, high and white, block after block,
the geometric world, the metropolis of tomorrow.

She was still staring when Hugo started to point out the
landmarks. Over there was the President's Palace. And
there was the cultural centre, and one of the concert halls
and part of the enormous library. Imagine, Brasilia had
four universities! She made a not very successful effort to
look interested. All she knew was alarm and strangeness,
the blinding sun and overhead the bowl of blue. The car
moved in the queue near to the motorway edge, and she saw
the red earth overplanted with those garish flowers.

Squeezing her hand again, Hugo turned to smile at her.
Joanna, always competitive, scrambled on to his knee.

Hugo had rung her four or five times after arriving in
Brasilia to tell her the news; he'd described the place as
'spectacular'. He never was one for large adjectives and
Eleanor guessed he was pushing it a bit. Now she saw she
had been right and Brasilia was everything she'd been
afraid of. What about their new home? He told her it was
a furnished villa, a previous member of the embassy had
lived there.

'Quite attractive and comfortable. We have a bonus too.

We can see the lake from our bedroom windows.'

She knew he was looking round at her as they drove along – part of that cavalcade of hot-looking automobiles – as if to gauge her reaction. It made her self-conscious.

Leaving the road-system, as Hugo called it, they took another motorway which was less wide, and in a few minutes had reached a road by the edge of an enormous lake. It lay immoveable in the still morning, its sheen, silvery, steelly, reflecting the cloudless sky. Although it was scarcely seven and without a breath of wind, there was a flotilla of yachts floating in the haze.

'Here we are,' said Hugo.

She had a moment of panic. Was she going to detest her new home?

Suddenly things shrank to her own size again. Across a stretch of lawns, remarkably green in such heat, was a large pleasant house with a red tiled roof; it was set in a garden shady with trees and cheerful with beds of tall yellow flowers. The flash of blue was a swimming pool. When Hugo lifted Joanna from the car, she ran straight into the garden and over to the water, looking down at its transparent depth.

'Dads, Dads, can I go in now?'

'After you've said hello to Zica and Esmeralda.'

'Who are they? Must I?'

'Yes, you must,' he said, adding to Eleanor, 'Darling, come and meet the staff.'

Eleanor's heart, which had risen, fell like a stone. Staff. He hadn't warned that there would be staff. On the front terrace of the villa a group of dark people, three women and a man smiling expectantly.

Hugo introduced them and Eleanor, feeling foolish, shook hands and smiled back. It was six years since at

Ferne Place she had been looked after by Luis and Maria. In London, Mirrén had been a visiting friend.

A dark young woman with a mop of curly black hair and huge brown eyes underlined with blue shadows, made a dive for Joanna, exclaiming in Portuguese. A young girl, scarcely fifteen, patted the child's hand. These were Zica and Esmeralda. Eleanor expected Joanna to have one of her attacks of shyness but, as both girls exclaimed over her and beamed at her, she began to giggle.

'They'll be looking after her,' Hugo said. 'That is all right, isn't it, Eleanor? They've worked here at the villa before; the family adored them. You don't mind Joanna being nannied, do you? Brazilians are crazy about children, and it will leave you much freer, darling.'

Proving the point, Joanna disappeared indoors with the girls, reappearing very soon in her skimpy red swimsuit. Eleanor remembered the number of their bags and cases and was impressed.

'We're going to the pool,' shouted Joanna, galloping ahead of the girls.

Hugo brought Fia, the elderly cook, who spoke a little English, to talk to Eleanor for a moment – a tiny worn-looking woman with gold earrings. And finally there was Henrique, strong and dark with frizzy grey hair, dignified and relaxed.

When they had left her, Eleanor stood on the terrace for a moment looking out at the garden. She felt like an animal transported to a world it does not recognise. The trees which stood in black circles of shade had leaves which were unfamiliar to her. Their very bark was unknown.

The house was pleasant although it matched the rigorous 1960s modernity of its day: concrete shelves, open fire-places also of concrete, admittedly filled with flowers. Along the window-sills had been planted a sort of indoor garden of cacti. The floors were very pale parquet, here and there covered with woven rugs. All the furniture was squared and the few paintings on the walls abstract.

Hugo was over-eager for Eleanor to like everything and although she made a real attempt to be enthusiastic he was not deceived. He said she looked tired.

'Help, you mean I look hideous,' she said, rallying enough for that. 'How cool this house is.'

There was a faint humming noise from somewhere.

'The air conditioning's on all the time. Does the sound get on your nerves?'

'Not a bit. It's soothing.'

When he had taken her into every room, including Fia's dazzling white kitchen, Hugo suggested they should go and see what Joanna was up to. 'She'll be talking Portuguese in no time,' he said, 'The children do.'

They walked out to the pool in the intense out-of-doors heat. Joanna had been joined by her two attendants in black swimsuits, and was splashing and shouting. She called out to her parents to come and join her. They laughed and shook their heads.

Eleanor's smile was strained and Hugo said, 'You're worn out. Zica says she'll start putting Joanna to bed in five minutes. You must go too.'

'I know I couldn't possibly sleep.'

'Try.'

Eleanor felt bothered at not putting her daughter to bed herself as she always did. She hung about and a short while later went in to look at Joanna. The child was already deeply asleep . . .

Thinking she wouldn't, thinking she couldn't, Eleanor went to bed and shut her eyes.

The shadows lengthened across the unearthly green of the watered grass, the sky stayed without a cloud. Mother and child slept on. Joanna was first to wake, and found her new unintelligible friends patiently sitting in her room. With gestures and smiles they indicated she must eat, yes? And then swim again.

At last Eleanor also woke to the dim curtained light. She remembered where she was, put her arms behind her head and lay listening to Joanna's voice somewhere in the garden. She stared into nothing for a while. Then her eyes focussed on a jug of thick-petalled flowers. They had a strong lilyish scent and orange stamens like tongues. On one petal was an enormous blue butterfly.

'I'm afraid I have something to tell you that you're not going to like,' Hugo said.

They were by the pool in the hot evening, after a sunset so swift that one moment the sky was crimson, the next a deep indigo spattered with stars.

'Oh Hugo, now what?'

'You do sound apprehensive, poor girl. It's about the name of our house.'

'Sure to be sentimental. Let me guess. Villa of Flowers?'

'Nowhere near.'

Refreshed by sleep, she giggled. 'You mean worse. Far Blue Horizon?'

'Alas.'

'Hugo! I can't think of anything soppier—'

'Eleanor, I am afraid it is VRN 27. P.'

Laughing at her face, he explained. Things here were named according to their position and distance, north or south, east or west, from the two main axes. (What is he talking about? thought Eleanor). Their house was Villa

Residencia North, 27, P. The P was for Lake Paranoa. It
was perfectly logical and totally confusing. As for locating
people who lived in the massive apartment blocks – well.
'Addresses are never written out in full and unless you get
local help, you could look for somebody for a week.
Foreigners can't bear all the letters and numbers, you
should hear the French on the subject.'

'Ah. They have the Road of the Great Sermon,' quoted
Eleanor. They'd seen that in Normandy once.

'London too,' he agreed. 'Hangman's Dock. Sugar Alley.
But we're living in an age of theory here. To be fair, the
Brazilians don't like it either. After all, in Rio you can find
a street called The Agony in the Garden. Well? Do you think
we could learn to love VRN 27. P?'

Hugo looked after Eleanor very particularly during her
first days; just as his father did with Mathilde. He did not
worry about Joanna who, in what seemed to her mother an
unbelievably short time, was completely at home. She had
already met some children from the next villa on her second
day. It was Eleanor, Hugo knew, who needed to be cared
for.

They had often talked about the time Hugo would be sent
abroad, and Eleanor knew it was the most interesting part
of his Foreign Office work, even though his time in Peru had
had so tragic an end. She had vaguely imagined that he
would be posted to Spain or Portugal, he spoke the
languages of both those countries so well. Eleanor, in her
thoughts, saw them living in countries of Moorish gardens
and ancient churches.

But she had not been given the easy move from one very
old country to another, however different the language or
tradition. She had been dealt Brasilia: a city created in the

red earth out of nothing. Every single worker, every piece of material, ton of concrete, every pane of glass had had to be flown from 'real' cities to make it.

She was too young to remember the excitement and virulent criticism when this extraordinary vision had been realised. Press coverage had been huge. It had been the most enormous gesture which a country could make, a flag thrown in the face of its destiny. The new capital rising out of an almost barren plain was to be the new centre of government. The decision to build it in this place, this far place, was to develop the vast empty spaces which had haunted Brazil for centuries.

To the fascination of the world, and the dismay of the Brazilians doomed to live here, Brasilia had made its bizarre, its stunning appearance. Its bold lines, they said, must be seen as symbols of the dramatic new start. Now in the 1970s it was already being called old-fashioned by the new city planners. But the country was stuck with Brasilia.

And so was Eleanor.

It was a country of extremes. Of the very rich and the very poor, Eleanor soon realised that Hugo had brought Joanna and herself into a life of privilege. The dark handsome servants were the under-class. Looking at the vivacious faces of Zica and Esmeralda and the others, in their spotless clothes, with their shining hair and huge eyes, she found it hard to believe that. Until, on a drive round the lake, Eleanor had her first view of the *favelas*. These were the shacks where the working people lived, shanty towns built close to the houses of the rich.

The *favelas* were not much worse than slums in other cities but they were more conspicuous, not hidden down shabby streets in a part of the town wealthy people never visited. The shacks were plainly visible to anybody driving five minutes from their homes. Flimsy, gimcrack, with corrugated-iron roofs often askew, they looked as if a strong wind would blow them to kingdom come. *Favelas* had little sanitation, no running water, and women queued at the taps with oil cans, which they then carried back to their pitiful homes. Some of the *favelas* had a look of half-starved respectability, like dilapidated stables. Others were filthy and falling to bits.

Eleanor was shocked and silenced when Hugo drove her past a great stretch of these squatters' camps, then almost immediately passing the tailored lawns of the golf club.

'But they are so poor, so poor, Hugo. I thought people said Brazil was the land of the future.'

'That's what they tell them.'

She knew enough not to ask – why isn't something done?

Years back, in Peru, Hugo had learned to accept the poverty, inequality and injustice. He was only a foreigner representing his country and dealing with the problems of his own nationals. What could he do, except treat the people he employed well and pay them more than he needed to. When he said that to Eleanor she thought – is Zica's devotion bought, then?

Believing she never would, she began to settle into the life forced upon her; and much of this was due to having a small daughter. Zica knew every other young woman working in the various villas built on the slopes and by the streams and little waterfalls running down into Lake Paranoa. Among the cosmopolitan people whose jobs brought them to Brasilia, the glue that fixed one house to another was children and the Brazilian girls who looked after them. The bond was as close as the clique of English nannies in Pont Street, but with a difference. Brazilians were not title, money or status-conscious. Such attitudes did not enter their friendly heads, and to boast of one employer against another would have shocked them as if they were committing a mortal sin. The girls were gossipy, spoiled their children and laughed a great deal.

Joanna soon made friends with half a dozen children – American, French, Brazilian, Dutch, German – who lived in the villas overlooking the great gleaming expanses of the lake.

Eleanor's first friend was Celina da Costa, known as Ceci. She had lived here longer than most, nearly six years. She was Brazilian and had come originally with her husband from Rio. Both her children had been born in Brasilia which gave her a certain cachet, a plus, among the VIPs. Her husband Oswaldo was a brilliant engineer, highly paid and likely to be more so. The government and the big business moguls needed men of vision like Oswaldo da Costa. He was in at the top of some of the mind-boggling enterprises for opening up the Brazilian interior: roads, mines, bridges, factories.

Oswaldo was short and thick-set, with heavy shoulders and hairy arms. When Eleanor first met him, she could imagine him as a king in the rain forests before the arrival of cruel invaders. His smile was full of good nature but it was absent-minded. His American clothes looked as if he would grow out of them at any moment, and he had the largest hands Eleanor had ever shaken.

Ceci was rounded and small and maternal, not only to her children, Shelley and Mitch, named after characters in American movies, but to Eleanor as well.

'You must come to me all the time. I will do everything you want. I will show you Brasilia.'

Eleanor said it was very kind of her new friend, but Hugo had taken her round the city already.

'Is different when with me. More beautiful.'

'Are you sure?'

Ceci looked at her humorously, knowing very well that her new foreign neighbour disliked the space city.

'Sure. I am sure. I collect you tomorrow morning, okay? At seven? That is a little bit late but will do.'

The habit of such early rising had already become as everyday to Eleanor and Joanna as it was with Hugo. The intense heat of the day came so suddenly. And you never thought – today there will be no sun. It was true she was told of heavy rains, but as yet she had not seen them. You rose in the dawn, you dined in the dark, you hid often in your cool house and came out during that thunderclap of the sunset. You never went for walks.

So it was not odd to be up before six and find Ceci before seven in her car outside the villa. Ceci, as usual, was in white. This morning a thin floating French dress, white with black dots, and a black bow in inky hair.

'Now you will admire,' said Ceci, patting Eleanor's hand. 'You have seen the cathedral, of course you have.' She was driving into the already shining day. 'But not up close to the ladies at the Palace?'

'I saw them from a distance. Terrific,' said Eleanor who was disinterested in the great art of Brazilian sculpture.

Ceci shook her head. She admired Brasilia, and – having left the incomparable Rio to which she and her family constantly returned – had taken Brasilia to her heart. It was Oswaldo's world and so she must love it.

The Guerrero's car, a Ferrari, was a convertible and, although the sun was already raying down, the air was cool enough not to drive with the hood up. The sky above was boundless, the light so pure that everything appeared to be supernaturally clear and shining. The skyscrapers rising in the distance seemed made of white marble, the flowers on either side of the motorway were jewels. Ceci was in informative mood, pointing at two vast towers. 'The congressmen work there. The other day, before you came, such a storm! The towers were struck by lightning and people very scared. Not Oswaldo. He says lightning is good.'

Eleanor tried hard to see the metropolis with her companion's eyes. It wasn't easy. Blinding acres and towers of glass; strange shapes and curves. The cathedral topped with a crown of thorns over a hundred feet high.

Ceci parked under a notice saying: 'No Parking' in four languages, and took Eleanor into the church. She fell on her knees, made the sign of the cross, and for a full half minute bent her head. Then giggled with Eleanor at a parrot shape in the blue and purple stained glass.

She was a lively guide, dragging Eleanor up to many of the enormous bronze figures outside the cathedral, sculptured men who stood there like guardians. Ceci said that they represented the workers who had built Brasilia.

'Our people,' said Ceci, standing dwarfed by one huge artisan of rugged nobility. But where, thought Eleanor, are the living people? A few tourists wandered around with cameras, but there was not a single stroller, no lazy lingerers, no open air cafés and no life in the streets.

When she and Ceci returned to their car, an official in uniform was waiting beside it with a menacing notebook. Ceci promptly burst into a passionate speech, laughing and indignant. She pointed at the cathedral. She appeared to be pointing at the sky. She gestured at Eleanor and at one moment she pressed her hand on her own bosom. The man listened, contradicting her but getting gloomy as Ceci volubly continued. In the end, heavily frowning, he waved at them to go.

'What *did* you say?' Eleanor remembered parking meters in London.

'What do you think? That he could not dare refuse to allow us to pray to the good God,' said Ceci piously. 'That you were a foreigner and needed to pray. Now we go to the palace.'

It was one of the largest of the many gigantic glass fronted buildings; it was shaded by white eaves which curved like the sails of some enormous three-masted clipper.

'And here,' said Ceci, 'are the President's ladies.'

Sitting on a white raft by a lily-covered pool in front of the palace were the two figures Hugo had briefly pointed out to Eleanor. They had been vague shapes in the distance, but now Ceci took her up close. They were real women, as massive as works by Henry Moore but boldly realistic and sculptured in black bronze. They had just washed their hair. There they sat, eternally holding their long manes at arm's length, interested in nothing but their hair. Graceful, enormous, mysterious goddesses of nature.

'I love them,' said Ceci, looking as if she would like to lean over and pat one gigantic knee.

Eleanor soon became acquainted with the many people who also lived in villas overlooking the lake. They were a heterogeneous group, speaking English with various accents, and restlessly social. There were American bankers with hospitable wives, Dutch engineers who spoke accentless English (the only ones), a serious-minded German couple, the woman an architect, the husband a diplomat. There was a French businesswoman hard as a diamond, and a sprinkling of Japanese people with strongly commercial interests; they kept themselves to themselves and had manners of eighteenth-century politeness. All the women wore wonderful clothes and the American men reminded Eleanor of Walter.

Her days began to fill up. Nigel Storey, who worked with Hugo at the Embassy, became a friend. He was an energetic easily-amused man, always ready to give Eleanor golf lessons at the club by the lake. His wife Jenny joined her for tennis, and sometimes the two women went sailing in the early morning on the great invented lake.

Sometimes she sat in gardens with these new acquaintances of hers, while the lizards which looked like sticks or little leaves would suddenly dart and vanish with the flick of a tail. And whenever she looked across the grass, up would spring the sprays to make rainbows.

Hugo was glad that his wife had settled down, and now he had done the same. He came to like Richard Selby, the Ambassador, very much. Selby had wisdom and panache. He was a man of many interests and something of a historian. He also collected Brazilian sculpture and liked to meet the contemporary artists. He deeply admired the country's tradition in popular painting and sculpture and 'what about their music, Hugo! Brazilian music is known and loved all over the world.' He and his wife became friends of Hugo's, but Eleanor was slightly shy with them. This was due to Katharine who might be relaxed and friendly, but was distinctly grand. It was a phenomenon Hugo had noticed many times – the wives of men in high positions put on the style far more than their husbands. Richard Selby was never grand. Indeed, he was rarely conventional and if circumstances forced this on him, submitted with something very like a wink.

Britain, alas, was not important to Brazil; Hugo realised that the most they could hope for was supplying technical help to some of the giant enterprises in the interior. But there was never a time when the intense complicated work of the embassy didn't fill each day to overflowing. Selby had to be briefed every morning with facts ranging from the awkwardness of a visiting minister to the plans of a British TV film unit with wondrous ideas and no money at all. Hugo needed all his skill. He was happy.

When work kept him late, the person Eleanor turned to was Ceci. She was as Brazilian as the dazzling blue butterflies; she was self-mocking, tolerant, funny, and as maternal as the holy picture of the Madonna in her bedroom. Ceci was very emotional. Her black eyes brimmed as often when things were happy as when they were sad. 'Oh, how beautiful,' she would exclaim and dab her eyes.

Her children, Shelley and Mitch, had two Brazilian girls to look after them, as Joanna did. Often, gossiping with Eleanor in the garden, Ceci would break off, run across the grass and slap one child or the other, then turn with angry instructions to the girls. Within moments they would all be laughing.

Ceci was an important part of Eleanor's new life. Eleanor did go with Hugo to receptions and dinners, to attend concerts or on occasion to parties to meet some visiting VIP. But she spent a great deal of her time with Ceci and saw more of her than she actually saw of Hugo, or, come to that, of Joanna.

The moment that Joanna and her mother had arrived at villa VRN 27 P. had been symbolic; the child spent all her days with Zica and Esmeralda. Of course, Eleanor saw her sometimes, but more often Joanna was away swimming with her friends, playing in their gardens, being taken on their yachts. Occasionally at home she was allowed to stay up very late as a treat to have dinner with her parents. But after a day in the open air, she stayed awake only for the first course. Hugo always had to carry the sleeping child to bed before the ice-cream arrived.

Somehow Eleanor began to feel that she had relinquished motherhood. Yet Ceci hadn't. Eleanor wished it was in *her* nature to shout and slap too. It was not. And how could she take Joanna away from the life in which she was flowering and flourishing?

Eleanor watched the groups of children when they came to play in her garden. They sat in circles, busy in some mysterious game and sitting together, indifferent to the sopping wet grass. They laughed and shouted and scuffled, and their attendant Brazilian girls interfered or joined in. All the children wore sundresses or shorts so fresh that it was clear they had been put on an hour ago, washed and ironed by the dark Brazilians who seemed to Eleanor like so many exotic ladies-in-waiting.

She asked about school to Hugo.

Of course he had done something about that.

'Didn't I tell you? They're beginning classes next month at the De Reyter's. Mrs De Reyter rang to ask if we'd like to put Joanna on her list.'

That, too, was out of Eleanor's hands.

One afternoon Eleanor confided her worries to Ceci.

'I know you'll think me stupid.'

'Never could I.'

Eleanor hesitated. 'It's just that I've always looked after Jo before. All my friends in England do. Hugo's sister has two but she's never had any help and couldn't afford it. I did have Mirrén, my Spanish girl, but she only came for an hour or two in the house, mostly. I did everything for Jo. But now she doesn't seem to be mine any more.'

'You wish to look after Jo. How can you, *quérida*? Zica

would lose the work if her *Senhora* took it from her.'

'I could do a little.'

'If you try, you will hurt. No, no, you cannot accept things. Jo is for Zica and Esmeralda. You must believe.'

'But you—'

'Yes, I shout and the girls pretend to listen but always they know Shelley and Mitch are theirs. I am the mother but to them that is nothing. The children belong to them. Later, yes, they will be mine. Never when they are little, and your husband chooses so nice: Zica. Everybody wants Zica.'

Eleanor walked pensively home after sunset along a short path covered with stones. The ground still radiated heat and she could hear the noise of little tumbling waterfalls.

By the time she was home the stars had come out, the lights in the garden were on and to her surprise, she saw Hugo's car in the drive. He was at his desk in the long sitting room, and turned to put his left hand out to her.

'Darling. I've fixed for us to go to Rio tomorrow for the weekend. You and I, Joanna and Zica. Esmeralda, Zica tells me, will spend the time with their family.'

'Rio!'

'Yes, we'll stay at the Bristol. Later perhaps we might run to getting somewhere permanent. I don't want you and Joanna having to languish here at weekends; she is always grumbling that her friends vanish on Fridays.'

'Hugo, how terrific.'

He liked to see her so pleased. It was true that Brasilia died at weekends. It might be the official centre, but Rio never lost its lure. Just as in a much smaller country, Londoners clogged the roads at weekends to get to their cottages, so officials and businessmen here streamed to the airport and took wing for Rio.

Eleanor went to the bedroom to shower and change. Everybody changed in the evening. She washed her hair, made up her face and was slowly opening the case where she kept her bracelets when Hugo came in, his jacket over his shoulder.

'Lovely, your scent smells.'

He stood behind her and looked at her in the glass.

'Hugo. There's something I want to tell you.'

'And what is that?' he asked in his easy way, looking caressingly at her face in the mirror.

'My mother lives in Rio.'

The hand on her shoulder stayed still. He spoke very slowly. 'Why haven't you told me this before?'

She was fast and defensive. 'I should have, I know I should have, but I didn't want to think about it until I got here and was used to everything. Anyway, I don't know her, do I? Not since I was six. I don't properly remember her even if I try. Giles gave me her address.'

'How did he have it?'

His voice had no expression; she had an idea that she had shocked him.

'Oh, Christmas cards. Apparently my mother writes to him every Christmas, for old time's sake I suppose. He said he thought I ought to know where she is, and maybe see her. Maybe,' she feebly finished.

'I still can't understand why you didn't tell me.'

'I didn't know whether I wanted to see her at all.'

'I think you should.'

She said like a child, 'Suppose I don't like her? My father didn't.'

His face had been grave but at that tone it cleared and he said quizzically, 'You could give the poor lady a chance.'

*

The idea of her mother had been shoved aside in Eleanor's thoughts for fifteen years. It did not acquire a new urgency now. Eleanor simply looked forward to Rio, and there was a flurry of packing. Zica filled zip bags with clothes for Joanna, who hopped about singing a Portuguese song Zica had taught her, a favourite at the carnival. Hearing his daughter singing away, Hugo translated it for Eleanor. They made her sing it again.

> I want to kill my longing,
> I am going to kiss you now, now!
> I won't be sad, masked dancer.
> Today is carnival, is carnival!

The child got her tongue round the Portuguese lisp and lilt.

Rio was everything Brasilia wasn't; crowded and lively, noisy, overwhelming and dangerous. The people who sauntered or surged down long avenues lined with palms were black or brown or white or pale and dark versions of all three colours. They stood in groups at street corners; they filled the street cafés. The expensive hotel had its own beach, and Joanna, used to the sedate swimming pools of Brasilia, charged into a sea so rough that Hugo had to run in after her, getting his trousers wet to the knee.

The weekend was the loveliest Eleanor could remember. Hugo was at his sweetest and funniest; Joanna, tired out from sea and sand, fell asleep early; and Zica, all smiles, was the child's shadow. It was not until Monday morning, while they packed for an early plane, that Hugo looked across the luggage piled on the bed and said, 'Stay an extra day.'

'But we're just going and you can't—'

'No, I can't, it's impossible. And Zica says Joanna is going to some birthday party this afternoon. But you could stay.'

She knew what he meant and her face was suddenly stricken. His heart smote him. But he'd thought about this.

'Get it over, Eleanor. You owe it to your mother and to yourself as well. Take just one day to see her, if she happens still to be at that address Giles gave you. I rang down, and there's a plane at half past eight tonight, so I'll meet you at the airport at 10.45. Well?'

She went round the bed to him, and understanding her, he took her in his arms and hugged her. He knew she would do what he suggested.

Quite suddenly, they were gone. And Eleanor in limbo.

She finished her half-discarded breakfast. She stood for a while, looking out at the sea which was covered in white rollers. She fetched the folded piece of paper. She won't be there, Eleanor thought. She'll be away. Then I can get the next plane home.

Picking up the telephone, she asked for a number. It was stupid how her heart began to pound.

The number did not ring for long; a woman's voice answered in Portuguese.

Eleanor said in English, 'Is Mrs Marquez there?'

The woman did not seem surprised at the different language, but replied in a heavily accented voice, 'Please to wait.'

There was a long pause. Eleanor's heart was now thumping so loudly that she could scarcely breathe. She almost slammed down the receiver – just as a drawling voice tinged with American said, 'Yes?'

'Mrs Marquez? It is Eleanor Lawrence.'

There was a silence. Then, '*Who?*'

'Eleanor Lawrence. I got married,' gabbled Eleanor, 'Didn't Giles tell you?'

'*Where are you?*'

'At the Bristol in Rio. Just for the weekend, we—'

She had no time to finish speaking for the voice interrupted in a tone between laughter and sobs, demanding that she must come 'at once, at once. Is your husband with you? Bring him too.'

The voice was as melodramatic as Ceci's might have been. Eleanor's heart had slowed down now and she said sedately that she would love to come sometime today. 'Would this afternoon be all right?'

'This afternoon! No, no, come at once. Don't waste a single second,' cried her unknown relative. 'I shall be waiting for you. You have my address, of course you have, I suppose Giles gave it to you. We aren't far, you can be here in ten minutes, well, maybe twenty, the traffic's awful. I shall be waiting. Unless I faint.'

When they had said goodbye, Eleanor hung up thoughtfully.

How could Walter have married somebody who went in for fainting?

The drive through Rio was indeed slow and she stared through the open taxi at the teeming streets. At one point they drove along the broad promenade. How crowded the beaches were, even to the very edge of the sea: swimmers, mothers, children and in the water, flotillas of little boats and pedalos. People, people. Then the car turned up a steep hill which reminded her of Montmartre, and she saw they were driving into a richer world. The villa where the taxi stopped was not unlike Eleanor's own but considerably larger and more glamorous. It was red-roofed and very modern, and overlooked the blue ocean where a distant island floated in the heat haze.

Eleanor was paying the driver when she heard a voice, and turned round to see a woman run full pelt down the steep flight of steps from the house.

'It isn't possible, it just isn't possible!'

Laughing and crying, she threw her arms round her.

She clutched at her so tightly that Eleanor found it quite difficult for them both, so linked, to walk up the steps. Finally Eleanor was released so that her companion could brush the tears away from her long, painted eyes.

'How good of you to ring. How kind of Giles to think of me.'

She led Eleanor into a spacious marble-floored room which was not cool, as Eleanor's villa was, but cold. It felt like going into icy water.

'Come and sit. Maria Teresa, drinks, drinks,' to a girl in a white apron who, hovering, obediently disappeared.

'Sit down and let me look at you.'

Apart from a muttered hello, Eleanor had so far not spoken a word.

Her image of the woman who had been her mother had always been vague. This morning after they'd spoken, an effort of memory had vaguely recalled a figure in an old and badly-taken photograph. A pretty face and fair hair, all out of focus; nothing motherly. This part, at least, was accurate. Sara Marquez had not a trace of motherhood in the sense of maternal warmth, the aura round Ceci or Agnes. She was beautiful and haggard and thin, with a strong jaw and a prominent *retroussé* nose. Her hair was short and fair, faintly tinged with something between fawn and very pale pink, and her eyes were as long and almond-shaped as Eleanor's, but with flecks in them like the flaws in china. Her skin was far paler than that of anybody European whom Eleanor had seen in Brazil until now. She supposed Sara disliked being suntanned.

If Paris, the Trojan youth of legend, had been called to judge the beauty of the two women, the only advantage daughter had over mother was her youth. And the years were being kept at bay by Sara Marquez.

The girl in the apron reappeared. Sara put a glass of red-coloured drink into Eleanor's hand.

'I'm such a fool. Why do I want to cry?'

Another feeble mutter from Eleanor who buried her nose in her drink. Strong Pimm's.

Sara Marquez, after a stare of hungry curiosity, went through the routine of the usual questions. Where was Eleanor's husband? Did Eleanor hate Brasilia? How long had she and her husband been in Brazil? Did she find the Portuguese language impossible? Et cetera.

'My questions will go on for at least a month,' she said, listening with an attention at variance with her ditsy manner.

'It does feel peculiar, suddenly turning into a mother again,' she impulsively said, touching Eleanor's hand. 'But I never was much of one, was I? For ages after I got here, I was sure Walter had told you I was dead. That was why I never wrote. I thought he'd tear my letters up. Did he say I was dead?'

'No. That you'd gone to South America.'

This amused Sara who remarked that it sounded as if somebody had kidnapped her and forced her into the old cliché, the White Slave Traffic.

She said pensively, 'How old were you when I left?'

'Six.'

'A baby. How could I have borne to give you up?'

'I don't suppose I was all that wonderful.'

Sara laughed. She seemed to have an unending lightness of spirit.

'How British you are. People I know here never say things like that. The Americans want everything to sound good: have you noticed how they always say "just fine" to whatever you ask even when it's disaster. And the Brazilians just want things to be beautiful, so they say that they are.'

She went on looking at Eleanor.

'Yes. I do remember you as a little girl: serious, adorable, and very sudden and impulsive. What a bitch to leave you.'

'We didn't know each other all that well.'

'You mean I was out most of the time.'

Unreality had come over Eleanor. Here she sat, clutching too strong a drink, and talking to the woman who had given birth to her, and was a total stranger. And who seemed more nervous than she was.

They went on talking. Sara was a chatterer, her conversation littered here and there with the names of people Eleanor was supposed to know. She heard a Rothschild mentioned, and at least two modern painters. Like Laurette, although she was clearly an egotist and presenting, as it were, her own invented portrait of herself, she was truly interested when Eleanor answered her questions. The only subject not welcomed surprised Eleanor.

'I haven't told you about Jo, she's four and a half. Your granddaughter,' said Eleanor innocently.

Sara gave a laugh with a certain raucous shrillness. Damn, I should have guessed, thought Eleanor. It's the name of grandmother she can't take. She turned to another subject, and her mother relaxed again.

It was well after three in the afternoon, and Eleanor was hungry, when her mother finally said she would talk to

Maria Teresa about lunch, and left her.

It was Eleanor's chance to examine the room. Like the other rich villas Eleanor had visited, the place had been built for big cool spaces. Stretches of marble tiles the colour of cream lapped and spread away from the room where she sat into a further room, a dining room with heavy carved furniture. Everywhere was striped by the light coming through Venetian blinds. At first Eleanor saw no doors, but then realised they were folded flat against the walls and painted the same shade, a pale straw colour. There were many pictures, four were portraits of Sara by different artists. The largest faced the huge open windows on to the terrace and showed Sara reclining on one of the many sofas in this room. She wore white, and there was a jug of white lilies beyond her shoulder. Her legs were bare and she wore no shoes. She looked out of the broad steel frame, fair head thrown back, eyebrows slightly raised, with the air of a woman listening to a joke she is not sure is funny. The artist had exaggerated the odd shape of her nose, the hollow of her cheeks. She looked intense; not particularly happy.

There were a good many shiny American paperbacks, compact discs, pieces of bronze sculpture. Not one photograph.

Sara came wandering back.

'You're dying with hunger,' she said.

Eleanor's buoyancy had abandoned her and she murmured without meaning it that she was not hungry, adding vaguely, 'I'm very happy.'

Sara pounced. 'Are you? Are you?'

Fortunately for Eleanor, the girl in the apron arrived and set a table on the terrace.

The food, salads and cheeses, some kind of cold meat, a great bowl of fruit, champagne, was delicious. Out of the range of icy air conditioning, the terrace was gratefully warm and Eleanor thawed out.

Sara ate almost nothing except to help herself to four black cherries which she covered in cream. She said suddenly, 'How long am I allowed to keep you? A week? A month?'

'That's very kind of you, but I'm afraid I have to go home on the 8.30 flight this evening.'

'Impossible!'

'It's very kind of you,' repeated Eleanor.

'Kind? Don't be crazy. Now I've found you, you've got to stay.'

For a moment she reminded Eleanor of Joanna.

Eleanor explained about returning to Brasilia where Hugo was expecting her. She was touched and troubled by Sara's dismay and spoke more warmly than she'd done until now. Her mother's affected actressy manner had in some ways inhibited her before this. Sara discerned the warmth and gave a big sigh. 'How selfish I am. Of course you have to go home to your husband and child.'

Jo, it seemed, hadn't a first name.

Sara leaned her chin on her hands and looked out at the sea which was dark and sparkling. One ship, a foreign battleship, loomed grey against the blue. Eleanor followed the look, envying her mother for the presence of the sea.

To her intense surprise, Sara said after a longish silence, 'We haven't mentioned your father once, have we? I suppose you've avoided talking about him because you think it will embarrass me. It doesn't. When things happened so long ago, they get unreal. You know?'

Like me, thought Eleanor. Like you.

'Giles wrote and told me Walter died a few months ago. I was sorry. Was he ill for a long time?'

Eleanor didn't say very much to that.

Her mother bit her lip.

'I know I treated him badly. Well, yes, I treated you badly too, but you were a child and that's different.' She ignored modern psychology. 'Poor Walter, I couldn't help it.' Pause. 'But I guess people always say that when they do what they want, and to hell with their partners.'

'Do they?'

'You haven't really forgiven me,' said Sara, turning her strange eyes on to Eleanor.

Politeness stopped Eleanor from telling the truth. She could scarcely admit to the woman looking at her with a sombre face that her mother hadn't been in her thoughts for months on end. At school Sara had been a subject of chat with her friends, soon forgotten. She had reappeared occasionally when Eleanor and Agnes talked about the divorce. But as a person, Sara hadn't existed, she'd been nothing to do with Eleanor's sad feelings. What had mattered – it still did – had been Walter's coldness.

'We moved after you went. We lived in Sussex in a huge old house Dad bought.'

'How like him.'

'Yes. Well. He was busy and I was at school and after that first time in London when he said you'd gone to South America, he never mentioned you.'

Sara grimaced.

'He wrote me a horrible letter. I wanted to keep it but José Americo, that's my husband, you must meet him, destroyed it. He said you must do that with poisons. Poor Walter.'

The next minute – which felt like thirty – passed in silence, until Sara said timidly, 'Do you think he had a happy life?'

'It was an important one. A success.'

Something moved Sara to lean across the table and pat Eleanor's arm. 'Were you good friends?'

'Of course.'

Later in the afternoon Sara again asked Eleanor if it would be possible for her to stay, and Eleanor, sounding more like the mother, explained that she really couldn't. She found now that she wanted to. To stay in this sea-haunted place, smelling a scent she did not know, with a woman whose heart she did not recognise.

She telephoned Hugo at the embassy.

He said at once, 'Where are you? Are you all right?'

'I'm fine. I'm here. You know.'

'With your mother.'

'Yes. I'll be on the 8.30 plane.'

A loud sigh from the listening Sara.

'I'm glad it's gone well, darling. I've been thinking about you all day. I'll be at the airport. Take care.'

When the time came for her to leave, Sara said she would send Eleanor back in her car with a driver. She herself did not drive.

'José Americo won't let me. He said I'd be a menace to man and beast. I won't come with you to the airport, I'd only disgrace you by crying again. But you'll find the car comfortable and Pietro will look after you.'

'Thank you, that's really kind. I don't want to be—'

'A daughter?' said Sara, widening her eyes.

They had a goodbye embrace. Sara stood at the door of the car, smiling and with tears not far off. Eleanor wondered what she and this stranger had in common. Nothing but the blood throbbing in their veins. Perhaps she betrayed the thought, for Sara said suddenly, 'How I hate goodbye. I won't say it,' and ran like a girl up the steps into the house.

Chapter Nine

The telephone was ringing as they walked through the dark garden. Hugo hurried into the villa. Eleanor followed more slowly.

He called through the open door, 'Darling, it's for you.' Putting his hand over the telephone he whispered, 'Guess who.'

'Eleanor? Me.'

'Oh, hello, how nice of you to—'

'Don't be like that. I wanted to hear your voice and prove I hadn't made up the whole thing. You did come to see me today, didn't you?'

'Of course. It was lovely,' said Eleanor, feeling uncomfortable.

'*Que bom*,' said Sara. Even Eleanor knew enough to recognise that meant 'great'.

'But the real reason I called you is – do you think it's time you gave me the fatal name?'

Again, Eleanor didn't need to wonder what she meant. Sara's face was before her just then in all its worn intensity.

'*Você entende?*' added Sara.

'Yes, I think I understand.'

'You don't sound too keen about what to call me,' said

the rather thrilling voice, 'And as it happens, I agree. It's a bit late to use it, wouldn't you say?'

Hugo had picked up a newspaper. He remained, paper suspended, watching Eleanor with a half smile.

'The thing is,' continued the voice, 'that though you are what you are, I don't really see myself with the fatal name. I guess I've been too long without it. As for that adorable child of yours—'

Why does she say Jo is adorable when she's never set eyes on her, thought Eleanor; she really is absurd.

'So I thought maybe you could use my first name?'

'I'd like that very much.'

'Hooray. Goodnight, lovely daughter.'

'Goodnight, Sara.'

Hugo wanted to hear everything about Eleanor's day with her mother. He listened, his eyes fixed on her with an expression of the most tender sympathy. Eleanor tried to be fair but found herself critical. Then Hugo disagreed, showing the woman he had never met to Eleanor in a gentler light. He was at his sweetest and Eleanor loved him for it. She was embraced by his imaginative goodness, and kissed him.

'I'm so glad for you, darling,' he said, when her story ended. 'It's important for you to have somebody close.'

'But you can't be close to Sara, Hugo. She's a dragon-fly.'

He was silent for a moment or two. The smile creased the corners of his eyes. 'Odd. I once thought you were.'

'Oh, oh. Aren't I any more?'

When Ceci and Eleanor first became friends, Eleanor told her about Walter's death and Ceci was full of warmth and sympathy. Eleanor was put out when the same kindness and a sort of pity was extended after Ceci learned that Eleanor's parents had been divorced.

'Is terrible,' she said, deeply sighing.

'People get divorced in Brazil, I suppose,' was Eleanor's tart reply.

Ceci said she supposed it happened sometimes, but she didn't actually know anybody who was.

'We have the second marriage now and then. Not in church you understand, and no divorce. Never. But often another woman the man has, and maybe more children. Some wives can accept. In Brazil the law has changed and no child is illegitimate ever. One of my Rio friends met the children of second marriage as we call it. Not the woman. Never would she meet *her*. But to have your own mother in divorce. Ah, *pauvrita*!'

She had sounded as if sympathising with Eleanor after she'd had a serious operation.

Eleanor couldn't wait to tell her the news.

'Now again you have your mama!' cried Ceci in delight, and during the morning kept returning to the subject. 'The answer to your prayer. You are a daughter now.'

Eleanor was none too sure. When she left Ceci after the idle day, she walked home as usual up the familiar lane. It was lined with trees bending down over the walls of neighbouring gardens. Many of them were covered with pink flowers which had fallen overnight, carpeting the path with rusting pink. She walked on petals. Arriving home, she saw that the garden lights were lit; it was now quite dark. Joanna, Zica and Esmeralda were home: she heard their voices.

She decided to have a final swim; she enjoyed being in the water at night. She was lazily floating and looking up at the stars when Henrique, the big grey-haired man who looked after the garden and the car and often drove Hugo into the city, came out with the telephone.

'Is for the *Senhora*,' he said, putting it on a table by the pool. Eleanor thanked him, emerging in a trail of wet footsteps.

'I behave like a lover,' said Sara. 'But isn't it just what I am? When will you see me? Can you come next weekend? I'm making up for all the time when you were not mine. I am greedy for you.'

Eleanor was in a quandary. Her mother's impulsiveness was engaging; it was touching too, but she did not want to see her again so soon. When she havered, Sara said she would speak to Hugo.

'After all, it's only right to ask him if I can steal you away.'

She rang late that night, and Hugo, rather flattered, needed no persuasion to 'spare' his wife for the following weekend. Eleanor felt herself pushed into the role of daughter, but Hugo was his delicate and reasonable self and she could not refuse.

In the Rio plane, this time alone, she did begin to enjoy herself. She was collected by Sara's driver at the airport in a different car from the previous one, a stretch limo which looked as if it belonged to a member of the Mafia. Eleanor realised, she hadn't thought of it until now, that her mother's husband must be seriously rich. Apparently Sara had instructed the driver to take her on a different route. A city of surprises: street markets ending in flights of steps topped by magnificent baroque churches; towering blocks side by side with elaborate ancient decorated houses; fountains, squares, and such a mixture of every race at every corner. The vast beaches were interrupted by mountains rounded like huge pebbles against the sky.

Sara was waiting at the top of the steps, wearing a fringed straw hat like a halo. She ran barefoot to greet her.

'I've been counting the hours. And I've got a surprise. José Americo waited specially to see you. He had to miss an awful American working breakfast, as they call them. Francisco's here too; he's a great friend and longing to meet you.'

Eleanor's mood clouded; she had come for her mother, not to meet strangers. Two men stood up as she was taken into the ice-cold salon.

'José Americo, here is my daughter.'

The man who bowed over Eleanor's hand as if he was being presented to the Queen was short, fat and about fifty. He was elaborately polite and looked up at Eleanor with black eyes like stones. His nose was aquiline, grizzled hair curled over his head, his lips were red and his skin as dark as a Sikh's. The stretch limo certainly was his. He had an air, thought Eleanor, of playing the lead in a Hollywood film.

'Sarita is so happy you have come to Brazil,' he said, flashing a smile. 'Remember to come here many times. Now I leave you to Sarita and our friend.'

'I'll see you to the car, *querido*' Sara said, taking her husband's arm. They left the room, talking in Portuguese.

The usual pause followed, which comes when strangers are left alone. The young man, as tall as José Americo was short, was still standing.

'Sara forgets her manners when she is excited. And finding you has been the great excitement of all. Or was it you who found her? I present myself, Madame. Francisco De Quiroz.'

He took her hand and gave it the brief non-kiss of the country. They sat down and began a conversation which was led at first by Eleanor, who wasn't shy. She spoke unselfconsciously about meeting her mother, about Rio – how beautiful the city was. She said she and her family lived in Brasilia.

'That is not your good fortune. Of course, I have been to Brasilia. We all must to see the showpiece of the age. But who would not prefer Rio?'

His accent in English was almost non-existent, although now and again, as in her mother's voice, Eleanor heard a faint American inflection. He used words that he was perhaps translating, saying 'of course' quite often, and 'isn't it?'

De Quiroz was everything that was Latin in looks and bearing. His skin was olive, his hair jet, his eyes black as ink. His nose was heavy and straight, his lips thick, curving – even when he was serious – into something like a smile. He looked as if nothing could make him hurry, put him out of countenance, make him blush, make him ill. In her mind Eleanor compared him to her husband, who couldn't help showing he understood suffering. This man looked as if he had not shed a tear since he was five years old.

'Your arrival for Sara was traumatic,' he observed. 'She did not tell her friends she had a daughter.'

'But surely her husband—'

'Oh of course José Americo knew. He was the one who brought her to Brazil.'

It was casually put and Eleanor was startled. So the gangsterish man who'd just left was the one who had stolen her mother from Walter. It was because of him that Walter had erased Sara from his life like a man sponging a blackboard.

'Sara and I have been friends a long time. Five years is long, isn't it? She is delightful but I must warn you, she is demanding.'

'Don't frighten me.' Eleanor's tone was flip. His air of taking over got on her nerves. He was so clearly used to women who were, from the start, overwhelmed by those good looks. Sara came back as he was smiling, and looked pleased when he told her what he had said and Eleanor had replied.

'He's right, darling. Nobody is more demanding than me.'

De Quiroz had to leave; he was rather late for the office, he said, and had called because Sara was good enough to ask him to meet her daughter.

'The great delight. We will meet again, of course.'

'We shan't be able to stop you,' said Sara, with the loud laugh.

When he had gone Sara called Maria Teresa to bring fresh coffee, did not drink hers and said suddenly, 'I've had a mad idea. Why don't we just stay home? I won't call up anybody and we won't go to the beach. Just have luncheon and swim and relax.'

It was obvious that remaining at home was the greatest novelty. She took Eleanor out on to the terrace, and they sat at each end of a long swinging seat.

'Now. What shall we talk about?'

The morning was warm, the sea spread and shone in all its glorious presence, and Eleanor saw Sara was as much in a quandary as she was. There was no such a thing as instant love. You could not make it by pouring boiling water on to air-dried granules formed from the divided past. They had nothing in common but their blood, and that fact was curiously difficult to take seriously.

Sara was actressy, over confident, nervous, pretty and sad. What shadowed the thin face and clouded the large eyes? Eleanor was willing to bet she would never be told.

Her mother's frank air was a deception, perhaps truth or reality or whatever made her so nervous, wasn't to be admitted because it would be unbearable. She thought Sara eager for love, but not knowing how to give or return it.

The talk between them soon ran out. There were no more basics to describe, nothing that might absorb the other. They fell back on little jokes and clichés, and Eleanor found herself avoiding the mention of Joanna, since Sara was frightened of being a grandmother.

At last it was time for the siesta. Both women went indoors to marble-floored Venetian-blinded bedrooms too cold for perfect comfort.

Before she lay down, Eleanor peered through the slats of the blinds at the land rising behind the villa. Strangely close up the steep hill she made out *favelas* like those in Brasilia, cheek by jowl with the villas built high up facing the sea.

Hugo had told her, when they talked about them, that the *favelas* grew and grew, as the blight of poverty increased. Almost a third of all Rio's inhabitants, he said, lived in the pitiful shacks. If a settlement of rich houses was built on a hillside, the slums would appear next to them almost overnight. The *favela* dwellers didn't want to live in the country, they wanted to be near the city. They wanted the excitement and the buzz of life, even if it meant queuing for water and being harassed by the police.

Eleanor lay down under a billowing white duvet. Riches and poverty: it was a tragedy, and it festered in her thoughts like a thorn.

José Americo and Sara were both in the salon when Eleanor reappeared in the early evening, still hazy with sleep. They were in elegant evening dress.

'My pet, you must change. I will lend you something. My Valentino will fit her, won't it, José?'

'You are thinner,' said José Americo, looking from his wife to Eleanor like a man in a paddock studying the horses.

Eleanor had brought a simple evening dress, black silk, but Sara insisted on coming with her to the bedroom, critically looked the dress over and then fetched her French one, clinging, white, Greek. When Eleanor had put it on, Sara studied her, head on one side.

'My daughter is beautiful,' she said aloud, adding that they were going into the city 'just to meet a few friends'.

Not exactly a few. Arriving at a big old house in a part of Rio not yet invaded by the skyscrapers, Sara and her husband joined a mass of people pouring through double doors into a room as large as that of the French Embassy in London. It resembled an embassy in other ways; chandeliers shone in all the adjoining rooms, marble and gilded furniture, tapestry chairs, heavy paintings of dark landscapes. Servants with loaded trays of champagne. The 'few friends' crowded round to greet Sara and José Americo. They smiled pleasantly with melting eyes at Eleanor. She saw that she was of no interest to them whatsoever. It was the exact opposite of the way she was treated in Brasilia, where she was welcomed as Hugo's wife. Here she had no identity except as a hanger-on of José Americo's. And there were far too many good-looking women, in dresses by famous French designers (with diamonds to match) for one young Englishwoman in a borrowed dress to have the least effect.

Eleanor was glad when she caught sight of De Quiroz. He came calmly through the crowd, stopped a waiter and took two glasses of champagne.

'I have looked for you. Come on to the terrace and see my city at night.'

From a broad balconied terrace hung with lamps and set about with tall palms, he took her to the balustrade to look at the glittering panorama. The mountains reared up behind the lines of shining streets, like lions asleep.

'Beautiful, is it not?'

'Very. I wish I knew Rio.'

'And also Brazil.'

'I think I am beginning to know a little about Brazil.'

'Brasilia is not Brazil. It was an invention of our president at the time; and the architect, of course. It is curious that people do not dislike to live there. I have talked to labourers and to professors. They all say they enjoy it. How can they? After all, for us Brazilians there is always the pull of the sea.'

He indicated the dark space, faintly lit by a rising moon.

'After a year you will want to live here always,' he said, 'but the first year will be hard. We seem easy. We are not.'

She did not know what to answer.

He turned his black eyes on her.

'You will learn to know Rio. I will show it to you.'

She feebly muttered how nice and that made him laugh.

Eleanor had flirted occasionally in London, but the encounters were mild enough and never went further than a kiss. Married to Hugo, with his demanding job taking up much of her life and with a daughter in her way just as demanding, Eleanor had never looked beyond the cards dealt to her by fate.

Her girlhood had been ended by pregnancy. After the age of nineteen she had quite lost all those years so enjoyed by the young girls who escape, or take flight, or turn to fight in the never-ending games of love. Now because Hugo was not making love to her as often as he used to do, she had started to believe that her Circean gift – she had at least held sway over *him* – was gone forever.

De Quiroz was more taken with her than she realised. She interested him slightly and attracted him more. She was good-looking, of course, but that was an essential for any Brazilian to remain in the company of a woman of his own age. He was born and reared a native of Rio, and to *cariocas* women were all-absorbing. The De Quiroz family were part of the old money of Brazil; Francisco's position in the family firm of mining engineers was already high, and work satisfied him up to a point; he knew he was cleverer than his colleagues. But as a true Brazilian, women satisfied him more. Any woman he chose must be young, beautiful, alluring, and see him as a kind of god. He could not count the hearts he had broken in the past. Fortunately Brazilian girls recovered quickly.

Eleanor Lawrence was a new kind of experience. His women were passionate but predictable, laughed much of the time and were dedicated to the sacred obligation to remain beautiful. In other ways, too, the Englishwoman did not resemble the women he was used to. He always chose *cariocas* like himself, married of course, in their early thirties. The affairs lasted quite a time and usually ended when the women went off on their travels with their husbands. They knew Paris and New York, London and San Francisco. Their tastes were also to travel richly in their own country, knowing its wildest places, the mountains and the white beaches where rivers and oceans join and there was not a footprint on the ridged sands.

This Englishwoman, her hair so thick (surely it should be thinned?), with her at times girlish manner, seemed unconscious that he was much attracted. She appeared to miss his compliments. When José Americo and Sara came to take her home at the end of the party and De Quiroz said 'I will call tomorrow', Eleanor supposed it was a Brazilian way of saying goodnight.

The following day, waking while the villa was still asleep, she went out to Sara's pool for an early morning swim. José Americo had gone to Mass at the cathedral. Sara never appeared until midday. The morning was hot and Eleanor was swimming lazily up and down when De Quiroz appeared.

She was very surprised.

'I hoped to swim with you,' he said, holding up some swimming trunks. 'Or have you had enough of the water at present?'

'I never have enough. Sure. Come and swim.'

He disappeared into the house as if it were his own. He knew Sara Marquez slept until noon. He knew the sleeping pills she used; he had suggested them – they were milder than those she had taken previously. He knew the reason for her passion to sleep many hours; her terror of losing José Americo and her looks. He knew everything about her although he had never been her lover. She was too old.

He found Eleanor sitting on the marble rim of the pool, her ankles in the water.

'Ah. You waited for me.'

Without clothes he was quite literally beautiful and Eleanor wished he was not. His shoulders were broad, his back strong and straight, his waist like a girl's. He was a hero: Roman or Greek. She slipped into the water but De Quiroz had to execute a perfect dive from the highest of the three boards, going into the deep end without a splash. Water was as much his element as land. He swam as otters do, turning into a long sleek shape, a flash of brown and black, popping up and shaking his wet head in a spray of glittering drops.

Suddenly and unexpectedly, she was intensely happy.

They came out of the pool at last, and Maria Teresa who had seen them went to make coffee. De Quiroz pulled their chairs under the shade of a parasol. Even in deep shade, their wet skins dried almost at once.

'Well?' he said enquiringly. He picked up her hand, pulled at the wedding ring without trying to take it off. He rolled it as far as the knuckle, to reveal a band of white skin.

'Already.'

'You mean I am getting brown.'

'Yes. I do not want you to be so. I like you pale.'

'Must I hide, then. Under parasols?'

'Of course.'

In the following silence – there was no birdsong as there would be in England in summer – she heard a whirr of wings. Two humming birds, flashes of metallic greenish-blue, were hovering over a tree covered in white flowers. Ceci had taught her the name for those birds. *Beija-Flores*, flower-kissers.

The coffee arrived. Maria Teresa looked, Eleanor thought, too knowing as she placed the tray between them, and slowly returned to the house. Eleanor picked up the heavy silver coffee pot.

'You are very beautiful,' he remarked in a critical tone.

'You don't have to pay me compliments.'

'But I do. I wish to. You must have them.'

He took her hand again. It was dry now but cold from the swim. He fitted it into his own: his hands were large. She sat very still.

'Besides,' he said, 'you and I are going to mean a lot to each other. Of course.'

Eleanor returned to Brasilia next morning and everybody,

Hugo at the airport, Joanna, Zica and Esmeralda at the villa, behaved as if she had been away for months. Joanna had one of her attacks of temperament, blushed crimson, refused to kiss her and hid behind Zica.

'She's been missing you,' said Hugo indulgently, at which his daughter pelted towards him and flung herself into his arms, possibly in revenge.

After the weekend, life returned to its Brasilia pattern. There was a reception at the Embassy for a British trade delegation, and the next day a small party in the Embassy gardens for some American visitors. Ceci invited her to a concert, and Hugo took her to the press club where he had to make a speech. Eleanor tried to put De Quiroz out of her mind. He wouldn't go. She kept seeing men who resembled him: the same blue-black hair, the same way of walking.

Days turned into weeks since she had been to Rio. Her mother telephoned often; Eleanor would have imagined Sara to be the sort of person easily offended if you put her off. Not a bit of it. She simply went on coaxing – when could Eleanor come again? When?

The truth was that thoughts of De Quiroz made Eleanor nervous. He was too interesting, and in a way this was also true of Sara. Eleanor did not want to be caught up in a life disturbingly different from her own. What kind of a mother, after all, was a woman who more or less refused to acknowledge Joanna? When Sara rang for long giggly chats on the telephone, Eleanor continued to slip out of promises that they should meet.

One evening when Hugo returned home very late, he found Eleanor in bed in the dark room which smelled of a lemon-scented Brazilian cologne Zica had produced from somewhere. Possibly it had belonged to the previous tenants of the villa.

Sitting on the edge of the bed, he touched one of Eleanor's bare feet.

'Your feet are like Jo's. So pretty. Poor love, is it your headache?'

'Yes. A bit horrid.'

'Too much sun.'

'No,' she said painfully, 'I stayed in the shade, truly, but Ceci gave me a violetta at lunchtime.'

It was a strong sweet Brazilian cocktail.

'That must have done it. Poor love,' he repeated rather absently.

Her head throbbed; she felt slightly sick. And since she had come home from Ceci's, she had lain on the bed with pillows not cooling, eau-de-cologne not working, aspirins having no effect, and her thoughts occupied with De Quiroz.

'I know you need to be left in peace and I shouldn't disturb you but I'm afraid I must,' said Hugo gently. 'Your mother rang me at the embassy.'

She gave an involuntary start.

'It's quite all right,' he said soothingly. 'Nothing to be worried about. She told me she keeps ringing but you can't see her because I burden you with so many social chores.'

He knew all about Eleanor's excuses. They amused him.

'The long and the short of it was that she rang to beg me, as she put it, to let you go and see her. She was so persuasive, Eleanor. I simply couldn't say no.'

'But I don't want to go. Not so soon, anyway.'

'Darling, it is well over a month.'

'I wish she wouldn't bother you. Or me, come to that.'

'Isn't that rather unkind? She *is* your mother.'

'She didn't remember that for the last fifteen years, did she?'

Hugo's tone was equable but it reproached her.

'When your headache's gone we'll talk about going to Rio again,' he said. 'I meant to take us more often. We'll all go. We enjoyed it, didn't we? And I confess I'd like to meet your mother, she sounds delightful.'

He went out. Eleanor, her head throbbing like an engine, pressed down into the pillows. De Quiroz walked again uninvited in her thoughts.

Hugo's embassy efficiency took his family to Rio again, with Joanna quite pink from excitement, and Zica bright-eyed. In the early morning of their arrival, Hugo suggested that instead of using the hotel's private beach they should go along the open seashore which was, he said, quite a sight to behold.

Crowds had already gathered by the time the Lawrences came out of the hotel and down to the shore. Or perhaps the people had slept the night by the sea; they were busy having breakfast, washing their hair under the showers, or, radios blaring, sprawling in the steadily rising sun. Life on the beach was very extraordinary: it was as if the Rio people didn't visit the shore for a swim or a sunbathe, but treated it as an extension of their homes or even their offices. They simply shifted to the edge of the sea. People lay reading or still sleeping, they jogged, did their exercises. Men under parasols sat round working out business deals, while mothers fed their babies nearby. Handsome *carioca* boys picked up dark near-naked girls. A few yards away there was a prayer meeting, the small congregation in bikinis. And always there were the slow-moving treasure hunters, painstakingly combing the sand to find rings or money, watches, chains, and all the lost treasures of the little children.

Hugo and Eleanor, arm in arm, wandered through the crowds fascinated, while Joanna ran ahead with Zica in pursuit.

In the evening Joanna was worn out with swimming and playing and was fast asleep before seven. Zica curled up with a tray of supper, content to watch dire American TV in her adjoining room. Luxury, to Zica, was a matter of astonishment; when she gave Eleanor her brilliant dark smiles, Eleanor felt more guilty than glad.

Hugo ordered a car to take them to the villa which, unlike the Lawrences' home, had a real name: the villa Sarita. The car was open, the air warm as milk, as they drove down the tree-lined boulevards.

'I'm looking forward very much to meeting Sara, darling. Are you nervous about us being together? I hope not.'

Saying no, Eleanor meant yes; particularly when at the villa Sara came running girlishly down to greet them.

When she was introduced to Hugo she cried, 'Why didn't you tell me he was so dishy?'

Hugo really laughed and Eleanor thought, Sara knows there isn't a man who wouldn't be pleased to hear that.

José Americo paid a great deal of attention to Hugo, the embassy guest. Almost immediately they were deep in talk; it seemed to be about the purchasing of land. During dinner, with Sara ineffectually darting in with frivolities now and then, the talk went on. Eleanor was bored. She knew little about Brazil's industries and felt like a schoolgirl who had strayed by accident into a conference of government officials. It wasn't her idea of a dinner party; it never happened like this in Brasilia. Laurette came into her thoughts. Would she hold her own with José Americo who, clearly indifferent to the women's boredom, went on with what he called problems and opportunities?

When coffee had been served, Sara dragged Eleanor away to a Hollywood-styled bedroom. She gave her a wink.

'My husband wants to talk to yours.'

'He seems to have been doing that already.'

'I know, I know, aren't they dull? I used to long to discover what men talk about when we're not around. Once I sat and eavesdropped in a bar: dull, dull, dull. But José Americo is really glad to consult your Hugo. It was great of you to bring him.'

She dabbed some scent on her wrist. Then, very sweetly, 'Am I being allowed to keep you after the weekend? Is Hugo due back in Brasilia?'

'I'm afraid so – meetings, meetings. Joanna too, she has a party. She positively lives at them, quite the social butterfly.'

Eleanor had begun to resent her mother's avoidance of a granddaughter and had decided to bring Joanna into the conversation occasionally. It did not work. Sara merely dabbed on more scent.

'Do you think they've finished the boring stuff by now? Do we dare go in?'

She sounded seventeen.

Apparently they had, for the rest of the evening was more civilised and Sara, glancing now and again at José Americo, looked curiously happy and relieved. When they said goodbye, it was very late. The driver of their car had been patiently waiting, probably for more than an hour, and smoking strong cigarettes which smelled like Gauloises, but he seemed quite relaxed as he opened the door for them. There was a huge round moon overhead; the night was balmy. As they drove back, Hugo said, 'I like your mother. I can see you in her.'

'Hugo, I'm not a bit like her.'

'Don't you think so? There are reflections . . .'

'My stepfather looks as if he belongs to the Mafia,' remarked Eleanor after a moment.

Hugo rubbed his chin. 'He's the sort of man you find in countries like this, where the division between poor and rich is so vast. Bigger here than anywhere else in Latin America. Apparently he's buying up Indian land and selling it at a high price. He didn't say so, but I wouldn't be surprised if he and his business staff didn't use threats to get hold of the land. He asked me loads of questions; I'm afraid my answers weren't as useful as he'd hoped.'

'He's a peculiar man,' Eleanor said.

'Possibly a dangerous one,' said Hugo.

The elaborate entrance to a huge white block of flats was guarded by two porters in musical comedy uniform. The lift was the size of Eleanor's sitting room in Brasilia. It wafted Sara, José Americo and Eleanor up to the twelfth, top floor. As they were taken upwards, Sara said 'Listen! The samba.'

Nobody who visited Brazil, let alone those who lived there, could escape the samba. Its thudding heartbeat could be heard long before the lift stopped and they had stepped straight into the music. Eleanor was used to the sound and liked it. She'd heard it coming from the *favelas* in Brasilia, from the radio, from Ceci's tapes. She knew about the samba schools in Rio where all the year round the people danced and planned their part in Rio's festival. The festival was the huge Dionysian revel which lasted for four days in a frenzy of dance and was known all over the world.

The hostess tonight hurried over to welcome them. She was tall and blonde and American. She kissed Sara and

José Americo and clasped Eleanor's hand hospitably. She was real glad to meet Sara's daughter, she said, examining Eleanor with sharp eyes.

'Franciso has been asking after you, Mrs Lawrence. He sure is an impatient man.' She laughed, showing beautiful American teeth.

On cue, De Quiroz appeared through the mass of dancers. 'Bernadette, may I steal your guest away?'

'Why not?'

De Quiroz kissed Eleanor's hand and led her on to the dance floor where there was scarcely an inch of space. The music beat on.

'You can do the samba?'

'No. We don't dance it in London.'

'I have seen the dances in London. Here it is different.' He took both her hands. 'Bend your knees – so. As if you are ski-ing. Keep your upper body very straight. Be proud. Yes. That is not bad.'

Eleanor loved to dance and seldom did so. Soon she was learning the first movements of the samba, and encouraged by the man facing her, danced with growing grace and pleasure. At last he stopped, and led her out of the crowd.

'One drink. Then we will start again.'

'I thought perhaps we'd dance later?'

She was accustomed to the sort of parties she went to with Hugo. There was more talk than anything else, except food and drink.

'It is only to dance we are here,' said De Quiroz. 'Bernadette has hired three bands, and we must squeeze the juice out of all three before we drop. Come along, beautiful girl.'

They drank something icy which tasted of peaches and went back to the samba. And danced. All night long Eleanor did not once see her mother or her stepfather. The music was seductive; it was inescapable. It never halted. There was no pause or roll of drums to indicate an interval. Relays of musicians appeared now and then on the stage, took the drumsticks from the hands of the previous group, sat down in their vacated seats, and on they went. De Quiroz was sweating and so was she. At last in mid-dance, he shouted over the deafening beat, 'We must have another drink.'

'Must we?'

'Yes we must, or we'll dehydrate.'

'What?' shouted Eleanor, deafened.

'Doesn't matter.' He pulled her out of the dance. They made their way between empty tables littered with tiny silver purses and empty glasses. Eleanor looked at her watch. They had been dancing for five hours.

De Quiroz fetched some glasses from the bar at the far end of the terrace and they walked to the balcony edge and looked out at a blackness which was the sea. No sign of the moon. The city still glittered and Sugar Loaf, dimly rearing, was a presence rather than a mountain.

'Shall we go to the beach and see the dawn?'

She felt a sexual frisson.

'But Sara will be looking for me.'

'She will not. She also will dance until she drops. José Americo, of course, is in the gambling room. They will go home eventually. Sara knows you are with me and that I will take care of you.'

She put her hot hands round the frosted glass, excited and afraid.

'Tell me something,' he said. She waited, longing to know what he would ask. It was not what she expected.

'Was it Sara you came so far to find?'

Eleanor did not know how to reply. The illusion that she

had come from England on such a quest was tempting to make her own. He did not seem to notice when she said nothing.

The tentacles of the samba still wound round her ankles, but De Quiroz said they would not dance any more. They left together, after looking in vain for their hostess.

'People disappear at parties,' De Quiroz said.

She had no idea where he drove her after they left the building. How was it that the pale-sanded beach was deserted when all the Rio poor slept along the edge of the sea? He parked the car somewhere, nowhere, and took her down to the empty shore. The long gentle waves came in, level and slow, scarcely two inches high. The ocean looked like oil. The waves broke and drew back with a dragging sigh.

He threw his white coat on the white sand and soon they were making love. She hadn't meant to, didn't think; she let it happen. She had no choice in her fate when she lay down on the hard sand with De Quiroz: it was the first time in her life that passion grasped her as the samba had done. She almost fainted with selfish pleasure and somewhere she could still hear the long sigh of the waves.

Hugo was at the airport next morning to meet her. When he kissed her, he said she looked tired.

'Sara wears you out,' he said indulgently.

He talked of her mother a little, and Eleanor described the party. But Hugo, who meant to listen, had his thoughts elsewhere.

Chapter Ten

Eleanor's love affair threaded in and out of her life, appearing and disappearing like a Lurex thread, harsh to the touch and over-bright.

It was impossible to see him often. According to Sara, De Quiroz was part of a large family, three brothers and a father – fabulously rich. The De Quiroz men were afraid of their mother who ruled them like some Portuguese aristocrat in the last century.

'She insists that they're at home whenever she wants them to be. Huge family dinners, apparently. José Americo had a gorgon like that too. Fortunately now in heaven,' said Sara, making the sign of the Cross.

De Quiroz, added Sara, always glad to talk about him, was rather important in the family business; there were millions being made in engineering and work swallowed up some of his time.

'But the rest, you'll see, he will keep for you.'

Sara appeared to know what was going on. Eleanor did not like that.

Although she had developed a guilt-free conscience, Eleanor could scarcely stay with her mother more than, at most, twice a month; especially since she'd made so much fuss about going in the first place. But Hugo encouraged her. He was more than usually busy, his days crammed with meetings, receptions, visitors, papers to be written, all the problems which kept him at the embassy until all hours.

'Darling, I am rushed off my feet. We have to be at the State Department this morning and then the Embassy people are all seeing the Minister of Culture. I don't want to bore you with it all; why not fix to see your mother this weekend? I know she would love to see you. Then I shan't feel guilty at coming home so late and being such a rotten companion. Don't worry about Jo. Ceci telephoned and asked if she could have her for the weekend. They're going to Copacabana.'

Eleanor did as he suggested. Inwardly trembling.

At the Villa Sarita, she was welcomed by Sara with the usual open-armed delight. Since her daughter did not spell out that she was sleeping with De Quiroz, Sara didn't either. But she enjoyed implying it, and smiled broadly when Eleanor pretended she did not understand.

Eleanor recoiled against being invited to talk about her love affair. It was hers, not something to be whispered into sounding sordid.

During drinks one evening when José Americo was out, Sara said teasingly that she was sure Hugo had started an affair by now.

'That's how it goes in this country – everybody's doing it. Well, let's say everybody but me.'

She gave her raucous laugh.

'Why not you?' Eleanor considered the subject of Hugo's infidelity ludicrous, and in any case wished to get her mother away from either him or herself.

'Don't think I haven't been asked. Brazilians are so sexy. But I wouldn't dare.'

'Because you'd hurt José Americo.'

'Mmm. I'll leave it at that. I just wouldn't dare.'

Eleanor's new passion affected everything: her love of De Quiroz's country, his tastes, his vices, the qualities missing in him as well as those in evidence, whatever was part of him she embraced. And it was a paradox that because of De Quiroz she saw Sara so often, and had began uneasily to love her too. Like De Quiroz, Sara was alluring and enigmatic.

At first she had backed away from the actressy manners and the exaggerations, but gradually she became affected by Sara's glad welcomes, and knew her mother meant the things she said, in a way. More and more Eleanor saw the similarity between her and Laurette. They were egotists to whom men were a necessity. Yet they had room in their selfish hearts for her, and so she loved them in return.

De Quiroz was formal with Eleanor when her mother was there. He stood around with a glass in his hand, talking of mutual Rio friends. It was unbelievable for Eleanor to remember the reason he was here.

'Off you go, darlings. Francisco, bring her home safely please, and not later than six.'

Sara in the role of mother.

When Eleanor and De Quiroz walked down the steps baking in the sun, she told herself she deserved the excited joy which went through her. Shouldn't everybody have the chance once in their lives to be treated as entirely sexy? She never had until now. Hugo was tender and concerned and gentle, but he had not, except at that one half-drunken party when she was nineteen, stirred Eleanor's frenzied desire. This man did so the first time they lay on a deserted beach.

Their time together was never, or rarely, in the same place twice. Sometimes they went to a borrowed apartment in one of Rio's luxury blocks of flats and De Quiroz produced, for that afternoon, a front door key. Or they would make love in the garden of a huge deserted villa, lying on the marble by water where nobody swam, with only the little lizards and the butterflies for company. He took her more often to La Favorita, a rich club where there were a series of chalets, each expensively fitted up with a bathroom, shower, Venetian blinds, a bed, creating a sort of miniature flat. The chalets, very discreet, were hidden at the end of hedged pathways or among tall flowering shrubs. Wherever he took her, it was for solitude and sex and nothing but.

De Quiroz did not talk much. He was there to make love. Once, breaking off from a kiss, he did say, 'You don't know your power. You should know it.'

'Have I any?'

'All there is.'

She returned to Brasilia in the happiest of moods. She could not do enough for Hugo. She took trouble with dinners she gave at the villa. Hugo invited the Ambassador and the queenly Katharine, Eleanor's golf companion Nigel, and the tennis-playing Jenny who reminded Eleanor of Joan Hunter-Dunne.

The Ambassador enjoyed his evenings with the Lawrences. He walked in the garden with Eleanor among the fireflies and talked to her of the wonders of Brazilian pottery. He told her about the time the country had been an empire with an imperial throne. Fortunately for Eleanor, Hugo took on the imperial Katharine.

Solaced by sex, Eleanor threw herself into her wifely duties. She was sweet-tempered and obliging and thought of ways to lift the social weight from Hugo's shoulders. She and Ceci gave a big cocktail party, a great success.

Eleanor went often into the city.

And she flowered.

As the months passed Eleanor saw De Quiroz often but never never enough. Their ardour did not cool and Eleanor began to understand that sex, like fire, increased by feeding. Very occasionally, after they had made love and were walking back to his car, or had stopped for a drink, he would – by ill luck – meet somebody he knew. De Quiroz presented Eleanor to who ever it was, but she knew he was displeased. The man or woman who had come up to greet them soon faded away. Eleanor hated that. She felt he was treating her as a disreputable secret.

When on one day, after a more than usually marked encounter, she felt raw and accused De Quiroz, he was astounded.

'Secret? Of course you are my secret. As if I would tell anybody about you or share you with the world.'

At the villa, Sara continued her half-implications but Eleanor was adept at ignoring them. She noticed that her mother never said anything like that when José Americo was present.

The more Eleanor saw of her stepfather, the more she was sure that Hugo was right and he was a dangerous man. Sometimes he was actually collected by two or three men who looked almost laughably like a heavy mob in a film. Sometimes when he talked on the telephone in Portuguese, José Americo looked ice-cold, threatening, and he sent shivers down Eleanor's spine. Yet when he and Sara entertained the high-ups in the Brazilian army or society, he was the soul of expansive Latin-American hospitality. Eleanor began to understand why her mother was slightly afraid of him.

Returning to Brasilia after a weekend in which she had

been lucky enough to spend two whole afternoons with De Quiroz, Eleanor was telephoned by Ceci.

'Is ages. A whole week. Come and swim.'

When Eleanor arrived at Ceci's villa, her friend, in one of her eternal white dresses, was waiting for her. But the swim was abandoned, for Ceci's thin white skirts were blowing like flags in a dry rasping wind which drove them indoors.

Sitting together, Ceci gave her a slow smile. 'You back from Rio only yesterday. Is that right?'

'How did you know? I was going to tell you—'

'No need. Always I can see.'

'What *do* you mean, Ceci?'

Eleanor was laughing.

'You are making love with a man in Rio, isn't it?'

Taken aback, almost alarmed, Eleanor wanted to deny it. But then came a longing for confession. Flurries of red dust blew in from the open windows, there was the melancholy steady sound of the wind. Jo, and Ceci's children, were away in a villa where the first classes were being given. Eleanor and Ceci were alone.

She began to talk. Her friend, like a plump-breasted pigeon, sat with her black eyes fixed on her. She did not look shocked or amused, just deeply attentive. She never smiled once.

And Eleanor saw that Ceci was Brazilian in her soul. She was tolerant. Why shouldn't Eleanor fall in love and was it not the most important emotion in the world? At last Eleanor had the luxury of talking about De Quiroz. A lover speaking of the beloved is famously boring, but not to Ceci. At the end of the story she gave a deep sigh. 'So you are happy.'

'Oh, very!'

'I can see.'

Another sigh. A pause.

'But you know what is important.'

'Not to be at his mercy, I suppose.'

'That also. But the real important ones are Hugo and Jo.'

She did not say it piously. But she was very serious.

'I know, Ceci, I know. I'm so careful, honestly. Hugo doesn't have any idea, I swear. I'm really nice; of course I am, I love him. And I am certain he doesn't know.'

Ceci nodded. When Eleanor finally stood up to walk home in the still-blowing wind, she gave Ceci the usual kiss but Ceci responded more emotionally than usual with the Brazilian *abraco*, the warm kiss first on one cheek and then on the other.

Eleanor continued to behave to Hugo with the eager consideration of somebody who, filled to the brim with joy for another reason, is profligate with time and good nature. She did think about Ceci's advice, but was positive she *was* putting husband and daughter first in the way she acted, if not in her thoughts. The days went by between one bout of passion and the next, and Eleanor was the perfect wife.

Hugo did not seem all that aware of her efforts. His work was hungrier than ever; he was very quiet. She recalled his friend, Nigel Storey, telling her that diplomats spend most of their time 'watching and advising and suggesting' various ways of playing a complicated game for Britain's advantage – if any. 'We seem so damn passive,' he said, 'but now and again our suggestions are useful. We have to be persistent. Sounds, dull, doesn't it? But Eleanor, believe me, that job of ours eats us up. Hours and bloody hours,' Nigel had said, laughing. When Hugo was at his most monosyllabic, confided in her little and came home late, she remembered what Nigel had told her.

Occasionally, over the months, he talked about the fact that their home leave was soon due; his first year of service was over, and the prospect drew nearer. He was enthusiastic. It would be so good to see his parents and to stay at Hillier's: he had begun to miss England. Every time he mentioned leave, Eleanor's heart plunged. Then somehow he seemed to talk himself out of the idea. They wouldn't go just yet; work at present was pressing. There were some minor British royalties due; there was a report which was already late, and other things.

In the lunatic way of the lover, Eleanor had got it into her head that if and when she left Brazil for a few weeks, she would lose De Quiroz. Sara had told her, during the early days when Eleanor had just met her mother and De Quiroz had first been introduced, that he was 'never without a woman. He's a great catch, of course: marriageable age and rich. There are a lot of Rio girls who long to marry him: I know at least four, poor things. But Francisco is as slippery as an eel.'

Eleanor thought, I shall lose him and I'll die.

The wind which had blown when she went to Ceci did not drop but continued, covering parked cars so that you had to wash the windscreen every morning; even touching a door handle was gritty.

Ceci came round to see Eleanor, and tell her they were going away for a couple of months.

'The place we go is beautiful. Forests of araucarias, the trees so tall, and a big river. We have stayed before; it is for Oswaldo's work.' She stood looking at Eleanor, who saw that her eyes were full of tears.

'Please miss us,' she said, running to her.

It was dull when her friend was gone. Brasilia seemed hotter and more airless than usual, and there was no comfortable little pigeon to suggest visiting friends or lessons in the samba. Even Joanna, who had dozens of friends, loudly wailed at missing Shelley and Mitch.

Eleanor felt low spirited. The sky looked as if it would never *not* be that pitiless blue and the only welcome sound was the water sprinklers.

One morning she woke feeling unwell, with pains in her stomach and slight diarrhoea. It must have been the mangoes at supper – they had been very ripe. Hugo had no ill effects, and when he had breakfast on the terrace, she decided to stay in bed. She felt languid and weak. When he came in to say goodbye, he did not sound particularly sympathetic.

'The only thing to do is to starve and drink a lot of water.'

She agreed sulkily. He had been off her, as she described it to herself, for weeks. She couldn't remember the last time they had made love. I suppose that happens eventually, but hell, he is still young and so am I. Hugo has never been very highly sexed. Perhaps it is the hot weather, she thought.

She drifted into the uneasy sleep of slight illness later. The house had a hush of quietness except for the familiar sound of the air conditioner. Her usually ebullient servants – Fia in the kitchen, Zica and Esmeralda in the garden – crept about without making any noise. She was restlessly asleep when the telephone loudly rang, the sound going straight through her.

'Yes?'

'Eleanor, Hugo. I have had a call from my mother. My father has been—' he stopped speaking and Eleanor was suddenly filled with fear.

'Yes? Yes?'

'He was killed yesterday in a car accident. In Scotland.'

She was speechless for a moment, and could scarcely take it in. John Lawrence dead. Recovering, she burst into sympathy. What a shock, oh poor Hugo, how terrible. What had Mathilde said? Had she been in the car? All the concerned questions came pouring out after the news of the sudden death. Hugo answered in short staccato sentences. His father had been in the Highlands visiting friends and no, his mother had not been with him, she was at Hillier's. He'd been driving home after heavy rain and apparently had skidded in the mud. The car turned over and went down a steep slope ... He did not finish the sentence but managed, 'I can't go on with this. I will be home soon.'

He put down the receiver.

Eleanor was very sick. The diarrhoea was, if anything, worse. She lay waiting for him, but the hours went by and he did not come. She was overcome with misery and shock to realise John Lawrence was dead. She'd always been fond of him, and she knew he liked her. He had seemed to give her a confidence that Walter had taken away. She simply could not imagine what life at Hillier's would be like without him. What would Mathilde do, robbed of his loving companionship? Her thoughts stretched out to Mathilde for a while.

But then what overwhelmed her was not grief for John Lawrence, or his wife, or Agnes with her loving spirit, or even Hugo, so devoted to his father. Knowing her own terrible selfishness she realised with despair that this was the end with De Quiroz. How could she leave him, lose him? Yet how could she not return to England with Hugo.

Illness gave her, at least, a reprieve. Would it be possible to stay on here until she was slightly better? The idea of travelling was impossible, she genuinely felt ill and – and if she *did* manage to stay, she would at least see De Quiroz just once more. She could think no further than that.

At last she heard Hugo's car, and his quick footsteps. There was a tap on the door and he came into the room. She found her voice.

'Oh Hugo, I'm so dreadfully, dreadfully sorry.'

'Yes,' he said, accepting the death. 'I spoke to my mother again. And Agnes. He – he is still in Scotland but Agnes is flying up, she'll bring him back tomorrow morning.'

'What exactly happened?'

'I told you. A skid.'

'And Mathilde didn't go with him to Scotland.'

'No, the Mathesons were friends of my father's, Mathilde never particularly liked them. She kept saying to me she wished she'd been there. Wished she was dead. She sounded dreadful – not crying – just dreadful.'

'I'm sorry, so sorry.'

He stood by the window and said without turning round, 'We're on the flight to London in the morning at half past nine. You'd better tell Joanna. I have spoken to Zica about packing.'

He looked at his watch.

'I must get back and look out some papers the Ambassador needs. I have a lot to do by this evening. I only came to tell you about the flight.'

As he turned to go she said in a shaky voice, literally feeling wicked, 'Hugo, I can't fly tomorrow, I really can't. The diarrhoea is worse than ever, and I feel ill. *I'm so sorry.*' She seemed to be saying that over and over again. 'I couldn't get myself into a plane like this. I'll follow you in two or three days.'

She screwed up the courage to look at him.

The force of the shock appeared to have hit him in the chest; he was not standing upright. She had a pang of love and pity for the haggard man; he looked prematurely old. But she wanted De Quiroz still. She read nothing in answer to what she'd just said. Hugo's face, shattered, was inscrutable. When he did not answer her she said weakly, 'Don't be angry with me, I can't help being ill, I can't come with you.'

'I'm afraid you must,' he said, and walked out.

She heard him calling Zica and speaking in Portuguese, and the girl's repeated '*coidado, coidado*' the word Brazilians all used for those in trouble. Hugo's voice was different when he talked to Zica. It was different.

He returned after midnight, came into her bedroom, switched on one light – the room had been in darkness – and packed in silence. Eleanor had spoken the truth when she had told him she was worse. She had been sick half a dozen times during the afternoon and evening, and could keep nothing down, not even water. Looking at herself in the glass as she returned from the bathroom, she saw with grim satisfaction how awful her face was, grey and drawn. It was very obvious that she was ill. But he did not ask how she was, he zipped up his travelling pack, went out again, and was on the telephone. But speaking in a very low voice.

Finally he came back into the room and shut the door.

She lay looking at him. She had convinced herself that she was too ill to travel, and in ordinary circumstances Hugo would have been the last man on earth to expect such a thing; Hugo so thoughtful and concerned when there was illness or trouble. But the man who came into her bedroom wasn't like that. He came bringing with him the dark shape of grief. He came with his father's ghost. He stood over the bed and said in a voice she scarcely recognised, 'I expect you to be with us.'

'*Hugo, I can't.*'

'Ariana at the Embassy went to the English chemist. She brought this.'

He produced a bottle of clouded liquid. 'It stops diarrhoea and sickness at least for a time. You can stave it off until we get back to England. Until after the funeral.'

'I can't,' she repeated in a half-hysterical voice and whether self-induced or not, ran to the bathroom to be violently sick.

He did not again say she must. She supposed his silence accepted her refusal. He did not sleep in their bedroom. Without explanation he went into one of the spare bedrooms. She was awake and nauseous all night, and heard him on the telephone at three in the morning, talking to Agnes. Hearing her friend's name was unreal to Eleanor, like hearing of a character in a film.

Early morning came to lighten Eleanor's room – slits of sunshine shone through the closed curtains. She was forgotten. She lay listening to Joanna excitedly talking to Zica, and Esmeralda's voluble chatter and then somebody, she thought it was Esmeralda, began to weep.

Hugo came into the room and stood at the door.

'Well?'

'I'm no better. Actually, slightly worse.'

'Have you taken the medicine I gave you?'

'Yes,' she lied. 'It doesn't work.'

'So?' he said without emphasis.

'I told you. I can't travel. It is cruel of you to expect me to. I will be back in England in a few days, the moment this horrible bug has gone.'

He didn't slam the door. Hugo never did.

As Eleanor, eyes enormous, lay listening with fear to the noises of departure, Joanna suddenly burst into the room shouting, 'Mummy, Mummy, I don't want to go. I want to stay with you and Zica. *Why* aren't you coming?'

She threw herself at Eleanor who wrapped her arms round her, hugging and kissing and smoothing the damp hair and kissing the plump wet cheeks. Joanna was loudly crying.

'Jo, Jo, come along, *querida*, there is no time,' Zica urgently called, in her recently learned and broken English.

With a final, 'Mummy, Mummy!' Joanna was led away still crying by the gentle Zica, who now talked soothingly in Portuguese, answered by the child who could speak it with lisping fluency.

Hugo was again by the open door.

Eleanor said weakly, 'Hugo, please telephone me. I shall feel so lost when you have gone. You will ring, won't you?'

'Yes. Goodbye, Eleanor.'

'Don't I get a kiss?'

He looked at her with a peculiar expression and made a sound which could have been a laugh. Coming across to the bed in two strides, he brushed her cheek with thin lips and left the room.

'Ring when you get to London,' she called after him.

She lay listening to slammed car doors, the rev of the engine, the '*Tchau, querida, tchau!*' from Zica and Esmeralda.

Then the awful silence.

She was ill for six days. The infection simply would not go. The doctor who attended the Embassy staff, a clever young Brazilian with faultless English, prescribed something, a powder dissolved in water, 'to treat the loss of salt and body fluids'. Of course, she must remain in bed, and when she asked if she could travel, she had a weak feeling of self-righteousness when he exclaimed, 'Impossible.'

Hugo did as she had asked, he rang from London Airport. The plane, he said, had been on time.

'How is Jo?'

'Fine. She slept for most of the journey.'

'Will you ring when you get to Hillier's?'

He did not reply, and she tried to force him to stay on the line, asking him to give her condolences to Mathilde.

'I will speak to you in a day or two,' was all he said. Then. 'How is your illness?'

He sounded as if he did not believe in it, and Eleanor told him about the doctor's visit.

'I see,' was all he said.

When he had rung off, she felt anxious and angry. Why couldn't he be the way he used to be? He didn't seem to care that she was ill. Because his father was dead, he had withdrawn from her. And she had been so sorry and eager to pour her sympathy over him.

Eleanor told herself many times, and said the same to Zica and to Sara who telephoned and learned what had happened, that she had been right to remain in Brasilia. Sara now rang every day, full of sympathy and advice and stories of friends who had had the same complaint. 'If you are not very careful, it can last for weeks!'

Eleanor was unused to being alone, and lonely as well as ill. The house felt extraordinary. There were four servants in the villa, but apart from Fia who catered for her (which meant bringing in fresh water by the jugful) and Zica who waited on her, she saw nobody. She told Zica that 'my husband and the little one will be back soon'. Zica looked solemn and said that 'we all in the kitchen' would run the house for the *Senhora*.

Sick and weak, eating nothing, Eleanor dragged herself

through the long hours. The staff quieted their voices in respect for their sick mistress and the death of their master's father. They were like dark kindly spirits in the villa. But the long long afternoons went by, and ill and fretful, bored and guilty, Eleanor turned on the radio for company. All Brasilia's main channel pumped out was news like the rattle of guns.

She lay listening to the incomprehensible voices for a while, and then quite suddenly, out came a pop version of the samba.

The samba. Even in this vulgarised version the beat contained all her desire. Since Hugo had left, she half believed it had been illness which kept her prisoner. But now, as she listened to the music, she knew she had stayed for De Quiroz. If it hadn't been a passion to see him once more, she would have swallowed down the medicine which would have temporarily halted her illness, and flown home with Hugo and Joanna. As it was . . .

She felt so ill and so lonely. People at the Embassy telephoned. Did she need the doctor again? Was she looking after herself? Nigel Storey offered to come round with champagne, but Eleanor persuaded him that she was rather ill, even now, and seeing nobody. His wife Jenny rang: surely there was something she could do? A kind message and roses came from the Ambassador and his wife.

Sara went on telephoning at midday, on the dot.

'How are you, poor darling? You still sound weak. But are you the tiniest bit better?'

Eleanor admitted that she was.

'When are you flying back?'

'When the doctor gives me the go ahead. I'm going into the city to see him this morning. I'm afraid I must have missed the funeral.'

'I keep thinking about Hugo. Didn't you say he was specially fond of his father?'

'Yes.'

'And you weren't?' was the somewhat mocking question.

'Of course I was. He liked me too,' said Eleanor pettishly.

Sara was calming. 'Look, if you feel better, why not come on Friday. Francisco keeps asking after you. He calls me up and complains that you have vanished.'

Eleanor's heart rose like a comet trailing stars.

She decided to ask Zica to come with her to Rio. Zica was radiant. She had scores of relations living in the *favelas* in the hills, and hadn't the chance to visit them when she had been in charge of Joanna. On the journey she was like a gentle nurse, and Eleanor felt herself really cared about. She needed that. It was arranged, when they parted at the airport, that she would come to the Villa Sarita to fetch Eleanor in two days' time.

It was Friday afternoon, and the offices and banks and government buildings were already closed, while the Rio streets seemed more teeming and jostling than ever. Eleanor was conscious of a curious change, something to do with the daylight, and then, looking at the palms and plane trees, she realised that for the first time for many months, the sky was growing dark.

Sara was waiting with her warmest welcome. 'Poor baby, you do look fragile. And you've brought the weather to match. José Americo tells me there will be a storm. I hate the rain, don't you? Come and kiss me, poor darling. How pale you are.'

Eleanor was still standing, circled with Sara's arms, when she felt the excited stab, the sensation of going down in a fast lift. De Quiroz was in the salon. He gave her an almost formal greeting, standing up and kissing her hand.

'Sit down, sit down. My poor child is too weak to stand.' Sara settled her among a heap of cushions, poured her a drink. 'Are you allowed my best champagne?' Sara enquired, and hovered round with all the sympathy Hugo had refused. Eleanor could easily have shed tears of self-pity. Sara gave De Quiroz a drink, and then consulted her tiny wrist watch set in emeralds.

'Bother, I have to rush. I'm meeting José Americo and I mustn't be late, though he always is!' She gave her loud laugh. 'Some of his horrible friends will be there too. Goodbye, my children. Francisco, take care of her or a breeze will blow her away.'

When they were alone, De Quiroz looked over at the girl leaning against the heaped cushions.

'You're as thin as a stick.'

'Aren't I?' She pulled at her dress to show the weight she had lost. He said, studying her, 'I rather like the *Dame aux Camélias* air. Tragedy suits you.'

'I *was* ill, as it happens.'

'Ah yes. Ill.'

He smoked for a moment or two.

'And you are well enough to swim on this dull day?'

'I haven't for ages, but I'd like to.'

She knew he did not mean for them to swim.

'Are you sure?'

'Certain.'

He lowered his eyelids, a trick he had. His eyes and thick lids were sexy, and she often thought he knew that. She supposed many women had told him so.

'Have you brought a swimsuit? No matter.'

He didn't say a word as he drove up the vertiginous mountain road, with its view of sea and ships under the lowering sky. The sea was a dull greyish green. Up, up, there was the Sugar Loaf veiled today in a cloud. He turned into an avenue of trees, and then through the gates of La Favorita. Just then the rain began. It didn't come gently but fell like hail on the car, making a thunderous deafening noise. De Quiroz muttered in annoyance as he drove through the intricate maze of little avenues among the thick hedges, until he parked at one of the chalets used by club members, officially, to change before a swim. Sara once told Eleanor that the place was a famous rendezvous. In Brazil, she said, you didn't get divorced, you paid your subscription to La Favorita.

As he opened the car door, the rain came down in buckets and in the few moments while they fled into the chalet they were drenched to the skin.

He locked the door and without speaking they stripped off their sopping clothes – and made love. There was a desperation in Eleanor's love-making that afternoon; she could not forget even in her highest moments that this was the last time. Soon she would be thousands of miles away, soon he would utterly have forgotten her. But for now he was hers. He, too, seemed more violent and excited than she could ever remember.

Afterwards they slept.

The afternoon went by to the noise of rain. The air grew cold and Eleanor, still asleep, groped for a sheet. She woke at last and turned to look at him. Indifferent to the chill air, he was sitting naked, leaning against the back of the bed. Seeing she was awake, he reached across her for his cigarettes, and then put one warm palm on her stomach.

'Where has the rounded Venus gone?'

'I shall fatten up again.'

'Of course.'

He lit his cigarette and snapped the lighter shut.

'You will go back to London, isn't it?'

'Sara told you.'

'That your husband's father died. I am sad for you and for him, very sad. Though I never met him.'

'Thank you.'

He went on smoking.

'When, then, will you fly?'

'The date has not been fixed.'

She stammered slightly, wondering with senseless temporary joy if he meant they could see each other just once more.

'But now your illness is gone, it will be soon that you'll go. I also. In two days I am going to São Paulo.'

Still leaning back, relaxed and easy, he began to describe the city which, he said, 'grew and grew', and so did its huge financial success, telling her his firm had a branch there. 'It's exciting.' For the first time since she had known him, he talked to her about his work.

With a bright false smile, Eleanor did not take in a word.

They drove back to the Villa Sarita in a rainstorm which seemed as if it was going to last until doomsday. It was as dark as night, the paths between the chalets had turned into rivers of mud, and the rain sprang up on the mountain road in a battlefield of water movement. When he drew up at the villa, De Quiroz took her hand to give it the old casual kiss, murmuring something in Portuguese which sounded caressing, and which she did not understand. But when she looked at him, she saw in his eyes that he had already gone.

Zica was shocked at her mistress's appearance when she arrived to collect her. Sara, also concerned and guessing the reason, tenderly bundled her into the car. Eleanor was too unhappy now to care what her mother knew. She spent the flight back to Brasilia with her eyes shut. Zica held her hand. She thought the poor *Senhora* had had a relapse, and that they should send for the doctor.

Certainly Eleanor was ill again, not from the stomach but from the heart. The pain which invaded her body was sensual and senseless. She had been obsessed by De Quiroz, had lived from one love-making to the next, and now it was over she lay like a boxer knocked out on the floor of the ring.

It was no pain-assuaging drug to know that De Quiroz was sorry to lose her, and had proved he was still attracted by his passionate love-making in the rain. He had, after that, simply packed her up; she was a possession not needed for the journey.

Worn out with misery, Eleanor made an effort to assure Zica that she was not ill, 'only tired and sad'. She needed company badly, and invited Zica and her sister to spend the evening with her. They accepted at once. Fia created a beautiful meal, and Esmeralda made special coffee spiced with cardamom. Zica then produced a surprise. It was a little bottle of liqueur made from sugar, known as *cachaça*. She told Eleanor that it was called the brandy of the poor, but had other more beautiful names.

'We sometimes call it the grandmother. Or the little blonde.'

'Or the thread of gold,' said Esmeralda, stumbling over the word 'thread'.

Zica poured a clear liquid into Eleanor's glass and told her there were many songs in praise of *cachaça*. They both laughed when Eleanor, at a first sip, gasped and nearly choked, it was so strong.

She was glad of them. They were concerned about her, argued about which day was best for her to fly home. Zica wanted her to stay at least another week, but Esmeralda declared it should be sooner, 'for the poor *Senhor* needs her'.

They discussed flight times.

'Oh, if we could be with you!' they cried. They did not mean that they wanted to travel to an unimagined Britain, they simply wanted to look after her and would count the days, they said, before the *Senhor* and *Senhora* and their little Jo came back to them. As they looked at her with their dark friendly faces, Eleanor had a sense of sad premonition.

Next morning, a large letter, sent Express, arrived for Eleanor. It was from a firm of London solicitors and informed her that Hugo was filing for divorce.

'My poor child, I will come at once.'

Sara did not wait for her sobbing daughter's invitation. She told her to do nothing until she arrived, not to try and get in touch with Hugo and not to ring the solicitors. She spoke as if her presence would solve everything.

For over a week Sara stayed with Eleanor at the villa in an atmosphere which was surreal. She was very certain of her opinions, and over and over again assured her stricken daughter that Hugo was bluffing. He wanted to frighten her. She knew those moves made by men, said Sara. Hugo could not seriously mean to break up their marriage, it was so – using the French word – exaggerated. She talked and pooh-poohed and comforted and drank a lot of champagne. But whatever she said and advised, Eleanor could not get herself together. She was stunned. Her marriage was a building supported by steel girders and, without any kind of warning, all the girders had been pulled away, and down the marriage had fallen into nothing but a mass of dirty useless bricks.

There had been De Quiroz for whom her body still helplessly longed. But this was far more terrible; when Eleanor tried to describe her feeling of nightmare, Sara answered in a lullaby, 'I know, *querida*, of course I know.'

Eleanor was sure she did not.

At the end of a week of talk, and God knew how many bottles of over-sweet Brazilian champagne, Sara made a move. She telephoned Nelson's.

They were in Eleanor's bedroom, where huge photographs of the granddaughter Sara had not accepted grinned from window-sills. A pretty child with curly hair. Sara sat at the end of the bed, barelegged and barefoot, wearing a pink and green sundress. The rain was gone. The sun had returned. She was waiting for London, gave a sudden jump, put her hand over the receiver and hissed, 'Got him.'

On the other side of the world, Giles seemed unsurprised to hear a voice whose timbre took him back twenty years. He was cordial and cautious.

'Yes. I've heard. Very regrettable. The solicitors sent me a letter, they suggested Eleanor might need some kind of help when she gets back. Their client, Hugo Lawrence, of course, thought I should get in touch with her. As a matter of fact I was writing to Eleanor this morning, I thought a letter better than a call.'

'Giles, the very idea of divorce is ridiculous!'

She seemed unaware of irony. He picked up a glass paperweight on his desk and put it down again.

'Giles? Are you still there?'

'Yes, Sara. I scarcely think we can call it ridiculous when there is evidence, which apparently has been given to the solicitors.'

'A mountain from a molehill. People here don't divorce for a bit of an affair, Giles.'

'They do in England. And Hugo is English.'

'I know, I know,' she said with the lulling sigh which meant nothing. 'But surely Hugo and Eleanor can sort this out. She really wants to. If you could see her, she's knocked out, poor love. And the—'

'Bit of an affair?'

'Totally finished. She's flying back tomorrow.'

'Give me her flight number. I will meet her.'

'Oh, would you? She's not feeling well. You know. Shock.'

Sara looked over at Eleanor and gave an encouraging 'things are looking up' smile which had no basis at all. Anxiously Eleanor returned the look. She did not believe it and she was right. All her mother succeeded in was to get someone to meet Eleanor in the desert of London Airport.

Eleanor asked Sara not to stay until she left Brasilia, and Sara, though not admitting it, was already hearing the siren song of Rio. She agreed. Perhaps it would be too miserable; they would say their goodbyes in advance.

'Then the nastiest part is over before you have to pack, darling.'

Eleanor drove with Sara to the airport and they parted as a mother and daughter ought to do and sometimes don't. They promised to ring and to write. When the flight was announced, Sara, her eyes shining, suddenly gasped, 'You won't give me up, will you?'

It was very early when it came to Eleanor's turn. Both Zica and little Esmeralda had been up since four, ironing the last of Eleanor's clothes, which they had washed the night before and were bone dry after being hung in the garden. They folded a ruffled blouse thin as a cobweb, a floating skirt. When would Eleanor wear those in cold England?

Eleanor had said goodbye to the other servants the night before, and given them generous goodbye presents. But Zica and Esmeralda were there to make her breakfast which she scarcely touched. The trio sat in the untidy bedroom. Nobody talked, except when Eleanor asked if they had remembered this or that. And every time they had.

She had a pain in her heart when she looked at the fine dark faces. She had only made three friends in Brasilia, and Ceci was still faraway and had been, all through Eleanor's miseries. Circumstances had stolen her out of Eleanor's life.

When the car drove off in the red dawn, Eleanor looked back to see two white-clad girls standing at the gate. Miniature fountains were already spraying their dewy benison on the grass, and she had a final glimpse of the swimming pool where Joanna's red and white ball still floated. Both girls were crying.

So was she.

Chapter Eleven

Everybody who knew Hugo, his mother and sister, his friends at the FO, his masters, people who had known him in Sussex from boyhood, thought he should forget about a divorce. He would not listen. His face had always been thin, but at times it had been handsome and humorous; now it became pinched and he had an air of resenting the world. He was very silent. His daughter avoided him, trotting off in a scared way to Agnes, like a chick anxious to hide under the hen's comforting wings.

It was Agnes and not Mathilde who first demanded the truth from Hugo on the day after their father's funeral. She was staying at Hillier's and came into his bedroom wearing the black dress she had bought for the requiem mass. Only Agnes and Mathilde wore black for death, it was a colour of chic and not of sorrow. Black suited Agnes, with her naturally pink cheeks and waving hair. She looked sad and still beautiful.

'Hugo,' she said at once. 'Where's Eleanor?'

'I told you and Mother. Still in Brasilia. Unwell.'

'Yes, I remember. But she hasn't rung us and you have not rung her. What's wrong with the poor girl?'

He gave a slight shrug.

'D and V.'

Agnes raised her eyebrows. 'Is that all? When David and I were in Hong Kong we practically lived on Doctor Collis Brown – Dave used to call it our cement. Come on, Hugo, what's really happened? What's up?'

He put his hands in his pockets. She foresaw an argument. She loved him and knew him impossible. What could you do with Hugo's reserve? She'd often marvelled that Eleanor put up with it apparently without difficulty. She knew from childhood that if you bashed against Hugo's reserve all you did was make the steel door thicken. Was there a key or a plastic card to fiddle the lock? And if so, thought Agnes, would you regret it when you opened it?

She was troubled because he was. It was terrible to lose their father so meaninglessly. A death like that was cruel, unnecessary. It had left Mathilde and herself speechless with disbelief. But she discerned another kind of trouble in her brother, not only grief but something ominous, and connected with the kind of man he was. Something to do with Eleanor.

'Hugo. I am still here.'

When he did not react she wanted to hit him. He was the only man in the world who made her feel like that.

'Well?' she said, more sharply than she spoke to anyone else.

'I am filing for a divorce.'

'You are *what*?'

'Eleanor has been – has not been what she should be.'

'For God's sake!' cried Agnes, starting out of her habitual calm. 'Are you saying that she slept with somebody else? Did she fall for them? Does she want a divorce? Tell me more about this!'

'I have no idea if she has fallen, as you call it. Or whether she wants a divorce. But that is what she is going to get.'

'Did you tell her you'd found out? Did you try to stop the affair? *Hugo*!'

'I don't want to discuss it with you, Agnes. I am sorry, but I will not discuss it. I have evidence.'

'How disgusting.'

'Yes,' he said, misunderstanding her, 'it is.'

Agnes looked at him searchingly. She saw nothing in the closed face which offered hope. She was horrified. Her life as the wife of a naval officer had taken her sometimes to the country, Plymouth, Portsmouth, and more often abroad for years at a time. She had lost a closeness to Eleanor, her oldest and dearest friend. When she *had* seen her there were times when Agnes was worried. Agnes had a particular method with invading insects, moths, bees, spiders, wasps: she put a glass over the unwanted visitor, slid a piece of paper under the glass and then, opening a window, threw the poor thing out into unbelieving liberty. She had once thought, meeting Eleanor at her London home, that she heard a frantic buzz from Eleanor's imprisoned wings.

After the useless interview with her brother, Agnes talked to her mother. Mathilde tried to drag herself from widowed misery to remonstrate with him. Even she utterly failed.

The immediate tasks which sudden death leaves for the survivors were sorted out. Agnes and David – he was on leave for a month – stayed in Hillier's with their two children. Mathilde accepted their presence with embarrassing gratitude. Agnes did not want her mother to thank her so often; it was unlike her.

Hugo was glad to leave Sussex. His mother and sister didn't mention the divorce again, but the expression on their faces, Mathilde's old and sad, Agnes's young and open, was identical.

The apartment in Saville Mansions, where long ago Hugo

had been able to stay occasionally, had been sold. Hugo went to his club, which was shabby and quiet. The food was similar to that at public school: boiled fish and overcooked vegetables. The porters and waiters spoke in hushed voices as if the club members were just coming out of an anaesthetic; but the place still smelled of Mansion polish, and all the serious daily newspapers were folded on a table in the draughty entrance hall. When a young member asked for the *Daily Mirror* he was told, 'We do not provide that journal, Sir.'

It was August, sultry and given to showers, the sky a mixture of grey and occasional blue. Hugo found the dull light of day a shock after the pure radiances of Brazil. So were the dull English voices and clothes, the lack of vivacity and laughter. Bustle and colour were absent. But so was grinding poverty.

He sat in a window seat overlooking the club's long garden, somewhere off Pall Mall, a newspaper on his lap, his eyes fixed on the same paragraph for ten minutes. He was thinking about Eleanor and what he had already set in train. He told himself that he was right. He wanted to be sure, but he was swept over the edge of a waterfall as terrifying as the Iguassu river pouring through a gorge 200 feet below. Helpless, deafened and half dead, he hated Eleanor. She had betrayed him. She had behaved like a whore.

In his secret heart, in his sex, in his most hidden emotions, it was not possible for him to conquer the jealousy which glared at him with the face of a devil. He had loved Eleanor and she had betrayed him; made his love cheap and of no account. He remembered their sex with shame. Had she been having that other man, the one in the evidence, at the same time? It made him shudder.

He used to smile at Mathilde for her attitudes, the monolithic rock of her prejudices about religion, morals. She had loathed the Sixties, never mentioned the existence of the pill. When Agnes tried sometimes to make her see things differently, the old look would come into Mathilde's face: a stubbornness, a mute immoveable resentment at being faced with many aspects of modern life. Hugo did not realise that his own reaction was exactly like hers. He probably would not have cared if Agnes had told him so. He was past caring what anybody said. He wanted to get rid of his wife. For the first time in his life, he understood Othello.

With Eleanor in his mind disposed of – the letter from the solicitors had been sent to Brasilia – he occupied himself late on Sunday night and early the next morning with the best way to deal with the divorce and his position.

The Foreign Office had moved with the times. It did not, like the old rules of Court in the past, ban divorce. But it didn't like any form of scandal, and the fact that Hugo's wife had been sleeping with a Brazilian high up in the business world was difficult. Hugo might be far gone in jealousy and suffering, but his mind still worked as far as his career was concerned.

Angular, distinguished, with a face of iron, he walked to the Foreign Office in the rain, sheltered under the usual black umbrella. London workers hurried by, their clothes like the garb of refugees. The streets were dirty and there were unremoved plastic bags in corners; to a man accustomed to Brasilia's blinding cleanliness banded with flowers, London was as dark as Hades. He turned with relief into the Foreign Office. His wet umbrella was taken from him by an egregious hall porter who prided himself on remembering everybody. Balding, with a ready smile.

'Mr Lawrence, nice to see you again, Sir.' Disappearance of smile. 'Tragic news about your father. My deepest sympathy.'

Hugo thanked him, and entered a newly-installed lift, a kind of gold metal box which took him, without a sound or light to indicate that they were even moving, to the fifth floor.

He was not looking forward to this interview. His wounds were unhealed, the dressing on them had stuck and he was sure Ward Bingham, his superior, would pull off the gauze and the lint, and then he would bleed all over the carpet.

Bingham was a thick-set olive-skinned man, short-sighted and tough. He wrote detective novels as a sideline. He nodded when Hugo came into his office, a comfortless place except for its carpet. The Foreign Office was on an economy drive. He said 'Sit you down', and ordered coffee which was brought in by a girl straight from Page Three in the *Sun*. Bingham always had secretaries like that. This time Hugo was unamused by the beauty who had legs yards long and fingernails like pearls. She withdrew in a trail of scent.

'Don't need to tell you how sorry we are about your father, Lawrence. The office was very shocked. So sudden. Tragic things, car accidents. A blow from fate. Such a good man, a first-class type.'

'Thank you, Sir.'

Ward Bingham picked up, from a desk on which there was no other piece of paper, the letter Hugo had sent him. It had been almost impossible to write. In his bedroom at Hillier's Hugo had tried draft after draft, until the final bald non-explanatory version which Bingham now held in his hand.

The older man looked across at him with a piercing

glance from behind spectacles which enlarged his eyes.

'I see you wish for a divorce.'

'I'm afraid so, Sir.'

Bingham studied the letter, as if reminding himself of the details Hugo had not given.

'You sure of this? Big step. Can be a mistake.'

'I'm quite sure.'

Bingham sipped his coffee. It was the reserve in Hugo Lawrence, the coldness which did not deceive Bingham, who recognised feeling and an almost feminine intuition in the man, which was useful. Bingham hired men with disadvantages: duodenal ulcers, stutters, hang-ups.

He stroked his well-bred aquiline nose.

'Can't stop you then, can we? But there is a problem. Diplomatically, there is a little problem. Do you think it might be simpler if you didn't – ah – happen to return to Brazil. Savvy? Suppose we box clever on this one. What do you say to a move? Richard Selby won't like it, I hear from Brasilia that he's very enthusiastic about you. But I can't see you, or him either, too pleased if you turned up at some shindig and found yourself sitting next to the man in question. Yes, I think a nice quiet transfer is what we need. There's an interesting vacancy you'll like the sound of. Progress in the service too. What about Political Councillor and Head of Chancery at Lisbon? Shall we say a couple of years? Then we'll see what we will see.'

When Agnes had visited her parents in recent years it was always a comfort and surprise to her to see how happy her mother had become. She was as busy and cheerful as a girl. Even Hugo's absence, after a first spell of missing him, did not dim Mathilde's smiling middle-age.

She and John Lawrence were the best of companions. She

studied him, as she called it, which meant she did everything for his comfort, fell in with his plans and enjoyed his company. When he talked about Catholicism, his favourite subject, Mathilde was glad to listen. She was more affectionate than when she had been young and Agnes's girls loved her and called her 'dear French Gran'.

As well as the usual countrywoman's love of gardening, she read a great deal in French, and her husband often found her, elegant in pearls and fine, if oldish, cashmere, not a still-dark hair out of place, with her feet up on the sofa, deep in a French paperback.

All the quiet pleasures ended when John Lawrence died.

It was a minor concession to the axe-blow of fate which struck Mathilde, that her daughter was in England at the time of the tragedy. David Lyttelton at once managed to get some leave, and drove Agnes and the children from Portsmouth to Hillier's.

'I'll help as best I can,' he said.

He was the man for it, devoid of sentimentality. He hugged his mother-in-law, took over the funeral arrangements. He was strong and quiet, and he was there. On the day of their arrival, and all next day, after the funeral, over and over, Mathilde talked to them about John Lawrence's death. She could not understand how it had happened. 'The police said the skid marks showed he had been driving very fast. John never drove fast. It wasn't like him. I don't understand it.'

David and Agnes let her talk. On went Mathilde. Had John fallen asleep? He had been to his friends in Kyle of Localsh but they said he had left at half past ten. When the body was found, the time of death was put at three in the morning. Where had he been in those lost five hours? There must, repeated Mathilde, be an explanation.

Agnes told David when they were in bed that she knew perfectly well where her father had been. Not to see some Highland mistress. Not drinking too much with people Mathilde knew nothing about. 'I'm certain my father just took a fancy to drive to the loch and sit,' Agnes said. 'He loved water at night. He told me so. He said he could watch it for hours. As a matter of fact I've often wanted to do the same thing myself.'

David kissed her and said nothing.

The following day when Mathilde once more dragged up the subject he said, 'I've been thinking, Mathilde. You mustn't stay in the house all the time.' He said he would like her to come with the family to a summer pageant being given at a ruined castle nearby. Mathilde meekly agreed.

The afternoon was a success mainly because heavy rain came pouring down on the audience, to the delight of Agnes's children and Joanna who was with them. They did enjoy seeing well-dressed country people rushing like rabbits into the tents.

Filled with merriment, they sang all the way home in the car. Agnes glanced at her mother. Mathilde wasn't listening.

When his leave was up and he was due back at Portsmouth, David asked Agnes to stay on at Hillier's with the children.

'The more noise they make the better. It will interrupt your mother's thoughts. I'll see you at the weekend, dearest. And miss you all very much.'

But despite shouts and laughter in the usually silent house, when David was gone Mathilde had a relapse. She'd made an effort because there had been a man about. Now she sat doing nothing, rolling and unrolling a lace handkerchief on her knee.

'Have you been sleeping much at night, Mother?' Agnes asked.

'Never more than four hours,' said Mathilde, rousing herself and speaking with a certain grim satisfaction.

'That's not nearly enough. Why not go up and have a nap before tea?'

'I'm not falling to pieces yet, thank you. In any case, Eleanor is due.'

Agnes was flabbergasted.

'When did she get back? Where is she?'

'I have no idea. She telephoned when you were out and said she was on her way.'

'But – but – did she ask to see Hugo?'

'No.'

'Surely you rang him!'

'*J'ai rien fait*,' said Mathilde coldly.

Agnes was thrown. She wanted to be ready for Eleanor, to sort out her own thoughts and try, God knew it would be difficult, to be of help. She'd temporarily taken on Joanna, poor child, who worried her very much, so quiet and withdrawn. She'd tried to reason with her brother and been told to mind her own business. She had a stricken mother to care for. And now Eleanor.

'Do you think she'll be arriving soon?' she asked. And at that very moment, to her dismay, a voice called, 'Anybody at home?'

Agnes ran out into the hall to give her sister-in-law an affectionate kiss. Eleanor hugged her convulsively. She was wearing a vivid blue silk dress which drained all the colour from her face. Sunburned, she was curiously greyish.

'It's lovely to see you,' exclaimed Agnes, trying to believe it. 'I'm afraid Jo is out. The kids have gone to a garden party. We didn't expect you so soon.'

'Aggie, I'm so sorry. I should've rung yesterday. How is Jo?'

'Oh, you know, missing her Mum,' said Agnes, thinking she sounded like a hospital nurse rallying a depressed patient. 'Come and see Mother.'

Mathilde showed no trace of Agnes's kind welcome; she was cold and Eleanor's grey face went slightly red. Agnes hurried into the gap and said Eleanor must come and talk to her in the kitchen.

The brick-floored kitchen was untidy, with the remains of biscuits and empty ice-cream tubs on the table. Free of Mathilde's stern presence, the children popped in to grab what they could find.

'Sit down Eleanor. You must be tired after that long journey.'

A little pause. 'I was so very sorry about your father, Aggie.'

'Yes. We miss him all the time. It was a shock. And Eleanor,' said Agnes, coming straight out with it, 'what is all this about you and Hugo? It's dreadful. It is not *you* who wants the divorce, is it?'

'Of course not.'

'So you don't mean to marry whoever it is.'

The idea of marrying De Quiroz came into Eleanor's mind in its grotesque unreality. She shook her head and said in a thin voice that she'd written to Hugo and asked for a reconciliation. No answer.

Agnes looked at her with pity and trouble.

'Perhaps he didn't get the letter.'

'Yes he did. His solicitors answered. They said Hugo "did not wish for any communication" from me.'

'My *stupid* brother,' said Agnes, crashing cups on to a tray.

'Aggie. Do you—' Eleanor faltered, 'do you think he'd ever take me back?'

'Do you?'

In the pause Eleanor knew then what she was afraid of.

'I kept thinking and thinking when I was on the plane, about how to make things right. I am so sorry, so miserably sorry that I hurt him. What I did was wrong and cruel but I can't go into that, I just want Hugo to forgive me. But forgiveness is so out of date. People now never do. They pack it in when the other one has an affair or something. They don't even want to *try* and make things all right again. They slam the door and you're outside.'

The kettle was boiling its head off. Agnes made a grab at it. She met Eleanor's eyes with intensity.

'Do you think Hugo still loves you?'

The reply did not come at once.

'No, Aggie, I'm sure he doesn't. The journey was so long and I was so tired, and I began to realise he must have known about the other man for months. I can't bear to guess how he found out, but I'm certain he did. I was such a fool not to see he was withdrawing from me. All right, it *was* my fault, but God, it was his as well. How could he sit and let it happen? It was awful of him. Why didn't he make a scene and force me to stop? They do in Brazil.'

'Do they?'

'Terrible scenes, my friend Ceci told me. But nobody gets divorced. Affairs are commonplace, they call them the second marriage. But they don't break up a real marriage. Never.'

Agnes made the tea and looked about for the sugar. She could scarcely bear to see her friend's sorrowful face.

'I expect you thought Hugo would take it in the Brazilian way when he did find out,' she said. Only from politeness.

Eleanor said nothing. She had never thought Hugo would take her affair in the Brazilian or any other way, she'd been so sure he knew nothing about it. It was true he stopped making love to her, and his manner changed. She'd put it down to her old adversary, his work. What had happened was that she'd lost her instinct with him; those tendrils which wind or wither when they touch the beloved. De Quiroz had made her immune from that awareness of Hugo.

Agnes picked up the tray.

'I think we ought to say some prayers. I will. And you must. Promise?'

Eleanor agreed. She knew she never would.

When they went into the drawing room to join Mathilde, Eleanor wished and wished that Hugo was here. She had come to fetch Jo, and had somehow imagined that he would see Jo and her together – his *family* – and he would relent. She'd made herself believe the impossible.

Agnes's Emily and Nicole, with Joanna trailing behind, returned after tea. Emily was small, neat and dark; Nicole, only three, still had a babyish round face and little dimpled hands. The children carried balloons and plastic monsters. Joanna, in a red dress, and with an odd set expression, carried nothing. She looked so waif-like that Eleanor thought her heart would break.

Seeing her mother, she came to a dead stop.

'Look who's come for you,' said Agnes.

Eleanor sprang up to kiss her daughter, but as she approached Joanna turned away, putting up her shoulder as a defence to keep her off. Eleanor, deeply upset, knelt down beside her but Joanna, escaping, rushed to Agnes. She clasped her by the legs, pressing her head against Agnes's knees.

Agnes patted her head, looking across at poor Eleanor. The child began to sob. Eleanor came over and knelt down by her again.

'I've come to fetch you, sweetheart. We'll go back to London together, shall we?'

To her alarm and pain, Joanna, face still hidden, violently shook her head. Agnes signalled to Eleanor who simply did not know what to do next, and then said gently, 'Jo, you can stay here with Em and Nicole for a while, if you'd like that.'

A nod. A sob. Joanna eventually stopped crying but she shivered and shook. Nothing made sense to Eleanor, and everything hurt her as it was hurting Jo.

The child was eventually coaxed by Agnes to go upstairs to bed with the other two. Agnes went with them, and when she came back she said gravely, 'Where are you staying, Eleanor?'

'In a hotel in Knightsbridge. You're thinking Jo is better here.'

'But she ought to be with you.'

'Aggie,' Eleanor said miserably, 'do you really think so?'

Mathilde suddenly said, 'A hotel will not do. The child will feel safer here.'

Her manner to Eleanor, during the dreary evening which followed, was as if Mary Magdalene, the harlot, not the saint, had arrived at Hillier's. Yet now and then when Eleanor met her eyes, she thought she sensed a faint sorrowful kindness.

Hugo rang before dinner to say he could not get back to Sussex until the next day. Mathilde took the call in John Lawrence's study; when she told her son who had arrived he said, 'She is not to take Joanna.'

'She is the child's mother,' exclaimed Mathilde, 'she will do as she wishes.'

'I forbid it.'

Mathilde, muttering *'Dieu'*, passed the telephone to Agnes and left the room. She did not know what her daughter said to him. Agnes grimaced when she came out of the study.

When the children were in bed, Agnes read to them. Eleanor, with an attempt at naturalness, sat on a window-seat. Joanna did not look at her. She was in a large double bed with Emily: the two children, not alike physically, huddled together like birds in a storm. Where was the carefree sunburned Brazilian child who had played in bright gardens?

Agnes closed the book. Eleanor bent down to say goodnight. Joanna put her arms round her neck. She wanted to love her – just then.

The evening dragged, and when it was time for Eleanor to leave, Agnes walked out to the drive with her. A plane droned overhead. The moon was full and very bright.

'I suppose it is best. And Jo should stay with us just for a little while,' Agnes doubtfully said. 'How do you feel about it, Eleanor?'

'That your mother was right.'

Agnes gave a long sigh.

'Yes. We'll keep her and you and I can talk every day. Jo seems to like Em, they do play together. Eleanor, you must write to Hugo again. Ignore that solicitor's letter. Just write and say how you feel. I'm sure it will work.'

But Agnes's hope went for nothing. Eleanor's second letter was answered by the solicitor; an identical reply to his first. There was no saving her marriage.

In the limbo in which Eleanor found herself while the

divorce was inexorably going through, all she could try to do was to find a home, so that she could have Joanna back. Not long ago she'd been married, with a husband she believed loved her, a little girl who hugged her, Brazilian girls smiling across gardens. There'd been Sara; there'd been Ceci; and the limitless blue sky.

Then so suddenly that it could scarcely be taken in, she was in a London swept by rain, in a hotel bedroom where the only possession which meant a thing was a snapshot of Jo and Zica in the swimming pool.

She had chosen to stay temporarily in Knightsbridge because part of her determination to mend Jo's life was that the little girl might be able to go back to her school in Pont Street. Eleanor visited the school and was received by the headmistress who, of course, remembered her.

Miss Thompson, short, blonde, and very brisk, was told about the divorce. She showed no surprise.

'Yes, Mrs Lawrence, sadly we have a number of children whose parents are no longer together. We do all we can for them. But of course we must work *with* the parents, their co-operation is essential. Stability, stability,' said Miss Thompson. 'You are wise, if I may say so, in choosing to send Joanna back to St Philips. Of course I remember her; a lively little spark.'

Not now, thought Eleanor, with a stab of the heart.

Eleanor explained that she was planning to move to somewhere near the school, but nothing was yet settled. Miss Thompson pursed her lips.

'I'm afraid term has begun. We do prefer the children to be back in time. So unsettling for the little ones. However,' with a steady glance, 'if there's no alternative, we must do our best. Five and a half? Then she will be in Class One. Shall we expect her in, say, two weeks? Your arrangements will perhaps be in order by then.'

Agreeing to the unrealistic date, Eleanor almost ran to the estate agents in Sloane Square.

The flat she finally decided on was in a building in Wilbraham Place off Sloane Street, less than ten minutes' walk from the school. It was a service flat, furnished, comfortable and over-chintzy. To Eleanor its main attraction was the room off the main bedroom; meant as a man's dressing-room. She felt its very smallness would suit Jo. Another reason for deciding on the flat, and one she would never have admitted even to Agnes, was that the gilt taps in an over-smart bathroom were in the shape of dolphins' heads. Surely Jo would like *those*.

The porter, a lugubrious man, told her his wife did the cleaning, and while the agent talked to him about keys, Eleanor went over to one of the tall windows, trying to imagine her life here.

It was strange.

Eleanor drove down to Hillier's to see Joanna two or three times a week, and sat around as if for all the world she belonged there as much as Agnes did. Mathilde thawed slightly, but then withdrew into a coldness and her own grief again. One afternoon Eleanor drove Joanna to Brighton; the other two children were already at school – Nicole at a playschool locally, Emily at a primary which was willing to have the child when she stayed at Hillier's. Eleanor drove a totally silent little girl across the Downs; in Brighton they went to the aquarium. She tried to interest Joanna in the brightly-lit tanks full of brilliantly-coloured fish, in the eels, the crabs. Silence.

Eventually, during tea, Joanna suddenly said, 'When am I going back to Zica?'

'I did explain, darling, that we aren't going back.'

Joanna took a biscuit. Her perfect face, a child painted by Greuze, became smeared with chocolate.

'Don't you remember, Jo? Aunt Aggie and I both told you.'

'No. I don't remember.'

Eleanor leaned forward and touched the sticky hand.

'Your Daddy and I—'

'Aren't friends any more. I don't *want* that!'

Looking straight at Eleanor, her beautiful face desolate, Jo opened a mouth full of biscuit and began to wail.

The lease signed, Eleanor was finally the possessor of a home. Real life, it seemed, was returning.

She had already spoken to Sara two or three times since coming home from Brazil, but the calls had been gloomy because she had been depressed. She knew she'd made her mother nervous. Now, at half past seven in the morning after the flat was settled, Eleanor rang again. The time difference was over four hours, and she wanted to catch Sara before lunch.

Hearing the news, Sara exclaimed in delight. She was clearly relieved, and immediately became the glamorous creature who had run down flights of steps towards a long-lost daughter.

When Eleanor gave her the address and telephone number, Sara cried gaily, 'I shall be in touch every hour on the hour.'

Later that morning Eleanor also spoke to Agnes, whose soft *hello* was a balm. She said news of the flat was the first good thing about the family she'd heard for months.

They talked of Joanna, of the other little girls, about Eleanor's move. And yet . . . did Agnes sound quite herself? Eleanor suggested that Agnes and her daughters might come to stay for Joanna's first weekend at Wilbraham Place. It would make things feel normal. Agnes agreed. Yet still Eleanor thought she did not sound quite natural.

Eleanor kept thinking about that when she went to the new flat, visited Peter Jones about deliveries, made lists. But the sun came out as she walked back to the hotel and she decided she must have imagined the check in Agnes's voice. I'm getting neurotic and who's surprised. She felt, now, happier than she had done for many weeks.

'Two telephone calls, Madam,' said the young hall porter as she came through the swing doors. 'Both from a Mr Thorpe. He said could you call back as soon as it is convenient. He has left his number.'

The porter then obligingly asked if he should get the number and put it through to her room.

All her nervousness rushed back as she took the lift to her bedroom, and her hand was clumsy as she opened the door. She sat down on the bed – the telephone immediately rang and she heard the lawyer's voice. 'Ah, Mrs Lawrence, good of you to call back so promptly.'

'What is it, please?'

'Would it be convenient if we met for a talk?'

'I came to your office two days ago. What has happened?'

Guy Thorpe, speaking like a cautious doctor, said he would be grateful for the chance of a word or two. Would she, perhaps, prefer him to come to her hotel?

'No,' said Eleanor, by now thoroughly alarmed, 'I'll come to your office. Right away?'

'That is very good of you indeed.'

When she rang off, she put her hands to her cheeks which were burning with excitement and a flickering hope. What did all this mean? Perhaps Hugo had changed his mind about the divorce. Something inside her unfurled, like a bud which she'd thought had been killed by frost. She thought of Hugo, for the first time since news of his divorce plans, with compassion and tenderness, and penitence. He wanted her back, he had seen, as she had, the dreadfulness of what it was doing to Joanna. He had forgiven her. That was what Agnes's tone had meant. She'd been told the news by her brother.

Eleanor took a taxi to Arundel Street. The traffic was bad and her impatience was stretched by every jam and every red light. She leaned forward, willing away the buses, trying to force the taxi forward.

At the lawyer's prosperous-looking office, she was taken at once into Guy Thorpe's large book-filled and impressive room. Thorpe was short, fussy and had a drawling voice. He shook her hand.

'Good of you to spare the time. Coffee, Mrs Lawrence? Tea? Orange juice?'

Thanking him, she refused all three. She sat down, leaning forward, hopeful and expectant. Thorpe regarded his client curiously. She looked young, eager, as she said in a soft voice, 'You wanted to see me, Mr Thorpe?'

'Why yes. The case is due—'

'Next Friday,' said Eleanor. She smiled nervously.

His heart smote him. Experienced at reading the human face which had been his book for twenty-five years, he discerned the hope there. He looked away, shuffling through his papers.

'I've received this. It came this morning. I confess, Mrs Lawrence, it was a surprise—'

And then he said something incredible: 'Your husband has raised the whole question of custody.'

She literally flinched. The colour drained from her face.

She looked haggard and her eyes were changed.

'*What* did you say?'

He explained, with all his tact, that this was not unusual. A good many husbands made such a demand but were persuaded to drop it. Little chance of success, the mother was in almost all cases granted custody and so on. 'Such requests can be prompted by animosity, resentment, a grudge,' he said.

'The fact is, Mrs Lawrence, he has put in a most unpleasant plea. I have talked to the other side about it, and they've agreed to try and persuade their client to drop it. I'd rather not upset you with too many details.'

'You mean that my husband says I'm not fit to have my daughter.'

'Something like that.'

'Let me see what he has said, please.'

Guy Thorpe hesitated. He had no right to refuse to show her the document. With a murmured, 'Remember, people in a divorce can say cruel things, I'm afraid,' he passed it to her.

When she read it, Eleanor heard Hugo's bitter voice. 'She was an immoral woman. She'd spent no time with their child when they lived in Brazil.' (Oh, cruel, cruel, when it had been *he* who decided upon Zica and Esmeralda, and as he well knew, all the children spent their time with their nannies.) He was gravely exercised at the prospect of his daughter growing up with the kind of person his wife had turned out to be. He was sure that his sister, Naval wife with two children of her own, would offer his daughter a home during the periods when his diplomatic duties took him abroad. He formally requested custody of his daughter Joanna.

Eleanor gave back the paper. Thorpe saw that her hand

did not shake, and nor did her voice as she said icily, 'How dare he say my daughter would be better off with her aunt than her own mother? She needs my love as I need hers. I refuse to let him have her. Let him just try.'

'He may do, Mrs Lawrence. He may well try very hard.'

'I will never give her up,' said Eleanor, her voice flat, her eyes fierce. 'Judges are willing to talk to parents in such cases, aren't they?'

'On certain occasions, yes.'

'Tell the other side that I'll see my husband in hell – put it any way you like – before he takes such a revenge. What time did he spend with our daughter? His work eats him alive and I can prove it.'

She stood up and held out that steady hand which was ice cold.

'I shall win this, Mr Thorpe. Because I've got to.'

The next week, with a sudden, inexplicable and almost terrifying change of mind, Hugo withdrew his demand for custody. It certainly wasn't, thought Eleanor when Thorpe (sounding positively jolly) rang her, due to a change of heart. She could only imagine that he had heard of her determination, and decided he could not win the fight. Or was it that a divorce, dragging on with appeals and much thrown mud, would damage his career? She didn't know and didn't care.

What she never found out was that Agnes was responsible for Hugo's withdrawal. She had flatly refused to take Joanna. Did Hugo really think he could use *her* to rob Eleanor of her own daughter? The scene between brother and sister, played out in Hillier's in the garden, well away from Mathilde, would have been melodramatic if Hugo had not been so iron-cold. In the end, giving her the look of a stranger, he agreed.

When Eleanor was informed by Guy Thorpe that the case
had been heard, 'decree nisi, Mrs Lawrence, we sailed
straight through. Custody to you with fair access,' Eleanor
thanked him. It was only after she put down the telephone
that she said aloud, 'Thank God.'

And, with the mention of the Almighty, she thought of
Agnes and rang her.

It was not until Joanna came to live with her in the
anonymous comfort of Wilbraham Place, that Eleanor saw
just how nervous and quiet the little girl had become. She
was shy as she never had been. She was much too quiet.
When told she was going back to her old school, she cried
in a heart-rending fashion. During the first week of school
she ate no breakfast, sobbing, 'I don't want to go, I don't
want to go', to the misery and alarm of her mother.

The class mistress whom Eleanor consulted was comforting. Yes, it was very upsetting and some children, apparently, *always* wept before going to school in the mornings,
and not necessarily children with broken homes. Yet in her
own experience she had seen them, minutes after their
arrival in class, perfectly cheerful.

'Persevere, Mrs Lawrence. It's best for Joanna.

Easy to say. But Eleanor resisted the longing to keep
Joanna at home, and took her to school every morning with
a heavy heart. Joanna had become not only difficult, but
demanding. Weak, wounded, she ruled a mother too
anxious to refuse her anything.

It began to occur to Eleanor that if she was to get back
to normal with Joanna, she must stop her own absorption
and glare of concentration on the little girl. She needed
other matters to think about. She needed to work. Yes, a
job would surely stop some of the worry, release her from

brooding and so release Joanna from an over-protective
mother. If she became happier, Joanna would be too.

One morning when Joanna had been taken to school,
Eleanor telephoned Giles to ask if she could see him.

He promptly asked her to lunch.

Eleanor took a taxi to Nelson's. It was a very long time
since she had been to her father's agency, which was still in
the same place, a solid white block in Baker Street. But
inside, there were changes. Nelson's had become self-
consciously smart in an increasingly style-conscious world.
The reception was in the command of a grey-haired lady of
noticeable elegance, called Merula.

'It's so original not to have somebody young,' said the TV
head of department. Merula's predecessor, only 20, had got
the importance of various clients somewhat confused.

Merula knew Eleanor was expected, and took her to
Giles's office.

'My dear child,' he said, standing up. He thought she
looked better. Her appearance, when he had met her at
Heathrow, had been dreadful. He had believed Hugo
Lawrence a reasonable sort of chap. What had possessed
him to break up his marriage so cruelly?

'Giles,' said Eleanor, smiling slightly at him across his
large desk, 'I think I'd like some sort of job in the agency.'

As it happened, he'd had the same ideas when he'd
thought about Eleanor, but had dismissed it. What would
she do in this highly-polished business which she partly
owned, and had never been interested in? He still acted for
her at Nelson's, she hadn't said she wanted to change that.

'Let's talk about it over lunch.'

They had a meal in his favourite restaurant, at the top of
a recently built skyscraper near the BBC. The head waiter
was reverent to Giles, as if welcoming the Pope on a

goodwill visit to London. Nelson's was Number 3 in the advertising league, and these things got about.

It was during the excellent meal that Giles had a brainwave. What would Eleanor say to a job as a stylist? After all, said Giles, 'You have quite a bit of style yourself.'

The work consisted of helping to dress the sets for advertising films, borrowing props from exclusive shops (often none too keen to lend), looking out for objects which were original, or beautiful, or odd. Things to enhance a set.

Eleanor was interested, but carefully explained that she could only work part-time.

'I have to deliver Jo to school at nine, and collect her at half past three. I suppose that means there isn't enough time for me to be at all useful?'

Giles thought so too, but assured her things might be arranged. He made a mental note to talk to his fellow director, Tommy Thompson. After all, this woman was half owner of the valuable business.

A letter for Eleanor arrived the next morning. It confirmed her appointment, set out her hours of work – and a modest salary.

She was ill-at-ease that autumn when she began to work at Nelson's, but slowly started to get the hang of it. Her job was made easier because the woman she worked for – big, humorous and bossy – was impatient but kind. Rose Clarke was clever and showed Eleanor how to be. When she met the writers, artists and executives, Eleanor remembered the days on the *Marie Cristine*. She'd become used to the graces of diplomatic life, and it surprised her to find that these people were harsher and coarser. They did not bother to hide their thoughts, or even to put them politely. Yet they were, in a way, her own. Everybody knew that Walter

Nelson had been her father and that she owned a large slice of the agency. Nobody mentioned that. In one way, at least, they were diplomatic.

The autumn was also brightened by the advent of Louise. Miss Thompson from St Philip's school, asked to speak to Eleanor one afternoon when she arrived to pick Joanna up.

'Joanna,' she said, fixing the child with a blue gaze, 'just run along to Class Two. Mrs Hames is there with one or two of the others. You can wait for your Mummy there.'

Joanna scurried off like a rabbit.

Eleanor's nerves were not as strong as she'd believed, and she wondered what the headmistress was going to say. Trouble? She was ushered into the head's office and given an uncomfortable chair. Miss Thompson sat down at her desk. She exactly read Eleanor's face.

'This is nothing to do with young Joanna,' she said. 'She seems to be settling down, I'm glad to say. Her class mistress says her progress is slow, and she is still very shy, which I judge is not her real nature. But she has made one friend. Abigail Potter. No, why I've asked you to have a word, Mrs Lawrence, is to make you a little proposition.'

A slight laugh.

'About my niece, Louise. She is taking a music course, and is looking for freelance work. Keen to find somebody for whom she could, perhaps, baby-sit? She is totally reliable, a nice lass, and experienced with children. Two young sisters. I can thoroughly recommend her.'

Never one to lose a good opportunity, the moment Eleanor said she would be interested, Miss Thompson put a call through to her niece.

The girl, whom Eleanor had imagined would be a younger version of the brisk Thompson, turned out to be plump and practical, rosy-faced, and as friendly as Agnes. Wisely, Eleanor invited Louise to tea. Joanna, covertly stealing glances at her, wouldn't eat a thing. But Louise suggested to Eleanor that 'if it isn't a nuisance', she might make an appearance every afternoon, 'just pop in so that Joanna gets used to my face'.

Treading as if on glass, Eleanor and Louise managed to get Joanna to accept the new arrival. Occasionally, so that Eleanor could work longer at Nelson's, it was now Louise who turned up at the school, and walked Joanna home.

'Eleanor? It's me. We're back in the West Country and it's pouring as usual,' said Agnes, one late autumn evening. 'Em has been moaning about not seeing Jo. No chance of her coming for half-term, is there?'

'Aggie, that's a lovely idea.'

Before Eleanor could suggest that she would love to stay as well, Agnes hurriedly added that Hugo was going to be in Plymouth during that week and was anxious to see Joanna. He had just come back from Spain.

'Of course. I've been expecting to hear,' said Eleanor, coolly enough. She said she'd bring Jo to Plymouth, return the same day and come back to Plymouth for Jo when half-term was over.

'But I do feel dreadful! You having to do all that travelling,' exclaimed Agnes.

'Aggie, I like trains. I shall read something long.'

'It would have been so civilised,' said Agnes, whose trouble was seeing more than one point of view, 'if you could both have met when Jo is here. But Hugo is still pretty low-spirited. He seems to have no resilience when it comes – you know – to matters of the heart.'

I'm not sure I have either, thought Eleanor.

Preparing for the trip, Eleanor packed a large plastic bag with things to occupy Joanna during the hours of travel. Sandwiches, biscuits and a thermos of orange, two favourite games, some puzzles and books, her bear and her Snoopy, pencils and paper.

The hours on the train went by with the child too busy to be bored, until she fell sleep, mouth open, and pencil falling from her hand. Eleanor sat and looked at her.

Having delivered Joanna to Agnes and a hopping Emily and Nicole, Eleanor took the train home – and realised she had brought the bag of goodies back with her.

Ahead of her were ten days alone.

The prospect was not pleasant. She had few friends, most of those from her previous life in London had moved or, somehow, had sided with Hugo. There seemed a good reason to work late on the day after she got back. Tommy Thompson found her in her office.

'Look who's here. I thought you were the devoted parent who buggered – sorry – left for school on the dot of three.'

Eleanor, not insulted, explained her presence. He hung about, talking and giving her that old familiar look of admiration she remembered as a girl. Tommy had become one of Nelson's leaders now, he and the agency had flourished together. Business, though good, was much changed since Walter's day. International companies were moving across the map of commerce, not unlike the way in which the British Empire turned the atlas pink in the last century: huge conglomerates keen on takeovers. Tommy, as well as Giles, kept his eyes skinned.

But that did not mean he had no time for sex. He was married, of course, but who wasn't? Walter's girl intrigued him, appealing to a romantic side of his cheerful and lecherous nature.

'With your child off your hands for a bit, why not come out for a meal? I've found a new place in Hampstead. The spaghetti is home-made.'

Eleanor accepted. She liked him and always had.

The Hampstead restaurant was smallish; they were given a corner table lit by candles, and served platefuls of spaghetti. Tommy regaled her with the story of his visit to Finland last winter.

'I was trying to get us the Finnish Cod Account. Do you know I agreed to go *by boat* in December? There were gales. I thought my last hour had come.'

The story progressed, the sea heaved; right in the middle of the drama a voice cried, 'Eleanor Nelson as I live and breathe!'

Coming towards her, wearing a trouser suit of hideous and expensive cut, short hair dyed the red of her youth, jade necklaces swinging, was Laurette.

Tommy sprang to his feet and so did Eleanor.

Laurette threw open her arms and pressed Eleanor against the knobbly jade. 'What are you doing in England? You're supposed to be sweltering in the concrete of Brasilia.'

'She got back,' said Tommy.

Eleanor introduced him and Laurette, in turn, introduced the man with her. He had not been looking best pleased at being ignored so far.

'Edward Cellier. I'm sure you both know Edward's column,' said Laurette.

He was dark and cadaverous. Tommy declared that he read the Cellier column every Sunday.

'You're sharp on our politicians, Mr Cellier.'

'Not near sharp enough.'

'People are terrified of him,' said Laurette, cooing. She

scribbled Eleanor's telephone number, and then, putting her arm through her companion's, was led to a table round the corner, apparently in a private nook.

'Edward Cellier,' remarked Tommy intrigued. 'And that clever-looking friend of yours. Just the sort we could do with at Nelson's.'

'She works for an MP, in the House of Commons.'

'Does she, now.'

Tommy visualised Laurette guiding MP's into the agency. Advisers and lobbyists for everything from cutting the tax on cosmetics to promoting low-tar cigarettes. Or unpromoting them . . .

Laurette rang Eleanor early the next morning at work. 'It's your one friend.'

'You're right about that.'

'Do I hear a bitter note? Is there news I'm missing out on? Why didn't you call me up when you got back. No, save it for when we meet. Would you like to lunch at the House today? The veal and ham pie isn't too awful. I always cut off the pastry.'

To her surprise, and pleasure, Eleanor found herself once again in the great echoing Gothic entrance hall, met by a Laurette so unchanged it was hard to realise that all Eleanor's life in Brazil lay between one lunch and the next.

When they were sitting down by a leaded window, Laurette asked at once why Eleanor was in London now.

'So you're divorced. Join the club. But did I gather from your voice that you never wanted to be? Now I *always* do. And I bet that Brazilian of yours was dishy.'

'Too dishy.'

'Come on, Eleanor. No man can be.'

Eleanor let that go; she said she was sure the Foreign Office must be pleased to have got rid of her. De Quiroz was part of big business in Rio, and the FO disliked high-up scandal. Laurette listened thoughtfully and then said, 'You still mind.'

'Yes. For Joanna more than anything. But for me too. I tried to persuade him not to divorce me. I begged him.'

'My poor woman, I can't approve of that! You don't love Hugo Lawrence and you never did. I remember when I came back from LA and you'd just married on account of you were stupid enough to get pregnant. You weren't mad about him then. Admit it. Of course you grew fond of him later. But what's-his-name, your Brazilian, was bound to happen. That's sex,' said Laurette. She looked at Eleanor and added mischievously, 'Tell you what. Come to my salon.'

'What *do* you mean? That's the word they use for a sitting room in Brazil.'

'In Paris too. I'm talking about Madame Recamier. I invite interesting people like you to my salons. They're quite a success ... What about the guy eating spag. with you in Hampstead. Shall we ask him?'

'Tommy Thompson is married and lives in Pinner.'

'All the more reason to visit with *me*.'

The Wilbraham Place flat seemed larger and quieter than usual when Eleanor arrived home that evening. Going to bed, she thought about Laurette; she supposed she should accept the invitation, it was cowardly to avoid parties. Suppose no one talks to me, was her usual thought. It occurred to her that there must be men with the same reservation. She hoped so.

Laurette still lived in her mansion flat in Swiss Cottage and, getting out of the taxi into a damp cold afternoon, Eleanor had a thin-blooded moment of regretting Brazilian sunshine. She was making her way towards the flight of steps which led to the flat's front door when a young man lounged up. Brazil still in her thoughts, she marvelled that he wore no coat, his jacket was unbuttoned and his shirt so thin it gave her goose pimples. To walk round London like that in winter was a new affectation.

'Coming to Laurette's too?' he said.

Eleanor answered that she was. He regarded her with a friendliness as open as that of Agnes's children. He was under six foot, his height lessened because he stooped rather. His gingerish hair flopped on his forehead. He had a handsome nose. Eleanor liked the youthful manner and felt less inclined to turn round and take a cowardly taxi back home.

'I've never been to one of these before, have you?' he said.

'Never.'

'Are you one of her new friends or one of the old?'

'Old as can be. We were at Oxford.'

'Were you? I thought she'd invented that. You must tell me what she was like. Did she come on as hot and strong as she does now?'

The door of the apartment was wide open, and a mass of people surged around, talking noisily. In the midst of these was the hostess in white jeans and a white T-shirt lettered 'That's my girl'.

'Eleanor!' she cried. 'And Sandy too. Have you introduced yourselves? Eleanor Lawrence, Sandy Trafford.' She put two glasses into their hands and vanished back into the press of people.

'Let's find somewhere to sit,' said Eleanor's companion and guided her through the crowd to a sofa under the window. Eleanor looked about; she had never visited Laurette's home. Walls crowded with paintings, shelves with books, a great many flowers. Even a log fire.

'To us,' said Sandy, finishing off his drink and grabbing another from a girl who passed by with a tray.

'Now tell me who you are and what you do and all about Laurette at Oxford.'

He stayed with her for the duration of the party. People drifted up and Sandy knew most of them: a loud-voiced businessman who boomed about the horror of subsidy for the arts; a beautiful Jamaican model who stood smiling down at him; a round-shouldered man Laurette brought over; a don at Cambridge who told them he was 'redefining T.S. Eliot'. Whoever they were Sandy was interested.

Once Eleanor said, 'Shouldn't you move around. I'm monopolising you.'

'It's mutual. Do you want to move?'

'No.'

'Neither do I.'

He told her that he worked for *Animus* and didn't expect her to know about it.

'Of course I do. A lot of influential people write for your magazine. And Giles Burnett, he's my godfather and we work in the same advertising agency, reads it from cover to cover.'

Sandy Trafford looked delighted.

'Burnett, MD at Nelson's?'

'Do you know everybody?'

'More or less. So Giles reads our mag. That shows he's as clever as I've sometimes thought him.'

'Now I feel guilty. I ought to read it.'

'So I should think. I'll send you a copy. Give me your address.'

The salon went on from four until half past eight. There was wine, coffee, tea and two enormous cakes which were polished off to the last slice. The hostess had no intention of providing supper. Salons did not include meals. Slowly the guests, couple by couple, began to drift away, to thank her and say goodnight. When Sandy and Eleanor had done so, and were leaving, he asked if she would have supper with him? She was pleased and accepted, and he bustled her off to a small restaurant somewhere nearby, which served inferior food and was not particularly comfortable. But Sandy was good company, and she enjoyed herself.

When he took her home in a taxi to Wilbraham Place it was late and very cold. The air was icy.

'Sandy,' she said, as she fitted her key into the heavy front door. She looked at his open jacket and thin shirt. 'Why aren't you dead with pneumonia? You must be a solid block of ice.'

'Try me,' he said and gave her a long sexy kiss.

The light from a clouded sky was faint. He looked down at her upturned face.

'Eleanor Lawrence,' he thoughtfully said. Then, 'I'll call you.'

'Oh do,' said Eleanor, and wished she hadn't.

Two days without Jo filled up with work, but Eleanor kept hoping Sandy Trafford would telephone.

Thinking about him, she saw that he was no De Quiroz. She was glad. There was something almost appalling in real male beauty: it was a disturbance, a vision. With it went a macho manner and great vanity. She had seen De Quiroz gaze at himself in the glass for a full minute. Sandy Trafford had no reason to wear that awful half smile which had characterised her Brazilian lover.

On her third evening, staying late at Nelson's again, she sat for a while looking at the telephone book. Then –

what have I got to lose? She rang.

A voice announced, '*Animus* Magazine.'

'Is Mr Trafford in, by any chance?' said Eleanor, hoping she sounded like a journalist. The operator did not ask who she was but merely said 'putting you through'.

'Hello?'

'Sandy. It's Eleanor.'

'*Hello*. How nice. Just what I need.'

They met for dinner that evening. And the next. Both times Eleanor suggested it, and Sandy looked as if it was exactly what he'd hoped to hear.

She asked him back to the flat. If he was impressed by its opulence, he didn't show it, but padded from room to room, asking questions. This must be her daughter's room.

'My God, what a lot of *things* the kids have now! When I was a kid I was lucky to have a train set and half a dozen toy cars.'

She fed him on scrambled egg and smoked salmon, and when he left, he gave her yet another of the sexy kisses. The following evening they went to a zany Hollywood film, Sandy clutched her hand and shouted with laughter.

Enjoying his company, attracted, almost happy, she looked forward to seeing him. He was fun to be with, his view of people unexpected and often quite hard. He talked of the men and women whom he interviewed; he told her of the latest scandals. He also boasted like a boy who has won a cup on Sports Day. There were other boyish qualities about him. His ginger hair flopped about, and when he got to his feet he didn't just stand up, he sprang. His face was youthful but slightly lined, as if he'd been ill as a child and the traces movingly remained.

On the last evening before she was due to go back to Plymouth for Jo, they went to bed together in her flat. They made love with pleasure, but for Eleanor with none of the delirium she had felt for De Quiroz. Sandy said she was – a favourite word – delicious.

Half-term in Plymouth, apparently, went well. Jo was bright-faced when Eleanor collected her. But she did not once mention having seen her father, and Eleanor did not ask. She did not even ask Agnes, much occupied with checking that Joanna was leaving nothing behind in the child-littered Plymouth flat.

Sandy was eager to meet Eleanor's daughter, and came round one Sunday for lunch. Eleanor was apprehensive beforehand, but she could not fault him with the little girl. He was breezy, romped with Jo, and at one time chased her, with delighted shrieks from Jo, right through the flat. He was clearly a success with the child, who was very good with him for most of his visit. Just now and then she stopped playing and gave him long, appraising stares. When they watched TV together – it was *101 Dalmatians* – he managed to pull her on to his lap.

Some little girls, thought Eleanor, are man-conscious from their birth and Jo reacted so quickly to Sandy, very differently from her slow acceptance of Louise, that Eleanor saw fully how much Hugo's absence and loss were missed by his daughter.

A comfortable routine was set at Wilbraham Place and Sandy Trafford became very much a part of it. Eleanor was solaced by the sex and easier in her mind about Joanna.

Laurette telephoned to ask if she could come round for a drink. 'I long to see you. *And* this flat with the smart address.'

When Eleanor opened her door, there was Laurette, wearing a black hat exactly the shape of the White Queen's crown in *Alice through the Looking Glass*.

Laurette said, with all her American charm, 'Why, Eleanor!'

She was shown over the flat, laughed over the dolphin taps, and said hello to a TV-watching Joanna who was not much interested in the visitor. Eleanor took her into the sitting room and poured the drinks.

'Champagne,' said Laurette appreciatively. 'You do yourself well. Now, how did you enjoy my salon?'

'I loved it! But I sent you a card, didn't you get it?'

'I don't count postcards, they're today's easy way out.' She looked speculatively at Eleanor. 'You seem to have changed since I last saw you. You have a glow.'

'Oh good,' said Eleanor, laughing.

'I'm serious. There's something . . . What is it? Or, to be exact, who is it? Not Sandy Trafford by any chance? I saw you both snuggled up together at my salon.'

Eleanor decided to go cautiously. Laurette was a mocker.

'Yes, Sandy and I have been seeing each other now and again. I'm not poaching, am I?'

'Good grief, no. I just like knowing journalists. They're useful.'

Eleanor had a moment of longing to confide. But she was convalescent, not strong enough to be teased.

'So he's responsible for the glow?' said Laurette.

'I didn't know there was one.'

'Oh, it's unmistakeable.'

Not a mock to be heard.

When Christmas began to glitter in people's thoughts and in the shops, when Jo was to be a shepherd in the Nativity play, just when things seemed settled, easy, Sandy asked Eleanor to marry him. She refused incredulously. She had never imagined such a thing.

But he was determined. The time was gone when, perhaps for self-satisfaction, he waited for *her* to make any moves. Now Sandy became the pursuer. When his work prevented their meeting, he rang early or late for long caressing talks. He turned up at Nelson's, flirted with Merula and made friends with Eleanor's colleagues. He was at home with the artists, executives, the young, the middle-aged. He had enormous appeal; his vitality was irresistible. And he went on asking Eleanor to marry him.

'We g∍t on, Eleanor. I want you with me. Say yes. You know you'll give in in the end. I shall nag you to the register office.'

Sandy was now part of the family at weekends – he saw to that. He was magnificent at Christmas, and as far as Jo was concerned, the reason for rushing to the front door, shouting, 'Sandy, Sandy!' She hopped up and down when he arrived.

On a cold day of early spring he appeared at the agency without warning, and told Eleanor he'd come to take her out to lunch. She was surprised and amused when, in the car in the Regent's Park Circle, all he produced was a packet of sandwiches. He stopped the car. The park was lonely. He put his arms round her.

'You've got to make up your mind to it and marry me. It's your destiny. Mine as well.'

They embraced. Eleanor thought this was just Sandy's usual loving persuasions. Until he said in a matter-of-fact voice, 'I've brought a special licence.'

'*You haven't!*'

'You know you like the big romantic gesture.'

They began to kiss and it began to snow. Twice while they were in each other's arms, Sandy had to break off and start up the engine, the car was getting so cold. After almost an hour, excited, frightened, half laughing and half crying, she agreed to be his wife.

She collected Jo from school and they walked back through an afternoon of snow which pricked their cheeks. At home Eleanor lit the gas fire and made tea, and after the meal Joanna fetched a jigsaw and scattered it on the floor. Eleanor sat down nearby. She waited a while, then said carefully, 'Jo, I have something to tell you. Sandy wants to marry me.'

What did she expect? A start? A rush of tears? The child went on with the jigsaw, muttering, 'More bits of sky. Sky's so boring.'

'Darling, did you take in what I told you?' Eleanor's heart suffocated her. Looking, not at her mother but at the fragments in front of her, Jo said, 'Does that mean he's going to live here?'

'He wants to be with us both. Very much.'

'All the time?'

'Yes.'

A pause. Then, 'Mum . . .'

'Darling?'

'This bit,' said Joanna, holding out a piece of the puzzle, 'is definitely a bicycle.'

Which Eleanor took for her daughter's agreement.

The only other person who must be told was Agnes. Eleanor knew that her marriage would surprise Giles who would disapprove, and Laurette who would laugh. Agnes mattered. Joanna was asleep that same evening when Eleanor telephoned Plymouth. David Lyttelton answered, sounding warm. Agnes, he said, had gone to Hillier's again.

'Mathilde has had quite bad flu. Do ring Aggie there, she'll be so glad to hear from you. How's Jo?'

Eleanor rang Hillier's and it was Agnes who answered.

She sounded glad to hear Eleanor's voice and said her mother was on the mend.

'Could you manage lunch tomorrow, Aggie? At the Luscombe?'

It was an old haunt of theirs, only a mile or two from Hillier's, an expensive country hotel.

'The Luscombe? But why not here? Could you bring Jo?'

'No, Aggie, she hates missing school, but of course I'll bring her soon. Tomorrow's different. I want to see you alone. Half past twelve?'

Puzzled, Agnes agreed.

When Eleanor rang her boss, Rose Clark, she explained that she couldn't come in to Nelson's next day because of 'family dramas'.

'Oh dear. Okay,' said Rose, controlling a desire to swear.

The Luscombe had hospitably lit all its lights to brighten the dull March noon, and as Eleanor went into the entrance hall, she thought the hotel smelled rich: a hint of fine cooking, the scent of lilies in a showy vase. In a small panelled bar, sure enough there was Agnes. And sure enough, she had brought a book. She sat quietly reading.

'Aggie.'

Here was a welcome as warm as Ceci's used to be. When they sat down, Agnes studied her sister-in-law, noticing the businesswoman's expensive suit of blackish burgundy, her shoes, an impression of money – and a certain strain. Both her brother and Eleanor, Agnes thought with an inward sigh, were so thin.

In the dining room they chose their meal. Neither young woman, thought the waiter, was as interested as she ought to be in the elaborate menu, or the descriptions he gave about creamy sauces, rare herbs and orange liqueurs. They weren't really listening.

When he had left them, Agnes said, 'Now *what's* the mystery?'

'Promise not to interrupt?'

It was the catchphrase of their girlhood.

'Cross my heart and hope to die.'

'I'm getting married again.'

Eleanor had expected a strong reaction and here it was. Agnes's eyes were enormous.

'Don't disapprove, Aggie, please don't! And don't think I am quite mad, I've thought about it so much. For months. Sandy is so nice—'

'But what about Jo?'

'She likes him. Likes him a lot. He comes to the flat every weekend, and they really get on.'

'That sounds good, at any rate.'

There was a moment's silence. Agnes simply did not know what to think. How eager Eleanor was to get her blessing was only too evident. During a meal they scarcely touched, Eleanor talked and talked about Sandy, describing him, giving details of his tastes, his work, not exaggerating, trying to sound detached but fair. The only thing Agnes could not like was that they'd only know each other six months.

'But you love him.'

'I'm afraid I do.'

'Don't sound guilty, Eleanor. You must forgive me for being – well – not too encouraging. I only want what is best for Jo and for you.'

She said nothing for another moment or two and Eleanor did not speak either. Finally Agnes said, 'Perhaps it *will* be best for Jo to have s stepfather. Single parents do concentrate so on their kids, it isn't good for the parent or the child.' She echoed Eleanor's own thoughts, ard again

Eleanor had the wit to say nothing.

'So when are you getting married?' said Agnes, with a change of tone, a different smile. 'Shall we have Jo while you are on your honeymoon?' she added, kind to the last.

It was in Capri, on a cliff-top overlooking the bay of Naples, sated with Italian wine, love-making and the blessing of a hot spring sun, that Sandy made Eleanor a proposition. He had been thinking a lot about it, he said. He was sure he would enjoy moving into the advertising business.

PART THREE

1993–4

Chapter Twelve

For a man who started with little, Sandy Trafford took to earning large sums of money like a duck to water. He swam in it. Naturally splashy, he was the epitome of the rich and successful character of the Eighties. He was older than the young men now paid high salaries for their quickness and their youth, but at just forty, Sandy still looked as if he were somewhere in his thirties. He never mentioned his age and his manner was not weighty: he was relaxed as well as clever. Easy to live with, he shared with Eleanor his pleasure in himself.

Giles and Tommy Thompson had both been dubious when Eleanor asked if they would consider Sandy at Nelson's. But they met and talked to him and soon saw that he was going to fit. Sandy rose and rose. He was appointed to the board; he made courageous decisions which paid off. He proved almost as good in a different way as Walter Nelson himself. The Eighties boomed and the man astride Nelson's comet was Sandy.

It took a long time for Eleanor to persuade him to let her at least try to have another child. He was absorbed in advertising now, and in any case didn't fancy a pregnant wife. They had Joanna, didn't they? Why wasn't one child enough? But in the end, eight years after their marriage,

Eleanor got her way and produced a little son. Sandy was bowled over at being a father. Paul was small and dark, no trace of Eleanor's copper or Sandy's ginger hair. His long dark eyelashes were like a girl's.

'Look!' cried Sandy, cradling the shawled bundle, 'he is exactly like me.'

Joanna, absorbed in school, absorbed in friends, had become a trifle arms' length with Sandy nowadays. But from the time that Paul could short-sightedly peer at admirers, when Joanna was around the baby looked at nobody else. And the same went for his sister.

She enjoyed being at home, but had never given up her attachment to the Lytteltons and often during holidays, when they were in England, she went to stay with them. She still loved Emily who was, she said, almost her twin. If she cut those Lyttelton holidays short, it was always because of Paul.

'I can't have him forgetting me,' she would say, falling on her knees beside the baby.

In her late teens Joanna developed a certain mystery. Between spaniel's ears of long soft hair, she looked out with a mixture of apprehension and critical judgement. You never knew what she was thinking.

'But you can bet your bottom dollar it isn't about us,' said Sandy. He added, changing the subject, that they were dining tomorrow night with some clients.

It did not occur to Eleanor, still in his sexual thrall, retaining some of her golden looks but no longer touched by the wand of youth, how much her life now resembled her mother's in the past. It was the very life from which Sara had escaped. Sara, too, had entertained bigwigs, spent hours at the Connaught while they drank Bloody Marys, danced on small floors with fat men. But Sara had not loved her husband. Eleanor did.

When Paul was old enough to go to playschool, and later to kindergarten, she went back to work at Nelson's. She had many friends in the agency, and had acquired some real skill at her job. She didn't want promotion, and although he didn't say so, perhaps Sandy didn't want it for her.

It was not until the early Nineties that Eleanor began to work full-time. Paul was eight and happy at a day school in Kensington. Joanna was eighteen and brushing up for her A levels. That same year the Lytteltons, together with their younger girl, the lively Nicole, left for St Vincent in the West Indies. Joanna saw as much of her beloved Emily as they could manage before Emily also left England. She was due to spend a year at Montbard with her French cousins, and would go to university at Auxerre.

Joanna sparred with her stepfather at times: she always spoke out, but he was interested in the fact that he had a teenager about the place. He listened to her opinions; she was today's customer, and although Eleanor and Joanna never knew it, he often quoted Joanna at the agency. He was attentive when she laid down the law.

'No, no, Sandy, you can't take that group seriously, their music's *awful*, we all think it's a load of rubbish now. They're finished.'

He had used his influence and managed to get Joanna into the City and Guilds school. Eleanor was proud of her husband's success at pulling this off; the school was exclusive. She told him so rather too often. But Sandy did enjoy being thanked; he was like a dog waiting to be stroked.

At work Eleanor often thought her job resembled that of a treasure hunter – she'd watched them on Rio beaches. She looked for things to catch the eye: what she wanted was to give colour, to lift a set which was inclined to look dull. As well as the many connections she had built up with rich London shops, she brought things from her own home, and from other people's. It was a joke in Nelson's that if you asked Eleanor Trafford to dinner, you would finish off lending her the clock in your living room.

At Nelson's things went well. Or they did until the end of the Eighties, when gradually at first and then more noticeably, Eleanor started to worry. It looked as if the good days were leaving them.

The agency began to sink down in the league; it went down to tenth and later, to the dismay of everyone at Nelson's, it fell as low as nineteenth. They lost accounts, pitched for new ones but were outstripped by new breakaway agencies founded by young men in their late twenties. One of the most successful of these was owned by a boy who had learned the job as account executive at Nelson's, and when he left had taken the plum accounts with him. The money which had gushed along Nelson's marble corridors had begun to lessen.

It was entirely due to Giles that Nelson's was not in a worse financial state. He had decided to buy the Baker Street building in the late 1960s at a bargain price. He managed to keep salaries at least reasonable, even if he lost a star or two. He remained in this business slavish to youth partly from whim and partly because he knew very well that it needed him. The young Turks complained behind his back.

But if Nelson's wasn't what it used to be, neither was Sandy. His huge appetite for advertising waned. So did his bosom friendships with the big clients, and the maddening yet attractive habit of picking up the telephone the moment he arrived home, to plunge into chat with some client whom Sandy had grown fond of.

When Eleanor was invited to one of the bigger agency meetings, she was surprised to see Sandy was absent. He was usually the first, and when you went into a conference room before a meeting, there Sandy would be, already writing notes.

One afternoon Eleanor was working in her office after a fractured morning. She had spent hours dressing a kitchen set for a washing-up liquid commercial. Kitchens were used much too often, and it was hard not to create another boring set. She had been pleased with the finished job. But the filming was postponed and early this morning all the flowers were dead; her assistant had forgotten to put water in the vases. Eleanor dashed out into Old Compton Street and returned with a great bouquet of freesias.

'You don't think I'd use those things, do you?' said the TV producer, who was in a bad mood. 'They're totally the wrong shape.'

She had been annoyed and half amused. Well, perhaps a quarter amused.

Now, catching up with desk work, she saw Giles at her open door.

'Could you manage a quick word in my office?'

'I'd like to.'

She was glad to see him and needed to talk; and wondered why *he* wanted to see *her*.

When they sat down and were drinking the usual disgusting coffee in cardboard cups, Giles glanced at her. The black sweater she wore didn't suit her, it made her look washed out. Didn't girls these days wear rouge? He said in a benevolent voice, 'How's that clever young chap, Paul?'

Eleanor gave some motherly details and then, of course, Giles asked about Joanna.

'I love having her with me now Aggie's abroad,' Eleanor said. 'And it was brilliant of Sandy to get her into the City and Guilds.'

Giles nodded. He did not say that he'd been the one who had pulled this off, and had passed the result to Sandy.

'She isn't working too hard, I'm afraid. She has a new boyfriend. She doesn't call him that, he is "a guy I go round with". Apparently he's gorgeous. But I haven't met him.'

Giles looked amused.

Eleanor paused for a little. She was with the one man she could confide in. She brought out clumsily, 'I think the reason Jo has stopped bringing her friends home is Sandy.'

Giles for the moment was bland. 'Surely,' he said, 'Sandy is in sympathy with the young?' Eleanor gave him a clear-eyed look; there was a nervous satisfaction now in speaking out.

'But Giles, Sandy's different. He used to be fun with Jo. He isn't now. And it's not only Jo. He never talks about work any more the way he used to do, fizzing away. Why not? And then the other evening he said something extraordinary. He told me he wants to go into politics.'

Giles was silent for so long that Eleanor became worried. Was she doing a dirty trick? Perhaps she shouldn't have told Giles. She might be damaging Sandy in his eyes. But if Sandy had been serious, surely this ought to be in the open.

'How can he want to get into politics,' she added, 'the people in it are so naff.'

'That sounds like your daughter.'

'Yes, I was quoting. Shouldn't I have told you about Sandy, Giles? I'm feeling guilty.'

'You don't need to. He mentioned it to me. If he *is*

serious, my guess is that he will succeed. When he puts his mind to a thing, it works.'

'But what about Nelson's?'

'Yes, Eleanor. We both have to think about that.'

On her way home to Kensington, Eleanor did. She'd seen that Giles believed Sandy was going to make this – to her – ridiculous move in his career. When Sandy had first spoken about it to her, she had actually laughed. The odd thing was that it had made him angry. He'd shouted that she knew nothing about it and had better shut up. Looking at the snarling face, she had quite hated him. But afterwards she had understood: it was the first time since they had married that she had laughed at one of his ambitions.

The house where the Traffords lived had been the first of Sandy's extravagances after he had married Eleanor and joined Nelson's. They had moved, after a year or two, from Wilbraham Place to a pleasant early Victorian house in Abingdon Villas, Kensington. It had four storeys, and from the first floor living room were French windows and iron steps which led to a small walled garden where camellias grew. The house's value had skyrocketed during the Eighties: it had been worth nearly half a million pounds. Sandy, triumphant, often talked about that. Its value had sunk since then, but it would still be high supposing, Eleanor had thought, they were mad enough to sell. She loved the house.

It was a sudden jolt as she turned the car into the quiet road to remember that Hugo was due this afternoon. He'd never come to Abingdon Villas before. During the first years after the divorce they had only met twice: once in an appallingly strained atmosphere at the solicitors', and then, no more comfortably, at the mews house they had put up for sale. After that there had been no reason for them to see each other. They wrote brief letters about Joanna now and again.

Hugo was back at present on a short leave, he was working again in Lisbon. He telephoned Eleanor's office and asked if they could meet.

'Let me give you tea at Brown's. Just a chat about Joanna. I would like to know how you think she's progressing.'

On an impulse, because his voice was suddenly familiar and likeable, she said, 'You've never seen our house. Come and have tea with me there. Sandy's away,' she added somewhat tactlessly, 'I shall have you to myself.'

She was late, after talking to Giles, and only had time to run upstairs and do her hair, and then run back again to lay a tray when she heard the front door bell.

She hurried to the front door. Hugo saw a girlish figure in black, bright hair still the colour of copper coins, pale face still with its scatter of a few freckles.

'Hugo, how nice.'

'Eleanor.'

She found her hand strongly pressed, almost wrung. They looked at each other for a moment as if both were holding scales. Critical on one side, approving on the other. They appeared to find each other less changed than they had feared.

'Do come in. Sit down. I thought we'd have a real tea. Not as grand as your mother's at Hillier's, but I actually have some scones.'

'How delicious.'

He followed her into the long room, where the late afternoon sun came through back windows which overlooked the garden. Eleanor took him over to admire the shrubs she had planted. 'You see the camellia? It is covered in pink flowers in early summer. I planted the vine too. It's doing well.'

'Do you ever get grapes? It's a marvel to me that grapes can actually grow out of doors in England,' he said, as they stood looking down at the walled green space.

'Poor vine, it does its best. Lots of bunches in September which the starlings love. They scream and fight over them,' Eleanor said. 'The grapes are tough and quite sour, but Jo always eats them. From loyalty to the vine, I suspect.' They exchanged a smile.

It was curious to sit and drink tea with the man who had once been her husband. Had their marriage only lasted six years? It seemed to her now as if they'd spent a whole life together, with a bad beginning and a sad end, and a plateau of happiness in the middle. Looking at him, she traced the deepened lines in his face. His eyes, meeting hers, had an almost expectant look. Her overriding feeling was how much she liked him.

'Are you well, Hugo? You look fine, but you're very thin.'

'A scarecrow,' he agreed. 'Going back to Peru, I was astonished how hot, hot, hot it was. It doesn't let up. I lost a lot of weight and I've never managed to put it back on again.'

'It suits you. You look interesting.'

He really laughed. He seemed strangely jolly, and laughter made his eyes water.

'Oh Eleanor, you are very kind.'

She asked him about his work, and he talked for a while about South America, mentioning her own time in Brazil quite casually. Things weren't any better, he said; in many ways they were worse. He talked thoughtfully, without a trace of conceit, and as she listened she realised that she had been tuned to expect this first husband to be like her second. Accustomed to Sandy, she'd expected Hugo to boast. She waited, as it were, for Hugo to launch into stories in which he figured as the hero, or at least as the one smart character among a group of fools. Not a bit of it.

Listening to him, in harmony with him just then, she remembered physical things that she had known: his long hands, his short hair, his voice. But she had forgotten a kind of grace in the things he said, and a compassion. That had always been part of him. Except once.

'It must have been really strange for you to be back in Peru. Did you have a pang?'

'Because of Edward. Oh yes. I haven't forgotten him, but you know how people go away after they die. It is the stretch of time, however fond you were – are – of them. When I first arrived at the Embassy, Eleanor – it is a much smaller set-up now, the staff reduced, but the atmosphere was the same – it was so familiar.'

'Not your job. You're – I mean you were – more important there, surely.'

She spoke with the instinctive and shameful flattery she used with Sandy. She was given a look of plain teasing.

'Well. A different office, certainly, too large and with horrible furniture, I don't know where they got it from. Lumps of gilt all over it. But when I went into my old office, there was the very desk I used to sit at when I rang Edward and we had long talks on the telephone. He was real to me again. That evening I drove out to see his grave. The slums are larger and worse, it took me an age to find where his grave was. They'd pulled down the little church and the presbytery. I'm sure the people used the bricks, real bricks, for gaps in the dingy houses. Edward would have approved. Do you remember how he felt when the people stole his plants? Anyway, I found the grave at last.'

He paused and gave a half smile. 'Such a pompous stone the Benedictines had put up for him, with the kindest and saddest intentions, Eleanor. There it was, with his name and date and a Latin inscription – a prayer. But it was scarcely readable, and simply stuck there in the middle of the dust and rubble.'

'Poor Hugo.'

He gave her a thoughtful look.

'Things heal, don't they? Edward is probably a saint by now. And we seem to be doing all right, wouldn't you say?'

They began to talk about Joanna enjoying her City school, and visiting Agnes, of course, whenever the Lytteltons were home on leave. Eleanor found a rare satisfaction in talking to him about Jo. It was as if they had stepped, for a short time, into a circle which until now both had tried to scuff out in the sand, but which was still deep and visible. Then the ease left him; he struck her for a moment as almost embarrassed.

'There's something I'd like to say, Eleanor,' he said. 'How grateful I am for all you've done for her. When Joanna came out that time to stay with me in Lima, she impressed me. She's a very special girl.'

'Did you find her easy?'

'Very good company. Fascinated by Peru. Going up in smoke about the poverty.'

'That's Jo.'

'An inexhaustible fund of righteous indignation. Good for her.'

Eleanor offered him another scone; she was thinking over his earlier tribute and said seriously, 'Hugo, I hope you're not thanking me for having her.'

'My dear girl! How could I possibly? But what I do think—'

He reminded her of a man picking out change from his outstretched palm. A pound coin? Fivepence?

'I think you have a generous heart.'

Ah. A pound after all.

'Yours isn't so bad either,' she said.

She refilled his cup and pressed him to have strawberry jam. She rather liked serving him.

'At present she does nothing but go on about an awful all-weekend pop festival she and a group of her friends are going to. Apparently there'll be about 20,000 people there. Can you imagine? Jo's excited. The only thing that worries her is the terrible prospect of not being able to wash her hair.'

'Poor Joanna,' he said, amused.

'Have you fixed to see her, Hugo?'

'I keep trying. I've rung every morning – I know you and your husband leave early and I thought I'd catch her then, but the number's always—'

'Engaged. What do they talk about? We've scarcely left the house before she makes a rush for the telephone. I know. I'll get her to ring you this evening. Where will you be?'

They continued to talk comfortably, and now and again Hugo teased her. When he was about to go – in his world people never overstayed – she walked with him out to the hall. It was Eleanor who detained him.

'I've had another thought. Just tell me when and where you want to see her, and she'll be there.'

He looked impressed.

'How do you know she'd turn up?'

'I shall make her.'

'You're brave, Eleanor. That child unnerves me.'

'Now that really would delight her.'

He smiled. 'Well – perhaps after all it would be better if you asked her to ring me.'

Joanna was home late from an expedition to Oxfam, to find clothes for the festival. She needed, she said, khaki jeans which wouldn't show the mud. She arrived home with four large plastic bags which she tipped out on the floor to show her mother: T-shirts, vests, shirts and jeans. Army fatigues, really, thought Eleanor. They were clean and ancient, mud colour, dark grey and a greyish washed-out black. Joanna held them up against her for Eleanor's approval, her face all smiles. Nothing she bought could extinguish her beauty.

Hugo and Eleanor's daughter was tall, with a bosom too large for her taste but admired by young men. Her olive skin was inherited from her French grandmother, and so were her dark eyes. She dimly remembered, like a dream, the time in Brazil. Life after that had changed – to a small child inexplicably. There had been that flat off Sloane Street, and a nice girl from whom she still had Christmas cards, called Louise. Then Abingdon Villas had become home, and still was. And, of course, there was her step-father. Many of her friends had parents who had married again, and when she talked about Sandy to them she usually said he was okay, 'sort of'.

At eighteen, Joanna was impatient, strong-willed, a mixture of bold and shy. She never argued with Eleanor, she looked pitying.

Eleanor and occasionally Sandy had tried and never succeeded in altering Joanna's tastes or opinions. She was certain about what she liked, what she thought was interesting and what – an overused word – was boring. When argued with she was as immoveable, but more charming, than Mathilde. She read nothing but the tabloids, a few magazines, and the study books forced on her by the City and Guilds. She spent most of her time on the telephone collapsing with laughter. But she was good at languages, and Eleanor wondered if there was a distant note of music in her, of a time when she chattered in Portuguese to a dark friend called Zica.

Collecting her purchases together, Joanna went up to her room to stow them away. Music started up at once and began to tumble down the stairs like water from an overflowing bath. Eleanor decided to follow.

Entering Joanna's room was to wade into the lake of sound.

'Darling, could you turn if off?'

'I'll turn it down.'

The music sank to a threatening mutter.

Joanna's room was as brilliant as a Chinese kite: orange, crimson, shocking pink and black. Eleanor sat down on the scarcely made bed.

'Your father called round. He'd like to see you.'

Joanna raised thick eyebrows.

'Were you expecting him?'

'Of course. We had tea. He's due back in Lisbon soon, so you'll have to fix to see him within the next three days.'

'Have to, Mum?'

'Of course. Don't you want to?'

Joanna gave one of her enigmatic looks.

'Yeah, I'm fond of Dad. He's funny. I don't mean he makes me laugh, I mean I never quite get him. Did you? When you and he were married, I mean. The idea of you two together always seems really strange. Did *you* understand him?'

'Of course.'

'Mum, you're lying. Keeping your end up. Aunt Aggie told me all about you and my Dad, at least she gave me the Aggie version, vital bits missing. Sure, I'll see him. Am I supposed to ring?'

Joanna was unusually obliging, her mother had recently paid for a pair of magnificent climbing boots. On the following day, dressed like a girl, she set off to see her father. She had bought a skimpy chiffon dress the previous week at Oxfam, black, red and orange flowers and short enough for a child of ten. She wore it under a huge black and purple anorak. It was cold that morning.

Her mind was full of Dave, whom she'd met at college; she was deciding whether to go to bed with him. He was smashing to look at but – problems, problems. She loped down Pall Mall, then up the steps into Hugo's club. The entrance hall was as lofty as a cathedral with a vaulted ceiling and a staircase from a Hollywood film. Marble. It was weird; a mausoleum or something. She had not been there for more than sixty seconds before her father appeared. Joanna gave him a warm kiss.

'Joanna. How kind of you to come.'

She never could get used to the old-fashioned manners, to the way he steered her over to a white-covered table in a restaurant large enough for an assembly hall, and about as intimate as an army barracks. He consulted her about food and wine. Her heart swelled.

Joanna liked older people. 'Oh, he's sweet,' she often exclaimed to Eleanor when they watched TV and an elderly, even a very old man appeared. Her father earned the description, she did think he was sweet.

But the questions of the old were embarrassing. They could not stop themselves asking you things you couldn't tell them, like what you had decided on for a career, or whether you remembered something which had happened when you were six.

Hugo asked such things. Joanna was kind. An angel on the other side of the table. All her best instincts came to the surface when faced with her father's simplicity. He was out of his depth, and swimming beside him the girl kept him afloat.

'So you're off to Portugal again,' she said, deciding to talk about his life as a way of avoiding him asking about hers.

'Tomorrow.'

'Are you glad?'

'I suppose I am. You will think it dull of me to say I like my work.'

'Somebody said to me yesterday that even in Portugal people are really poor,' said Joanna, with the usual attack of righteousness. 'But I expect it's no worse than London. Honestly, Dad, I don't know how you can bear a government which lets cardboard city happen. Shouldn't we all try to do some good?'

Her father agreed. He explained how little influence the foreign service had on home affairs, or other countries and their problems either. He talked as if she were his own age. Perhaps it was a pity Joanna did not listen, for what he said was worth hearing. But her attention span was short, and although she smiled and nodded to her father, it was from good nature because she thought him sweet. Her eyes strayed across the expanse of the Victorian room. Was that someone she recognised?

Seated under a lofty stained-glass window decorated by an elaborate coat of arms – a herald on horseback blowing a horn – were a man and a woman. Just as Joanna looked over, a beam of sunshine came through the window and shone straight down on the man, turning his hair into flame. It was Sandy. To Joanna's fascination, he was leaning forward – he picked up his companion's hand and held it. She was laughing intimately at him. Something in her, something in him, made the girl stare.

The woman was Laurette Jacobs.

Chapter Thirteen

Laurette had always liked Sandy Trafford. But Laurette liked men and it was that, not her undeniable skill, which helped her – a shameful reason – to succeed at her job. Members of Parliament calling in at her office were certain of a welcome. Her intimate '*Hello*' was full of pleasurable surprise. Ever since she and Sandy had met years before when he worked on *Animus* magazine, he was in the habit of asking her advice. And when he moved to advertising the advice became even more useful. 'Laurette', he had said to Eleanor, 'gets the point before I've finished speaking.'

From researching for a not very brilliant MP, with whom she had an affair and a lot of expensive entertainment, Laurette now worked for a man who was already a PPS, and was almost guaranteed a junior ministry in the next reshuffle. She liked him and her job; relished the drama, bitchiness and the big stakes. How often the men round her used or were bruised by the sharp elbow of ambition. Influential men were interested in Laurette, and asked her why she did not take out British nationality. How kind of them, she said, to want her to be a Brit. She was afraid she was soppy about the good ol' USA.

Her taste, however, did not run to Americans in her love affairs.

286

Over the years there had been a series of these, every one
of which had begun in bliss and ended in acrimony. She had
described, to Eleanor, a positive cavalcade – lover after
lover. There had been an actor 'so selfish', an academic
'work-obsessed'; the heavily-married MP had got on her
nerves. There had been a publisher or two. Laurette's sex
life ranged through a large-small world and at the time
Eleanor and Sandy married, she had returned to her early
passion for academics.

'Dyson has this brilliant reputation at Cambridge. He is
their king-pin on Russia. ITV have started using him on
their discussion programmes, you must see him next time,
Eleanor. You'll love his eyebrows.' She reflected for a
moment. 'You'd never think it to look at him, but boy, is he
good in bed.'

Scarcely a month from the time Eleanor had returned
from her Capri honeymoon, Laurette had taken her to
lunch.

'We must go to the Swiss Centre. I just got back from *the*
most romantic holiday in Montreux.'

Greeting Eleanor with delighted smiles, Laurette had
summoned a waitress in an embroidered blouse, and
ordered bitter black bread and some kind of cheese which
looked like soap.

'Full of mountain vitamins. The reason I wanted to see
you today, Eleanor, is to tell you my news: first you, then
me. Dyson and I are getting married.' She had clasped both
hands on her breast in a familiar gesture, adding, 'I'm just
kerazy about him, and he thinks I'm Christmas.'

At that moment the waitress had reappeared with a small
floor sweeper and began to push it round their feet to
remove a few crumbs. Eleanor had been amused. The Swiss
might be dedicated to cleanliness but this was going too far.

She had waited for Laurette to hit the roof; all her friend did was to go on blissfully describing her feelings.

'Third time lucky, Eleanor.'

Married quietly, which meant inviting nobody but the register office porter and his wife as witnesses, Laurette had then given a salon. It was a terrific party, Eleanor and Sandy enjoyed every minute and were among the last to leave, and Laurette, seeing them off, had been so warm and happy it gave Eleanor a little pain in her heart.

It was decided she would not give up the Swiss Cottage flat, her husband commuted to Cambridge, 'alternating' said Laurette, 'married happiness and University hush'.

Eleanor and Sandy were often invited to smart dinner parties chez Laurette, which were written up in the *Evening Standard* diary.

It did not last. On a spring day of heavy rain the following year Eleanor saw Laurette in the coffee bar at Simpsons. She was sitting grim-faced staring out into Jermyn Street.

Eleanor hurried over to say hello. Laurette did not smile, but spoke as if in the middle of a sentence, 'Do you know what he's done? Accepted a post at UCLA, lecturing on Russian politics. Being paid a fortune.'

Laurette's voice was harsh. 'Some of his work is to be linked with cable TV. He's as flattered as hell. You know what academics are like, sneering at the media until they get asked by them. And he expects *me* to go with him. To that hell-hole, LA. I'd rather be dead.'

Eleanor heard this in silence. She was not brave enough to ask why Laurette's birthplace had now metamorphosed into the infernal regions. Was it something to do with Laurette's rarely-mentioned sister? She said tentatively, 'Shall I stay for a bit? Just five minutes.'

'Okay,' said Laurette, her good manners gone.

She was not recognisable as the woman too happy to care when a waitress swept the crumbs round her feet. Whatever Eleanor said was answered in a hard bitterness. Her face was angry and sad.

Sandy heard about the meeting without much interest; he was absorbed at the time with a successful deal for Nelson's and was pleased with himself.

'Don't sound too bothered about it,' he airily said. 'Laurette will get a divorce and then marry the solicitor.'

He was right when he took for granted that Laurette would divorce her third husband. She did. And in time was quite back to her old self, giving dinners and salons. Now in her mid-forties, she still had her taste for exaggerated and costly clothes, great black hats pulled down over her at-present blonde hair. Like girls at Henley Regatta, Laurette went in for hats. When she came to see Eleanor and Sandy, she always wore some new and extraordinary creation – Arab or Red Indian, Japanese or Parisian.

She never disappeared for long from Eleanor's life, although she went on distant holidays with whoever was her current beau. She travelled to the Galapagos Islands, to the Gambia, to the Great Barrier Reef. Once, it was odd for Eleanor to hear of it, to Brazil.

Not long after Eleanor's meeting with Hugo, Laurette invited her to lunch at the old haunt of the Writers' and Artists' Association in Half Moon Street. She was as bright as a button in a grey suit with enormous lapels, her hair tucked into a baseball cap.

'My one friend. Sit down, sit down, I've ordered you some Châteauneuf-du-Pape, I know you like it.'

'I hope you do too.'

'Alas, my aerobics teacher has forbidden it. She has this list, "Positively Condemned" which includes lovely wine and digestive biscuits, would you believe. I'm told to drink the new mineral water,' lifting her glass. 'It has the most disgusting taste and the ads imply it's full of substances to encourage the sex drive.'

'Then you'd better not have too much of that.'

'Flatterer.'

They gossiped during the meal about her boss: 'He has a demonic eye.' But at the end of the meal she said, raising her eyebrows, 'You're distrait, Eleanor. I wonder why?'

'Sorry.'

'Don't be, just tell me what's bothering you.'

'Nothing very much. A feeling, really,' said Eleanor, floundering.

Laurette was too experienced to say anything at this point, but sat looking at her with such tempting attention that Eleanor finally came out with, 'It's Sandy.'

'What's wrong with that attractive husband? Not ill, I trust?'

'No, he's okay, it's just that, I really do sound stupid, it's just that he seems different.'

'In what way?'

'Difficult to describe.'

'You can do better than that.'

Eleanor tried again.

'He seems to have lost his enthusiasm.'

Laurette's attention deepened.

'For you.'

'Oh no, not that,' said Eleanor too quickly. This was not true but Eleanor would not confide about sex, least of all to a three-husband-expert, a female Bluebeard. She tried to explain how Sandy seemed changed. It was mainly the way he was about work; he used to be so crazy about it, he really loved it and had so much success.

'We all know about that. Brilliant. So?'

'So it seems to have gone. He scarcely talks about it now. And his face never lights if *I* do, in fact I almost feel he wants me to shut up.'

Laurette pondered for a while, fiddling with her rings, lost in thought. She finally came out with, 'Isn't the real point how Nelson's is doing right now?'

'Oh, the agency's very busy. Things are going well,' Eleanor lied for a second time.

'So not to worry,' said Laurette simply. It was then that Eleanor realised her instinct had stopped her from telling Laurette about Sandy's interest in politics.

After she'd met her, and Laurette had been so relaxed about things, Eleanor told herself she was making something out of nothing. But the truth was that she had become sharply aware of Sandy, and he bothered her. One evening they settled down to watch late TV: a courtroom drama, just the sort of film he enjoyed. She spoke to him twice and when he didn't answer looked to see if – it rarely happened – he'd fallen asleep.

On the contrary, he was very much awake; but his eyes were not on the screen. Mouth slightly open, he was staring intently at the carpet. Above the sound of American voices she said, 'Hey! I bet you've had an idea for a new campaign.'

'What?' He roused himself from thought. 'No, no, nothing like that.'

The movie ended in the old-fashioned way, all the wrongs righted and the main couple coming down the steps of the court house to meet a gathering of enthusiastic reporters. Sandy walked out of the room, leaving Eleanor to clear away his newspapers and the coffee cups. She grimaced.

When she was in bed, he emerged from the bathroom

with that spotless new-washed look of his before he went to
bed. The short white towelling dressing gown suited him —
how attractive he still was. But physically drifting away
from her. Mentally too. He threw off the dressing gown,
climbed into bed and punched his pillows. Conscious that
she was looking at him, he casually said, 'Remember I said
the other night that I might, I just might go in for politics?'

She nodded, feeling strangely nervous.

'I've decided to do that.'

This time she didn't laugh. She said in a thin voice, 'Are
you really sure?'

'I've just said so. Ronnie Hislop, a guy I met recently,
wants to introduce me to the chairman of the local
Conservative party at Potter's Bar.'

'Potter's Bar,' repeated Eleanor faintly; he'd spoken as
if it were a great cathedral city.

'One hundred per cent cast-iron Tory and the MP's due
to retire — he's ancient and not too well. Hislop introduced
me to the chairman this evening, man called Belwood.
Guess who we met at the H of C bar? Laurette. We bought
her a drink.' He grinned. 'There's nothing that girl doesn't
know about party politics.'

Laurette's cleverness wasn't what was being discussed
and after a long moment Eleanor said, 'What about
Nelson's?'

'What *about* Nelson's?'

'You can't have two jobs.'

'Don't be bloody silly, of course I can. Nobody can live
on an MP's salary except those awful holier-than-thou
Labour MPs. Don't start making objections, for Christ's
sake, before I've even started.' He switched off the light.

He was grumpy next morning, ate little breakfast and left
the house early. His BMW was parked in the paved space,

once a little garden, in front of the house. He drove showily away, roaring the engine.

Paul had left for school in the company of Eleanor's Spanish help, Gloria. Louise, such a friend to Jo (she still sent her Christmas cards) was long gone. She had taken her music course, played for a while in a touring orchestra, and then married. Now she had a daughter of her own.

Gloria was no rosy-faced English girl with a taste for taking her charge to the Natural History Museum, but she lavished attention on the little boy, a love very similar to Zica's in Brazil. Joanna was eating muesli and drinking strong red tea.

She flicked back her long newly washed hair which had mauveish lights and looked like heavy silk.

'Sandy is a pain when he's in a bad mood,' she said, giving her mother a look of teenage sympathy.

'He has a lot to worry about,' said Eleanor, despising the excuse.

'Like what? Himself? *You* have things to worry about. I mean, there's me. And there's my Dad.'

'Why,' said Eleanor with impatience, 'am I supposed to worry about him?'

'He's away such a lot. How could we get him quickly if we needed him?' was the obscure question. 'And then,' continued Joanna after some thought, 'he doesn't lead a full life. That time ages ago when I was in Peru with him I saw the sort of thing. My dad is a worry.'

'Jo, that really is a lot of rubbish. I can't spend my time worrying over Hugo.'

'Maybe you should,' reproved Joanna. 'I do. French Gran does. It would be nice if you did as well. Then another thing. Paul.'

'And what's the matter with Paul?' Eleanor was

thoroughly provoked – Joanna loved putting her in the wrong.

'His earache.'

'*What?*' Eleanor sprang up, shouting that if he had earache why hadn't she been told and what was the child doing going to school?

'Gloria wanted to tell you but he started to cry. Then I said I'd tell you, but he cried even more, poor chap. I begged him, but he kept crying and saying his Dad looked cross. He's scared of Sandy sometimes, dunno why. I keep telling him there's nothing to be afraid of.'

Eleanor ran down to the kitchen where Gloria was cleaning the silver. 'Is *asquerosa*' she said, glancing up.

'Gloria! Joanna says Paul is not well – why—'

'I want to tell you, Mrs Trafford, but he cry and many time say "I am better". Maybe is better now—'

Eleanor did not wait for her to finish, ran upstairs, pulled on a jacket and left the house. She drove off as fast as Sandy.

Paul's school, Saint Mark's, was a sober, expensive and reasonably reputed place near Onslow Square. Eleanor was soon, through urgent enquiries, shown into Paul's class-master's study. Mr Denny knew all about the ear.

'The pain, apparently, is much reduced; we put him in the sick bay. A brave little fellow. Matron gave him an aspirin and hot tea. We didn't telephone at once, Mrs Trafford, we wanted to give the aspirin time to work before you drive him home.' A big blond chunky man, he looked at her over his glasses.

The small drama took most of Eleanor's day. She drove her son, white and silent, home. Her heart smote her. What sort of a mother didn't know when her boy had miserable earache? She telephoned Nelson's to say she wouldn't be in until very late, and took Paul to the doctor. The ear was not badly inflamed; the aching had nearly stopped. Soothing drops were prescribed, and Paul was congratulated on his stoicism.

Sandy's son had no trace of his mother's Rossetti colouring or his father's gingerish tints. He was dark, on the small side, with large grey eyes, a dignified manner and wild arm gestures. Sandy had been set on putting Paul down for a top boarding school. Eleanor disagreed and they'd argued about it for months. Then Sandy's opinion crumbled in a moment when Joanna remarked, 'You can't. It's so out of date.'

With Gloria to look after him and pet him, Eleanor felt she could leave Paul and get to Nelson's. It was after six when she drove into the agency car-park. She hurried down the corridor to her office. Her desk was covered in messages.

'I got six tins of the fake lumpfish stuff we can use for caviar.'

'No go at Liberty's, it's Indian week and not a Japanese vase in sight.'

'The Stockwell house is okay. It's great!'

Eleanor worked for an hour, then felt she needed tea. By the machine, she was holding a scalding hot plastic cup, when she met Tommy Thompson, who gave her the flirtatious up-and-downer; no feminist had yet succeeded in stopping that habit of his.

'You're working late.'

'So are you, Tommy.'

'Aha, but I just got back from Glasgow. If I don't do my report tonight, by tomorrow I'll have forgotten every blind thing they said.'

Eleanor explained about the earache and Tommy, shamelessly disinterested, said, 'I'm off to a meeting with

Giles. Why not come and join us?'

'You don't need me.'

'As a matter of fact we do.'

He bustled her along so fast that the hot tea slopped over her wrist.

Giles was at his desk, grey head on his hand, studying sheets of figures as intently as a scholar with Shakespeare's first folio. He glanced up.

'Tommy. And Eleanor, my dear child.'

'When I saw her, I thought it is going to come to us three getting together, so why not now?' said Tommy, sitting down. Both men treated Eleanor with their usual camaraderie; they never missed the chance to show how much she was part of the agency, how they did not forget that she owned a big slice of it. The fact that she worked as a stylist, was represented nowadays at board meetings by Sandy, had won their affection. She was an old-fashioned sort of woman, not a threat apparently. Were they fond of her because of that?

There is something about offices at night. They are different from the bright morning, the used-up afternoon, the surge as people crowd into lifts and stream out of the building. Time in the office at night is relaxed.

Table lamps shone on the desk strewn with papers, the dark carpet, Eleanor's bright hair and Tommy's black shoes polished at the Glasgow hotel.

The tie between Giles and Eleanor was strong. It had been Giles she had gone to for help when she returned from Brazil; Giles who'd given her support, encouraged her to work at the agency: and Giles who had accepted Sandy. Tommy, too, had played a part in her life, backing up Sandy's entrance into advertising, recognising a fellow spirit.

But things were not the same.

Giles's concentration on the balance sheet had actually been that of a man looking at his house after it had been bombed. When Tommy enquired if the figures were as bad as expected, Giles said, 'Worse.'

'And I had no success in Glasgow,' said Tommy, 'God knows I sold hard enough. Hopeless.'

Giles folded up the balance sheets.

'There's a lot more news, none of it good.'

'Christ, any moment we'll be talking crap about making a leaner and fitter agency,' said Tommy, 'which in plain language means sacking people.'

Giles rubbed his long nose and said nothing.

'There's something else we've got to face,' said Tommy.

He looked at Eleanor and she heard herself saying, as she went an uncomfortable red, 'Do you mean Sandy?'

Giles looked embarrassed. He was thinking that the old act was re-acting: Walter on Concorde, Sandy heaven knew where. He spoke carefully, 'I don't expect you realise, Eleanor, how little time he actually spends at the agency now. You're out on location or in the studio here . . . Does he tell you where he goes most days?'

'I thought he was in the office.'

'No, he ain't,' said Tommy.

'But—' she began.

'He just isn't around, Eleanor.'

'We presume,' put in Giles, 'that it must because of that new interest you and I talked about.'

'He's told me too,' said Tommy, 'I'm afraid I laughed. We had quite a row when I said he had turned into an absentee landlord at Nelson's.'

'He does keep in touch,' said Giles, seeing her face.

'Usually from his car,' said Tommy with what Giles

thought unnecessary lack of tact. But Tommy had made up his mind to speak out. 'The nasty fact is, Eleanor, that Nelson's can't afford him any more.'

Giles was more the politician. He was also kinder-hearted, speaking about Sandy's past skill and flair and the accounts he had won for the agency. 'One of the main reasons for our considerable success in the Eighties was certainly Sandy.'

'But I'll tell you what's happened now,' said Tommy, going on with the story. 'You must know, Eleanor, that your husband's the guy for what's new. What's growing. June bustin' out all over. Now we're doing badly he just isn't interested. He's bored with Nelson's. And he's looking elsewhere.'

When Tommy said that, Eleanor knew it was true and desperately wanted it not to be. Still staying cool, even detached, she looked round for something to say in her husband's favour.

'Tommy, loads of MPs have two careers. They're in the House, and they have business interests as well. Not just names on writing paper, real jobs. Well, some of the cleverest ones do. Surely it would be useful for us if Sandy did get a seat.'

Tommy looked at his hands. He wore a wedding ring and did not live up to it. He was remembering Eleanor's friend in the Commons. Sandy always had a sharp eye for contacts.

'When Sandy talked to you about changing gear, did he happen to mention one vital point? About exactly when he plans to start at this thing seriously.'

'No. He didn't say.'

'Mmm,' said Tommy. 'That's the point, isn't it? We all know Sandy never hangs about.'

Silence.

Giles said in a different tone, 'Eleanor, we need to talk about you. Your shares are still in your name, of course, but you gave your husband your vote on the board. You made him, as it were, your representative. If he is going to go, we'll have to alter that.'

Both men looked at her and she said hesitantly, 'I suppose so.'

'Good,' they said together.

When she was back in her office she rang Gloria.

'Is asleep,' was the answer to her anxious question, 'Much better. Nobody here. Only me.'

'I'll be back very soon.'

'Not to worry, my boyfriend he wait.'

When Eleanor arrived home, she thanked Gloria, who scampered off to the Spanish club, and went up to Paul's room very quietly. She stood looking at the little boy. The feeling which came to her then was as sharp as the most excruciating pangs of being in love. He lay on his back, one cheek red from lying on it for too long. He clutched Joanna's old bear. All its fur was gone from face and chest; it stared steadily up at the ceiling with brown glass eyes.

Too tired to eat, she went down to the sitting room and collapsed into a chair, overwhelmed by thoughts of the past. It must be the bear, she thought. How ridiculous I am! She remembered the toy, brand-new in Brasilia. For months she forgot she had ever lived there, forgot the bright air, the instant sunsets, the impression of a larger world under an enormous sky. She thought of the rounded mountains, the hooped blue bays, the fireflies which rose and fell. She had never forgotten Ceci, but could you keep love alive with letters and photographs of children now turned into adults? Things were better with Sara, who came to stay in London sometimes. Clearly, her dubious husband was doing better than ever: Sara always stayed at Claridge's. She was older and thinner, still girlishly eager, still wanting love and missing the point.

It was on her first visit to see Eleanor, when mother and daughter were alone, that Sara said, with one of her raying smiles, 'You remember Francisco De Quiroz?'

'Of course,' said Eleanor, mentally adding, I'd scarcely be likely to forget him. That horrible divorce. And then ... for other reasons ... his name made a sort of music. Did you always feel a reaching-out to someone because you had once loved them?

'You *were* rather éprise, weren't you, darling? I only mention him because José Americo and I went to his wedding last month. The hugest show, about 400 people. Francisco is getting on, ridiculous to think that he's nearly forty. He's been an eligible bachelor much too long. Apparently the aged mother, rich as rich, finally put her foot down. So there was Francisco walking down the aisle of the cathedral with his bride.'

'And is she rich too?'

'What do *you* think? Rolling. And all of 17.'

'Oh dear.'

'I agree. Very beautiful. Huge eyes. But you know how girls in Brazil put on weight unless, like me, they have wills of steel. Now, what's on the agenda today? The RA?'

Sara had developed a positively American enthusiasm for London, and never criticised it or compared it unfavourably with Rio and New York. She was delighted with the city. She expansively invited Giles to lunch, not with her daughter who was happy to be left out: her mother and Giles would only bore on about old times.

Both of them had a shock of relief to find the other in

many ways the same. Of course, thought Sara, Giles was now as grey as a badger, but he was lovely and it was good to see that he still thought *she* was. Giles was his gallant out-of-date self. He was glad Sara had managed to keep some of her looks, he was rather moved by the little crow's feet round her flecked eyes, and it intrigued him to notice that when he asked about her husband, she was nervous.

'Oh,' she said, 'I've no idea what his business is, exactly. Something to do with land or gambling, I don't know. José Americo is quite a mystery. That's what's fun about him. I never ask, and he never says.'

Giles said José Americo was fortunate to have such a wife and she gave her loud laugh.

It interested Giles, when he walked back to Baker Street, to realise that both Sara's husbands had slightly frightened her.

If Sara was a success with Giles, she won gold medals with her daughter's husband. Sandy was bowled over, laughed at her jokes, paid her compliments and kissed her. He took her about with Eleanor. The trio, man, wife and glamorous, if elderly, arrival from South America, went to theatres and galleries and restaurants. Sara decided to teach her son-in-law the samba. She took a lot of trouble to find real Brazilian music, brought it back to Abingdon Villas, kicked off her shoes, swayed invitingly and smiled at Sandy with eyes like her daughter's.

Sandy had no rhythm and couldn't dance a step, and it was while Sara, singing in Portuguese, was encouraging him, and the Brazilian beat thudded round the room that Joanna came in.

Sara and her granddaughter had never met in their lives. In Brazil, Sara pretended she didn't exist, and on her first London visit, Joanna had been away.

Looking at her sternly from between the curtains of long hair, Joanna declared loudly, 'I think you must be my grandmother.'

Sara laughed.

She set out to be charming to the girl. She took an enormous fancy to her. Joanna made her feel not grand-motherly but up to the minute. She took Joanna shopping and bought her an outrageously expensive jacket Joanna had coveted as 'my impossible dream'. Sara confided to Eleanor that she thought it hideous but oh, had Eleanor seen Jo's face? Joanna did not shy away when her grand-mother kissed her, she accepted the embrace and smiled sweetly. She was willing to be fascinated by the exotic stranger while suspecting that, generous and affectionate as Sara was, she perhaps secretly wished Joanna had never been born.

They looked most odd when they were together, the over-elegant Sara dressed by masters, and the girl in Oxfam clothes and boots, with a skin like a camellia.

At London Airport, seeing Sara off, Joanna had watched the plane rise in the air and sighed.

'I hope she's going to be all right.'

'You're not nervous about her flying, surely?'

'No, no, Mum. Of course not. I mean her life: that husband. I just hope she'll be okay, that's all.'

Eleanor thought that somehow her mother always was. In her own odd, nervous and secretive way, she managed to have a life which perfectly suited her. I wish she was here now, she thought. Sara's advice during the divorce had been hopeless, but that didn't mean she wouldn't be a help now when Eleanor badly needed her . . . Eleanor shut her eyes.

*

Suddenly there was a blaze of lights.

'What *are* you doing?'

Sandy, in a dinner-jacket, was standing beside her. 'Why aren't you in bed? You weren't waiting up, were you?'

'Of course not.'

He yawned. 'Anything to eat?'

'Haven't you had a meal?' she said, with that immediate instinct to look after him. He looked pleased.

'Not a bite. I was with Bob who was in full flood, saying what was needed was "a dynamic new man, not the usual lobby fodder. A man with tomorrow's ideas. Thrusting. Consequential." He'd marked me out as just that, he said.'

Sandy grinned shamelessly as he repeated all this. 'I sat and looked dead keen. He'd already eaten so I pretended I had. Didn't want to stop the enthusiasm. Shall we go down to the kitchen?'

He didn't ask her if she had had any supper, but then Sandy never asked questions like that, and if you reproached him, he'd say he supposed you were sensible enough to look after yourself. And so, thought Eleanor, you should be. But she felt slightly faint with hunger, she hadn't eaten at lunchtime because of Paul's earache. They went down the stairs to the basement. Gloria had left everything in order, breakfast laid, curtains carefully pulled across metal shutters. The house had twice been burgled.

Sandy helped himself to a strange meal of the kind he enjoyed late at night when they returned from films or theatres. Reverting to childhood, he had a bowl of cornflakes as high as Mount Etna, sprinkled with brown sugar and slopping with milk. He said with his mouth full, 'What have you been doing today?'

Eleanor told him about his son's earache, and he reacted at once in the way which was Sandy at his best: he was for specialists, Harley Street, an interview with the headmaster, he even left Mount Etna as if about to run up to the child. When his fatherly love was uppermost, nobody was warmer. She dissuaded him, repeated what the doctor had said, calmed him down.

'If you're sure—'

She was. She promised. Comforted by the display of affection, she felt brave enough to say, 'I saw Giles and Tommy tonight. We had a meeting.'

'Oh?' Crunch, crunch of the cornflakes.

'Did you know the agency's lost the hairspray account?'

'I thought they might.'

And it was then, while her husband enjoyed his childish meal, and the clock struck midnight, and the summer night grew deeper, and the traffic died, that Eleanor knew Sandy did not care a straw, a pin, for the work he'd done so well, or the firm that had fascinated him, her father's firm, still bearing his name.

The old old love was still somewhere in Eleanor's daughterly heart, and she hated it when Sandy spoke of Nelson's and did not say 'we'. He said 'they'.

Chapter Fourteen

Like a good many children of divorced parents, Joanna Lawrence grew up without showing her feelings to older people. She appeared happy and well-balanced; she was certainly cheerful. And an iron will indicated that she did not see herself as a victim.

Her French grandmother was fond of her and sometimes Joanna invited herself down to Hillier's where the elderly lady still lived with little domestic help and much lost grandeur. Mathilde listened for Joanna's car an hour before she was due, cooked *boeuf bourgignon* in the Montbard fashion and fussed over her in a – to Joanna – comical and satisfactory fashion. She saw Aunt Agnes, surrogate mother, whenever it was possible, as well as her cousins, beloved Emily and the younger Nicole. She was still part of the Lyttelton family and in a way had two mothers.

But was there a scar somewhere? Eleanor couldn't tell. She noticed that her daughter was an espouser of causes. The girl loved the old, the weak and the disadvantaged. She collected for charity and bullied her friends into giving generously. Once Eleanor remarked that she should be a social worker. Joanna looked at her with pity. 'Really, Mum.'

Joanna loved animals, and had never had the chance to own one. She had tried often enough: she had wheedled and groaned. One glorious weekend when she was twelve, she had been lent a well-behaved and serious-minded spaniel, called Binker, by a schoolfriend who was going away for two days. The presence of Binker was a disaster; Sandy had hit the roof, and the poor animal had to be practically hidden from him until the weekend was over.

When she was older, Joanna tried again. 'I *need* a dog. A cat would do.'

Sandy put his foot down. Animals scratched the furniture and left hairs on the carpet. He refused to put up with a beseeching dog or an unfriendly cat. Recently, to her mother's relief, Joanna had stopped groaning about a house without an animal not being a home. She appeared to have forgotten her yearning. Little did her mother know a secret shared by Joanna only with her young brother. It was about Ruffles.

Ruffles was a neighbour from three houses away, half Persian and the colour of milky coffee with bands of cream round the neck. He had a life of his own on the rooftops. One autumn evening of heavy rain, Joanna was in her room struggling with homework when she heard a strange noise at the window – and saw a wet reduced face looking pitifully in. She rushed over to welcome a half-drowned cat. His ruffles were flat; he looked like a wet rag and was utterly miserable. She put him by the radiator, gently patted him dry and talked to him in a soft monotonous voice. 'How lovely you are, there, lovely cat, there.' The ruffles magically dried and the cat's beauty returned. Fluffing him round the neck, she named him. As Joanna knelt worshipfully beside him, their friendship was sealed. He became a regular visitor, usually at night, and when she saw his face at the window-pane she would rush to welcome him. Deafeningly purring, he sometimes slept on her bed leaving, like Eros, at dawn. She adored him.

Joanna was undemonstrative, except to Ruffles, occasionally to the current boyfriend, and always to her brother Paul. She was his champion. He did not need one: his parents spoiled him, but Paul became Joanna's cause from the day she saw him in the maternity home, a scrap with a creased face and a parrot's nose. Her heart grew large when she looked at the baby and as far as Paul was concerned, it had never returned to its right size.

After a night with Ruffles, Joanna came down to breakfast late one morning. In the kitchen Gloria's Radio One was at full blast. Sandy had gone, and the house had loosened its stays; Eleanor was also relaxed. She waved a letter at her daughter.

'What do you think? Your grandmother keeps saying she wants to sell Hillier's.'

Joanna sat down and helped herself to muesli. Her family's ancestral home, that Sussex pearl, meant nothing to her except embarrassment. She never dared to tell her friends about it.

'I suppose Gran can't cope with anything so huge any more.'

'Perhaps I ought to go down and talk to her about it,' said Eleanor doubtfully.

'That's not a very bright idea, Mum. French Gran isn't one of your admirers, is she? I could go. I'd quite like to. Anyway, who told you about Gran? I bet she didn't.'

'Your aunt Agnes.'

'Really? Why didn't she write to me?' Joanna was possessive about Agnes and looked annoyed. Eleanor handed her the letter which contained nothing new, it was a re-cap of one Joanna had received last week, except for the mention of 'Mother talks about selling Hillier's. Hugo thinks she does it to have an effect'.

But thinking about French Gran made up the girl's mind. City and Guilds' term wasn't starting until next week, so she was quite free. Before Eleanor left for work she heard her daughter non-stop on the telephone, doing what she called some unhooking. She laughed a good deal. She never does nowadays when Sandy's around, Eleanor thought and sighed.

When her mother was gone, Joanna went up the steep stairs to her brother's bedroom. He was building an expensive kit Sandy had bought him. Pieces of brightly coloured plastic were all over the floor.

'The young inventor,' said Joanna.

'Don't make me turn round yet.'

'Okay,' said Joanna peaceably. The boy muttered to himself. 'That's the one. And then that one. Help, where's the wiggly bit? Oh, there it is . . . but isn't there another?'

Joanna threw herself on his bed and picked up the old and rakish bear. Downstairs Gloria's music thrummed as loudly as at a fair.

'Done the bottom of it. What do you want, Jo?'

'To ask if you'd like to come with me.'

'Where?'

'To Sussex. Hillier's. You know that old place which belongs to Dad and Gran.'

He blushed. 'I've never been there,' he said cautiously.

'No reason why you shouldn't come now, is there? Mum wouldn't mind, I'm going to stay with my Gran and it'd be a change for you from smelly old London.'

'I had my holiday.' He was still red. The idea of going away with his grown-up sister excited him. He was fussed.

'Look, you don't need to come if—'

'But I want to.'

'Thought you would. I'll ring Mum at work.'

'What about Dad?'

'He's not here, is he?'

Joanna rang Nelson's and pushed her mother into agreeing, by her old technique of presenting the trip as an inspiration. Paul was crazy to come! French Gran hadn't met him, wasn't that stupid? They'd only stay the weekend, and they'd help in the house.

Oh, would they, thought Eleanor. But there was no reason to say no, and Joanna sounded delighted.

Joanna's car, small and shabby, was a French Deux Chevaux which had seen better days. It actually looked as if it had come, already old and battered, from some French factory dedicated to producing cars for the young. It had a humble look and Eleanor said Joanna used it as a tip. Paul fastened his seat belt and asked twice if Joanna had packed his kit. He scrabbled at the luggage. 'Can't see it.'

'The red plastic bag.'

'Oh yeah. Great. Are you sure your grandmother won't mind if I get on with it?'

'Gran won't mind anything when she's got us,' said Joanna. She concentrated on the traffic. Where was everybody else going, and why just at this particular time?

Paul's eyes were like saucers when his sister hooted the horn and drew up at the old house. September is the month for houses which have grown like trees into the landscape. Hillier's lay basking and russet. It had put out every rose. They hung from the brick front, looped round doorways and opened their hearts in a garden filled with weeds.

Ma chère enfant.

Mathilde came through a gate in the wall and the girl ran

up to give her a hug. Mathilde, always embarrassed, managed awkwardly to accept Joanna's smacking kisses. She was too fat nowadays but still strangely elegant in an old silk dress, her hair by a quirk of nature's still dark, worn long, in a pleat on the back of her stately head. She looked tired.

'And here is Paul?' She pronounced it 'Pol'. She shook his hand politely, and took them into the drawing room where tea was waiting.

Joanna and Paul never had a real tea, the meal of Mathilde's youth as a bride coming to England in the late forties. Joanna thought, sitting down, what a lot of washing-up. Mathilde had produced some old Derby china and had washed every cup and little plate. She had even cleaned a cake stand, an object Eleanor's children had never seen until now. The grandeur and oddity deeply impressed Paul. As for Joanna, seeing the tiny sandwiches, she had a moment's heartache but sternly banished the emotion.

'Tell me all about yourselves,' said Mathilde, sitting down heavily.

It took all Joanna's determination to cope with such a conversation stopper. She described the pop festival, while her brother wolfed the sandwiches. He hadn't realised he was hungry until he was given a lace-edged napkin, a plate with a gold dragon on it, and offered cucumber, egg and cress, Marmite, or banana: a feast. He concentrated on his tea, and the worry of whether he had packed his plastic screwdriver.

Mathilde listened courteously to Joanna's tale of enormous crowds, collapsed tents, men dressed as Druids, and people selling what the girl called alternative medicines.

'It sounds rather a muddle,' she said when the story was over. She turned her face, noble in its age, set in its prejudices, strangely sweet, to her granddaughter. Then glanced at the boy who was not her blood and murmured encouragingly, '*Encore un petit morceau?*' and cut him more cake.

When the meal was finished, Joanna took charge and carried away every piece of the time-wasting grandeur into the kitchen, saying she'd do the washing-up.

'No, no,' said Mathilde. 'Mrs Maffett comes in at six, from the village.'

All her life, Mathilde had found a Mrs Maffett from the village. Eleanor used to suspect there was a deep snobbery in the English which produced elderly women glad to work for a real live countess. She had said it to Hugo, who looked annoyed and said did she imply that the village people were not fond of his mother, which they most certainly were. But Eleanor had still thought country people were snobs.

With tea out of the way, Mathilde asked another show stopper: what would 'Pol' like to do? Joanna was ready for that one and explained about the plastic bag. She and Mathilde took the little boy into John Lawrence's old study and Mathilde sat him down at Lawrence's huge old desk, with the Victorian silver inkwell, empty, and the blotter, clean.

Forgetting everything, Paul set out his kit, his back to them both. Mathilde hung about but Joanna touched her arm.

'He's fine for the next two hours.'

'Three,' said Paul, without turning round.

Mathilde and Joanna returned to the drawing room. The old woman said slowly, 'Did your Aunt Agnes mention that I'm going to sell this house?'

'I heard that you'd mentioned the idea.'

'It is not an idea. It's true I have talked of it in the past. But now I am starting to arrange things. You will find upstairs *un peu dégagé.*'

'What do you mean, Gran?'

'I am already packing up.'

'Wow! Can I help?'

'That is kind of you, darling.'

'No, it's not. Paul will as well.' Joanna looked round and noticed for the first time that, in a far corner, some of the pictures had been taken down. And there were parcels along the top of the bookcase. 'I've had a brainwave, Gran. Why don't I ask Mum to come down and lend a hand? She's really good at organising things; it's part of her job at Nelson's.'

Joanna's suggestion was not without guile, and when her grandmother's face looked very cold, she said disapprovingly, 'Honestly, Gran, you are awful. Isn't it time you buried the hatchet?'

'I do not know what that expression means.'

'Oh yes you do,' Joanna was at her most schoolmistressy. 'You ought to forgive Mum after all these centuries. My Dad has, and when they meet they are quite civilised.'

'Good.'

'Gran, you really are hopeless.'

Mathilde looked pleased and asked why. She loved conversations about herself and nowadays nobody indulged her in them. She listened to the girl's strictures with interest, while Joanna had the rare and satisfying chance to lecture a lady of rising seventy.

When Mathilde went out to talk to Mrs Maffett, Joanna looked round the room again, thinking that every single object she saw was a leftover: portraits, silver, furniture, chair covers – one had a hole in it. Yet she liked the room very much and felt as comfortable as in her own crimson and orange kingdom at the top of Abingdon Villas.

Mathilde came back.

'If you really mean it, about helping, could we perhaps start with some books?'

'Lead me to them, Gran.'

Mathilde looked through the open door across the hall to her husband's study. 'Would Pol mind if we went in?'

Paul did not take a blind bit of notice when his sister and the elderly lady with the French accent began taking books down from what looked like a million shelves. Here, in this strange house with the strange woman Jo seemed so fond of, he was left in glorious peace. Mathilde eyed him now and again, but Joanna mouthed, 'He's okay.'

So many books, thought Joanna. European Royal Houses, French history, hunting; there was even the old cliché, *The Decline & Fall of the Roman Empire*, the dust on which made her sneeze. Mathilde fetched trays and they took the books in piles out into the hall and stacked them on a long chest. Mrs Maffett, pink-faced and breezy, came out, not to lend a hand, but to say, 'See you on Monday, my lady.'

Golly, thought Joanna, struggling with the *Roman Empire* which seemed to want to slide on to the floor. Mathilde suggested the books should be divided into those she, Hugo or Agnes might want and those to be got rid of.

'You mean Chuck or Save?'

Chanting the phrase, Joanna worked on.

Later, seeing her grandmother looked rather alarmingly pale, she asked if there was any hope of some supper, and Mathilde went into the dining room to see if Mrs Maffett had laid it. Joanna dragged Paul away from his task. He was tired too and even docile.

'Paul. When you go to bed, your room's next to mine. Is that all right?'

'Well. . .' He'd been thinking about that.

'Keep the door open and you'll hear us.'

'I won't. This house is a . . . like a . . .' His imagination failed. All of a sudden, he looked as if he might cry.

'You'll hear okay. I slept there when I was here with aunt Aggie.'

'But you had your cousins. You had them.'

'No, I didn't. I was on my own, can't remember why. I was in your room and thought I'd be spooked. But Aunt Aggie wedged the door open and I heard everything they talked about. As a matter of fact, they talked about me!'

The little boy couldn't laugh. He was realising the upstairs frightened him.

'Will you give it a go? If you positively hate it, I promise I'll come to bed same time as you.'

Reassured – his sister never lied – he went to bed after supper. She propped open his door with an outsized book. Mathilde was surprised when her granddaughter then swooped back down the staircase, leaping the last four stairs, and began a loud conversation.

'I say, Gran. All that dust! I saw four spiders.'

Pause.

'Okay.'

Faintly the boy's voice called, 'Okay.'

'Goodnight, then.'

'Are you coming up?'

'All right. I'll bring Gran.'

With the child snuggled into an overlarge carved bed, Joanna came over to kiss him. Behind her was the stately and to Paul impressive figure of the old woman. If he was shy, so was she. She leaned over to pat his head and Paul suddenly threw his arms round her neck.

She's pleased, thought Joanna, and so she should be.

Mrs Maffet had gone long ago; the silences of the country

set in. Books lay about, silver on a tray, photographs face downwards. Joanna liked the disorder and plumped down on the old sofa.

'I'm glad I'm here.'

'So am I, dear child.'

'Do you like my brother?'

'Mais, voyons!'

I suppose that means she does, thought Joanna, adding, 'He really likes you.'

Mathilde poured coffee and they were quiet for a moment or two. Then, 'Why did you come, Joanna?'

'To see you.'

'Yes, but the other reason. Do not think you offend me. To have you here is a joy no matter why you came. But you did not visit me for *mes beaux yeux*, my child.'

'What a cynic you're getting, Gran.'

Maltilde's worn face had a self-regarding smile.

'I suppose I am. Well, Joanna?'

Her granddaughter fidgeted and stared at her enormous feet. Mathilde had controlled the desire to ask why the army boots, and because she hadn't commented, had unknowingly scored points. Looking for boot inspiration, Joanna said, 'Fact is, I'm rather worried.'

'About your examinations.'

'Oh, oh, that's so like you! Of course it isn't about that. Work's okay when I work and sometimes I don't. It's about Mum, actually.'

The blank expression at once returned to her grand-mother's face. Joanna leaned forward, her hair hanging on either side of her cheeks like the ears of some exotic dog. She looked for a moment uncannily like Eleanor as a girl.

'You're so against Mum, Gran. Why can't you get used to the fact that it's all finished. It's *old*. No-one cares about the ancient history: not my Dad, not Aggie, not me. You carry on the campaign all by yourself. Everybody else has forgotten.'

Silence.

'Well, and what is the trouble with her?' said Mathilde very coldly.

Joanna groaned and threw herself about. She picked up a patchwork cushion which Mathilde had made thirty years ago. It needed repair, but what didn't? She squeezed it; filled with feathers, it dented and then slowly regained its shape.

'If you aren't going to be sensible, I can't tell you anything, and I want to. Yes, that is why I came in a way. Of course, I always need to see you and I know I don't come often enough and more fool me. But I can't explain anything if you put on that face.'

Mathilde capitulated. Resisting the vanity of asking 'What face?' she said in a slightly trembling voice, 'You are not very kind, Joanna, but you are right. I am *prejugée* against Eleanor for treating your father badly. I have always found forgiveness hard, *c'est une erreur de ma part.* I am sorry. Tell me why you worry and—' it was a generous offer, greater than Joanna knew, 'if I can help.'

Evening had fallen, and the dusk smoothed out the colour of silver panels and golden floors, blending them to a uniform dullness, mixing the old past and the impatient present. Joanna's heart was touched, she would have liked to take the freckled hand loaded with diamond rings. She searched for words which would not upset this ancient friend.

'I think Mum's marriage is cracking up.'

Mathilde's eyes widened.

'What makes you think so?'

'Not from her. She'd never confide in me and probably hasn't admitted it to herself. But something's changed in the house. It doesn't feel right any more. And it's Sandy.'

'Do you dislike your stepfather?'

Mathilde had never even discussed Eleanor's second marriage, let alone the second husband. She had no idea what kind of man he was and until now had not cared.

'I used to like him a lot. He was fun – funny and fun. He bounced around. And he was real. He isn't now.'

'Is he – is he unkind to your mother?'

'Oh, he doesn't yell at her or beat her up or anything.'

'*Dieu*, I should hope not!'

'Grandmother, it happens.'

'I prefer not to think of such things and am shocked you should know of them, Joanna. May we please speak only of your mother's husband if he is the person who troubles you.'

'Okay. Right. No, he isn't nasty to her but he's sort of cold. He has this habit of blowing a trumpet.'

'*He does what?*'

Joanna had to laugh.

'Oh, oh, Gran, how I love you! Not a real trumpet, that would just be great. I mean when he's irritable he's so cold you practically catch pneumonia being round him, and when he is annoyed, and he often is, he goes like this.'

She pursed her lips, blowing an invisible instrument.

'Years ago when I was little and we were still at Wilbraham Place, he did it once when I spilled ink on a beastly white carpet. Then for ages not a trumpet sounded. Now he blows one all the time.'

Mathilde took it in.

'How does Eleanor take this?'

'She gets nervous and sometimes drops things. Once a

coffee pot half-full. She isn't happy, and now I know why.'
Joanna paused, wondering if she should take the plunge.
The desire to tell was too strong to resist. 'I'm sure he's
having it off with somebody else.'

Mathilde's face registered disgust.

'Joanna, if we are to talk about your troubles—'

'They aren't mine.'

'Very well, your mother's, then I insist you do not use
such expressions. They offend me.'

Joanna looked sulky and then amused. She couldn't help
liking Mathilde for hanging on to the old rules. It made a
change.

'I've seen Sandy with Mum's so-called friend. She's an
American called Jacobs whom Mum and Sandy have both
known forever. She was at university with Mum. Jacobs
sometimes comes to the house, but I'm sure she's the sort
who doesn't much like other women. *She* prefers guys.'

'Guys?'

'Men, Gran.'

'I recall a Mademoiselle Jacobs who came to dine here
once with Hugo and Eleanor.'

'Wow. As long ago as that! Anyway, I'm sure Sandy is
having – having an affair with her. It's obvious, but Mum
doesn't see it. What bothers me is ought I to tell her?'

'You mean tell Mademoiselle Jacobs? Go and see her and
tell her it must stop.'

'How could I do that?'

A sense of absurdity came to Joanna. She imagined
herself as a character in Edwardian drama – she'd seen one
of those at the National: 'Never dare enter our house
again.' Jacobs would rip her to shreds, and she'd be right.

'What I mean is Mum ought to know, surely? I can't
prove anything but I'm positive it's time. As I said, I've

seen them together and it's obvious,' repeated the girl. 'And it's always better to know the worst. Isn't it?'

Mathilde said nothing for a long minute. She was remembering Eleanor, and how much Hugo had loved her. Mathilde was tired. The enormous weight of the move she had crazily decided upon, the past too heavy for her, the absence of the son who was never here when he was wanted, pressed her down. And here was a beloved granddaughter offering her yet another burden. Mathilde intended to refuse it. Besides, nobody wanted advice. They only wished to talk, and whatever you said, they had decided beforehand what they would do.

'I can't give you the answer to this,' she said.

'But Gran!'

'No, Joanna, I cannot. I do not know your mother any more and I am not sure I ever did. When she needed advice, she had her own father and turned, I suppose, to him.'

'She never talks about him. But Gran,' not to be put off, 'I'm only asking a simple thing – should I tell Mum what is going on?'

'I do not know.' It was difficult to resist speaking of herself. 'If it was my decision, I would not.'

'Why?'

A Burgundian shrug. Mathilde wanted to end the conversation. It was getting nowhere and wasting the little time she had with her granddaughter.

'What matters is the truth, isn't it?' said Joanna.

The question was too strong for Mathilde who did not reply. 'Well, I think it is,' said Joanna sententiously.

Mathilde's thoughts strayed upstairs to a row of packing cases. Joanna jumped to her feet. 'I'd better go and see if Paul is asleep.'

Next day was Sunday and Mathilde went to Mass. The

weekly taxi arrived in good time, drove her to the Catholic church and waited to bring her home. While she was out, Joanna and Paul discovered some peeling ping-pong bats and a slightly cracked ball, and played on the dining-room table with books for a net.

Mathilde, carrying three prayer books and wearing a black lace mantilla she had bought at nineteen in Montbard, heard shouts and laughter when she came into the house. Two grinning faces.

'I nearly won,' the boy cried excitedly. 'It was only a couple of lousy bounces which beat me. Gran, do stay and watch my wicked serve. You could borrow Jo's bat and play me if you like.'

The rest of the day continued to be a success. Mathilde asked her visitors if they'd help upstairs. Joanna took on more books: there were shelves in the corridors, beside beds in empty bedrooms, even ranged along window-sills. Paul went from room to room pulling out drawers. He tottered down the main landing to lay them at Mathilde's feet, like a dog offering his mistress a treasured bone.

The drawers were crammed with fascinating things. Table linen and yellowing blouses of fine lawn with heavy embroidery. Rolled stockings (eaten by moths), and handkerchiefs patterned with violets. One drawer was weighty with old magazines and writing paper. Another contained nothing but leather belts. Paul loved to be praised, and Mathilde's praise was lavish.

'Fine, "Pol", but how do you manage? How heavy that must be.'

'No, no, Joanna, leave Pol to do it, he is now our expert.'

Brother and sister had scarcely dented the gigantic task by Monday evening when they were due to leave. They'd had a great deal of fun and Mathilde's non-stop admiration. They were beaming and dusty. She came out to the drive to see them off, giving Joanna a big bunch of newly-cut roses.

Paul put his arms round the old lady's stout waist and pressed his head against her. 'Gran, can I come again?'

It was Mathilde's moment of triumph.

High spirits, a mess, admiration, and the knowledge that their youth had put them in command, evaporated the moment brother and sister went into the house. Joanna had stopped on the drive home: Paul was hungry, and they'd had sandwiches and Coke in a motorway café. It was nearly ten when they finally arrived.

'Mum, we're back!' shouted Joanna.

An angry voice said, 'So there you are.'

'Hi, Dad,' said Paul cheerily, caught sight of his father's face and hurried upstairs, lugging the red plastic bag.

Sandy plunged his hands in his pockets. He wore one of his expensive suits and very over-smart he looked, thought Joanna, as well as being in a filthy mood.

'Where have you been?'

'At my grandmother's, of course.'

'Don't be cheeky, there is no of course about it.'

Joanna put down the roses and the zip bags and said, throwing her eyes up to the ceiling in martyrdom, 'I just said. We were at Gran's. At Hillier's, my father's house in Sussex, right?' She spoke in an adult-to-idiot tone. 'I told Mum where we'd be. Actually, I left a note with our phone number. All right?'

'Don't use that voice with me, I will not have it,' he rasped. Joanna saw his unpleasant expression with interest and not a trace of fear.

'Look,' she said, 'I'm not going to stand here while you

yell. Where did you think we'd been? On a rave-up? Why didn't you ask Mum?'

'She's out.'

Joanna pushed past him into the living-room in search of the note, which she intended to wave under his nose. He followed her, slamming the living room door behind him. He was a door slammer and this was the loudest yet. The house shuddered. He said in a more controlled voice, 'Listen to me. Don't turn your back, turn round!' He shouted it like an army command and from sheer surprise she obeyed.

'I don't give a fu—, a damn,' he never swore in front of women but it did not stop him from being ready to bully them, 'I don't care where *you* go or with whom—'

'Oh thanks.'

'Will you shut up? But I will not have you taking my son—'

'My brother,' she cut in, now as angry as he was.

Her contemptuous voice infuriated him more.

'I will not have my son taken God knows where without you asking my permission.'

'For Christ's sake. My grandmother!'

'I don't believe you were there. I telephoned.'

'So you did find my note.'

'I found a ridiculous piece of paper, if that's what you mean.'

Joanna recalled then that it had been very facetious.

'Understand?' he said, determined to get the last word.

Joanna looked at him steadily, thinking, you're pathetic: a bullying, unfaithful, pathetic slob. She did not know why he was angry, she was sure it was nothing to do with her taking Paul away for the weekend. Something had upset him and she'd been handy as somebody to yell at.

'If you rang my grandmother, then she must have told you we have been with her.'

'She wasn't there.'

'Oh bollocks.'

'Don't you swear at me, Miss,' he said viciously. 'There was no reply from that number you gave, and as far as I am concerned you never went there at all. I shall ask Paul.'

'You leave him alone!' shouted Joanna and literally rushed over and stood in front of the door. 'You scare him. You're so grouchy and you don't take any interest in him like you used to do, and when he *does* talk to you, you don't listen. Don't you dare go up and take it out on him. If my Gran didn't answer, it's because she didn't hear the bloody phone, she's quite deaf and jolly old. Whatever put you in this shitty temper,' she glared at him like a Fury, 'it isn't me and it isn't Paul. You make me sick.'

She went out of the room. She'd had the last word, and left Sandy furiously banging round opening drawers and boxes in search of the cigarettes he'd given up three months earlier.

The storm blew over, but it left its mark. Sandy only spoke to his stepdaughter in front of Eleanor, and Joanna replied in monosyllables.

Her mother could scarcely miss the bad feeling and tried unsuccessfully to make things better. She was uneasy too about the delicate problem of her Nelson shares. Giles had made up his mind that he didn't want Sandy any longer at board meetings. Eleanor was sure Sandy was going to be very nasty when he heard of this. The falling-out between him and Jo could only make things worse.

Eleanor longed for peace, for the time when Sandy had shown how much he loved her, and when he'd been heart and soul for Nelson's; when she had believed he was fond of Jo. She supposed, now, that she had fooled herself, and that neither of them had much liked each other. They had tried. But now their real feelings were out in the open.

Even Paul was bothered by the way his father and sister behaved to each other. One evening after term had started, he asked Joanna to help him with his maths. 'I'm muddled, Jo.'

She came obligingly up to his room, sat on the floor and began to work on the sums.

'Jo,' said a small voice, 'I wish you wouldn't be so cross with my Dad all the time.'

'Don't get heavy, Paul. We're just fine.'

It was the glib American phrase still used in soaps, often by characters fatally ill, just arrested or, on some occasions, about to get shot.

'Are you really?'

'Positively, absolutely, certain-sure. Don't give Sandy and me a thought; we only pick at each other. Now, about your maths, it's easy if you do the sums like this.' She showed him, and then planted a kiss on his pink cheek. He tried to believe her about his father. He loved her.

Joanna was back at the City and Guilds, travelling by underground and with one shoulder weighed down by books.

'Look. I'm Richard III.'

She met girlfriends for orange juice, and talks about men. She and Dave had now parted; Joanna had a new admirer. His name was Kon – thin and bespectacled – and she thought him irresistible.

Kon asked her to a club to learn how to rap. You had to string rhymes together which matched the rhythm of Reggae music. It was tricky, and Joanna enjoyed it. They went to a Chaos Bop night and danced wildly. In contrast they also agreed to go climbing in Glencoe in the spring. Joanna (who told her mother Kon was 'a bookish guy') even queued with him to get into a violent seventeenth-century Spanish play which she described as brilliant. Joanna told her mother that Kon inspired her. He also happened to work hard and – competitive still – she began to do the same.

Having preached holy forgiveness to Mathilde, Joanna had no intention of forgiving Sandy. She was certain his bad temper was something to do with Laurette Jacobs, but had not yet mentioned her suspicions to her mother. Much as Joanna now disliked Sandy, he was quite nice to Eleanor. Perhaps the affair had petered out. She hoped so. French Gran's advice, to do nothing, might be right after all.

One evening, coming in to the house wrapped in thoughts of Kon, she heard Sandy on the telephone. The tone of his voice made her stop and listen. It was soft, caressing, quite unlike the voice she knew.

'Is that you at last?' he said, 'I was worried.' Silence. 'I understand. It must be difficult, but I was pretty sick. Do you know, Laurette, I sat outside your flat on the doorstep for two hours!'

Another silence. A laugh.

'Do you mean it? Sounds perfect. I can be with you in twenty minutes . . .'

Another pause. A sexy laugh.

'Mmm. That's what I like.'

Joanna fled upstairs, moving silently and remembering which stairs creaked. She arrived at her own floor, her heart thumping. 'Pig,' she said aloud. 'Pig. Pig.'

Downstairs, the front door slammed.

'Pig,' shouted Joanna.

*

Lately Sandy had begun to come home impossibly late or, more often than not, simply not come home at all. At first Eleanor was cross and there was a row. But when he went on doing it, often without the courtesy of ringing to let her know, she accepted it. She knew she shouldn't, knew what she was doing was wrong, but she so hated rows. Where was Sandy? Potter's Bar, that mecca, came again and again into his tedious excuses. She was sick of him and his politics.

'I was at the Garrick and we've been discussing my chances.'

'I have to go to Potter's Bar, to get the feel of the place. Belwood's idea.'

'I'm being introduced to Marie Stothard, she's a local Tory battleaxe with a lot of pull. I shall stay locally somewhere.'

Oh really, thought Eleanor.

She did not want to prove he was lying. And if he was, why? Everything now was connected with his new career, nothing was connected with Nelson's which he was two-timing. The agency went on dropping accounts like a man with paralysed hands, and what did Sandy do? Go to Potter's Bar.

When Eleanor arrived home, Gloria called from the downstairs kitchen, 'I make casserole. Does not spoil.'

Now Sandy was away so much, and Eleanor often late back from work, Gloria's repertoire for the evening meal was pretty limited. She tried to ring the changes, chicken, vegetable hot pot, lamb, but the result was familiar.

'Kids,' called Eleanor from the bottom of the stairs. They came down to the dining room, and with Gloria safely gone, chorused 'Not stew again!' before asking for second helpings. Neither of Eleanor's children mentioned that there was no sign of Sandy.

After supper Joanna said she would read to Paul while he had his bath. He toiled up to his room carrying the entire set of C.S. Lewis Narnia books.

Eleanor cleared up, went to the sitting room, poured herself some wine and forgot to drink it. She stood by the French windows looking out into the garden. October had come quickly. It was already dusk and the leaves had begun to fall, the flower-beds were moist from the autumn rain. She kept thinking about Sandy, whose absence seemed ominous.

How much of his feeling for her had run parallel with his feeling for work? It seemed as if he had fallen in love with her and with Nelson's at the same time, taken them both on with the same energy. Work and love had been a pair of spirited horses which Sandy controlled in his own chariot race. Now, knees bent, he was gathering himself to leap from the old chariot to a shining new one, in which some stranger offered him the reins.

Who said that time was cruel? It seemed to Eleanor that it could turn dirt into a pearl. She didn't remember her misery when she fell into that trap as a girl, but she recalled now with a little spasm of the heart how Hugo had rescued her. She had learned to love him. He had never excited her, but he had been so tender and there had been years when she'd known she held complete sway over him, and that it was both beautiful and undeserved. She faltered now, wondering if the way he'd felt when she first refused him, with so much sorrow, had stayed somewhere in his love-making. Was that far-fetched? When she and Sandy had come together, and De Quiroz was in her past, all had been desire and triumph.

What now? Tommy said Sandy wasn't interested in things when they began to fail: Nelson's, their marriage? It hurt her to think that, but the pain was not as intense as it ought to be.

When Joanna had finished reading too many chapters of *The Horse and His Boy* aloud, she came down to find her mother in the sitting-room, staring at nothing.

Joanna frowned and said loudly, 'Mum!' Noticing the untouched wine she took a long swig.

'Is Paul asleep?' asked Eleanor, rousing herself.

'Dropped off during Chapter Seven; kept saying "Go on," and then started to snore. I practically crept out on my hands and knees. I say, Mum, isn't it lucky he is not one of those kids who keep appearing in pyjamas whingeing for a glass of water? A girl in my class has got a sister of six who does it all the time.'

Eleanor murmured something. Then, in a tired voice, 'I'm glad Sandy is not home. It gives me a chance to have a word.'

Joanna looked wary.

'Darling,' Eleanor said, 'it isn't on, you know. And don't pretend you have no idea what I mean. You really are very rude to him these days.'

'He's rude to me.'

'Don't give me that. In any case—' She stopped.

'Yes?'

'Oh nothing.'

Eleanor thought she had not made her point strongly enough and Joanna had certainly not accepted it.

'Look, Jo. You're still living with us. I know you want to go off on your own, but you can't until you finish your exams and manage to get a job. In the meantime your stepfather is very good to you. He gives the family a home. He helped to get you into the City and Guilds, and the least you can do is to be civil to him.'

Joanna did not mean to flare. But when her mother added how generous Sandy was and repeated how good he was to them all, that did it.

'How can you say he's good to us when he's behaving like a pig?' she burst out recklessly, and before she could stop herself, 'When he's sleeping with that so-called friend of yours. Is that good for any of us, least of all for *you*?'

She saw the colour drain from her mother's face and became angry with her victim as well as with herself.

'You must have known! I was talking about it to Gran—'

'What has your grandmother got to do with this?' Eleanor's voice was like ice.

'Wait, wait, let me explain. I only asked her if I should warn you and she said don't. She said it wouldn't be right. Anyway I'm sure you know. You must see what's going on under your nose, anybody would. What's the use of us pretending Sandy's good when he is nothing of the kind. He isn't, he isn't! Lorelei Jacobs or whatever her stupid name is must have been having it off with him for ages. I saw the way they were together when I was at Dad's club, and then last week I came in from college and he was on the phone to her. I was nearly sick. He didn't know I was there and I listened.'

'Joanna!'

'Why not? If you're cheating on someone, anybody has a right to listen and I did – to find out if what I suspected was true. He made a date with her there and then, you should have heard him all kissy-kissy, and then he left to go to her. Anyway,' finished Joanna, really frightened by her mother's face, 'where is he now?'

'Potter's Bar, with the constituency.'

'You can't believe that! He's with *her*, with Jacobs. He's there all the time, I'm sure of it. And what are you going to do to stop them?'

Joanna was half crying with guilt and misery.

Eleanor couldn't speak. The autumn evening had darkened at a stroke. She saw with clarity all the lies she had been fed, remembered calls cut short when she came into a room. He had stopped talking about Laurette at all now, and that was the worst sign of all. She thought of Laurette's bright, fixed expression when she and Eleanor were alone.

'How's Sandy? Tell me how you're both getting on. You know I always enjoy hearing about you and that clever husband.'

Joanna ran over, knelt down and tried to take her mother's hand.

'Don't look like that, Mum, oh please don't look like that,' the girl pathetically wailed. 'Isn't the truth always best?'

Chapter Fifteen

They were making a commercial for a new soap and Eleanor came home from the studio covered in dust. The studio was cheaper than those generally used by the production company and was slap in the middle of what they would call refurbishment. This meant walls of hardboard newly arrived from the factory and shedding something like pollen over everybody. The crew coughed and sneezed and moved to another studio in the basement.

It had been the usual day. The model was young and spoilt, had the face of a flower and decided to be difficult. The TV director had just signed for a real movie, and got into a rage over the pollen. And to end the pleasures of the day's work, Eleanor found that somebody – oh who? – had stolen an antique hairbrush, silver-backed and valuable, on loan from a Bond Street jeweller.

At Abingdon Villas, she felt in need of a bath and a hairwash. Her daughter's music thundered. She'd once asked Joanna how she could work to heavy rock, and Jo answered how could Eleanor work to *Eugene Onegin*. Impossible to win with Jo, or to escape when she thought it right to tell you the truth.

It had been horrible to learn something from her daughter which her own instincts should have told her

weeks ago. Why hadn't she known? And what the hell to do
about it? For Laurette she felt a dull disgust, remembering
her so eager to discuss Eleanor's problems. She had known
all the details, of course, of Sandy's new venture. She'd
taken on the job of explaining his absences to Eleanor.
They were to be expected. She pooh-poohed Eleanor's
anxiety when Sandy had begun not coming home at night.

'He's networking. You can't get anywhere if you don't,'
she said. Laurette was versed in the curious job of getting
oneself chosen as a candidate. She knew the egregious
Ronnie Hislop, who in turn had led Sandy to Belwood,
chairman of the local party at Potter's Bar. Laurette had
been enthusiastic.

'It's a tough fight, but that's what your husband enjoys.
The local party members vote for their choice, and I'm sure
Sandy's determined it will be *him*. Anything like that is a
battle, Eleanor – tooth and claw.'

'Sandy says the majority is about 14,000,' Eleanor had
said. She'd heard it often enough.

'Exactly. Whoever gets it has a job for life,' Eleanor had
listened to Laurette's sympathetic laugh.

To accept that she and Sandy were lovers was the second,
most unnerving shock of Eleanor's life. As if she'd driven
down Abingdon Villas and suddenly, a yawning crevasse
had opened up in front of her. She felt as if she'd shoved
on the brakes just in time.

When she was dressing, she saw from the bedroom
window that Sandy had come home. Through the almost
bare branches of the cherry tree, she watched him climb
from the car and lounge casually to the front steps.

In the living room, he threw down the briefcase which
bulged more every day, poured himself a gin and switched
on the answering machine. Wandering round the room, he

drank and listened. 'Sandy? Ronald. Could you call me?'
'Sandy, this is Tommy Thompson. I've been trying to
contact you since yesterday.' It was sheer melodrama that
as Eleanor came in, it was Laurette's voice.

'Hi there. Me again. Ronnie says what about tomorrow
and he likes your idea about the 15th. Call me. I'm at home
tonight and we can sort it out. Incidentally somebody said
you're a real power-house. I agree.'

Sandy was grinning as his wife came in. He switched off
the machine.

'Things are picking up,' he said in a relaxed way. 'Let me
give you a drink and I'll fill you in with what's happening.
White wine and fizz?'

He put the glass into her hand.

She looked at him with real curiosity. Is it so with
everybody, she thought, that the things they do simply do
not show? I guess we are all hypocrites. I was with Hugo.

'Sorry, give me a moment,' said Sandy, switched on the
machine again, listened to the rest of the tape and began to
enter and change dates in his big *Economist* diary. He
finally turned off the quacking voices and said good
naturedly, 'How was work?'

'A mess. The bath soap commercial.'

'Yeah,' he said, not listening. And then with an obvious
effort, 'You know I got the *Arbeitskräfte* tyre account? I'm
glad I managed that.'

'You didn't get it. Tommy did.'

If the sofa had piped up, he could not have been more
surprised. He said sharply, 'Tommy Thompson loves taking
the credit for my work.'

'What work? You're never in the agency. You're a dead
loss. Why? Because you're with Laurette.'

There was a moment's pause. Sandy, who had begun to

look unpleasant when his boast was disbelieved, changed tack. He was cool.

'What is that supposed to mean?'

'Sandy, do me a favour. We both know you're a good liar but don't waste it on me. And don't think me such a fool. You are sleeping with her, so why not admit it?'

He sipped his gin again and considered. He was used to being the one who called the shots and didn't, at present, quite see where this was going. He gave her a boyish smile.

'How long have you known?' he asked, like a fellow conspirator.

'Long enough. What do you propose to do about it?'

Sandy found himself rather comforted by the turn in the conversation. He had expected that when she did find out, Eleanor would make an appalling scene. Women did. He had had many affairs away from home, but never like this one, while he was with Eleanor. It rather excited him. Eleanor's reaction to him in sex and in their life together was always hot. He was the lynchpin of her life and that suited him. No scene. Passion later, maybe.

'Look, girl, you can't really be surprised. You know her so much better than I do.'

It was a line natural to Sandy. Seduced by female wiles. 'And she's up to her neck in my political stuff. She's the key. She's very smart, Eleanor. Sure, we've been to bed a couple of times but it doesn't mean anything. Don't make it into a big deal. Forgive?'

He gave her, this time, rather a sexy grin.

Does he really believe I will accept that? thought Eleanor in wonder. She could just see them laughing over poor old Eleanor. She remembered how easy the house became when he wasn't here.

'Friends?' he said, looking at her in a certain way and clearly thinking she would come to his arms. Eleanor finished her drink and said thoughtfully, 'Sandy, I'd like a divorce.'

He actually grinned. 'Come on, Eleanor. What rubbish.'

'I don't think so. Didn't it occur to you when you started up with her that it might lead to this?'

'Don't be a fool, of course we won't divorce. I never heard anything so ludicrous.' As he stared at her, realising she had meant it, she saw something wolfish in his face. He said with a sneer, 'Do you think I'll risk my future because you have hysterics?'

'But I'm not having them, am I? Yes, Sandy, I shall divorce you. I certainly don't intend to sit here while you go off with my erstwhile friend. I take it you won't give her up?'

'For God's sake,' he shouted, 'how can I do that, even supposing I wanted to, which I don't. I'm on the verge, which you haven't bothered to ask about, of getting a safe seat. Laurette's responsible for fixing a lot of my most valuable contacts. Do you think I'll risk my reputation now it matters? Have some sense. You usually do.'

'Divorce,' said Eleanor calmly. 'I won't stay married to you now that I know—'

'That another woman's got me?' he said, jeering.

'About the sort of man you really are.'

'Oh thanks,' he weakly said, but his eyes were wicked. 'I have no intention of giving you a divorce so just get that into your head. If you think I'll ruin what's taken me over a year to set up, just because you won't share—'

'Share?'

'Won't put up with something which doesn't mean a thing.' His usual skill with words had deserted him. He sprang to his feet, went to the window and turned to face her.

'I repeat. I refuse to be involved in a divorce. It would damage me and do you, and her, no good. And that's final.'

He walked out, inevitably slamming the door.

Joanna appeared later and looked into the living room. 'Mum. Kon and I are going to a horror movie. Kon says he hopes I shall scream. *He's* the one who'll be petrified, he was last time. Won't be too late.'

She lingered. 'You okay?'

'Of course,' said Eleanor, summoning a smile. She hadn't moved since Sandy had left the room half an hour ago.

The bell rang and Joanna ran off to open the front door and greet her friend. Eleanor heard their laughing voices as they walked away down the street.

She went upstairs to look at Paul. He was nearly invisible under his duvet, one lock of dark hair sticking up like a feather. She trailed back to the living room. The evening was already nearly dark, but she did not turn on the lights and stood looking out at the dim garden. Summer's gone. My summer too, thought Eleanor.

Mathilde believed the old house, her dead husband's family house, knew she was deserting it. She could feel the sorrow and silence while she toiled about, ineptly filling tea chests. Mrs Maffett helped in the unending job, but she talked too much and was tiring. Her elderly husband, an enormous man who had been a carpenter, came in to carry the heavy things. He was voluble too: his loud voice boomed down ancient stairways as he staggered down into the hall now so cluttered that Mathilde could scarcely make her way across it.

At half past nine one autumn morning she telephoned Bryan Fairfoot, owner of the largest estate office in Haywards Heath. She had met him once or twice at the local church. He was by way of being a Catholic, a fussy red-faced man doing badly in the property market. She made an appointment to see him. It did not take Fairfoot two minutes to guess why.

Wearing her diamonds, Mathilde arrived by taxi. Fairfoot was polite, gave her some coffee which Mathilde thought undrinkable, and offered no hope at all. Of course he knew Hillier's and its famous history. He had come to a charity fête there on one occasion, and to an open day.

Mathilde asked him if he would be good enough to come and see round the house this morning. Fairfoot was forced to agree. He accompanied her on a tour of the place, noting that she was unrealistically in the process of moving. He took in the house's Tudor beauties and money-guzzling spaces, the out-of-date kitchen and two sculleries, the cobwebbed stables, the conservatory with its broken windows, the enormous overgrown garden, the lake with its flock of winter birds. Hillier's represented this lady's life. He had seen over many historic houses not as beautiful but certainly as shabby. What Hillier's needed as a thirsty plant needs water, was money. But so did everywhere else.

Ignoring Fairfoot's pessimism at any prospect of a buyer, Mathilde persuaded him to put her house on his books.

She then continued, stubbornly, with what she had planned. She had decided to move into the one property still owned by Hillier's: a poky thatched place with the unlikely name of Fuschia Cottage, five minutes walk away. It had been empty for a year. Her previous tenant, a young banker, had enthusiastically smartened it up with her approval, planned to make it his weekend home, paid for half the new thatch, whitewashed the walls and added a *Country Life* kitchen. After which, to his dismay, his job took him abroad. He came to a generous agreement with her over the money he had spent, and Mathilde now owned a tiny house smartened out of recognition.

Scarcely a piece of Hillier's furniture was going to fit into it, but Mathilde ignored that. She went on taking down pictures and packing books. She and Mrs Maffett ventured into the attics. The Maffetts, husband and wife, thought the move daft. But she was, after all, a countess.

Climbing nervously up the ladder into a boxroom, Mathilde spent an afternoon sitting on a mouldy trunk, reading letters a hundred years old.

When the telephone rang on a wet late autumn morning, she expected Fairfoot, and was all set to ask about Fuschia Cottage's electricity when, 'Mother?'

Mathilde was startled. 'Agnes! Are you in Plymouth?'

'No. London. I rang to ask if I can pop down this evening. The girls are on an archaeological dig on Dartmoor and David's doing another computer course. I'm on my own: a lovely chance to see you and have a real chat. I'm sorry I didn't let you know sooner, but things before the girls went were chaotic. Is it all right if I come this weekend?'

'*Of course, darling.*'

'I'll have somebody with me.'

'Emily? Nicole?'

'No, Mother, I told you. They're on Dartmoor enjoying themselves and drenched to the skin. Em said the Dart is in flood. It is somebody else. Can we arrive before supper?'

'You're being very mysterious.'

'Oh I love to keep you guessing,' said Agnes and laughed.

When she rang off, Mathilde had to sit down. She looked with real alarm at the tea-chests and a sensation she had never felt before came over her, a great wave of guilt.

Hillier's had been her home for nearly half a century, since starry-eyed and anglophile she had come here with John from liberated France, leaving her French life, her parents and her brother. Recently she had not been back to Montbard. Her parents were long since dead, and Jean-Claude had converted the château into three apartments. His married children, how unlike the English, were glad to live still under the château's storybook turrets. Agnes stayed with her French cousins whenever she could. She retained her love of photography and came back with dramatic shots of the country which was Mathilde's: its wide rivers, its fields thick in spring with cowslips, its churches where too few people prayed. But Mathilde did not go back. She thought in English, she was rooted in England, she did not long for Montbard. Yet in her bones she was deeply eternally French.

She had no sentimental attachment to Hillier's. Her love for John Lawrence was in her heart, not in his house. It exhausted her, and it was absurd for one old woman to live in a mansion of fourteen rooms, six acres and a lake. She had often said, 'Some day I will leave.'

Now, suddenly and out of nowhere, her desire was as fierce as the swallows' urge to migrate. She thirsted to move, to get the house's Elizabethan weight off her shoulders, to clear up, to clear out. She did not want to go back to France. The fanciful little cottage beckoned. They were the same size.

She was too unsettled to go on with the packing after Agnes had telephoned. She broke the news that she was expecting visitors to Mrs Maffett, who bustled off to sweep two bedrooms and find hot-water bottles. Mathilde had no electric blankets and didn't like them.

Out in the garden, Mathilde walked the full length of a long herbaceous border. It was the picture of autumn, with late flowers, dropping leaves and tall weeds. Her high heels sank into the damp earth as she picked some roses and peony leaves which had turned crimson. Back in the house, she unwrapped two vases and arranged a bunch for each bedroom.

It was not easy for Agnes to get through to Eleanor. Agency people answered, said they would go and look, and kept her watching the flickering figures in the telephone booth for what seemed half an hour. At last there was Eleanor, satisfactorily surprised. 'Why, Aggie!'

'I'm passing through London on my way to Hillier's to see Mother. Are you desperately busy? It sounds as if you are.'

Eleanor, who was, made crosses and exclamation marks across the day's appointments. She wasn't going to miss the chance of seeing her friend; they had not met for a long time.

'Aggie, if you have to rush off quite soon, why not lunch here in the office? Much quicker than in a restaurant and more fun, really. And I'll have you to myself.'

Agnes had never visited Nelson's. Knowing all about the agency, it had never seem quite real and she was very amused when she arrived. All the floors were of black marble, the ceilings pricked out with tiny points of light and you walked on stars. It looked very rich and stylish. A receptionist like an American doll (Merula had retired in glory some years ago to marry a rich widower) rang through to Eleanor, who appeared at once, hurtling across the wide areas of Reception to embrace her. Both women laughed in delight and the receptionist buried herself in *Hello* magazine.

No black marble in Eleanor's office, but a lot of papers

and untidyness, sandwiches, white wine and storyboards.

'It's fantastic to see you, Aggie. How do you manage to be so brown when you said it has been pelting with rain? How are the girls? Can you stay more than an hour?'

Agnes answered in her tranquil way, and during the picnic of smoked salmon, Eleanor calmed down. She had been, Agnes thought, too hostessy and too talkative, which had the effect of rendering Agnes calmer still. Eleanor went off to get coffee, and when she returned, Agnes stood up and closed the always-open office door.

Eleanor looked slightly caught.

'What's happened? Something has,' Agnes said.

Eleanor hung fire. She had told nobody: not Joanna, not Giles. Her mind was filled with Paul and the future was impossible to contemplate. But she was still set on her decision.

Agnes sat with an improbable background of advertising proofs on Eleanor's pinboard. 'Winemakers of the world!' shouted one. 'Ozone friendly every hour of the day!' yelled another. Half hidden by Agnes's curly head was a promise of 'One month's *FREE TRIAL* for this special. . .'

Eleanor could not have said later why her reserve crumbled, why she gave in. Was it simply that Agnes's tranquillity upset her because she had none. She blurted out, 'Sandy's got somebody else and I want a divorce.'

Decidedly her placid friend was older, she did not start, but only made the familiar "tt" with her tongue. 'Does he want one too?'

'That's the rub. Definitely not.'

Agnes was struck by this.

'Then don't people usually come to some sort of agreement? Defended divorces are impossibly expensive, apart from getting the evidence—'

'You mean hiring a private detective to sneak about after
the guilty parties. It does sound absurd.'

'Isn't it odd, it used to be commonplace,' remarked
Agnes.

Eleanor waited for her to come up with a solution. All she
did was turn her eyes on Eleanor and ask the question she
had asked many times of people whom she loved.

'Are you getting enough sleep, Eleanor?'

'Probably not. Things go round and round in my head.'

'They do for all of us.'

'Never you.'

'Don't be mad, Eleanor, I sometimes lie awake worrying
in the most imbecile manner: about David, Nicole, Em,
your Jo. Talking of whom, where is Jo? And little Paul?'

Eleanor was offended that Agnes seemed to have relinquished looking at the enormous fact she'd dumped in front
of her among the sandwiches. She said shortly that Jo was
away for the weekend, and Paul at home. It was half-term.

'Great. I've got this idea. I told Mother I would be
bringing somebody and I came here to persuade you to let
me drag you off to Hillier's. Will you come? We can bring
Paul, and Mother can teach him croquet.'

The unlikely suggestion was the best news Paul had had
for days, and when told, he shouted, 'Wowee!'

Eleanor explained to Agnes that he had recently been to
Hillier's, while Paul himself had rushed up to fetch the red
plastic bag. He came down and announced, 'Last time,
Gran let me build my kit.'

Neither Eleanor nor Agnes missed the 'Gran.'

'So I'm bringing it again,' he added unnecessarily. Agnes
peered into the bag and asked why there were only three
wheels; was it a three-wheeler? That sent him upstairs
again.

Eleanor had to cancel a lot of appointments to go to Sussex with Agnes, but she had a superstition about her. Agnes had always been her oracle.

Nobody talked much during the drive. For company, Agnes sat at the back with Paul beside her and when, after some high-pitched talk, he feel asleep, she pulled him close and spent the rest of the journey thinking her own thoughts. As for Eleanor, she just drove. She hadn't seen Mathilde for fifteen years and was not looking forward to it; Mathilde's feelings about her would not have changed.

Driving through Balcombe Woods, she came finally to the village which was nearest to Hiller's and noticed that it had been much primped up: freshly painted or white-washed cottages, (one was actually bright pink). There was that film-set smartness which commuters give to the country. Eleanor thought that Sandy would approve.

'We're near Ferne Place,' Agnes said. 'Do you ever go back there to see it, Eleanor?'

'No.'

'I can't remember if you sold it or not.'

'Didn't I tell you? Sandy was keen for us to keep it: he said it would rise in value. In the Eighties it certainly did: the price if we'd sold then was quite mad. But we let it instead. It's empty now.'

Soon they came to the rusted open gates of Agnes's old home. In the distance there was the glint of the lake. It was dark, and the windows shone. Mathilde must have been listening for the car, the front door immediately opened and light shone out on to the driveway. Agnes ran over to her mother. 'Oh darling!'

As Mathilde accepted the kiss, she looked beyond her and saw a small figure climb out of the car.

'Why, you've brought Pol!'

'Yes, he's been longing to come. Somebody else too.'

Mathilde and Eleanor came face to face and Eleanor held out her hand. Mathilde, with the plain air of wishing she did not need to, gave it a brief pressure. Eleanor said something about it being very kind of Mathilde to let them stay. But Mathilde was not listening. She walked over to Paul and the old woman and the boy were at once in animated conversation. Agnes caught Eleanor's eye, and winked.

It was the last peaceful minute of the evening: the four standing in the cool dark lit by a flood of brightness from the front door, the arrival, the promise of future hospitality. Agnes walked eagerly through the front door, and gave a real scream.

'What's happened?' gasped Eleanor. Mathilde did not even start, she replied sombrely, her French accent very pronounced and every 'h' forgotten.

'She 'as seen I am leaving this 'ouse.'

Agnes's vision of a cosy evening with her mother in her beloved old home, of discussing her children and later talking seriously with Eleanor, utterly vanished. She stood facing chaos. Agnes was not only flabbergasted, she was cross.

She darted back outside to exclaim and scold and Eleanor grabbed Paul, who, in his turn, dragged her indoors to the study saying it was where he'd built his kit last time.

Eleanor said curiously, 'Paul. Had all this packing up begun when you were here last?'

'Sure. Jo and me helped.'

'Why didn't you tell me about it?' asked Eleanor, knowing her question was a waste of breath. He said vaguely, 'Didn't we?' and began to arrange rows of yellow

screws and blue bolts on the desk. He always hummed when
he was happy.

'Eleanor, where are you?'

It was Agnes. Out in the hall, Eleanor edged her way past
boxes and packing cases. A large rusty nail was sticking out
of one of them and she missed it by inches. There was no
sign of Mathilde. Agnes was sitting on the bottom stair of the
staircase. Her da Vinci face had lost its calm.

'It really is too bad of Mother; she could at least have
warned me when I rang. Honestly, Eleanor! To make things
worse, apparently Hugo's due home very soon. He's got
some unexpected leave. He'll be charmed, won't he?'

'Perhaps it's a good thing he's coming. He can talk to
her.'

Eleanor had made up her mind that she was in the way.

'Aggie, I really think I'd better take Paul home.'

'Go!' exclaimed Agnes, laughing with exasperation.
'You'll do no such thing. I suppose Mother was scared when
I said I was coming, and hadn't the guts to stop me. The
only thing she's pleased about is that we brought Paul. As
for you, don't you dare to go back to London, I need you
for moral support. Imagine walking in just now to *this*.
Okay, she has a perfect right to leave Hillier's, though I
don't know how she can bear to. But I'm certain she can't
sell the house, it belongs to Hugo. And as for starting to
move like *this*—' and she looked round with high disdain at
the muddle made by a woman of seventy-five.

Eleanor sat down beside her.

'Where is Mathilde?'

'Gone to get Paul's tea. She's making sandwiches.
Apparently he and Mother have started a big affair, you
must have noticed the "Gran".'

'Of course.'

'Do you mind?'

'Now Aggie, how could I possibly?'

There was, thought Eleanor, a single plus in the disorder which had taken over the house. Mathilde's stuffy formality couldn't stand up to it. The dignity which had ruled her life, and which years before had told on Eleanor's nerves, could scarcely retain its power when every table had to be cleared of packages and every chair resurrected from dust sheets. But Mathilde's manner was still chilly to Eleanor who was deeply interested to see how warm it was to Paul.

'Now Pol, sit down and eat the tea I have made for you: peanut butter – you said last time you like the smooth kind – and the *gâteau au chocolat*, and this little plate of "cheeps".'

'Oh Gran, it's chips, not "cheeps"', said Paul, giggling through the peanut butter.'"Cheeps" are what sparrows do.'

Awful child, thought Eleanor, impressed.

The scolding and reproaches from her daughter had subdued the old woman. When not waiting on Paul, she thanked Eleanor for offering to fetch some hot water. Agnes recovered from her irritation and asked about her brother's arrival. 'He's only been on leave recently. Why again so soon?'

Mathilde explained in a gloomy voice (Agnes had thoroughly depressed her) that a Lisbon colleague had had to cancel his leave as his wife had developed chicken-pox. He was taking leave in his place.

'So poor Hugo is coming back to all this. Honestly Mother, you really should have warned us,' said Agnes, for about the fourth time.

Eleanor stole a glance at her mother-in-law and saw the expression of someone expecting another wigging. Mathilde replied humbly that she 'ated the telephone for anything you 'ad to talk about seriously. Looking at her, Eleanor thought how Mathilde was more and more like a countess in a nineteenth-century play. She did not like seeing her so subdued and hoped Agnes wasn't going to bite her head off again. Perhaps Eleanor's own expression worked, Agnes never missed anything. She said, after a pause, using her old peaceable tones, 'Mother, Mother,' and actually smiled.

The familiar voice, the smile, had its effect. Mathilde quite perked up, cut more cake for Paul and began to talk about his school to him, a subject usually banished by Paul with a 'Yuk'. He answered as if to someone of his own age.

'No, Gran, we don't call it arithmetic, it's maths. And we do art and PE and reading and—' he spoke through the cake – '*science.*'

'*Ah, bon?*'

'We've got a thing called a Floor Roamer which sort of walks all over everything and we programme it with a computer.'

Mathilde nodded. Nothing about Paul surprised her. 'Do you learn French yet?'

'Oh sure. It's awful.'

'To learn a foreign language. Yes. I thought learning English 'orrible.'

They exchanged looks.

'Finish your tea and then show me your kit. I will talk in French, very slow, and you can answer in English.'

'Shan't understand a word!'

Youth and age left the room together.

Agnes and Eleanor exchanged looks.

'That is just how she was with my brother. Completely at his mercy.'

'She loves the young.'

'No, Eleanor, she loves *boys*: little ones, big ones, always boys. She is mad about them, they can do no wrong. When Hugo got up to mischief as a boy she only laughed. She used to say "what a rascal". She wasn't like that about me. Of course we know she's fond of your Jo, and Em and Nicole. But. You see how it is. I imagine your friend Laurette is like that, about men, I mean.'

'Scarcely my friend.'

'You were very fond of her.'

'Not anymore, Aggie, I'm not a canonised saint.'

When it was dark, Mathilde went round switching on table lamps, which shone on the old split oak panels, on floors of uneven boards covered here and there with worn Turkish mats. Lines of packages were in a row on a far table. Books were piled up, some with broken spines. A china owl, badly packed, looked out from a twist of newspaper. The room was like the study of a don who had decided to leave his college. Eleanor was not aware that the disarray affected her, just as it had done Joanna the other day. Things loosened. They didn't seem to matter. Even the paintings, unhooked and facing the wall, removed seriousness. You were down to basics when you took a home to pieces. A life as well?

Agnes looked out of the latticed windows. The curtains had not been drawn, and a long spray of rambling roses knocked against the pane in the night wind. She picked up a cup of stone-cold tea and finished it.

She was looking at Eleanor rather fixedly and finally came out with, 'May I ask you a question?'

'I think I know what it is.'

'Are you sure?'

'Almost.'

Agnes looked at her again as if for help and Eleanor smiled. 'Go on, ask.'

'Yes. I will. Forgive me, but do you still love your husband?'

'Oh Aggie. Of course it's what I've been asking myself. But isn't it confusing, really to *know*?'

'I can't think so.'

Agnes's words were a sigh, and the roses tapped at the window as if they wanted to get in.

When Eleanor spoke she sounded more detached than Agnes had ever heard her. She said pensively, 'It was lovely once. I do promise you. But it's been different for longer than I realised. I mean, I don't think he has really loved me the way he used to do. When we've made love I've almost thought it *was*. But you know how unobservant I am, you used to tease me about it. And you said I only saw what I wanted to see, not what was there under my nose. Wasn't I blind, Aggie? When Jo told me and I saw what a fool I'd been, I was angry. But the terrible thing was I didn't feel as if I was going to die. Not once. Do you think,' she falteringly asked, 'you can catch falling out of love the way you catch a cold?'

Eleanor was due to drive back to London early on Monday morning and Mathilde, always awake by six, made her some breakfast. Eleanor now found herself in Mathilde's good books.

'Agnes tells me you say that Pol may remain.'

She was humble again. Eleanor wished she wouldn't be.

'Of course he can. He'll be so pleased. He finds half-term in London so boring, and he loves it here with you.'

'He does seem to,' said Mathilde, carefully pouring coffee. She looked over the kitchen table to be sure Eleanor had everything she needed. Then began to lay a tray, with a row of tiny cereal packets: Crunchies, Whirls, Puffs, Munchies. A faded mug was patterned with the alphabet. Mathilde arranged the tray meticulously, leaning forward in concentration. She had fallen in love again.

Before she left for London, Eleanor went into her son's room to say goodbye. He was wide awake, the breakfast tray in front of him, books all over the bed, and tucked in beside him his two inseparable companions, the bear and the frog. Joanna's nearly bald teddy had a certain melancholic style, but the frog was another matter. Someone had given it to Paul when he was six months old and it rarely left his side except at school. It consisted now mainly of darns in green wool by Eleanor and Gloria, over its kissed and slept-with frog face and body. It looked like a patched-up soldier straight from the trenches.

Paul had heard the news of his prolonged stay.

'I say, Mum, brilliant. Gran says I can go out in that old boat on the lake if Aunt Aggie comes with me. I bet it's got a hole in it. What'll happen to us then?'

All the way back to London, first in the leafy lanes and then joining thick traffic, Eleanor thought about Paul, his father, and the ugly fact of the divorce. She was determined to be free of Sandy but the enormous problem was – how? She must speak to Giles. She was afraid he would be pleased at the news. He was clearly as sick of Sandy's behaviour at Nelson's as he was devoted to her; it was going to be humiliating to listen to him. And losing one's husband to a close friend was not exactly helpful to self-esteem either.

When she arrived at the villas she decided on a bath and a change of clothes. She had already had one bath, but Hillier's went in for lukewarm water. She fancied a long soak in water – hot, scented and deep. She let herself into the house, wondering if Sandy was here. Somehow she felt that he wasn't, and in the drawing room she saw that his briefcase was not on the floor by his desk, or the *Economist* diary in its usual place. The deserted room smelled of star-gazer lilies: Agnes had insisted on buying her a big bunch before they drove down to Sussex.

Calling to Gloria that she was home, Eleanor went to her room. She turned on the radio for the 9 o'clock news, and was peeling off her sweater when the telephone rang.

She was expecting to hear from Agnes about Hugo's arrival. Eleanor had decided that if by chance he came to Hillier's earlier than they expected, she would not be there. What with the tea-chests and the drama, Hugo wouldn't want an ex-wife around as well. Agnes had laughed and, hesitating, agreed.

Eleanor picked up the telephone by the bed and said cheerfully, 'Hello?'

'Is that my one friend?'

Eleanor was filled with rage.

'I refuse to speak to you.'

'Don't ring off!' cried the American voice, 'I realise you want to, but don't. Don't escape, Eleanor. Honestly, we ought to meet.'

'No.'

Wanting to, she didn't ring off.

'I know I'm several sorts of bitch, but I need so much to see you. We can't talk on the phone, surely you agree about that? Look, will you see me? I have this idea. We could meet at the Hyde Park Hotel and they'd get you a cab from there. You could be at Nelson's in ten minutes.'

Only Laurette would suggest a meeting which took Eleanor's job into account.

Eleanor couldn't help her voice altering.

'I really don't think . . .'

But Laurette had located a soft spot between the joints of the armour and pressed through it. She promised she wouldn't take more than fifteen minutes, maybe less. She truly needed to see Eleanor and maybe Eleanor was going to find that *she* needed it too.'

'I haven't told Sandy about this. Is he around?'

'Isn't he with you?'

'No. Ah well. Guess he must be in that limbo married man get into, have you noticed? They're not with their girlfriends and not at home either. Fun if we could discover exactly where they *are*.'

Eleanor took a taxi to the hotel. There had been rain in Sussex early in the morning, but it had gone and the sky was full of clouds, grey, white, with blue in between. A wind made them race. When she went up the steep flight of steps, through the heavy swing doors and into the lounge, she remembered that Laurette had said, 'They call it the Ferrari bar,' adding her favourite, 'would you believe it?'

Laurette had already arrived. She wore coffee colour with a jade green knitted scarf tied round her neck like a pirate's, and some jade earrings Eleanor had not seen before, and one of her baseball caps.

'Eleanor,' she said, as if they were still friends. She beckoned to a waiter. 'You like your coffee black, don't you? You're so brave.'

The waiter knew somebody who over-tipped when he saw her, and hurried over to serve coffee and some expensive-looking biscuits. Laurette poured out, picked up her cup and said, 'Hi there.'

Eleanor looked at her as curiously as she'd looked at Sandy.

'I'm not sure why I agreed to come.'

'Because we're fond of each other.'

'That can't possibly be true any more.'

'Don't see why not. I may have taken up with your husband but he was never exactly a faithful guy, was he?'

This was news to Eleanor, who said nothing.

'You know me,' confided Laurette. 'A pushover for the attractive man. I'm not proud of my track record. Remember Lee? No, you wouldn't, he was before your time. Lovely muscles. Now your guy—'

'Do shut up.'

'Eleanor. The only answer to that is shucks. Sandy *is* attractive, and kind of concerned, and as pushy and ambitious as any man I've met. The way we like it in the States. I know I shouldn't have egged you on about him the way I did. I'm sorry. That wasn't nice. But I wanted to find out, really, how *you* felt about him. How serious it would be for you. It was no good asking Sandy, isn't he a liar? I kept meeting you, and you kept telling me more or less that it was going badly, and in the end I'm afraid I decided you wouldn't be too shaken up.'

'Oh great.'

'Come on, Eleanor.' As she leaned forward, the carved jade earrings swung on either side of her cheeks. 'You've proved it isn't such a big deal by wanting this divorce. If you loved him to bits, you'd hang on for grim life.'

'You didn't with your husbands.'

'Exactly. Because I got over them. Lee. Dyson. The others. I wanted to forget them and start again. My guess is that's what you want.'

Eleanor was again silent. Now that she was with Laurette, she couldn't see her as a bitch, an adulteress, a cruel schemer, a husband stealer. There she was with her round face and her round eyes, blue flowers in the windows of a house. She shared with you her own flaws. And she remembered that your office was ten minutes away by taxi.

'One way and another,' said Eleanor, not showing her hand, 'I want the divorce. Sandy has refused it.'

'That's what I want to discuss. I can talk him into it – if I talk him into us getting married. I mean, they do have these little troubles in the House. MPs have the odd affair ... wives get swapped, that kind of thing. Even a baby appears occasionally who wasn't exactly welcomed. Sandy and I could' – Laurette waved one hand – 'provide you with evidence.'

Eleanor was staggered. Gulping black coffee as bitter as poison, she marvelled at the ease with which Laurette proposed to acquire her husband. But there was somebody else in all this – the person who gripped her heart.

'There's Paul.'

'Yeah. How old is he now?'

'Eight.'

'That young?'

'Laurette, I will never give him up.'

It was the first time during the interview that Eleanor saw her out of countenance. She repeated, 'Give him up? My poor Eleanor, you don't suppose I'd want your boy? Sure, I wanted my own once, God knows how many years ago that was. But now I'm hopeless with kids. I'm like W.C. Fields: can't stick them at any price, and they certainly can't stick me.'

Eleanor couldn't help laughing.

'You're a monster.'

It was scarcely twenty minutes before she saw Eleanor off from the hotel steps, waving as the taxi drove away.

No wonder, thought Eleanor, as they turned into the

park; no wonder Sandy's hooked.

That evening when she arrived home after another session of re-shooting the soap commercial – they'd returned to the dusty refurbished studio – she was met by Gloria whose face was dramatic. She was bursting with news.

'Is gone, Mrs Trafford. Is gone. All his luggage, clothes, even one shirt still damp. I tell him do not put on—'

Eleanor stood in the hall wearing her jacket covered with studio pollen. It was a strange way to learn that her marriage was over.

'He go after lunch. Come back and shout I want you Gloria and all afternoon I pack. So much clothes,' added Gloria with admiration. 'You knew he was going, your husband?'

'No, Gloria, I didn't. But we are getting a divorce.'

'Oh, *Dios mio*, now I understand.' Gloria was impressed. She'd known about Laurette for weeks, had often heard her employer on the telephone to that woman who had actually come here to see him when Eleanor and the children were out. She had been enraged and had confided to her boyfriend at the Spanish Club, 'Often I wish to break a plate on his head.'

Now her way of showing loyalty was to say something about supper, and go down to the kitchen.

Laurette moves fast, thought Eleanor. The speed left her slightly disorientated. It was as if Sandy had never existed: not a letter, not one sign of him except a smart carrier bag pushed into the paper-basket – Gucci. Clearly Laurette had taken him shopping.

There was no time to get her thoughts organised before Eleanor heard Joanna's key and the customary, 'Hi, I'm back.'

She came into the living room looking happy, and gave her mother a smile to match. She was wearing jeans the colour of mulberries, one of her dark sweaters, and had tied a trailing black scarf round her neck. The sombre colours made her all the brighter.

'Kon took me to his home, Mum. He has three brothers older than him and they're really nice. We went to the skating rink. I kept falling down.' She gave a blissful sigh.

Eleanor had a pause while her daughter collapsed on to the floor and leaned against her mother's knee.

'Don't think I can manage any homework tonight; didn't get to bed until three. And school today was dire. What's on the telly?'

'Jo. I have something to tell you.'

The classic opening, thought Eleanor. Parental and pompous, even scary. But Joanna was still in her dream of young men and only murmured, 'Yeah?'

Eleanor said quietly, 'I am divorcing Sandy.'

Joanna spun round in a movement of such violence that she almost fell over. The dream vanished as if it had been scraped off her face.

'Divorce! *Who gets my brother?*'

Eleanor was stung. 'Do you imagine I'd give him up?'

'He isn't a parcel!' shouted Joanna, beside herself. 'And now you're going to say it's all my fault for telling you what was going on.'

'Of course it is not your fault, don't be so stupid.' Eleanor was glad to be annoyed. 'I never heard anything so ridiculous. If you hadn't told me, it would have been Gloria. When I spoke to her just now I could see she already knew. How many other people? Probably every one of Laurette's friends in the House of Commons. Anyway, Sandy and I are parting, which is what he wants and certainly what I want. He left this afternoon.'

'But I only told you—'

'Stop blaming yourself. The thing will be painless. She's practised enough at divorce, for goodness' sake.'

'It won't be painless for Paul,' said Joanna, her voice rising again and her eyes angry. 'He loves his father. Christ knows why.'

'They'll see each other whenever they want.'

'You mean whenever Sandy wants – not whenever Paul wants.'

It was true. Eleanor couldn't deny it. She simply looked at Joanna in silence.

The girl's mood changed. Her face became desolate.

'Poor Paul. It's awful. It's so awful.'

Eleanor felt she could not bear much more. It hurt her enough to think of Paul missing his father. Joanna was making it worse.

'Oh Jo, have some pity.'

'Who for?' demanded Joanna. 'You? That American? My stepfather? I'm not sorry for any of you. I know it isn't *your* fault, but you're forty next month, you aren't eight years old.'

Her eyes brimmed. She gave a loud sniff.

'Have you told him?'

'Not yet. I—'

'Then I shall. I'll do it now.'

Joanna sprang to the door. Eleanor said quickly, 'Darling, Paul isn't here. He's at Hillier's with Mathilde.'

'With my grandmother?' said Joanna, much taken aback.

'With his too, apparently,' said Eleanor.

There was no word from Agnes about the definite date of

Hugo's arrival, and it was with tired relief that Eleanor looked forward to the weekend in Sussex.

Since she'd been told about the divorce, Joanna had been very depressed. Eleanor longed to comfort and reassure her, although she knew that in time, when the shock wore off, Jo would be her cheerful self again. Her heart ached to see her usually spirited daughter so withdrawn. She was cold to Eleanor, who pretended not to notice, and spent more time than ever with Kon. At night, unknown to her mother, Joanna was solaced by midnight visits from Ruffles.

Eleanor decided to take the opportunity, one evening, to call in to Giles's office and tell him about the divorce.

He listened, very concerned and grave. He showed none of the satisfaction she'd expected, but said he would speak to her solicitors if Eleanor would like him to do so. And that he was always there to help in any way she wanted.

'You're really kind, Giles.'

'Of course I'm not. And I'm still your godfather, remember?'

He added that he had had good news. Sandy was leaving Nelson's and a golden handshake had been agreed; Giles did not say how much. I bet it is handsome, thought Eleanor; one way and another Sandy's doing well. But when doesn't he?

Looking at her in his thoughtful way, Giles said he would like her to take more part in running the agency and be an active member of the board.

'You will find it interesting,' he said.

Is that my future? thought Eleanor. She wondered if her self-deprecating attitude to work in the past had been partly because Sandy had to be the one to shine: too simple a reason and probably true.

She telephoned Hillier's before she left London. Mathilde was polite, almost welcoming.

'We look forward to seeing you. Pol would speak, but he is in his bath.'

'Give him my love. Lots.'

'I'm afraid I will have to keep your dinner hot, Eleanor, we eat early for Pol.'

Hillier's, it seemed, now revolved round somebody of eight years old. How did he do it? thought Eleanor, impressed.

Sussex was leafy, not yet seriously turning to orange and yellow. The smell of wet leaves came through the open car window as she drove through the woods. These were the roads which she knew as well as her own name. She remembered her father driving her to London in his Rolls. She had wanted and dreaded the journeys. He had never said a word.

When she was a few miles from Hillier's, an impulse came to Eleanor out of the sweet-smelling dark. She suddenly wanted to see Ferne Place again. The house still belonged to her. It was empty now – the tenant last year had written to the agent with apologies. He was afraid the house had proved too large for his family and himself.

How many times had Giles told her she was mad not to sell?

'Do you ever go and see it, Eleanor?'

'I don't particularly want to.'

'Then why keep that big old place. It is simply a liability,' he had said, looking at a bill for repairs.

But 'Keep it, keep it,' Sandy had said, 'the price will only go up.' And it had – in the Eighties – by leaps and bounds. Then all of a sudden that wasn't true any more and the price went down.

She came at last to the sloping drive, opened the gates which were slightly rusty, and drove towards the lightless house. She had forgotten its size, its formal eighteenth-century style meant for grandeur. There was nothing homely and higgledy like the Lawrences' house. How often she'd revved the engine just here by the high box trees, and Luis had appeared to greet her. Like Ceci, Maria still wrote. She sent photographs of Luis and herself, fat and prosperous, with four children bright in the bright sun and behind them a spacious white house built with Walter's cheques.

Parking the car, Eleanor got out. How eerie houses are, she thought, when nobody lives in them. She wondered if they had a soul of their own, or whether they needed human beings to make them come alive. It was dark, but the sky had begun to clear and the moon came sailing from behind a cloud, lighting up a wide pale stretch of unkempt lawn. She went through an arch of overgrown yews to the terrace where she and her father had sat sometimes, and Walter had never been glad that she was there. Weeds, very small and very strong, had grown up between the paving and here and there had lifted the stones, like the lids of tombs in Highgate cemetery.

She walked slowly along the terrace, with the great presence of the house on her left. To London ears the silence of the country was very strange. The distant hoot of an owl. Then quiet lapped back again.

Would she meet her father's ghost? She imagined seeing him. Could you embrace a ghost? It would be air, thin air. She sat down on the edge of the low wall which was smothered with saxifrage, looking up at the blind windows. Where was the girl she used to be, and was her present self better or worse than the old headstrong Eleanor? She couldn't tell.

Suddenly she gave a violent start and the hair on the back of her neck rose like the fur of a cat. She'd heard a footstep. She turned round, almost expecting that a shadowy broad-shouldered figure would stand facing her . . .

Against the moonlight was a tall thin man.

'Surely that is not Eleanor?'

'Hugo!'

'Did I frighten you?' he said, half laughing. 'You certainly frightened me.'

'But what are you—'

'Doing here? I'll ask you the same question.'

'I think I came to pay my respects.'

'So did I.'

It was easy to talk in the dark. He came over and sat beside her on the same piece of wall.

'We didn't expect you this weekend, Hugo.'

'I know. I'm early. It looks as if it's a good thing Agnes and I are around at present, doesn't it?'

'Poor Mathilde.'

'Oh, I wouldn't say that. Not with your son about.'

'She does love him, doesn't she? I'm so glad.'

'Are you?' he said quite earnestly. 'Are you?'

As he turned towards her, out came the moon from behind a cloud, shining straight down on his face. Eleanor saw it and saw, just then, all its sorrow and its kindness. She remembered him.

All he could make out was the bright hair. The silence was interrupted again by the cry of a hunting owl.

'This is quite odd, isn't it?' Hugo said.

'Nice, though,' said Eleanor.